LUCY'S BLADE

John Lambshead

LUCY'S BLADE

John Lambshead

LUCY'S BLADE

Copyright © 2007 by John Lambshead

A Baen Books Original

Baen Publishing Enterprises
P.O. Box 1403
Riverdale, NY 10471
www.baen.com

ISBN 10: 1-4165-2121-6
ISBN 13: 978-1-4165-2121-1

Cover art by Clyde Caldwell

First printing, May 2007

Distributed by Simon & Schuster
1230 Avenue of the Americas
New York, NY 10020

Library of Congress Cataloging-in-Publication Data:

Lambshead, John.
  Lucy's blade / John Lambshead.
     p. cm.
  ISBN 1-4165-2121-6
  1. Great Britain--History--Elizabeth, 1558-1603--Fiction.
  2. Dee, John, 1527-1608--Fiction. I. Title.

PR6112.A53L83 2007
823'.92--dc22

2007002004

Printed in the United States of America

10 9 8 7 6 5 4 3 2 1

Acknowledgements

I would like to thank Jim Baen, who always believed in *Lucy's Blade*. He helped me work out the background and plot and he gave me the chance to write it. Jim sadly died before the book was finished. Wherever you are, Jim, I hope the novel pleases you.

I must also express my gratitude to Toni Weisskopf for her editorial skills. She improved the novel tremendously.

A very special thank you must go to David Drake, for his wisdom and many kindnesses. Please drive your motorbike carefully, David. The world of science fiction and fantasy has taken a big enough blow this year.

I would also like to acknowledge the contribution of my wife and daughters; the latter's university fees supplied the motivation to be an author.

—John Lambshead
Medwaytowns,
Southern England, October 2006

There too Lilith shall repose,
and find a place to rest.
There shall the owl nest
and lay and hatch and brood in its shadow.
                                        —Isaiah 34:14

Dramatis Personae

Doctor John Dee—scholar and royal magician

Elizabeth 1st—Queen of England

Gwilym—Sir Francis Walsingham's man

Doctor Alice Harding—London University history lecturer

Captain William Hawkins—sea dog

Lady Isabella—Spanish lady

Lilith—a demon (sort of)

Earl of Oxford—aristocrat

Master Christopher Packenham—gentleman adventurer

Master Simon Tunstall—secretary to Sir Francis Walsingham

Sir Francis Walsingham—statesman and spymaster to the Queen

And, of course, our heroine:

Lady Lucy Dennys—niece of Sir Francis Walsingham

Contents

Prologue,
A Room in Queen Elizabeth's Palace

The trouble with magic is that it consists of ninety-nine parts boredom and one-part undiluted, gut-twisting terror. At the moment, they were still in the boredom stage; the terror would come later. Simon Tunstall didn't mind boredom. He was a secretary, a "keeper of secrets" for Sir Francis Walsingham, who was one of the Queen's greatest statesmen. Boredom was in the job description. Secretaries attended meetings and made notes. They kept records and archived papers. Occasionally, when feeling particularly energetic and daring, they might index something. Simon had been considering reordering the documents in the large trunk behind his desk. These were the files marked "English families with sons training as Jesuit priests." Most of all secretaries kept their mouths shut.

All the shutters in the room were tightly closed to keep out the summer sun. A brazier burnt in each corner; the fumes contributed to the general fug. Simon's eyes stung and the smell of wood smoke and burning herbs was too acrid for comfort. Slim rays of light surreptitiously penetrated through cracks in the shutters to illuminate the rolling banks of incense in shafts of light.

Doctor John Dee meticulously traced a pentagram in chalk on the floor, using a rule so that the lines were straight and the angles

1

perfect. The magician consulted a large volume that had been newly bound in cow's leather. Simon sneaked a look at the book's title, which was written in Dee's own hand across the spine. There was just one word—*Necronomicon*—the Book of the Dead.

The magician applied great caution to his movements so that his long brown robes did not smudge the chalk. "The unguents," he said.

Simon held the bowl of oily liquid out for Dee, who dipped the point of his athame, his conjuror's dagger, into the mixture. The liquid ran into the glyphs that were inscribed on the blade.

The magician marked each angle of the pentagram in unguent, while repeating a phrase in a language Simon had never heard before. It seemed to consist solely of consonants and tongue clicks.

"Is that the first language? The one spoken by Adam in the Garden of Eden?" Simon said, taking a wild guess.

Dee stopped what he was doing and looked in astonishment. "You have heard of the Tongue of Angels?"

Simon felt smug. The other thing about secretaries is that they read. People often forgot that.

"No. That language has not been heard since the Fall but one day, perhaps, if I can find the right skryer and skrying stone . . ." Dee's voice trailed off. "This language is also old but not as ancient as the Tongue of Angels. It comes from Africa. An Egyptian priest taught it to Plato, who recorded it for the wise. It is the Tongue of Summoning."

That word, *summoning*, was too explicit, too descriptive of their purpose. Simon could not suppress a shudder of apprehension. He felt an urge to talk as a way of normalising the situation.

"I suppose the spell will not work if the markings are flawed?"

"The spell will work," said Dee, flatly. "I translated it from the *Necronomicon* myself. The mad Arab's spells always work, God help us."

"Then why the exact precautions, Doctor Dee?" asked Simon, still confused.

"This issue is what happens after the demon is summoned. We are tearing a hole between the spheres, so upsetting the natural laws that govern their separation and concordance. The pentagram limits the size of the tear and constrains the demon from too deep a penetration of our sphere. I will take other precautions as well. An unchained demon in our world would be disastrous."

"How disastrous?" asked Simon, nervously.

Dee stared at him. "Abdul Alhazred, who wrote the *Necronomicon,* died in 778 AD. He was ripped to pieces in the market of Damascus by demons that only he could see."

Simon licked his lips nervously. "We risk our lives then, Doctor Dee?"

"Your life, Master Tunstall?" Dee seemed to find the comment amusing. "You risk much more than that, secretary. You risk your very soul."

Leaving Simon to reflect, Dee continued his preparations. When he had finished marking the angles, he placed candles at a precise distance from the pentagram and lit them. Then he carefully chalked symbols on the floor, glancing at the book every so often to refresh his memory.

Finally, Dee looked up at the third man in the room who sat patiently in an oak chair. If this man had any nerves or doubts then they were well hidden.

"We could stop now, Sir Francis, with no danger to ourselves or to others. Once I start the ceremony, there will be no turning back," Dee said, a trace of pleading entering his voice.

"You seem worried, old friend," said Walsingham.

"Worried! Why should I be worried? I am about to summon a demon, for which the punishment is death. I am to raise him in a Royal Palace with the Queen in residence, which is most certainly treason punishable by disembowelment. And just to affix my neck firmly to the block, I am to do all this witnessed by the Queen's spymaster." Dee wiped his dagger carefully on a rag before sheathing it.

"It is the last point that shall protect you from the axeman. Come, I cannot believe that the man who made the giant dung beetle of Cambridge fly is worried by a little demon." Sir Francis placed the tips of his fingers together in a characteristic pose.

"The beetle was a mere stage prop activated by a cunning contrivance of mirrors, ropes, and pulleys as you well know," said Dee, testily. "The University Proctors cleared me of all charges."

"I know that it cost Lord Burghley and me a great deal of money and influence to see that the Proctors reached the right decision," said Sir Francis. "Soothing the shattered nerves of the poor actor who played Trygaeus took an entire flagon of my best ale."

"The script said that Trygaeus was to fly up to Zeus' heavenly palace on the back of a flying scarab," said Dee. "I simply arranged it."

"And Cambridge University has not had the nerve to stage a play by Aristophanes since." Walsingham waved his hand. "Too much is at stake for any squeamishness on your part, my friend. The Queen herself demands that we proceed."

"So be it," said Dee. "If you are resolved. As you value your souls, stay in the places that I have allocated to you. I intend to use a dog as the vessel."

"Which demon do you intend to summon?" asked Walsingham.

"Choronzon," Dee replied. "Choronzon is a demon of knowledge who always answers truly. But be warned, Sir Francis, Choronzon is subtle and manipulative. The truths he speaks will be designed to mislead and confound, as he did to Eve in the Garden of Eden, in his manifestation as the Serpent."

Simon slowly released the breath he had not realised that he was holding. The Serpent in the Garden! Dee played with dangerous forces. He consoled himself with the thought that his master, Sir Francis Walsingham, was as clever, devious, and ruthless as any demon.

Dee pulled a wooden cage into the centre of the room and lifted out a puppy. The magician soothed the animal, which looked at him trustingly and wagged its tail. Dee took fresh strips of meat from a basket, sprinkled white powder on them, and fed them to the dog by hand.

"Poison," Dee explained. "The demon will be removed from the earthly sphere by the death of the host, should my wards fail."

The animal gulped the meat down greedily then sniffed about for more. Dee replaced the beast in the cage and positioned it within the pentagram. He was very careful not to disturb the chalk lines. He then knelt down, extended his arms straight out parallel to the ground, and chanted in the same guttural language that he had used before.

Simon blinked. The herbal fog grew more acrid and Dee disappeared into it. His voice grew fainter and farther away and yet was all round the room, whispering from the oak-panelled walls.

Flames shot out of the braziers, illuminating the room and lending Dee's face a satanic cast. The dog froze stiff-legged and howled.

Dee clapped his hands. "Choronzon! I know your true name and by the power of that name I command you. You must obey. Speak truly."

"Now, Sir Francis. Now!" Dee said, urgently. "We only have a short time before the poison takes hold."

"Who is behind the plot to murder the Queen? When will they strike? Where?" Walsingham leaned forward, his eyes glittering in the light.

The dog twisted, its back arching into an impossible angle, and howled in pain. Dee cursed and threw some orange-coloured powder at the dog, which made it howl again.

"Answer, demon. I command you by the power of your true name, Choronzon. I invoke the pact as a child of Eve's line," Dee said.

Simon had assumed that the dog would sound like a dog. Instead, when it opened its mouth, a clear piping voice emerged.

"Will you stop doing that, it hurts?" the voice said, petulantly and in a distinctly feminine tone. Dee's head snapped up. It was clear that something was unexpected.

"Who threatens the Queen?" asked Walsingham.

"Queen. Female head of a state organised on monarchical lines. Could be anything from a dictatorial ruler to the head of a constitutional democracy."

The dog paused before adding, "That sort of Queen or did you mean the popular band?"

Dee threw more powder over the puppy, which screamed like a woman in childbirth.

"Stop, please stop. This biological structure can barely sustain me and is decaying fast."

"Tell me about the Papist plot against the Queen. From where does the threat come?" Walsingham refused to be diverted.

"The portals. The power to cross the Shadow Worlds threatens your whole species." The puppy lay down on its side, panting. Its tongue lolled out of its mouth and deposited spittle on the bottom of the cage.

"I don't understand," said Dee. "The dog is dying too quickly."

The door burst open and Lucy ran into the room.

"Stop her, Tunstall," Dee gasped out.

Simon reached for Lucy but he never had a realistic chance of grabbing the girl before she reached the pentagram. As she crossed the chalk, there was a flash of white light and a clap of thunder that flung the men across the room. A great wind sucked the shutters off the windows, flooding the room with sunlight.

Lucy lay facedown on the ground beside a very dead dog. In its last moments, the animal had twisted in muscle tetanus strong enough to break bones. Simon reached the girl first and turned her over, lifting her head and shoulders off the ground in his arms. She groaned slightly and her eyelids fluttered.

"Thank God, Sir Francis," said Simon. "Your niece yet lives."

Dee drew his dagger and advanced on the girl, weapon raised. "Kill her. Kill her now, while we still can."

Act 1, Barn Elms Wildlife Park

It is sometimes said that the past is always with us, but in England the past has a habit of lurking in dark corners and jumping out at you at unexpected moments with a cynical grin on its face. In Alice Harding's case, the dark corner that history lurked in was a wildlife park, on the south bank of the River Thames, in the early hours of the morning.

The clatter of falling equipment was bad enough but Hammond had to compound it by shrieking like a girly.

"Oh hell, oh bloody hell, my knee," he said, writhing in pain.

"For God's sake shut up," Alice hissed at him. "What part of the phrase 'covert operation' don't you understand?"

"It's all right for you Alice," he said, huffily. "I have to hump all the equipment. Just a torch, that's all I wanted. Would it have hurt you to carry one little iddy-biddy electric torch?"

Hammond wasn't being completely unreasonable. The night-lights of London, reflecting off the rippling surface of the Thames and the lakes, cast just enough shifting illumination to drown the park in pools of shadow. He had disappeared into one of those pools.

"Where are you?" Alice asked, wearily.

"Down here." A head popped out of the ground at her feet. "I'm in a trench. What sort of bloody fools leave unmarked trenches lying around?"

"Archaeologists?" she said, with heavy sarcasm, "this being an archaeological site."

"Don't get cute with me, Alice, or you will be carrying out your own survey."

"Sorry, Hammond. I'm a bit on edge." Alice regretted snapping at him as soon as she had done it. Hammond was only here as a favour to her personally and he had turned out at a couple of hour's notice. He was a geek, not a field agent.

"Here, cop hold of this." Hammond's face appeared over the lip of the trench closely followed by his geophysics pack. Alice took the equipment off him and he disappeared again.

"What's the matter now?" she asked.

He replied, but at that moment the pilot of an Airbus, lining up for the descent into Heathrow Airport, advanced the throttles to power wheels down. Anything Hammond had said disappeared into the howl of Rolls Royce turbines.

"What?" she mouthed pointlessly into the darkness.

"I'VE LOST MY GLASSES," he shouted back into sudden silence as the plane retarded throttles and disappeared over the West London suburbs. A flock of wildfowl, startled by his yell, erupted from the water's surface and followed the jet.

"Tell you what, Hammond. Next time, why don't we just send out circulars? 'Dear residents of South London, please excuse the unusually loud noises in the middle of the night but the Commission is running a secret, covert operation.'"

"Sorry, Alice."

"Never mind. Move over and I'll help you look."

She jumped down into the trench, landing on her hands and knees.

"Hammond."

"What?"

"Why didn't you tell me the trench was waterlogged?" she asked.

"You never asked," he replied, distractedly. "It's okay, I've found them."

He held his spectacles up, triumphantly. "Look, they were still on the chain round my neck the whole time."

Alice resisted the urge to strangle him. Her jeans were wet through and something squishy had got under her fingernails. Hammond trotted off none the worse for his adventure and she followed carefully. He threaded his way into the centre of the dig without further mishap.

Alice ducked as a ghostly, underlit, white shadow flew over her head. I must be getting jumpy, she thought, to be spooked by a barn owl. A barn owl at Barn Elms, she chuckled to herself. Who would have thought it?

"Alice, I've found them. The cellars are here." Hammond peered down at a hole in the ground.

"Stand still, I'm coming. For heaven's sake don't fall in."

Hammond kept a dignified silence.

"Can we get down?" she asked. The hole looked vertical and steep-sided from where she was standing.

"I think so. They've started putting up scaffolding and we can climb down. It doesn't look too safe, though."

Hammond handed her the equipment and disappeared. She lowered it down to him then followed on. The scaffolding creaked and wobbled, causing her heart to jump, but she made it to the bottom. Once they were safely belowground, she took out the torch that he thought she had not brought, and put it on the "diffuse light" setting. He didn't seem to notice and continued to set up the gear.

He extended the two probes on the geophysics analyser and connected up the laptop slung round his neck. Hammond flicked a switch backwards and forwards, looking at the machine like a midwife looking at a recalcitrant womb.

"What's the matter?" Alice enquired.

"It won't boot up." He stabbed buttons seemingly at random. "I think I may have jarred something loose when I fell on it."

"Oh great. Do something."

He took a deep breath then struck the delicate equipment sharply. It made a *chukka chukka* noise and sprang to life, lights blinking. Hammond grinned at her. "The trick is in knowing where to hit it."

Hammond was like a lot of geeks. Socially inept, he came alive when there was a task requiring his beloved gear.

"So how does this thing work?" Actually, she couldn't give a damn but, in her experience, men liked to talk about their equipment.

"You just push the electrical probes into the target and pass an electrical charge between them. The analyser measures resistance across the gap. Even you could do it, Alice." He grinned at her.

"I am bowled over by your superior technical knowledge," she said, with wasted sarcasm.

Alice decided that geophysics analysis was never going to be a major spectator sport, not when watching ink fade in the sun was an available alternative. Hammond plonked the probes against the floor, took a reading, moved the probes twelve inches, took another reading, and moved on. Alice positioned herself on the scaffolding and wriggled, trying to find a comfortable position. There was an interesting smell hanging around the cellar suggesting that one of the TV crew had a dog.

"Alice?"

"Hmm?"

"Why am I geophysing an old cellar in Barn Elms Wildlife Park?"

"That's a long story, Hammond. But we are hardly pushed for time. You will recall that Barn Elms was the home of Sir Francis Walsingham," she said.

"No."

"Well, it was."

"And Walsingham was . . . ?" His voice trailed off.

She saw he was going to need the full picture. She mentally rotated through her lecture notes and settled on the one she gave to second-year Politics undergrads.

"Walsingham is remembered mostly as Queen Elizabeth I's great spymaster. He is credited as being the father of the English Secret Service. The Commission files record him as also controlling demon hunters. So they took an unhealthy interest when *The History Show* announced Barn Elms as the site of their next televised dig. If the television company 'had only three days' for their excavation, the Commission had only twenty-four panic-stricken hours to check through their records to see what the TV crew might turn up," she said.

"That doesn't seem a good enough reason for us to be here," Hammond said.

"Not on its own, no. But the Commission despatched me up to Oxford to check through the Dee records at the Ashmolean Museum. It's all the fault of a Robert Jones who lived at the Sign of the Plough in London's Lombard Street in the seventeenth century."

"I knew I would regret asking," Hammond said. Actually, he didn't really mind. He was not paying much attention to what she was saying so much as how she said it. Alice was the most exciting and "alive" person that he knew. It was going to be difficult to give her up.

She was in full lecture mode now. Never ask an academic a question about their subject. "One day, Mr. Jones was moved to buy a wondrous cedar wood chest from a carpentry shop in Addle Street. It took him two decades to find the papers and other objects hidden in a secret compartment in the base. Clearly, Mr. Jones had all the investigative skills of my old professor."

"I remember your old professor," Hammond said, with an unbecoming smirk.

She was not to be deflected. "Half the papers were lost when the kitchen maid discovered that they were just the right size to fit her baking tray, but the remainder survived Mr. Jones' death and the Great Fire of London to be sold to the collector Elias Ashmole. He recognised the records as the lost work of Doctor John Dee. He was Queen Elizabeth's court magician, and the man who, according to Lovecraft, first translated the *Necronomicon* into English. Dee was also a brilliant code-breaker working for Walsingham's spy network."

"No offence, Alice, but why you? You're a history lecturer for London University, not Emma Peel."

"I wish I was back at Royal Holloway College right now," Alice said, with feeling. When she was not attempting to drum knowledge into sprawled ranks of hungover undergraduates, she spent her quality time in the university library researching her next book.

"So why aren't you?" asked Hammond.

"I have generally found it politic to obey smartly when the Commission makes a polite request. Otherwise, my research funds could suddenly dry up and I might find myself assigned to teaching Media Studies students how to use joined-up writing." She wasn't going to tell Hammond, but the Commission knew too much about Doctor Alice Harding. So she found herself clambering around an archaeological dig at the dead of night.

Ironically, Alice hated archaeology. It was true that she had wanted to be an archaeologist once, but that dream had died in the mud of her first summer dig. "Student volunteer" turned out to be another name for unpaid labourer. She shifted more earth that summer than a royal engineer at the Battle of the Somme. She ruined her nails and tangled her hair into something that Alexander the Great would have taken a sword to. Then there were the lice. Even now the words "archaeological investigation" made her want to scratch.

As she was a romantic young fool, she also fell for the dubious charms of her professor only to have him snub her in the college corridors the following term. She thought that he loved her but found out that he had an unsavoury reputation as the college swordsman. To add insult to injury, the swine only gave her a C minus for her summer project report. If that was not taking advantage of a girl, then she did not know what was. He soon raised it to an A when she threatened to add in details of certain nocturnal investigations that he had undertaken, and to send his wife a copy. She had earned her A the hard way. Her only regret was that she wished she knew who had dobbed her in to the Commission. The organisation had maintained a hold over her ever since.

"The Commission didn't really expect me to find anything in Oxford or they would have sent one of their top torpedoes. Even when decoded, Dee's papers make less sense than Bob Dylan's lyrics. They include his fabled *Liber Mysteriorum* and never was a work better named. Thank God the museum has scanned them into digital records. At least I could run a computer search for any reference to 'Walsingham' or 'Barn Elms.'"

"Presumably you found something," Hammond said, distractedly. Every so often he stopped and checked the downloaded data on his laptop. The first few times he did this, Alice caught his eye enquiringly but he always shrugged and shook his head.

"A number of the works were diaries so there were various references of the sort 'Had supper with Sir Francis Walsingham. The man is a frightening bastard of the first order.'"

Hammond laughed. "He wrote that?"

"I paraphrase but that was the gist of it. What he actually said were things like 'Sir Francis did question me about the summoning. He did'th make my bowels clench like a virgin on her wedding night.'"

Alice readjusted herself on the scaffolding to transfer the dull ache to another part of her bum.

"I struck pay dirt right at the end of the diaries. This was an unhappy period in Dee's life. He returned to England from his years at Prague to find Queen Elizabeth's court changed out of all recognition. Most of her old advisors had died and a new generation was running things. Dee must have seemed to them like an antiquated fossil returned from the grave. The extract in the diaries read 'Good Sir Francis is near death.'"

"Good Sir Francis? Walsingham must have lent Dee money."
Hammond laughed again. At least someone was having a good time.
Alice felt more than a little guilty. She tended to turn up in
Hammond's life at irregular intervals and demand favours, but he
always seemed pleased to see her and happily acquiesced in her
requests, or at least he had in the past. She made a mental note not to
trade on his, undoubted, affection for her quite so ruthlessly in
future.

"Or maybe it was an old man's nostalgia for past times. Anyway
the quote continues, 'I have entrusted him with certain items of
power concerning Lilith. Sir Francis assures me that all is safely
hidden below.'"

"That could mean anything, Alice."

"Yeah, well, the next day The History Show proudly broadcast the
discovery of unknown cellars below the ruins of Walsingham's old
house at Barn Elms and the Commission had a collective fit."

The silent white shadow flew over the top of the cellars, attracting
Alice's attention. It clutched something small and furry in its claws.
The something wriggled and squeaked, desperately. The bird must
have a nest nearby. Alice decided to take it as a good-luck omen. The
average Londoner might never see a wild owl in their whole lives and
she had seen one twice tonight.

Alice wedged herself back into the scaffolding, closed her eyes,
and prepared for a long night. She wished that she had worn
something warmer. The night air was turning decidedly chilly. She
must have dozed off, because the next thing she remembered was
Hammond shaking her.

"Alice, Alice look at this."

He shoved the laptop under her nose. On the screen was a sort of
diagram filled with dots of varying intensity.

"That close cluster of dots in the top right of the screen. Is that
some sort of hole?" she asked.

Hammond looked shifty. "Well, actually, um, close dots usually
indicate a region of superdense material." He shrugged. "Maybe the
gear is playing up."

"Maybe." She tried to sound convinced but the hairs on the back
of her neck stood up. This was usually a sign that her body was
spooked even if her brain was still in a state of denial. "Show me
where you took those readings."

The entrenching tool bit into the cellar wall. The bricks were old and the steel was new so it was an unequal contest. She went at the wall like Schliemann went into Troy.

"Ouch." She put her finger in her mouth before remembering the squishy stuff.

"Are you okay?" Hammond asked, concerned.

"I broke a nail," she said, finger stinging.

The wall collapsed to reveal a cavity. Hammond flicked the torch onto "direct beam." An old steel-bound wooden chest stood illuminated in the shaft of light.

"I found it, Alice. I told you that if something was there I would find it." He hopped from foot to foot like Pooh Bear around a honeypot.

"Yeah, you found it, Hammond. You're a star." Impulsively, she threw her arms around his neck and kissed him. "Now give me a hand getting it out."

She danced like she was on the surface of the moon. Every small movement of her legs kicked her body high off the ground. She wore a long dress that swirled around her legs as she jumped. Someone threw her a large knife, a dagger. The weapon spun glittering towards her in slow motion but she was quicker than fire. She snatched the blade from out of the air, the hilt smacking firmly against her hand. Things loomed in front of her, things monstrous and evil. She wanted to run but her body disobeyed and stood its ground. Her body attacked despite her fear, slicing the things in ribbons of gore. Great claws raked at her.

Alice screamed, and screamed, and screamed.

"It's okay, Alice, okay, you are just having a dream." Hammond held her tight in the dark until she stopped shaking. He stroked her face, which he knew she loved. She stroked him back, which he always seemed to like. When they had finished with all that stroking, it was dawn.

Hammond, hmm, she had not exactly intended this but he had helped her carry the chest home and it was true that she could not have found it without him. She invited him in for a drink to celebrate and, well, Hammond was kinda cute for a geek. Every time she returned to London, she vowed that she would treat him purely as a colleague but then he'd look at her with those come-to-bed eyes and her resolve melted with her knees.

He also made one of the best breakfasts in England and that was up against some pretty stiff competition. As Hercule Poirot had once said, "Dinner in England is generally execrable but the English are without peer when it comes to breakfast."

Pulling on some clothes after a quick shower, she found the man happily pottering in the kitchen. The chest sat innocuously on the kitchen table, just where she had placed it the night before.

Obviously, the Commission had forbidden her to poke around in anything she found. So she told herself that she had only squirted penetrating oil into the lock last night just to help the Commission. She had absolutely no intention of opening it herself, honest.

"How many eggs do you want?" Hammond asked.

"Only two please as I'm on a diet."

"Whatever are you dieting for, Alice? You are perfect as you are," he said.

She knew there was a reason she liked Hammond so much. He was always good for her morale.

Alice sat and looked at the chest and it sat back and did nothing. Somehow, it seemed to call to her, nonetheless. A crunch of breaking crockery announced that Hammond had breakfast underway. Hammond was a great cook but he tended to leave a trail of devastation behind him in the kitchen. The delicious smell of frying bacon filled her flat.

She rationalised that it would be embarrassing to deliver an empty box to the Commission. Better to have a little peek, just to make sure there was something in it. After all, a little peek could not hurt, could it?

Alice inserted a pick in the old lock and levered. It was rusted in but the oil had done its magic and the catch ground reluctantly over. She opened the chest with the proper reverence due to something that had been shut away for half a millennium. Inside were a bunch of musty papers, and something wrapped in a rag and a bulky, yellowed, linen bag. She briefly glanced at the papers but they were in cipher so she turned her attention to the other items.

The oiled rag unwrapped to reveal an Elizabethan dagger. It was a workmanlike tool, rather than a gentleman's prop. Arcane astrological symbols marked the blade, such as the glyphs for Mars, now used as the scientific sign for male, and Venus, the scientific sign for female. The central glyph, around which the others were placed, was complex. It looked like the Venus glyph, a circle with a cross coming out of the bottom, but two arches were placed at the bottom of the cross. In the centre of the circle, which was bisected by an upside-down arch, was a dot.

Alice's mouth went dry with excitement. This glyph was the symbol invented by Doctor John Dee to summarise the *Monas Hieroglyphica*, his mathematical and magical treatise. Doctor Dee had given a copy to Queen Elizabeth and he had taught the Queen math so that she could understand the work. This was not just a dagger; it was an athame, an astrologer's knife associated with the element of fire, which was used in magic ritual.

Behind her Hammond tuned in the radio to the local breakfast news. "A tanker has spilt acid on the westbound M25 motorway south of Heathrow Airport. The queue now stretches for fifteen miles."

Alice reluctantly set the dagger to one side. Inside the linen bag was a large polished crystal, the size of a cricket ball, set on a black iron frame chased with silver. Four arms crossed over the top of the crystal to support a silver cross. Stamped in the silver was the monad glyph.

The newsreader on the radio finished the transport update and moved on to the human interest story. British news reports tended to be on the heavy side so they liked to end with a light, uplifting piece, preferably involving a cute animal. This was known in the trade as the "skateboarding-duck slot" after a story of especially revolting sentimentality.

Obviously no ducks were skateboarding today, as they closed the news report with "Vandals attacked *The History Show*'s archaeological dig by the Thames last night. Presenter Rupert FitzHenry described the damage as a wound in the flesh of Olde Englande."

Alice filtered the drivel out. The object in front of her was wonderful, literally invaluable. She knew what it was. She had seen a drawing of this artefact in the British Museum penned by Dee's own hand. The curators at the BM would sell their souls to get their hands on this for their collections. This was Dee's skrying stone, the crystal ball with which he talked to angels to learn the secrets of the universe. Alice ran a hand over the smooth surface. It looked as if Dee had packed it away only yesterday.

A ray of light from the rising sun slid slyly through a gap in the clouds. It thrust through the kitchen window and illuminated the translucent mineral. The stone glowed from within with a fierce flickering aquamarine intensity. An image coalesced into life like an old TV locking onto a distant signal.

A woman looked at Alice through the crystal. She had fair skin with vaguely Asian eyes, and cheekbones like Kate Moss. Her jet-black hair was cut short at the front and sides but curled long onto her neck at the back. Her face was young but her green eyes were old peoples' eyes that knew too much.

The woman wasn't just an image; she looked at Alice directly. The historian was making eye contact with a face in a crystal ball. Alice tried to jerk back but couldn't move. She tried to scream but her mouth wouldn't open. She tried to close her eyes but her eyelids were frozen. Alice drowned in the crystal and her mind unravelled like the thread of a cheap dress.

"My, my, Alice. You have been a naughty girly, haven't you?" The woman chuckled, admiringly.

"Who are you? What are you?" Alice asked.

"You can call me Lilith. I'm the Queen's demon." The woman laughed out loud. The title obviously amused her.

"How can I talk to you without speaking?" Alice asked.

"I'm in your head, Alice. I have been having a look around. It always amazes me how you humans manage to cram so much into such a small space."

"Why hasn't Hammond noticed that I'm frozen?" Alice was more puzzled than scared. She should have been frightened but she had experienced too many strange events in her short life to be unduly worried by a demon in a magic ball.

"Our conversation takes a microslice of time. Your friend will notice nothing," replied the woman. "I know all about you so I will tell you something about me. Look deeper into the crystal, Alice. Deeper."

Act 2, A Dark Universe

It was a lovely day. She basked in gravitons. Immensely strong gravitonic waves in space-time flowed past in an endless stream, causing her to bob gently up and down in the eleven dimensions of reality. She had an absolutely prime position on—well, to human perspectives it would have been a low orbit around a tightly spinning black hole but to her it was a beach, a beautiful, exclusive, private beach.

Beaches like this were reserved for the Elders but she was special. She was special not because she was old but because she was very, very young.

The sky was completely dark. It had been dark forever. That was what the Holy Word said. The sky had always been dark and the People had always existed. They lived within the disruptions caused by the interaction of strong floods of gravitons and the space-time matrix. The People fed on the energy differentials between gravity waves. A whole art form depended on subtle gravitonic manipulation of gravity waves to produce different complex waveform cuisine.

She curled herself in and out of the eleven dimensions tasting the different flavour of each. With her gravitonic senses pulled in tight she could pretend that only she existed. She liked this game. She was the only being in the whole universe and she could do whatever she

19

wanted. She had been created as a loner, to be entirely satisfied with her own company. But it was just a game because she rarely got to do anything she wanted. Her life was circumscribed by instructions and restrictions and she was closely observed.

When she extended her senses into the higher dimensions, she became part of a universewide communication web. Dancing space-time strings stored and moved the data that made up the culture of the People. She was not permitted to access that data without close guidance. Unstructured learning would confuse her and impede her education. That was what her instructors said.

She was young and inexperienced and her instructors were old and wise, so she acceded to their wishes. But, sometimes, she would have liked to follow up the interesting ideas and theorems that floated tantalisingly on the edge of her constrained education. She loved to find out. She had been constructed with a need to amass information.

She had chosen her own name. No one could deny her that privilege. Her name was not a formation of modulated sound frequencies but the product of the interaction of a burst of high-frequency gravitons on the matrix of the ninth dimension raised to the seventeenth power. The fractal pattern produced by the interaction was very pretty, so she had a very pretty name. The raising to the seventeenth power wove strong disharmonics into the matrix, giving a hint of contradiction and rebellion.

Her instructors ignored the disharmonics in her name. Their view was definitely that "a rose by any other name would smell as sweet," assuming that they had ever heard of roses, which they had not, or that they had any concept of scent, which they had not.

The arrival of an instructor ended her rest period. "Access data point binary 7783. We will consider the holy data on the Involution of the Dark."

She sighed, more religious indoctrination, but did as she was bid. She was young so she was not completely efficient at hiding her thoughts. Her instructor must have noticed her reluctance because he disrupted her slightly, causing enough pain to focus her attention. She had been slapped. Suitably chastised, she concentrated on reordering the data stream in her consciousness.

The lesson dragged on interminably. The Creed of the Dark, the Catechisms of the Dark, and the Closed Loop of Being. She had been through all this material before. Finally, her instructor pronounced himself satisfied and departed. She was left to bask gently in gravitonic radiation. She spiralled outwards on the radiation current before surfing a gravity wave back into her allotted orbit.

A portal opened in the same plane of orbit. She drew herself in tightly and adopted the frequency of expectant submission. A portal meant that someone very old was coming, someone very old and very, very important. Her instructors travelled by quantum displacement. Portals were complex to open and maintain so only the most skilled could acquire the knack.

A very large powerful example of the People emerged from the spinning tear in space-time, an Elder.

"Ah, there you are young, um, person."

She gave the frequency of genuflection. She knew who this being was. He ranked so high as to be beyond reproach. He had clearly not bothered to find out her name so he did not know how pretty it was. More importantly, he did not know about those stubborn disharmonics.

"Your instructors inform me that your performance has been adequate. I have, therefore, given my assent to your deployment. No doubt you have wondered why you were created?"

Actually, it had never occurred to her. She surfed, she rested, she learnt and she did as she was instructed. What else was there to know? She had not really been asked a question so she did not venture to answer. The Elder was clearly more used to talking than listening.

"In a way, this whole business is about the whys of life." The Elder paused, lost in his own thoughts. Then he said, "Tell me about the Shadow Worlds."

She gathered her thoughts. It would not do to waffle. "At each intersection of the eleven planes of existence, echoes of the real universe fade back into the hypothetical quantum multidimensions. These echoes are the Shadow Worlds."

A textbook answer, she was rather pleased with herself.

"And the properties of the Shadow Worlds are what?"

"The closest are mirrors of the real universe. Further away the images in these mirrors become more and more distorted and unreal." She had no idea where this was going.

"Yes, yes." The Elder made an impatient flick in the space-time matrix that bounced her up and down. "But what is the most consistent change?"

She thought furiously. "Time slows progressively down along the Shadow Continuum," she said, timidly.

"To travel back into the Shadow Worlds is to travel backwards in time," he confirmed. "Time travel within the real universe is forbidden. Do you know why?"

She felt on firm ground and answered confidently. "To avoid a time paradox. Time travel could set up ripples that could destroy everything the People have built, even cause the People themselves never to exist."

"Correct, but now we need to investigate the past. That is why we created you. You are going to jump down into the Shadow Worlds further than any of the People have ever been. You are going to travel to the furthest reaches of time to confirm the Sacred Truth."

The Sacred Truth, she repeated it automatically—*the Dark is eternal and the People are one with The Dark, now and for evermore.*

"But I don't know how," she started to say but she realised she did know how to travel through the Shadow Worlds. Citing the Sacred Truth had unlocked a block in her head. Her instructors had shown her how and then hidden it from her conscious thought.

"There is a heresy." The distaste in the Elder's data stream was so strong that it shrivelled her distal body function forcing her to withdraw into a tight sphere. "This heresy denies the Sacred Truth."

The Elder continued, "It all started with the Shadow Worlds. I should never have permitted their exploration. My only excuse is that it seemed harmless at the time. The first explorations of the nearer Worlds were innocuous enough, showing only shadows of the People at an earlier stage of cultural development. But then came the long jumps that revealed the People living in decompressed matter-based constructs."

"I don't understand." She was completely confused. Matter was something used to create black holes.

"When matter is decompressed outside of a black hole, it can assume complex and strange forms that interact by the exchange of tiny charged particles, particles that behave like photons or gravitons." The Elder sent her a personal data stream that showed a bewildering variety of forms and processes. "Research into the Shadow Worlds suggested that the People might have once used these properties to construct living space using a lost science called 'electronics.'"

This was a new and disturbing thought. The Elder let her process it before continuing.

"Heretical scholars have used this minor detail to construct an imaginary universe based on decompressed matter. Tenuous wisps of matter that interact to produce a blaze of photons so there is no Dark but only Light."

She adopted the frequency of great shock but the Elder pressed on with the mode of finishing a distasteful duty.

"Worse that this, these same heretics postulate that the People themselves were once constructed of decompressed matter. That we have not been eternally as we are now."

She pulled her wave functions in tight with shock.

"So now you see why we constructed you. You must jump back into the far past of the Shadow Worlds to demonstrate the truth and put these heresies to the lie. The alternative is a new religious war."

She had been taught about the religious wars. The People had no logical reason to fight. Certainly, they never fought over resources. The population size was fixed, few died, few were born, and the black holes poured out more energy than could be used. But the People had fought wars; they had fought over religious doctrine and the death rate was awful.

"Do you have any questions?"

"Why me? I am new and inexperienced. Surely there are many others older and wiser who could do such an important task?" she asked.

"So we thought. But every person who has tried this journey has failed to return. The dimensional engineers have become convinced that flexibility rather than experience is the key. So we created you."

She thought it sounded like a suicide mission but she had been carefully constructed and trained for service so she did not protest. However, she could not resist pointing out the logical flaw in the Elders' plan.

"Suppose the heresy is true? My mission could have disastrous consequences," she said.

The Elder struck her hard. "Heresy is by definition untrue. You will prove that and return to witness it. Then I will deal with the core of this conspiracy." The Elder adopted the mode of merciless retribution.

So this was a matter of faith. To question the Elder's view was to doubt the Word. She decided to keep her questions to practicalities. "How do I return?"

"You have been loaded with that information already." He spoke a code word releasing the information from storage.

She reviewed her memory. All the information she needed for the journey was now available to her, including the technique to return to the real universe.

"I will have to exploit an energy source to open a return portal. That could do immense damage locally."

The Elder waved a lobe languidly. "That is of no consequence. The natives will only be Shadows. Personally, I doubt they even exist when there is not a true member of the People there to observe them."

She asked the key question. "When do I go?"

"Now," he said.

She entered the Elder's portal. The novelty would have been exciting but she was numb. She was about to leave the universe before she had even seen it. Entry to the vortex was a new sensation. She was cut off from all contact with the People or the external universe. This was like her game, except that this was real. For the first time in her short life, she was truly alone. She was not sure that she entirely liked the feeling when it was for real, but she supposed that she had better get used to it, all things considered.

The vortex spat her out into the centre of a complex construct. Five equally spaced black holes rotated around a common centre in a single plane. The gravity waves were breathtaking. They crashed over her body, spinning her in surges of energy.

A dimensional engineer approached.

"Greetings, Master of Constructs." She spoke to him with the frequency appropriate to a technical specialist.

"Greetings, Traveller," he said.

His body flicked between modes from the genial contempt shown to youngsters, to the respect due to a personal emissary of an Elder. She sympathised with his confusion.

"I trust that you are ready?" he asked.

Actually, she was not sure she would ever be ready but there was only one reply possible to that question.

"Yes," she said.

Dimensional engineers manoeuvred her into a gravity scaffold rigged vertically above the disk. The engineer tagged her with a data stream and downloaded launch vectors.

She had a question of her own, "How far am I going?"

"As far as we can send you," he replied. The Engineer noted her pose of inquiry and elucidated. "In theory, the distance that we could send you is limited only by the power of the energy source. However, in practice there appears to be a barrier that we cannot penetrate."

"What causes the barrier?" she asked.

"I hope that you will tell me when you return." He initiated the launch procedure without further preamble.

She dropped down the plane towards the rotating structure. The buffeting from the gravity waves increased until it was almost unbearable. She could not breathe or, to be more precise, she could not exchange gravitons with the space-time matrix. Despite pulling her function in tight, small sections of her existence were shaved off by gravity disruptions. She reached the exact centre of the spinning construct and the universe disappeared.

The buffeting stopped and was replaced with nothingness. This was not the emptiness of unoccupied space-time or the tunnel of a portal. This was nothing. She did not appear to be moving. She received nothing; she gave out nothing. There was just nothing. All she could detect was the protective gravitonic field that she generated around herself.

She paused for a while, just experiencing nothing and wondering what to do. Her internal clock still ticked away but she had no idea whether it meant anything real anymore. Outside possessed no time. It was not only the spatial dimensions that were lacking.

Checking and rebooting all her various systems occupied her for some little time. She had been badly shaken up but functioned fully. She did not need a diagnostic, however, to confirm that her emotional condition was—terrified!

One of her receptors picked up a flicker of energy. She ran a diagnostic but the sensor was performing adequately. It really was a flicker of energy. Isolating the input and analysing it gave her something to occupy her mind. The energy source went *click, click, click* at regular intervals. She analysed, extrapolated, and modelled it. When the model ran, she saw the Shadow Worlds.

Each click was her body momentarily phasing with a Shadow World before moving on. This was tremendously exciting. She had made her first discovery. The data programmed into her had given the impression that transit between the Shadows was smooth and continuous. This was not so. It was subject to quantum fluctuations just like everything else. Perhaps the Elders were right. Perhaps a young mind was better suited to exploration. Already she had proved her value to the People.

The Shadow Worlds ticked away endlessly. She tried to extract information from the signal but the small energy quanta carried too little data for her to determine much. Still, it was comforting to have these echoes of the sacred Dark on her strange journey. After a while, she got bored and let the information just flow into a memory store while she played mathematical games with prime numbers to base seventeen. She had a peculiar fondness for this, the most unloved of bases.

Even the delights of base seventeen faded with enough repetition. She decided to check the data stream that was still clicking remorselessly with quantum delight in the background. The Sacred Dark had gone. In its place was light. The universe was a blaze of light. Her philosophical world picture imploded. She desperately rechecked and recalibrated, but the result was always the same. The Dark had gone.

She metaphorically curled up in a ball and put her head between her knees. She was still in this frame when she arrived.

Her world went from nothing to—everything.

Gravity was so weak that she had to work hard to breathe, but her body was bombarded with electromagnetic radiation on a scale that she could barely believe. Floods of photons modulated, coded, radiated, stored, and reradiated in more ways than she could measure. She dropped into a sea of electromagnetic radiation and she struggled and fought. But the more she struggled, the more she drowned. She was dying of energy starvation in a universe of plenty.

Defying all her instincts, she stopped struggling while she still had some energy left and floated. And float she did. She drifted in some sort of electromagnetic decompressed-matter construct. The construct sustained her function. She did not need huge washes of gravitonic energy to warp space-time around her. The machine took the place of her gravitonic body.

The wisdom of the Elders was again apparent. An older person would have been unable to adapt to the strange environment, even if they had survived the emotional shock of seeing heresy confirmed.

Shadow World travellers were usually selected from among those who showed strong religious orthodoxy. She was not old enough to be orthodox about anything.

The machine construct was diffuse, a complex of multiple lines that crisscrossed through energy nodes. Streams of coded data flowed backward and forward. She considered her options. The safe strategy would be to recoil back home immediately to report. There was easily enough energy in the complex to power-launch. But that coded data was so tempting. She could learn so much.

Another issue nagged at the back of her mind. If she left now she would soon be in the presence of the Elder, telling him that the heretics were right and that the Sacred Truth was wrong. How would he react? Probably by destroying the messenger as a closet heretic. It did not occur to her to simply lie and tell the Elder what he wanted to hear.

So she stayed and learnt. The data were surprisingly easy to decode but the messages inside were almost meaningless. The concepts were so strange and alien. She intercepted and decoded, stored and cross-indexed, analysed and interpreted and built her conjectures. Before long, she had made another exciting discovery.

Now she could answer the Engineer's question. She knew why this was the furthest that the People could penetrate into the Shadow Worlds. The machine construct that she inhabited had only recently been built. It was called the "Internet." The important goal now was to find out who or what created the Internet since, logically, it could not have been constructed by the People.

She pursued her investigations relentlessly until she had the answers. Living things that were made of decompressed matter had built the construct. Whether they were Proto-People or not, she would not conjecture, but it was clear that they preceded True People and that the People could not have come into existence without them.

She should have left then but still she hesitated. Her love of knowledge, combined with her fear of facing the Elders, worked to hold her in the Shadow World. She wanted to know more about the Shadow creatures, what they thought, how they lived.

So she worked feverishly, totally consumed by her researches. She watched the creatures make mighty machines and fight terrible wars. She saw the matter beings live and die. Their lives seemed so short but so brilliant. They blazed like particles entering a black hole and they were gone just as quickly.

They shared their living space in the Light with a wide variety of other living things but only one species was the builders. She watched a builder fight another living thing, an "animal," that was four times his weight. The fighter wore a suit that reflected electromagnetic photons brilliantly, a suit of light. He enticed the horned animal to charge and then spun away, allowing the animal to thunder harmlessly past his back. He repeated this until the large animal was tired whereupon he forced a pointed weapon vertically down into its body, killing it instantly.

She was enthralled. She played the clip over and over, spellbound by the beauty and grace of the builder, or "human" as they called themselves. Spookily, sometimes they called themselves "people." Were these people early matter-based versions of the People or did they create them? She would have loved to stay and find out but she had also been created with a strong sense of duty. She would have to go back and make her report. She suspected she would be executed on the spot for heresy but she had to go.

She would allow herself just one more study. She found a data point at a place called Oxford University, English Literature Department. It recorded great histories of the humans by a genius called Shakespeare. The stories he told were masterpieces of emotional conflict. She strode to glory with Henry the Fifth and wept with Romeo.

The humans lived in a fire of emotion, especially their emotions connected with reproduction. Because they had such short lives, they all reproduced frantically. The People were divided by gender but the humans had sex. Many of their deepest motivations and desires were bound up with an incandescent desire for sex.

But she had to go.

She made her preparations, set up the invocation, took a deep breath, and jumped. Computers all over the world crashed simultaneously. The last messages that she picked up passing across the Net all blamed a being called Bill Gates.

Her spell ripped a hole in space-time and she moved into it to begin her long journey. For one moment, she saw the way stretching upwards towards home but then the universe opened beneath her.

Something seized her and pulled her down. She fell and fell and fell, ever deeper into the Shadow Worlds.

Some force held her in a tight grip and then there was light. She emerged into another Shadow World of light. This time there was no Internet. This time she really drowned.

She repeated the trick of relaxing and shutting down as many functions as possible, while she searched for an energy source. She was held tight in an energy matrix of unknown form. The matrix interfaced her body with the matter universe and, for the first time, she saw the universe of light directly.

Energy flowed backwards and forwards across the face of a structure that reflected light, a "mirror." Crystalline nodes, set around the edges of the mirror, powered the matrix. She tapped into them and managed to draw enough power to stabilise her body, at least on a temporary basis. Once the initial panic was over, she took stock of her surroundings. To her delight, she could identify many of the objects around her from the records in her databases.

The mirror stood off the ground in a clearing amongst lush green vegetation. Insects droned around it. When she concentrated on sound waves she could hear other things, wind caressing the vegetation and the distant roll of waves onto the shore. She could also hear humans.

A group of humans sat around the mirror and chanted,

"Lilith, Lilith, Sister from the Dark, sister strongest.
"Come to us, Lilith, we summon you by the pact.
"Sister strongest, we summon you with blood."

A woman lay sprawled on a stone in front of the humans. Blood flowed from a neck wound along a stone channel into a silver chalice. The chant continued.

"Dark light, Lilith, sister strongest, who cleaves the walls of hell.
"When at my lightest, when at my darkest, you hold my soul.
"Lilith, Lilith, sister strongest, made from dust,
"Dark sister, we summon you with blood."

A different stronger voice cut through the repeated chant, "Sister strongest, first born woman, greet your sister, come to me, Lilith. I, Isabella, summon you with a sister's blood."

The owner of the voice, a woman in a black satin cape, moved in front of the mirror, blood still dripping from a knife. "Answer me, Lilith. I am of Eve's line. The mirror opens to your cave. By the ancient pact, you must answer."

She had not a clue what the humans meant. The woman held a whip with multiple scourges. A tiny subroutine from one of her databases identified the object, a cat-o'-nine-tails, used to punish unruly sailors.

"Answer, Lilith," said the woman, whipping the front of the mirror.

It hurt; the pain was acute. She screamed and was astonished when sound erupted from the mirror. The phasing allowed her to communicate as well as listen. Most of the humans retreated in fear at the sound of the scream, but the woman in front of the mirror was made of sterner stuff.

"Answer me, Lilith. I am of Eve's line. Honour your pact with the Avenging Angels. I, Isabella, summon you."

Isabella drew the whip back again.

Another whipping like that might kill her. She had to humour this lunatic. "I am here, Isabella. Lilith is here. What do you want?"

If they wanted a being called Lilith she had better be Lilith.

"My God, it works. The sea diamonds can turn a mirror into a gateway to the Other World." Isabella stood in astonishment, her whip forgotten.

Lilith's data acquisition subroutine filed away another important fact. The crystalline energy nodes were sea diamonds. She automatically cross-indexed with the data she had purloined from the Internet. *Sea diamonds, <query> aquamarine diamonds, rare, once mined from the northeast coast of South America.*

The humans cowered in fear and even Isabella was distracted, so the spell that had activated the sea diamonds began to dissipate. Lilith's body started to dissolve. Desperately, she sucked the last faltering power from the diamonds and attempted to open a portal. There was so little power.

She created a way through the Shadow Worlds and jumped but the energy was insufficient. She bounced off the dimensional wall as the portal failed and fell back into Isabella's Shadow World.

Her mission was over; she was dying. The records would only show another failed long-distance jump. The People had invested so much into this experiment that she suspected no one would ever follow her. Travel to the Shadow Worlds would cease and the People would turn inwards to a new religious war.

She fell backward, until something grabbed her and pulled her in.

Complex matter interacted all round her, exchanging tiny charged particles that released sparkling little bursts of energy. She gratefully absorbed chemical energy. The flavour was like nothing she had ever tasted, with endless subtle variation. She explored her new home and found structure, endless complex fractal structure. Structure at microscales built up to even more structure at macroscales. The whole complex was a machine to regulate chemical reactions and the transfer of chemical energy.

She made a critical discovery. The chemical structure was exchanging particles with the "outside." So there was an outside but how could she access it? Gravity was still weak here but she could extend gravitonic senses. Chemical energy sources flared in her immediate vicinity. Some were simple energy release mechanisms while others were complex, like the thing she inhabited.

She understood. She was in a body and the three larger, complex things around her were also bodies, human bodies. Her body was the wrong shape for human so she inhabited an animal of some sort. She needed to think and run through her data. The body should have sensory structures with which she could investigate the world around her. Running through the body was a webway that reminded her of the Internet. Electrochemical signals flowed along protein membranes. She phased with the signals and perceived the outside world.

Auditory receptors picked up human speech. The voice was deeper than Isabella's so he must be a male according to her stolen Internet data; for some reason he reminded her of an Elder.

"Who is behind the plot to murder the Queen? When will they strike? Where?"

The words made absolutely no sense to Lilith. Right now she was more interested in working out how to mesh with the body's data network. No, not data network, prompted a small subroutine, it was called a central nervous system. She could tap into the signals that streamed along the nerves from sense organs but she could not work out how to activate the motor system and get control.

After some study, Lilith thought that she understood the process. The body was controlled from a complex mass of nervous tissue near where the primary senses were clustered. She meshed into the system and she got it wrong.

The nervous system went into shock. It released a burst of incoherent signals. Chemical energy flashed and all the muscles in the body went into spasm. She felt the pain and howled.

She ran various diagnostics but her own structure seemed unhurt. She siphoned chemical energy from the body to restore her power levels.

One of the humans threw something at her. She saw the material quite clearly through the animal's eyes. The particles contained strange energy that attacked her fusion with the body. She howled again in pain.

Lilith ran diagnostic subroutines to check the damage to her host. The report was chilling. Blackness spread through the body, destroying membranes and chemical pathways. She modelled the damage and made a simulation. The blackness, the "poison," would cause accelerating damage until the body failed. There was nothing that she could do to stop it.

Think, think, she needed time to think.

"Answer, demon. I command you by the power of your true name, Choronzon. I invoke the pact as a child of Eve's line." The human spoke again.

Choronzon? Isabella had christened her Lilith. Couldn't the wretched creatures make their minds up?

She sucked energy greedily from the little body. She needed power to jump into a new host. She extended gravitonic lobes to probe the three humans around her to select a new host.

The lobes were blocked. She was surrounded by a field of strange energy, rather like that in Isabella's mirror. She couldn't jump through this energy barrier. Lilith was close to panic. Talk to them, she thought. Keep them occupied until you can find a solution

"Will you stop doing that, it hurts," Lilith said, using some of her precious power reserve to shape the animal's vocal structures.

Success! Lilith found a small frequency loophole in the energy barrier around her. It was too small to squeeze her body through but she could extend a communication pseudopod out. There was a fourth human some little distance away. This human sang. She sang songs that vibrated the air in harmonious patterns that opened a channel for Lilith to exploit. Now Lilith needed to find a way into the human's nervous system. She checked her stolen database. The eyes were the key. Humans were visual animals and visual information connected directly into the forebrain. Lilith expended a whisper of gravitonic energy to excite the vibrating air molecules in front of the human's eyes. Lilith made a flickering light, a light that flickered at a carefully calculated frequency.

The human must have a nervous system rather like the dog. She might be able to take partial control if she could just find the right frequency. Come on, come on, she thought. There, the light flickers matched the electrochemical waves in the target's nervous system. She had contact.

She projected an image that spoke to the subject.

"Come to me, come to me," it said

"Who threatens the Queen?" asked the human Elder, interrupting her concentration.

Why could they not leave her alone? She *ran* a quick run through her purloined data on the word *Queen*. She had many picture clips of a woman being treated with great deference by her subjects. She was Queen Elizabeth II, the Chief Elder of an English-speaking community. She had almost as many clips of a young man called Freddie Mercury singing. Surely, they must mean the Elder.

"Queen. Female head of a state organised on monarchical lines. Could be anything from a dictatorial ruler to the head of a constitutional democracy," she suggested, helpfully.

All the time she kept the flickering image in the fourth human's eyes. "Come to me."

Her data search revealed more pictures of Freddie Mercury. He seemed more popular than the Elder. Perhaps she should ask for clarification.

"That sort of Queen or did you mean the popular band?"

They threw more of the energy-charged powder at her, causing more damage to the rapidly fading animal body that she inhabited. She screamed in pain again.

"Stop, please stop. This biological structure can barely sustain me and is decaying fast."

Why could she not reason with them? They seemed completely irrational for supposedly intelligent beings. All the time, the subroutine she had set up flickered light at her hypnotised subject and commanded, "Come to me."

"Tell me about the Papist plot against the Queen. From where does the threat come?" The human Elder refused to be diverted; he was implacable. He would have made a good Elder of the People.

Tell him something important, she thought, something that might mollify him.

"The portals that cross the Shadow Worlds are the danger. They threaten your whole species."

Her host body was in the final stages of failure. She could not speak again. She sacrificed precious energy reserves to keep the light flickering in her subject's eyes. The subject moved towards her. Lilith was low on power. It was going to be touch and go.

The subject touched the energy barrier and it exploded. Lilith grabbed the energy released. There was just enough power to jump to the nearest target.

Act 3, Barn Elms House

Simon stirred, then woke, as doors banged closer and closer to his bedroom. Morning light streamed through the gaps in the shutters. The erratic English weather had decided on summer sun, at least for the next few hours. He climbed out of the wooden bed and padded over to open the window to partake of the morning air. The new sun had not yet driven the chill from the air so he was glad of his full-length nightgown and nightcap.

A servant pushed open the bedroom door.

"Mornin', sir," said the man, in a rustic Surrey accent.

"Morning," replied Simon politely, and gestured for the man to set the tray down on a table.

"Cook has instructions that you like to breakfast frugally, sir. So I have just brought a little rye bread, a few slices of ham and chicken, a couple of boiled eggs, a piece of game pie, and a bowl of fruit from the orchards."

"Thank you," said Simon, with resignation. He had long given up debating the meaning of the word *frugal* with the cook.

The servant beamed at Simon with the air of a job well done. He departed, slamming the door hard to wake any remaining sleepers. Most of the Barn Elms household would already be awake. Simon was important enough to have a room at the front of the building, overlooking the ornamental gardens rather than the farmyard at the

35

back, but he was far enough down the pecking order to be at the end of the east wing.

Barn Elms was a working farm so the food was fresh and good. It was said that an English peasant dined on better quality food than did a duke on the Continent. That may have been an exaggeration but the agricultural richness of the island gave the English a reputation for idleness. Gluttony was supposed to be the English sin, as lust was the French and drunkenness the German.

Simon ate with his fingers, cutting the food up with a steel knife. A household in England had to be very poor indeed not to be able to afford a good blade of Sheffield steel. The meal was washed down with ale from a wooden mug. No one but the desperate drank water in England. The poor drank water and died of typhoid. The last administration in England that had delivered clean water supplies to the cities had owed their allegiance to Caesar.

When he had finished breakfast, Simon washed his hands and face and dressed. Law in Elizabethan England tightly controlled who could wear what clothes. There were strong consumer laws that guaranteed quality. Of course, the laws only applied to cloth sold to Englishmen. One could sell any old rubbish to foreigners. Clothing also denoted social rank. In a world without identity cards, to wear clothing more suitable for a higher rank was to commit identity fraud. Elizabeth's government solved this problem by forbidding credit sales for clothing.

Simon was a gentleman so he wore a shirt, breeches, and a doublet. He was also entitled to wear an open, knee-length robe to show that he was an educated man, who worked with his head rather than his hands. Simon opened the door to go to work and bumped into a servant come to clear away the breakfast debris. The man looked pointedly up and coughed discretely.

"I think sir has forgotten something."

Simon blushed and grabbed the nightcap off his head. He carefully positioned his circular cap and retreated with as much dignity as he could muster from the presence of the smirking hireling.

Queen Elizabeth herself had given Barn Elms to Sir Francis Walsingham. It was a gentleman's villa on the south bank of the Thames, a few miles upstream from London. As a working farm, it had some of the most productive eel ponds in England. But Barn

Elms was much more; the house was the headquarters of the Secret Service.

Simon had an office in the centre of the building at the back. It contained a small desk and chair by a lead and glass window, so he could still work in the light when the weather was inclement. The window was a major status symbol. The rest of the room was full of trunks and bookcases stuffed with the records of the Secret Service. The Spanish ambassador would have sold his soul for an afternoon alone in this room.

Simon worked steadily filing new papers and adding notes of their location to his various storage lists. This was an infinite task and he was still working assiduously when Walsingham entered.

The spymaster dressed all in black with a small white ruff under a neat pointed beard. Simple, unostentatious clothing was the mark of Elizabeth's closest ministers. There could only be one sun in the sky, and in the English sky that sun was the Queen. In any case, Walsingham hardly needed clothes to demonstrate his importance.

"Ah, there you are, Tunstall. Clients have arrived for an interview and I need you to take notes."

"Of course, Sir Francis."

Simon followed the statesman down the back stairs to the audience room on the ground floor. Walsingham seated himself in the middle of the room and Simon sat at a desk to one side. The room smelt of wax polish. A servant knocked and ushered in a portly visitor who was dressed in the fashion of a senior member of the merchants' guilds.

"Master Mascall of London," the servant announced the visitor and backed out.

"Please be seated," said Walsingham, pointing to a wooden upright chair.

"Thank you, Sir Francis. This is a most delicate matter. I hardly know where to start."

The man waffled on for some time. Walsingham sat patiently. Mascall was one of his more important clients.

"Calm yourself, Master Mascall. Come, my secretary will pour you a glass of malmsey."

Simon did as he was bid. He produced a piece of Venetian glass and carefully filled it with the expensive Greek wine. The sweet smell filled the room. The merchant took it without looking at Simon or offering thanks.

"A woman dressed as a lady came to me with a letter of introduction from another guild member. She called herself Judith Phillips." The merchant paused for another sip. "She told me that she had irrefutable evidence that there was treasure hidden somewhere in the grounds of my town house."

Simon almost groaned aloud. Not another treasure hunt. It was true that the ancients had been in the habit of burying their wealth in moments of crisis but most of it was either found or forever lost under some new building. Nevertheless, the lure of easy gold still drew fools, like the North Star dragged a lodestone.

"The witch Phillips claimed that she could find the treasure with the help of the fairies."

"The fairies?" asked Walsingham, enquiringly.

"Yes, Phillips claimed to be a white witch who had the goodwill of their Queen," said Mascall.

"The, um, Queen of the Fairies," said Walsingham, thoughtfully. "Ah yes, Titania."

"You know her?" The merchant seemed to think it quite possible that Walsingham might well be on intimate terms with supernatural royalty.

"Not personally," said Walsingham, solemnly.

Simon noted down "Titania, Queen of the Fairies."

"This Phillips woman promised to use a magic spell to locate my hidden gold in exchange for a share."

Simon noted that the hypothetical ancient treasure had become "my gold" in the merchant's thinking.

"Would you describe the spell, Master Mascall?" asked Walsingham.

The merchant flushed. "Is that really necessary, Sir Francis?"

"If I am to help you then I need to know it all," Walsingham said, firmly, slapping his hand down on his knee, for emphasis.

"To appease the, um, Fairy Queen, Mistress Phillips had me dress in horse harness."

"Horse harness?" asked Walsingham, faintly.

"You know, reins and a saddle and things," said the merchant. "Then she rode me on all fours around the house calling out Titania's name."

Simon wrote down "horse harness" and worked very, very hard at maintaining his composure.

"She whipped me quite hard as well," said the merchant, with a touch of self-pity.

The laugh bubbled up but Simon just managed in time to turn it into a cough.

Walsingham pinned Simon with grey eyes. "I trust you haven't picked up a chill, Master Tunstall? It would be so inconvenient to train a new secretary."

"No, Sir Francis. Sorry, it won't happen again." Simon busied himself in his notes.

"Phillips instructed me to wrap up a goodly pile of sovereigns in linen and leave them in the centre of my garden as a lure. She said the fairies would add the lost gold to the package." The merchant ploughed on. "I waited two days but no fairy gold appeared so I took back my package."

"Let me guess," said Walsingham. "Your sovereigns had been replaced by . . . ?"

"Metal scrap!" The merchant wiped his brow.

"And I suppose Judith Phillips has disappeared," said Sir Francis.

The merchant nodded.

"You enquired with the guild member who had written the letter of introduction?"

"It was a forgery," said the merchant, heavily.

Walsingham sat pondering, touching the end of his fingers together in a characteristic pose. Simon knew this was theatrics for Master Mascall's benefit. Walsingham had already decided what to do.

"I fear your money is already lost, Master Mascall," said Walsingham. "The knaves likely have already spent it, but I think we can get you justice."

The spymaster turned to Simon. "Send a message to Pooley in London, Master Tunstall. My 'projectors' are to pass the word around the London taverns that Master Mascall has come into a great fortune."

Walsingham preferred the English word *projector* to the French word *agent*. "Send another message to the Constable in London. Tell him that I would deem it a great favour if he would station a couple of men in Master Mascall's house."

"What for?" asked Mascall, in bewilderment.

"Why, to arrest Mistress Phillips when she comes for her share."

"You think that this woman will fall for such a simple trick?" asked the merchant.

"Greed makes fools of us all," said Walsingham, dryly. "In my experience cozeners are fantasists who half believe the lies they spin. That's why they are so convincing."

After more platitudes, the merchant was ushered out. Walsingham placed his head in his hands and his whole body shook. "Queen of the Fairies!" he guffawed. "Whipped around the house like a recalcitrant stallion!"

He wiped his eyes. "You see the cunning of the woman, Tunstall? Most men would be too humiliated to report the loss and just shrug it off. She misjudged both Mascall's greed and stupidity. Both exceeded her expectations."

The steward entered and coughed discreetly. Walsingham indicated he should speak.

"The heads of the Montague and Belmont houses await on your pleasure, Sir Francis," said the steward.

"In different rooms, I trust," said Walsingham, dryly.

The steward looked puzzled but Walsingham waved away his question before it was begun. "Show them in."

Masters Montague and Belmont were well-to-do farmers with considerable land holdings near Barn Elms. They were involved in an acrimonious land dispute that had dragged on for more than a year now. They entered the room, each studiously ignoring the other.

"I have had my clerk investigate your conflicting claims to Green Acre Farm. He tells me that both of you lack convincing proof of ownership," said Walsingham.

"But I have proof of purchase—" both men said simultaneously before leaving off and glowering at each other.

"Yes, yes, gentlemen," said Walsingham, impatiently, drumming his fingers on the table by his chair. "You both have proofs of purchase but from different vendors. And there is little evidence that either vendor could legitimately sell. My clerk tells me that this case could drag on for years in the courts. That should cost a pretty penny in lawyers' fees. Of course, the farm could revert to the crown if neither of you can demonstrate a legitimate claim. My clerk also thinks that a likely possibility."

Walsingham gave both men time to digest the implications.

"Do you have any advice for us, Sir Francis?" asked Montague, eventually.

"Well, I have had an idea," said Walsingham. "I seem to recall that you have a comely daughter, Montague."

"Er, yes," said Montague, clearly struggling to discern the significance of the new direction of the conversation.

"And you, Belmont, have a second son. A clean-limbed boy, as I remember."

Belmont nodded.

"Then the solution is obvious. You, Montague, give your claim on Green Acre as a dowry to your daughter and you, Belmont, give your claim as a wedding present to the fortunate couple. Second sons are always a tricky problem. That way, you both have your grandson inherit and with no legal bills either."

"But the couple have never even met," said Montague, stubbornly. Belmont, however, looked thoughtful.

"Excellent," said Walsingham. "Then they will not have had time to develop any unfortunate prejudices about each other. I always think too long an acquaintance before the wedding spoils the marriage. Introduce them, gentlemen, and promptly."

He signalled that his steward should show the men out.

"Montague," said Belmont as the men left. "I generally throw a feast for Saint Swithin. Why don't you join us this year? You may wish to bring your charming daughter."

The steward returned with a leather saddlebag. "The post, Sir Francis."

Sir Francis looked through the bag. It was stained with wear. "This letter is from my spy in Edinburgh," said Walsingham, placing a document on the desk in front of Simon.

Superficially, the letter was an ordinary communication from a wine merchant in Scotland to his agent in London. It contained various opinions of wines and delivery dates and prices, coupled with family news and harmless gossip about King James's court.

Simon retrieved a sheet of stiff paper from a drawer and laid it over the letter. The paper had rectangular holes that hid certain words but revealed others. Simon copied the revealed words and then moved the paper down the letter by three lines to reveal new words and so on. The agent in Edinburgh who had written the letter had a piece of stiff paper that was identically cut to the one in Walsingham's office.

Walsingham's secret service relied heavily on codes and used the most sophisticated and modern methods. The best codes were steganographic, where the secret information was hidden in plain sight. The letter from Edinburgh was an example of a new steganographic code known as a Cardano Grille, named after a Milanese mathematician. Doctor Girolama Cardano was one of Dee's friends, so the English secret service had full access to his latest ideas.

Simon's notes built up into a new letter that contained the secret message. The beauty of the Cardano Grille is that the original letter looked so innocuous that it passed unnoticed. A mathematician could break even this code in time, but first he had to know which of a batch of harmless-looking letters to spend the time on.

Simon handed the revealed message to Sir Francis without comment. The spymaster would draw his own conclusions but to Simon it was clear that King James was treating secretly with the French again.

"Tunstall, remind me. What was the value of goods seized by our bold sailors during the last political crisis with Scotland?"

The art of being a good secretary is to anticipate your master's wishes. Simon already had the records on the table.

"Some thirty-five thousand pounds, Sir Francis."

"That must have made the Scottish merchants howl. And how much did we lose to Scottish pirates?"

"Five thousand pounds," said Simon.

"An acceptable rate of exchange," noted Walsingham. "Draft a letter for me to send to King James noting these figures and expressing my satisfaction that a state of peace exists between England and Scotland. Explain how distressed I would be if the political situation deteriorated and Her Majesty was forced to unleash the sea dogs again. And make sure you praise his good relations with France, so the royal whoreson knows that we know."

"Yes, Sir Francis," said Simon.

"That should give His treacherous Majesty something to think on," said Walsingham, with satisfaction. He leant back in his chair. "Ludicrous fellow told me once that a king's every utterance was sanctified by a divine right and could not be questioned. I wonder how divine his utterances would seem to his subjects with Drake's men plundering the Solway Firth?"

Walsingham stared out of the window. "At least the fellow is a protestant, of sorts, and he is the Queen's natural heir. But I cannot help but pray that Her Majesty enjoys a very long reign."

"Yes, Sir Francis. I think we all hope that," said Simon, loyally.

A paid man, even one who had been educated at Cambridge, normally found it wise to keep his political opinions to himself. But a long life to the Queen was a sentiment that could be safely endorsed by any subject.

Walsingham smelt the next document. "An expensive perfume, Leicester's, I fancy." He slit the seal on the next document and read it. "Leicester is concerned that Drake is still missing. The Earl will lose a tidy sum if Drake has been lost."

Drake had left in great secrecy in '77, for a voyage to the Pacific to intercept the unprotected Spanish silver trade. Both the Earl of Leicester and Walsingham were among the financial backers for the venture. So, in great secrecy, was the Queen herself. Many in England, including Lord Burghley, disapproved of the more spectacular naval enterprises on the grounds that they were a needless provocation to Spain, hence the need for secrecy.

Simon consulted his notes. "There was an intelligence report from your spy in the maritime ministry in Madrid. Drake was certainly operating in the Pacific a year after he left. There were squeals from every provincial governor in South America."

"Yes, the political results were most gratifying. Hopefully, Drake will cause money to be diverted from the war in the Low Countries to shoring up defences in the New World," said Sir Francis. "I am concerned that we have heard nothing since. Even the Spanish appear to have lost track of Drake's ship. Send a message to Leicester reporting no news. Then answer all the routine correspondence. Tomorrow, I intend to ride to Nonsuch."

The stallion gave Simon the evil eye and shied when he tried to mount, causing him to slip down in the mud. A groom helped him up. Simon examined the stable lads carefully but they all adopted studiously blank faces. Simon had a notoriously unsafe seat.

"Up you get, sir," said the groom. "Don't worry, the lad will steady the horse."

Simon climbed back into the saddle and adjusted his cloak. Walsingham had already mounted and the two men rode slowly from the stable enclosure. Their horses picked their way carefully around the chickens and the bored farm dogs. A solitary pig watched their passing and snorted, before resuming his endless rooting for edibles.

Two mounted men waited for them at the gate. The one in front wore the coarse smock of a farm labourer but the rearward was a gentleman.

"What are you doing here, Gwilym?" asked Sir Francis. "I don't recall requesting your company."

"No doubt an oversight on your 'ighness' part," said Gwilym, raising his hat. "You being so busy in affairs of state and such."

"About your business, man. Think you that I need a nursemaid?" Walsingham made a shooing gesture. Gwilym ignored it.

"With respect, Sir Francis," said Simon. "They did try for Lord Burghley last month. You could be next."

"Stuff and nonsense," said Sir Francis, but he raised no further objections to an escort.

"I would also like to join your party, Sir Francis. The Queen has given her assent for me to travel to court."

"And welcome you are, James. You can tell me of your father's new enterprises as we ride. No doubt you will want to see Lady Dennys when we arrive." Walsingham kicked the flanks of his horse.

Simon sighed. James Sydney was the latest of Lucy's suitors. Sydney was entirely suitable, being upright and heir to a noble name and fortune.

Lucy herself was an eminent catch. She was a Dennys, a lady of gentle breeding and inheritor of the Dennys estates. Also, it had not escaped the notice of English aristocracy that marriage to Lady Dennys would connect a family to Sir Francis Walsingham. In uncertain times, the favour of the Queen's spymaster might be an invaluable asset to even the highest. So the sons of the noblest houses in England were paraded before Lucy.

And then there was Lucy herself, fair of face and bonny of character. Simon felt his heart lurch in the familiar pattern but ruthlessly suppressed the thought. Lady Dennys was not destined for the likes of him. Sir Francis had a duty to arrange that she married well and that did not mean to an impoverished scholar with no connections. When the time came, Simon would choose a bride from among the daughters of merchants or the more prosperous yeomanry.

The riders followed the muddy track that wound through forests and fields. Where possible, they rode two abreast, Sir Francis and Sydney in front and Simon and Gwilym behind. Often the track narrowed between bramble thickets, forcing the riders into single file. Sometimes the surface was so cut up by farm carts that the men took to the fields and rode parallel to the road, merely using it as a guide. No road had been built, or even maintained, in England since the legions left.

Nonsuch was irritatingly placed in that it was not on the River Thames, the great highway of southern England. The Palace was about ten miles south of Barn Elms, in the land surrounded by the great southern loop of the Thames. One could take a boat upriver to Kingston and then go a-horse southeastwards to Nonsuch but that would save no time. There was a Roman road, Stane Street, that ran from London southwest to Nonsuch, but it was a little too far to the east of Barn Elms to make it worthwhile seeking out. Nonsuch was just plain in the wrong place. So the party were forced to trek overland.

By midafternoon, the travellers were within a short ride of the palace. Walsingham led the way single file through a thicket. Simon had found the journey tedious beyond belief riding alongside Gwilym. The man refreshed himself often, from a beer jar slung around his saddle. He sang continuously, mostly a ditty about the amorous adventures of a Little Pixie.

"Rye-over, rye-over, rye-over, aye-ay,

"I up's on me shoulder, me shoulder away,

"For when she was only an unkissed sixteen,

"I showed 'er..."

Simon dreaded to think what the Little Pixie showed her.

Two men rushed out at the spymaster and thrust weapons at him. Walsingham's horse reared in panic, throwing the rider over the tail. The horse took the billhook meant for the spymaster's throat, but the fall left Walsingham helpless on the forest floor.

Young Sydney screamed a battle cry and rode straight into the fray bowling over Walsingham's attackers. Six generations of aristocratic breeding paid off. Two more bandits appeared and Sydney took them on as well. He punched a hole through a throat with his sword but a blade caught him a nasty gash in the thigh. He lost his weapon and slumped over his horse's neck in shock.

Simon froze.

Gwilym rode past him at the gallop.

" 'Ave a sip on me, sunshine," said Gwilym.

He felled one attacker with a single blow from the jar, which smashed, spraying the man.

"My beer! A pox on you tosspots," said an enraged Gwilym.

In fury, he engaged the other two with his sword. Simon unfroze and rushed to Gwilym's aide, waving his sword over his head and screaming. The attackers took one look at the charge of the wild man and fled, retreating into a thicket where the horses couldn't pursue. Gwilym roared abuse after them, flicking his thumb against his teeth in a gesture of contempt. Simon fell off his horse into a bush.

"Are you all right, Sir Francis?" Simon spat out leaves.

The statesman sat up and flicked mud off his doublet. "Yes, yes, look to Sydney. He took a bad blow."

The young gentleman held tight to his horse's neck. His face was white with shock and blood ran down his leg. Simon and Gwilym lifted him from the saddle and placed him flat on the ground.

"Hold him, Gwilym, while I stop the bleeding." Simon cut open Sydney's breeches and tied a tourniquet around his leg.

"Tight now, Gwilym. I am going to put pressure on the wound and it will hurt."

Sydney moaned. His eyes rolled up in his head and he fainted.

"Can you save him, Tunstall?" asked Walsingham, concerned.

"I think so," said Simon. "The bleeding is slowing."

A groan sounded from the ground behind them.

"Broke my beer jar and the villain don't even have the decency to die cleanly." Gwilym pulled the fallen man's head back and placed a dagger against his throat.

"No, Gwilym, hold," said Walsingham. "I'll have that one alive."

"As you want, your 'onour." Gwilym reversed his dagger and struck the bandit carefully on the temple with the pommel, knocking him out.

Gwilym's quick eye alighted on a pouch at the belt of the man killed by Sidney. He pulled it off and handed it to Walsingham, who unlaced it. Gold sovereigns spilled out into Walsingham's palm.

"A rich purse for bandits. I wonder who gave them these?" asked Walsingham, suspiciously. "Just reward for you, Gwilym. You earned every pennyworth today." He tossed the coins to the Welshman.

Walsingham turned to Simon. "Your bravery did not pass unnoticed either, Master Tunstall. I had no idea you were so fierce with a sword."

"In truth, Sir Francis, I have no skill with the weapon," said Simon, ruefully.

"Then what would you have done if they had stood and fought?" asked Walsingham with a laugh.

"I had not thought things through to that point," admitted Simon.

Walsingham's praise did not fill him with pride. He recalled that moment of weakness when he could not move with complete, shameful, clarity. Without Gwilym, they would all be dead.

Gwilym tied the semiconscious prisoner to his horse and they resumed their journey. Simon led Sydney's horse. One hundred and forty-three more verses of "The Little Pixie" brought them into the estates around Nonsuch.

The lands around the palace were extensive. Old King Harry had demolished a whole village, Cuddington, and diverted several highways to create the thousand-acre park. The King died before the palace was complete and Queen Mary subsequently sold it to the Earl of Arundel. The old Earl died a few weeks ago and the palace had passed to his son in law, Lord Lumley.

Elizabeth, and hence the court, was a frequent guest.

No matter how many times Simon saw Nonsuch, it always took his breath away. King Harry had hired Italian architects to work with his English master masons. The result should have been a disaster but instead it was a triumph. Ornate Italian towers soared airily over dark, brooding, English Gothic halls.

The riders threaded their way through ornate tents outside the palace. Nonsuch lacked sufficient guestrooms for the royal entourage, so the minor courtiers and servants were consigned to canvas. This made Nonsuch an unpopular destination for all but the Queen, but her opinion was the only one that counted.

Walsingham hailed a guard captain at the gate. "Get Master Sydney to a bed and see he is attended by a physician."

"Yes, Sir Francis."

"Gwilym," said Walsingham. "Take the prisoner to the guard house and patch him up. I want him put him to the question."

"Yes, Sir Francis."

"You, fellow." Walsingham gestured to a steward, who stood wringing his hands in the middle distance.

"Yes, Sir Francis."

"Where would I find Lady Dennys?"

"In the Italian Garden, Sir Francis."

Lord Lumley had created an Italian garden, the first in England, to complement the Italian features of Nonsuch. Walsingham strode off in search of his niece, Simon following.

"I have been far too indulgent with that girl, Tunstall." Walsingham set a brisk pace for a man of mature years.

"Yes, Sir Francis."

"This time I intend to have my way."

"Yes, Sir Francis."

"I spoil her because she reminds me of my daughter, Frances, of course. That the same plague took my wife and child as well as Lucy's parents seemed an omen that God intended me to be her guardian."

"Yes, Sir Francis."

High hedges laid out in a halfhearted maze shielded the Italian Garden from the wind. Walsingham and Simon entered at the lower garden below the long pool. Inside the green walls, the air was still and warm. The garden was alight with the buzz of insects visiting the flowers. Lucy sat reading on a stone bench in the shade of a small folly.

"Lucy!" called Walsingham.

She looked up and leapt to her feet. Abandoning dignity, the girl ran the full length of the long pool. As she was at court, she wore a formal gown even in the garden. It split down the front as she ran, her legs kicking out her white petticoat in front. The effect was exactly as the French dress designer intended, which was an act of great imagination on the designer's part, as he preferred boys.

She threw herself into her uncle's arms and he whirled around with her. The girl disengaged and curtseyed.

"Greetings sir," she said to Walsingham. "I hope you had a tolerable journey?"

"Well, actually . . ." Walsingham began but Lucy was not listening. She kissed her uncle and then Simon formally on the lips in the way that an English lady greeted or took leave of guests or a host. The freedom given to English women was the scandal of the Continent and nothing aroused more comment than the "English kiss."

"Now, Lucy. I want a serious talk with you," said Walsingham, leading her back into the folly. Simon waited politely outside but he could hear every word.

"You were sixteen this summer, well past the age you should be betrothed. You have not lacked for offers from men that I consider suitable. I have been more than patient but this cannot go on. I shall just have to select a husband for you if you do not make your own choice soon."

Walsingham would be quite within his rights in ordering Lucy to wed; indeed, it was his duty to her dead parents. Young women were delightful creatures but absurdly flighty and inconstant. It was said that the love of a maid was like the spring rain—it was as like to fall on a cowpat as a rose. Left to her own devices, Lucy would probably waste her fortune and her maidenhead on the first rascal that gave her a pretty smile and a beguiling story. That was why the law quite rightly insisted that she should have a male protector, responsible for both her money and her future.

Lucy's lip trembled. "Please, Uncle, don't scold me so. I have so been looking forward to your visit."

"Now, now, Lucy. Don't take on. I have your best interests at heart," Walsingham said, patting her hand.

Simon thought that it was just as well that Elizabeth's enemies could not see the fearsome spymaster being moulded like fresh clay by the young girl. Lucy had that effect on men.

"I mean, take that young Sydney. He is eminently worthy and the man clearly adores you. Probably too much for his own good, I'll warrant. He would never be complete master of any household that included you despite being brave and valorous as a lion. The boy took a terrible wound defending me on the way here to see you."

"Master Sydney hurt . . ." The girl put her hand to her mouth in shock.

That was the trouble with Lucy, thought Simon. She was essentially good-hearted as well as beautiful, so men were drawn to her like drunkards to a keg.

"I have sent a physician to him," said Walsingham.

"Poor James, I must go to him at once." She picked up her skirts and ran out of the garden.

Walsingham leaned back on the bench and grinned at Simon. "I thought that might do it. Nothing like a wounded hero to win a young girl's heart."

"Yes, Sir Francis," said Simon. He held his council, as he thought otherwise. Sir Francis seemed not to have noticed that Lucy had adroitly removed herself from a conversation that she wished to avoid.

In the last two years, Walsingham had paraded a small phalanx of suitable men in front of the girl. She had seemed struck with a number of them but, like a frightened filly in a steeplechase, had always shied away at the final fence. Simon suspected that poor Sydney was about to be another casualty in the quest for Lucy's heart.

Act 4, The Palace of Nonsuch

Why are these places always underground? thought Simon. Is it simply tradition or is there a natural tendency for such functions to gravitate toward Hell? It was damp and cold belowground. His torch lit Walsingham's back, throwing the spymaster's flickering shadow onto the cellar wall. Walsingham pulled open the heavy wooden door with a thud that echoed down the stone walls.

"Oh God, oh God, oh God, please no more." The scream cut through the air.

The captured assassin was stretched over a wooden frame by ropes attached to his wrists and ankles. The wrist lines were wrapped around a drum that could be turned by a large wheel to increase the tension. The assassin's joints already strained.

"You should have thought of God, matey, before you tried to stick a blade in my gut." Gwilym gave the wheel of the rack another tenth of a turn eliciting a loud pop from a knee joint and more screams.

"I told you, I don't know who paid us. We met him in a tavern. He told us where to set the ambush. The gentlemen must not reach Nonsuch, that were the instructions. That's all he said. They mustn't reach the palace."

Gwilym went to give the wheel another turn.

"No more, he has nothing more for us." Walsingham called off his man.

"'Ee might just need a bit more encouragement to name names, your 'onour," said Gwilym.

"I don't think so," said Walsingham. "Any more would be pointless cruelty. Cut him down and give him to the hangman."

No experience seemed to affect Walsingham, but Simon needed no encouragement to leave the torture room. He wanted fresh air to get the stink of blood, bodily wastes, and fear out of his nose.

"That was a waste of time," said Simon, in disgust.

"Not so, Master Tunstall. We learnt two important facts." Walsingham placed the tips of his fingers together, so Simon knew he was in for a lecture.

"The first is inconsequential. They knew exactly where and when to wait for us. We have a spy at Barn Elms. Someone is passing information. Well, Gwilym can be relied upon to ferret that out. No, it's the second point that bothers me more. 'They must not reach Nonsuch'—that's what he said. Why, Master Tunstall? Why must we be prevented from reaching the Palace? What is going to happen here?"

Walsingham led the way into the heart of the main building. Simon followed a respectful three steps behind. They passed a number of guard stations but Walsingham was waved through each time without breaking step. The final set of guards stood in front of a long corridor that led to the audience room. Walsingham proceeded up the corridor at his normal measured pace. A gaggle of men appeared at the far end. The Earl of Oxford, a thin, stooping man dressed in expensive finery, led them. He sported a royal blue doublet with fashionable peasecod belly and tight Venetian breeches. The costume was stitched through with gold thread. A ruff, so large that it fell upon his shoulders, completed the ensemble. Simon thought the Earl looked like a peacock that someone had kicked in the rear so hard its tail had become stuck around his head.

The corridor was not wide enough for both parties. Walsingham strode on, forcing the Earl to stand to one side with his entourage.

"My Lord." Walsingham inclined his head ever so slightly.

"Sir Francis." The Earl spoke civilly but his eyes blazed.

"Why does the Earl give way to a mere knight? We should thrash the fellow." One of Oxford's young protégés, freshly in from the provinces, expressed anger at his master's humiliation.

"Shut up, you fool or he might hear you. That's Walsingham," said a more experienced member of Oxford's retinue.

"Why does he hate you so?" Simon asked Walsingham.

"A simple question with a complicated answer," said Walsingham. "Elizabeth's sister, Queen Mary, assembled a ragbag of nobility to act as her councillors. Most were appointed on a whim that usually had little connection to their political views or abilities. So they had no common policy and spent most of their time arguing with each other and competing for the Queen's attention. Elizabeth, on the other hand, secretly assembled a government in waiting even when Mary still ruled. She selected her statesmen largely from the alumni of Cambridge University and she chose capable people who shared her views on the world."

Simon understood that to mean people who supported the New Religion.

"Some of those people were nobility, like my Lords Burghley and Leicester, but others were of humbler stock."

Walsingham smiled grimly at this point, since he was one of the latter. His mother was a Dennys but his father was a prosperous merchant who acquired respectability by buying a manor house in Kent.

"Of course that disenfranchised many nobles, traditionalists, and fools. Oxford encompasses all three in one body. To put it at its simplest, he hates me because I have the Queen's ear and he doesn't."

"I see," said Simon.

"Some years ago, the noble Earl of Oxford bent in the throne room before Her Majesty and broke wind with alarming vigour. The court erupted in laughter. I thought Elizabeth would break her stays. Humiliated, the Earl withdrew and sulked on his estates. It was some little time before he reappeared at court. Do you know what Her Majesty said when he bent to kiss her hand?"

"No, Sir Francis," said Simon.

"She said, 'Fear not, my Lord, I have quite forgot the fart.'" Walsingham shook his head. "'I have quite forgot the fart.' Of course, he hates her as well for the sport she made of him. Poor Anne Cecil, Burghley's daughter, is married to the man. He treats her abominably. I thought Burghley ill advised to consent to the match."

The spymaster pondered, his face suddenly without humour. "Do you not think that he has a lean and hungry look? All plotters seem to share it. Give me fat men who are content with their lot."

The irony, thought Simon, was that Walsingham himself was one of the leanest men in Christendom. Walsingham strode into the audience room with Simon behind him. Both men bowed low in the direction of an improvised throne. On it sat the Queen of England. She was deep in conversation with a man dressed in the robes and skullcap of a scholar. Areas where the robes had worn threadbare thin suggested that the man had the typical scholar's indifference to wealth. Walsingham waited patiently at the back. One did not interrupt a queen; in particular, one did not interrupt this queen.

"Look at the colours and glitter on the fine clothes of the courtiers," whispered Simon to Walsingham. "The court shines."

"It shines with the glow of rotting wood," said Walsingham. "This is the most dangerous place in the land."

"The Queen's gown is spectacular," said Simon, still enthralled despite Walsingham's cynicism. "She must spend hours with dressers every morning."

"We must allow her the vanity of her sex," said Walsingham. "Her sister, Queen Mary, cared but little for her appearance but indulged her vanity in her rule. No argument or fact could sway her as she believed that her every whim had the endorsement of God. So good men burned at the stake because they opposed her will. Even her husband, Philip of Spain, cried halt but could not dissuade her."

Simon could not remember the reign of Bloody Mary but he knew that Walsingham had fled England for his very life.

"So let Her Majesty indulge her vanity in her appearance," said Walsingham. "She knows she dare not indulge it in her politics."

"I see Dee is at his most unctuous," Walsingham said, nodding in the direction of the scholar. "Looking at him now, you would not believe that he was one of the more drunken revellers at Cambridge. His party trick was knife throwing. He used to pin tavern wenches to the wall by their skirts."

Simon tried to picture the sober scholar pinning tavern wenches to the wall by anything, but his imagination failed him.

While they talked, Sir Francis had been edging them inconspicuously closer to the Queen, until they could follow the conversation.

"A fine scholarly work, Doctor Dee," said the Queen.

"The British nations have historical claims to the New World that predate the Iberians. The voyages of your illustrious ancestor, King Arthur, are one example. Then there is the visit of your kindred, the Welsh Prince Madoc, to the Americas in 1170 AD. The Pope's division of the world between Spain and Portugal is little short of theft." Dee was in full flood.

Simon cricked his neck to get a glimpse of the title of Dee's new book. It had *Brytanici Imperii Limites* in gold on the spine. Simon translated it as "The Extent of the British Empire." *British* Empire! Dee clearly thought big.

"I have marked Your Majesty's territorial claims on this map. It includes a great part of the seacoasts of Atlantis—the continent that the ignorant call America—that are next to us and all related islands from Florida to the northern seas."

"What say you, Sir Francis?" The Queen deigned to acknowledge Walsingham.

He dropped on one knee until bidden to rise.

"Well, Your Majesty," said Walsingham, putting his hands together as if at prayer. "Doctor Dee's scholarship is unquestionable but I fear a violent reaction from Madrid to any English colonies in the Americas, sorry, Atlantis. Spain can put two hundred warships into the water. Have you calculated how many ships we might need to protect an American empire of our own, Doctor Dee?"

"I estimate that Her Majesty would need a Petty Navy Royal of just sixty tall ships of one-hundred-and-sixty to two-hundred tons," said Dee. "A Spanish fleet of two hundred is a chimera. Firstly, they need to station considerable forces in the Mediterranean Sea, so as to deter the French and guard against the Turk. Secondly, a goodly number of their warships are galleys that are suitable only for coastal and harbour defence."

"Still, sixty royal galleons," murmured Walsingham.

"Supported by twenty barques of twenty to fifty tons. They would need to be very strong and warlike, not river barques," Dee developed his theme.

"How many warships did we inherit from our Royal Father, Sir Francis?" By convention, the Queen tended to forget the reigns of her siblings.

"Some twenty-two, Your Grace, not counting ancient hulks unsuitable for modern warfare," said Walsingham.

"And now I have thirty or more, many of them race-built galleons of the most modern type, thanks to the efforts of John Hawkins," said the Queen proudly.

Hawkins was a product of the democracy of the sea, where men of talent could rise far above the station in life allotted to them by God.

He had risen to be Treasurer of the Navy, an unprecedented position for a provincial commoner. A Plymouth man, he was drawn from the same cluster of interrelated families from the County of Devonshire that had also thrown up Drake.

Traditionally, warships were crewed by merchant seamen who were commoners, while the captain was a member of the ruling classes, a gentleman amateur who had no inclination to learn ship crafts. This state of affairs still prevailed in Spain, France, and even Scotland. But in England, the commoners who built, sailed, and fought in the new sailing ships could achieve status and position in society. They could become captains or even admirals commanding from the deck of a royal warship. Similarly, older gentlemen competed to fund the new warships and younger gentlemen competed to serve in them.

Drake demanded that the gentlemen must haul and draw with the mariner and the mariner with the gentlemen. So sons of the English ruling classes, who would literally have rather starved than demean themselves to push a plough or mend a wall, proudly showed the rope scars on their hands and boasted of the famous captains under which they had served.

This social and technical revolution threw up a new breed of men, the sea dogs. Continental princes professed to despise England's Virgin Queen, who ruled but half an island, and they talked darkly of when she would be brought to heel, but it was all hot air. Elizabeth's realm lay in the ocean, and in the seas around England, the sleek, culverin-armed ships of the sea dogs had the final word.

"Of course Her Majesty can also draw on the ships of her loyal subjects in times of crisis. John Hawkins alone can add a further sixteen warships to Her Majesty's forces," said Walsingham.

"True, but an American empire would need a larger core force of royal ships constantly available," said Dee. "The Plymouth ships are mostly employed in trading."

As the Spanish had declared it illegal for English ships to trade in the New World, "trading" in this context tended to be a euphemism for piracy.

"And how many men would be needed to crew these new ships of the Navy Royal?" asked Walsingham, changing the thrust of the debate.

"I calculate we would need a professional force of six thousand and six hundred men," said Dee, with the air of a man asking for an extra egg for breakfast.

"What think you, Sir Francis?" asked the Queen, with a clear hint of challenge in her voice.

"I doubt the Royal coffers could extend to funding such a force, Your Majesty. Currently, you spend only about sixteen thousand pounds per annum on naval defence which, if memory serves, is about one twentieth of Your Majesty's income."

"But Doctor Dee has considered how to finance the project," said the Queen. "As the Navy Royal would benefit all the kingdom, Doctor Dee suggests that the money be raised by general taxation. What say you to that, Sir Francis?"

"I say that a new general tax would be a very brave decision by Her Majesty, given the attitude of Her Majesty's subjects to new taxation."

"You see, Doctor Dee. Our loyal subjects expect our protection for them and their enterprises, but the ungrateful wretches don't want to pay for it."

Simon got the impression that the Queen was enjoying herself hugely. She liked to set her councillors against each other. Simon doubted that Sir Francis had said anything that she had not worked out for herself. Elizabeth was one of the most formidable politicians ever to have sat on the English throne.

"I regret an American empire, although a great enterprise, is beyond our current resources but this book is a valuable work and we are much pleased with it. One day perhaps."

The Queen gazed right through the court as if at some far horizon. Her eyes took on a steely glint. An old courtier had once told Simon that she was the image of old King Harry when she got that look.

Dee took that as his cue to depart. Sensibly, he decided to quit while he was ahead. He bowed deeply and walked backwards away, until he disappeared into the crowd that always surrounded the throne.

"Your Majesty, I would have leave to speak of the plight of our coreligionists in the Netherlands," said Walsingham.

"Go on, Sir Francis," said the Queen, in a dangerous tone.

"The Duke of Parma's Catholic forces are on the move again. They have captured many Protestant towns and inflicted divers horrors on the inhabitants. Parma has consolidated Spanish power on the whole region south of the River Schelde. Soon he will move on Antwerp. Our friends need money and troops urgently."

"Not this again, Sir Francis. You want us to spend the reserves of our treasury on equipping idle mouths to go a soldiering in the Low Countries. Five years ago, I turned down the offer of sovereignty of that unhappy place. Have not your own spies reported that the Spanish treasury is too bankrupt to support a new offensive?"

"Indeed, Majesty, but the Duke has paid the Army of Flanders from his personal resources."

"Men like you persuaded us of the Havre enterprise. It cost a quarter of a million pounds from the Royal Treasury and do you know what we received for our money? Shall I tell you, Sir Francis? Nothing! No doubt you have some friend in mind to appoint general so he can chase glory at our expense. You expect us to use our money to set up a Caesar to challenge our own authority." The Queen was shouting now and the court had gone very quiet.

"I calculate the cost is affordable, ma'am," said Walsingham.

"You think that with your head and our purse that we could do anything," said the Queen.

"No, Your Majesty. Some money spent now will save you spending much more at some later date. I want you to save the New Religion. You must—"

"Must! Must!" screamed the Queen. "*Must* is not a word you use to princes, little man. You would not have dared used such a word to our father and you shall not dare use it to us."

"No, Your Majesty. I humbly beg Your Majesty's pardon." Sir Francis dropped to one knee. Simon shrank down as well, lest the Queen notice his presence.

"Gentle cousin, you presume too much on your kindred with our mother." The Queen's anger seemed to leave her at the mention of the unfortunate Anne Boleyn. She sank back in her chair and waved a hand.

"You have our leave to depart, Sir Francis."

Walsingham stayed where he was.

"I regret my duty forces me to trouble Your Majesty a little further, on the matter of Your Majesty's security."

"More plots, spymaster? You see plots everywhere." The Queen spoke harshly but she did not order Walsingham out.

"Yes, Your Majesty. But there is less danger in fearing too much than too little," said Walsingham.

One had to look very carefully to see the small motion Walsingham made with his left hand. Simon was expecting it. Only the Queen's most trusted inner circle knew this hand signal. Men like Burghley, Leicester, or Walsingham.

"Enough, sir, enough of your endless plots. We will listen to no more of them. We are fatigued."

The Queen stood and all the men in the room dropped to one knee while the ladies curtsied.

"You, sir," she said to Walsingham. "You are the knave that has worn us out, so you will give us the privilege of your arm to lean upon while we walk."

"At once, Majesty." Walsingham climbed to his feet and held his arm out.

"I believe I will take a turn down the long gallery to catch the sun." The Queen slipped from the royal pronoun "we," indicating that she was now expressing the personal opinion of Elizabeth, rather than a royal view as head of the English state.

She rested her hand lightly on Walsingham's arm and they walked to an elaborately carved door. The rest of the court stayed low and pivoted to face her as she passed. No one turned his, or her, back on the Queen. No one.

Guards opened the door for her. Simon followed the couple through. He was not an individual in his own right at court but an appendage of Walsingham, so he was not challenged. Once the Queen's party was through the door, the guards snapped their halberds across it, denying access.

The long gallery was an extensive narrow hall, with leaded windows down one side, and paintings and tapestries down the other.

"Well, Sir Francis, what is it this time?" asked the Queen, wearily.

"That is the problem, Your Majesty. I don't know." This admission was not one you heard often from Sir Francis and it clearly pained him.

"They tried for Burghley earlier and then plotted to assassinate me on the way here. It's as if someone was trying to strip Your Majesty of her security. I believe that something evil is to happen here at Nonsuch, and soon. I suspect it will be another attempt on your life, ma'am. Ideally, I would like Your Majesty to leave this place today."

"What! Leave just like that? Impossible." The Queen stared at Walsingham in astonishment. "Do you know how long it takes to plan a move of the court? Where would I go? Nothing is ready for me at any of the other palaces. And I will not leave without my court. Think you that Elizabeth will slip away like a thief in the night, like some scallywag cozening a tavern keeper?"

"No, Your Majesty. I thought it unlikely but duty bade me try. My alternative suggestion is that I employ extraordinary methods. It is convenient that Doctor Dee is at court."

"Stop," said the Queen. "You must do as your duty guides you, Sir Francis. But we do not wish to know your methods. We do not need to know."

Simon noticed that the Queen was using "we" again. Sir Francis was being given an order.

Queen Elizabeth was a subtle and many-layered personality. She would equip ships for an enterprise to the Spanish Americas and then forbid them to sail south of Biscay. And if a disloyal subject ignored her and sacked some Spanish treasure town, well, it was hardly the Queen's fault. When the Spanish Ambassador complained, she would be sure to promise to root out the guilty. As an indulgent ruler, however, she would probably restrict punishment to a tongue lashing—provided the royal share of the loot was adequate.

The Queen and Sir Francis continued to promenade down the long gallery.

"All this spying and counterspying, Sir Francis, we like it not," said the Queen. "We grow weary of the subterfuge. Sometimes we think it has tenuous connection to justice and we have no wish to be a despot to our subjects."

"Not the one of your subjects thinks you a tyrant, ma'am," said Walsingham. "But some kind of despotism is essential for the protection of Your Majesty's person and your subject's liberties. Spies are like tax collectors, an unpopular necessity. Spies placed strategically are less dangerous than an army that can band together. A country without a standing army needs a strong government, otherwise civil war and invasion will surely follow."

"Your niece is bonny, Sir Francis," said the Queen, changing the subject. A subject was closed when the Queen decided it was closed.

"Indeed she is, ma'am," said Sir Francis, warmly.

"I like her well. She is a good girl and an ornament to the court but I do not understand why she is still a maid. Marriage is the proper state for a young lady."

"Yes, ma'am," said Sir Francis.

Simon winced. He knew that the advantages of marriage for a lady were not a subject that Walsingham would wish to expand upon to the Queen. At the start of her reign, all the Queen's councillors had agreed that she should marry while young in order to produce an heir. The world was an uncertain place. Without a clear heir, England might tear itself apart in civil war as different applicants put forward their claims to her throne in the event of the Queen's death. Spain and France could hardly resist interfering if such a calamity unfolded. There might even be a resumption of religious conflict.

So the Queen must marry, every one who mattered agreed upon that. The Queen herself was not adverse to the idea as she had been an energetic girl who was fond of men. But whom should the Queen marry? Under English custom, her husband would not be merely a royal consort but King of England, with all the advantages and privileges of his rank. Each privy councillor enthusiastically suggested applicants from his own family, and fiercely resisted contenders from other clans. In the end, all agreed a truce. Elizabeth would stay the Virgin Queen, married only to England.

The Queen herself eventually came round to this view. She would have found it irksome and intolerable to hand her throne to a lesser prince while devoting her life to childbirth and household affairs. And anyone who married Elizabeth was likely to be a lesser Prince.

This still left the problem of an heir. An acceptable candidate had gradually emerged in the body of the Protestant James of Scotland. Typically, Elizabeth refused to discuss the matter, yet at the same time allowed her councillors to open diplomatic channels to James. That Mary Queen of Scots was Elizabeth's prisoner and James's mother complicated the situation.

"She is past the age where you should have found her a husband by now. You are lax in the discharge of your responsibilities, Sir Francis," said the Queen, teasing.

The dour Walsingham was never lax when it came to duty.

"Yes, Your Majesty," said Walsingham.

"I must take the matter in hand myself," she said.

Matchmaking was one of Elizabeth's hobbies. It deflected her harmlessly from her own barren condition.

The Queen glanced at each painting in turn as she walked down the gallery. Most were portraits of Arundel's respectable but boring ancestors and relatives. The late Earl was a typical product of the line. A less exciting man would have been hard to find. He was entirely disinterested in politics, an attitude that Walsingham found much favour in. An aristocrat who was disinterested in politics was an aristocrat who presented no threat. Walsingham had taken great interest in Arundel when the court became a regular visitor to Nonsuch. Simon had filed many reports from various spies who had investigated the Earl most thoroughly. They were now working on his son-in-law.

The Queen stopped at one portrait to study it most carefully. It was of her father, King Henry VIII, in the middle part of his life. The King stood in a characteristically confident pose, with legs placed firmly apart and fists upon his hips.

"Have I Your Majesty's permission to withdraw?" asked Walsingham.

The Queen did not reply or take her eyes off the portrait but she waved a hand casually to indicate the audience was over. Walsingham and Simon bowed low and backed away. As he retreated eyes down, Simon overheard the Queen whisper to herself.

"Father, Father, what a mess you left for me."

"We are going to have to use extraordinary methods to protect the Queen, Tunstall."

"Yes, Sir Francis."

"We shall need Dee's help," said Walsingham, gesturing with his hand as they walked through the endless corridors of the palace.

"Dee, the code breaker?" asked Simon, somewhat confused.

"The good doctor is so much more than a code breaker," said Walsingham. "As well as an intelligencer for the Queen's Council he is also one of the foremost authorities on supernatural beings in the land. He has in his possession one of the three known copies of Johannes Trimethius' *Steganographia*. Lord Burghley supplied Secret Service funds so that Dee could purchase it from a bookseller in Antwerp."

At that point, the scholar appeared around a corner. Pretending not to see Walsingham, he put his head down like a man advancing into a gale and made a dash for the door.

"Doctor Dee," purred Walsingham. "Just the man I was looking for."

"I regret that I am rather busy, Sir Francis. Possibly another time." Dee attempted to disengage but Walsingham held him firmly by the forearm.

"Now, Doctor Dee. I am on the Queen's business."

Dee looked resigned; there was only one answer to that. "I am at Her Majesty's disposal, of course."

"We have a little problem. I need information about a threat on the Queen's life," said Walsingham.

"You require me to transcribe a coded letter for you?" Dee asked, obviously pleased at the challenge that breaking a new code would bring.

"No, Doctor Dee. I need information and the supernatural is my last hope."

"You should try a disciple of that quack Nostradamus then," sneered Dee. "He could stare into the water and have one of his visions for you."

The scholar tried to walk off but Walsingham tightened his grip on Dee's forearm, bringing a gasp of pain.

"I want you to do a summoning." Walsingham fixed Dee with grey eyes.

"Keep your voice down," said Dee, looking around. "Trafficking with demons is punishable by death."

"I know that," said Walsingham. "Nevertheless, you will do it. I speak in the Queen's name."

"You have the wrong man, Sir Francis. I lack such skills," said Dee, licking his lips nervously.

"Don't try to gull me, Dee. I know Trimethius dealt with demons. He raised the shade of Maximilian's dead bride so the Emperor could talk with her one last time." Walsingham was implacable.

"There are no spells in the *Steganographia* that would summon a demon. On my life, Sir Francis."

"On your life, Doctor Dee, Trimethius' decoded writings led you to another hidden work. You know of what I speak. The work of the mad Arab, the *Necron*—"

"Don't say that word, Sir Francis. Please, the very pronunciation of the name is dangerous." Dee glanced around again. "I suppose this means that you have a spy in my household."

Walsingham did not waste his breath answering. Dee was incredibly naïve if he imagined that someone so close to Her Majesty as himself was not under surveillance.

"Very well, Sir Francis. You will need to send someone to fetch a certain wooden box from my cottage at Mortlake."

Simon was waiting at the front entrance when the royal messenger returned. The man would have changed horses at Mortlake but even so, steam rose from the horse's body and foam flecked its lips.

"Have you got Doctor Dee's property?" Simon asked the messenger.

"Here," the rider said, handing down a modest container. "I hope it is more important than it looks. I have ruined two good mounts today."

"I believe it is of the utmost significance," said Simon. "Of course, I do not know what it contains."

The two men exchanged the sympathetic looks of one small link in a chain acknowledging another.

Simon took the wooden box, which was surprisingly small. In his imagination, it had grown into a large wooden chest full of strange devices and leatherbound tomes of great portent.

"You, boy," he said to a servant. "Find Sir Francis Walsingham and Doctor Dee. Tell them the messenger has returned from Mortlake."

Simon made his way around the central building of the palace to a small quiet peripheral annexe that largely consisted of storage facilities. His route took him out of the complex through the cottage garden. A familiar voice sang quietly among the scented herbs. He calculated that the servant would take some little time to locate his master so he could tarry for a while. It would be pleasant to inhale the scent and converse with the garden's occupant.

"Good afternoon, Lady Dennys," Simon said.

"Hello, Master Tunstall," she said. "Have you come to rescue me from boredom?"

"Were I so gallant," he replied. "But I am on Sir Francis' business."

The girl nodded. She was used to living in a world that revolved around Walsingham's many interests.

"But this is a pleasant spot, Lady Dennys. Surely it can lift any black mood."

"I had thought the gardens of Nonsuch the finest that I had ever seen but I expect even paradise palls with time. And time hangs heavy here." The girl sighed.

"You have your duties, surely, as a lady in waiting to Her Majesty," said Simon.

"The Queen is very kind," said Lucy, carefully, "but she has few tasks for me so I am left much to my own devices."

Simon was not surprised that the Queen declined to have Lucy on display around her. There could only be one sun in the sky. He had no intention of speculating out loud on the Queen's motivations, however, so he changed the subject.

"Master Sydney is recovering, I trust?"

"I believe so," said Lucy, distantly. "He is in the care of the Palace physician. I can't be expected to waste my time on every aristocratic young sprig that is foolish enough to take a tumble while indulging in boyish heroics."

So much for the wounded hero, thought Simon. Another suitor gone, he concluded. Walsingham would not be happy. Her tone shut down further discussion.

"I fear I must take my leave of you, Lady Dennys." He raised his cap politely.

The room chosen for the summoning was an outbuilding on one side of the garden. As he entered, he could hear Lucy singing again.

"Come, heavy sleep the image of true death,
"And close up these my weary, weeping eyes.
"Whose spring of tears doth stop my vital breath,
"And tears my heart with sorrow's sigh-swoll'n cries."

Simon did not have long to wait before Walsingham and Dee joined him inside the annexe.

"Your property, Doctor Dee," Simon said, holding the wooden box out.

Dee took it and examined the seal carefully before breaking it and opening the lid. A pungent smell filled the room. Dee took out several small vials, a book, and some geometrical devices.

"I must prepare everything very carefully," said Dee, pedantically. "It has been many years since I attempted to summon a demon. Close the window shutters and lock the door. We must not be disturbed."

Simon sealed off the windows, plunging the room into gloom. There was no lock fitted to what was an insignificant building but he shut the door tight to humour Dee. A lock was hardly needed, as the only person around was Lucy and she knew better than to disturb Walsingham's meetings.

Through the door, he could still hear Lucy singing in the garden.
"Come and possess my tired thought-worn soul,
"That living dies, that living dies, that living dies."

Act 5, Queen Elizabeth's Apartment

The summoning had not gone well. Lucy lay on the floor unconscious. Dee drew his dagger and advanced on the girl, weapon raised. "Kill her. Kill her now, while we still can."

"What in the name of Hades do you think you are doing?" asked Walsingham, grabbing Dee by the arm.

Dee tried to shrug him off but Walsingham held his arm in an iron grip.

"There is no time to explain," said Dee. He looked at Simon. "Cut her throat, now. Please God, don't argue, just do it."

"Are you mad, Doctor?" asked Simon, shocked.

"You don't understand. She is already dead. Kill her body before something else claims it. Do it for her, do it for all of us." Dee pleaded with Simon.

Walsingham pulled his dagger out and held it against Dee's breast. "Dee, you will be silent or I will kill *you* now."

He flung the scholar across the room. Dee stumbled then stood, head bowed.

"I know what you fear, Dee, but I will not let your fear kill my niece. What happened in this room will remain solely between the three of us. Do you understand?"

"I understand," said Dee.

"I know I can rely on you, Simon," Walsingham said, almost with affection.

"On my life, Sir Francis." Simon met Walsingham's gaze.

Walsingham nodded. He picked Lucy up in his arms. "Come with me, the pair of you."

A maid put Lucy to bed, still unconscious. Walsingham sat at her bedside. The girl slept deeply, breathing steadily and slowly. She did not moan or turn but just lay there, auburn hair spread on the pillow. When Walsingham was exhausted, Simon persuaded him to his bed and took over. Every few minutes, he held a candle by the girl's mouth to confirm that she still lived.

Not long after dawn, Walsingham returned accompanied by Dee.

"Any change, Tunstall?" asked Walsingham.

"None, Sir Francis. She sleeps still but she breathes strongly," said Simon, hopefully.

"This is most unusual," Dee said, looking closely at Lucy.

"Unusual?" Sir Francis snarled, spinning Dee round. "Unusual? Nothing has gone right in this enterprise, Dee. I hold you responsible."

"I told him to lock the door," said Dee pointing at Simon. "How did Lady Dennys get into the room?"

"The door didn't have a lock," Simon protested.

"This is getting us nowhere," said Walsingham. "Stop squabbling, the pair of you. Dee, what can we do?"

"I don't know, Sir Francis," said Dee. "This is unprecedented. If the girl was possessed, then I would have expected her to be already dead, or trying to tear our throats out."

The men stared at each other helplessly.

Lilith swam in chemical energy. The endless clicking of electrons, the making and breaking of chemical bonds, supplied the power that sustained her information functions. She occupied a structure like the dog's body only on a larger scale. The main differences were in the central nervous system. The primary node was vast, with layer after layer of complexity. She was in a human, a sentient being.

The body was organised into three levels. At the lowest level coexisted a bewildering array of molecular interactions. Lilith's stolen database from the previous Shadow World gave her the basic tools to log and track these. All chemistry originated in molecular biological databases that were located all over the body. These information stores held coded instructions to control all other biochemical pathways. Molecules zippered down the codes to synthesise chemical messengers that then bonded on to amplifiers, spreading their impact throughout the system.

Lilith was struck by the resemblance of these databases to the core subroutines that stabilised her own processes. The mechanism was different but the principle was essentially similar.

The most important structures in the body were charged lipid membranes. Ions flowed backwards and forwards setting off cascades of electrochemical energy. The membranes branched and divided, enclosing central databases in cells that were filled with ionised chemicals. The cells danced in biochemical energy, extending processes that kissed other cells to exchange ions and electric charges. Lilith identified more than two hundred different types.

The dancing cells were organised into blocks, <query search subroutine>, functional blocks of cells are called "organs." Some of these organs consisted of a single cell line while others were matrices of two or more cell types in various patterns.

The body produced an abundance of energy that Lilith could use to open a transdimensional portal. She could go home. There was only one snag. The disruptive flash of energy release would inflict terminal damage on the body that she inhabited. She knew what the Elder would say. That it was only a shadow thing of no importance. That it probably wouldn't exist without a member of the People to observe it. That it had such a short insignificant life that it should be proud to lose it at the disposal of the immortal People.

But the body was real, and it was not an it, but a she. Lilith had read Shakespeare's stories and she understood how much love and hate and life humans packed into the few days granted them. They should not be denied a single second of their allotted span. Lilith couldn't do it. She couldn't kill one of these wonderful biological creatures for such a selfish reason. She had not the right.

The woman was in shock. The brain functions were all on standby. Lilith cautiously explored and checked, taking each step very carefully. She compared each piece of new evidence with the material in her stolen database. She did not want a repeat of the disaster with the dog. Her host seemed in good condition but in quiescent mode.

It was not long before what Lilith knew exceeded the information she had filched. Even the twenty-first-century humans knew so little about themselves. These bodies were so powerful, so wonderful, and so chaotic. They were also amazingly inefficient. Lilith started tweaking and improving a bit at a time. She found a cell whose central code was corrupted, such that it was multiplying uncontrollably. Lilith killed it with constructed toxin.

The body's mitochondrial energy output systems could be so easily upgraded. The bone structure was inelegant and weak. A tiny adjustment to the molecular structure could increase the strength-to-weight ratio enormously. The muscles could be made to contract harder and faster. Small changes in the membranes could speed electrochemical impulses making the nervous system respond more quickly.

The problem, from Lilith's perspective, was what to do now. Her options were limited if she rejected taking the female's life. She could take over the body and hold the owning personality unconscious but what would Lilith do with a strange body in a strange world? A better alternative was to revive the female human and hide within her. Lilith could meld with her nervous system sufficiently to monitor everything the female experienced.

Lilith moved slowly and carefully. The host body was still on standby but Lilith now knew how to turn it on. Eventually, she pressed the switch.

A small voice said, "I'm thirsty."

The men turned and looked at the bed. Two large brown eyes gazed back at them.

"What are you all doing in my room?" Lucy looked puzzled.

Walsingham rushed over and sat beside her. He took her hand in his. "How do you feel, Lucy?"

"I'm thirsty, Uncle, and hungry. Why is everyone staring at me?" she said, nervously.

"But how do you feel, Lucy?" Walsingham persisted. "Are you all right?"

"Of course I am. Why wouldn't I be?" The girl pulled herself up in the bed and then, remembering her modesty, pulled up the blankets so the men could not see her nightdress.

"Shall I fetch a physician?" asked Walsingham

"God, no," said Lucy, looking frightened. Simon did not blame her. After King Harry destroyed the monasteries and their resident doctors, medicine in England was left in the hands of barbersurgeons, wisewomen, and physicians. And the most frightening of the lot were the physicians, whose every cure involved leeches.

"What do you remember?" asked Walsingham.

"I was in the garden." She paused thoughtfully. "I remember speaking to Master Tunstall and I saw you and Doctor Dee. Then I woke up here."

"Can you remember anything else?" asked Walsingham. "Try, Lucy."

"Not really. I think I dreamt. There was a bright flickering light." Lucy looked sharply at Walsingham.

"It's nothing, child, nothing. Tunstall will arrange breakfast for you. I want you to spend today resting. You fainted in the garden." Walsingham glared at the other men as if daring them to contradict him.

"Tell me, Lady Dennys," said Dee. "Can you hear voices?"

"Voices?" repeated Lucy, wide-eyed. "I can hear you."

"In your head, girl. Voices in your head telling you what to do," Dee said, impatiently.

"What does he mean, Uncle? He's frightening me." Lucy clutched at Walsingham for reassurance.

"That's enough, Dee," said Walsingham. "The girl is fine. She was just stunned by the blast. She would be screaming in rage by now and trying to kill us if it had got her. You said so yourself."

Dee walked to the door and turned to face them. "I hope you are right, Sir Francis. You might be, nothing else in this business has proceeded as normal. However, if I am right, then I doubt if we could kill her now anyway."

Lucy followed this exchange with incomprehension.

Dee's conjuring dagger appeared as if by magic. Dee tossed it idly into the air and caught it by the tip. Dee drew his arm back and threw in a single fluid movement. There was a flicker of movement from Lucy too quick to follow. She held the blade of the knife between her thumb and forefinger, the point inches from her breast. A small trickle of blood ran down her hand where the blade had cut.

"You see," said Dee. "I suspect all discussion of what to do about her is now academic. I doubt we could kill her even if we tried."

There was a long silence during which Dee opened the door.

"Don't you want your knife back, Doctor Dee?" asked Lucy.

"You keep it, Lady Dennys," said Dee. "When you hear the voices, and I think you will, you might want to use it on yourself rather than your family."

With that Dee walked out.

Lucy said nothing but a single tear rolled down her cheek.

"Go and find a servant and arrange a meal for Lady Dennys, Tunstall," said Walsingham, speaking evenly as if nothing had happened.

He examined Lucy's hand carefully. Even a small cut could kill in a world without antibiotics. "It must have been just a nick, child. It has stopped bleeding already." He wiped the trickle of blood off. "Indeed, I cannot even find the cut."

"I feel well, Uncle. I think I would like to get up now," the girl said.

"Very well, child. I will leave you to your toilet."

Lucy was left alone holding the dagger. It was a beautiful piece of craftsmanship. The blade was covered in astrological symbols. Lucy tilted it backwards and forwards so the light reflected hypnotically off the glyphs.

Lilith was in a panic of indecision. She had patched into Lucy's sensory input system as she woke the girl. The men's conversation was chilling. They must guess that she was inside Lucy and they ascribed evil motivation to her.

She knew enough about Lucy to influence her nervous system directly. She could phase with the sensory nerves and create false electrochemical waves. The girl would hear or see what Lilith wanted her to hear and see. The dangers were immense. She had no idea what the girl might do but Lilith had come to a decision. She had to make contact with Lucy. Lilith thought that Lucy would react badly to a voice in her head after Dee's warning. There was nothing else for it. Lucy would have to "see" her.

Lilith had Lucy see her open the door and walk into the room. Lilith chose the way she would look with great care. She selected a mixture of features that she liked the look of, from various races of human. It was a surprisingly difficult decision. She settled on north European skin with emerald Asian-shaped eyes and high cheekbones. Jet-black hair, cut short at the front and sides but curled long onto her neck at the back, completed the look. She decided to be petite, as humans found that unthreatening.

Now for the dress, and she had so many styles to choose from. Of course, she could keep changing it just like a human. She finally decided on a cream dress with red panels. It was high at the front and low on the ankle but slit up the side to allow her to walk, appear to walk, comfortably. She felt sexy. That was the word. She felt attractive to human males. Lilith was confused. Why should she want to appeal to human males? Something of Lucy's emotional responses must be leaking over along with the sensory input.

"Have you brought breakfast?" asked Lucy, to where Lilith appeared to stand. Then the girl took a closer look at the fine clothes. "I am sorry. I am half asleep. I thought you were a servant." The girl giggled in embarrassment. Clearly someone dressed like Lilith was a lady, albeit a rather strange one.

"No, Lucy, I need to talk to you. We have a problem," said Lilith.

"Do I know you?" Lucy was surprised by the informality.

"No, but I know you. I am Lilith. I am afraid I have played a foul trick on you. My excuse was that I was dying." Lilith sat on the side of the bed.

At that moment the door opened and Millie, her maid, entered with a tray.

"Breakfast, my lady, with Master Tunstall's compliments."

"Thank you," said Lucy. "Put it on the side." The maid bustled around. "It is a nice day, my lady. Master Tunstall says you have been unwell and will be inside all day but what do men know? If you are feeling better then, if I were you, I should take some air in the garden to clear away the foul vapours. I will help you dress when I come back for the tray."

"Thank you," said Lucy again, as the maid let herself out.

"Can you pass me the tray?" Lucy said to Lilith.

"I'm afraid not, Lucy."

"No, you can't touch anything, can you? The maid never once looked at you. She couldn't see you could she?"

"No, Lucy. Only you can see me."

The girl nodded. "What are you, a ghost? In those clothes you must be a spirit from a faraway country. Why am I not more frightened?" The girl frowned, "Mayhap this is all a dream, or I am bewitched."

Lilith's subroutine interpreted. A <ghost> was the insubstantial remains of a dead human.

"I am not a ghost, Lucy. I am alive but I am from far away. You are not dreaming or bewitched. You are looking at a portrait that only you can see. I am really in your head. You are calm because I am deliberately damping panic reactions in your body." Lilith tried to put the situation into terms that would suit Lucy's world picture.

"Sweet Jesus. This is what Dee meant. I have something inside my head. Something that will make me a monster." The girl's hand curved around the knife.

"Lucy, stop. Dee was wrong. You are not a monster. I don't want you to kill anything. I am not in favour of killing," Lilith said, primly. "At least, not of unnecessary killing."

Honesty forced her to add the qualifier at the end. The People were invariably honest. Their physical structure made it difficult to be otherwise.

"No killing?" asked the girl.

"Not into killing," said Lilith, firmly.

Lilith ran through the events of the last few days with Lucy. The girl bolted down an enormous breakfast while listening intently. Higher energy output required a higher calorific input, noted Lilith. She should have thought of that. Oh well, Lucy would never get fat.

The explanation took much longer than expected because Lucy's and Lilith's concept of how the universe was put together differed in several important areas. Eventually, the girl translated Lilith's story into terms that were familiar. She sat up on the bed and hugged her knees.

"So, Doctor Dee was attempting a spell to summon a demon for my uncle?"

"Yes, Lucy. He wanted information about an attempt on your Queen's life."

"Someone tried to kill Uncle earlier," said Lucy.

"Really? That is interesting," said Lilith, thoughtfully.

"So something went wrong and he got the wrong demon. You are from a far country in the Other World and, unlike our local demons, you are not evil."

"No more than you humans," said Lilith. She had given up trying to explain to Lucy that she was not a demon. Maybe *demon* was the best word Lucy had to describe her.

"Oh dear," said Lucy. "I have met some vile humans. Uncle has tried to marry me to some of them. And I am stuck with you in my head because it would kill me if you left?"

"Yes, Lucy," Lilith said, patiently.

"I am not sure I like that," said the girl.

"No, Lucy, I am sorry. I was dying and had nowhere else to go. I have made a few improvements to your body as rent, so to speak."

"What kind of improvements?" asked Lucy, suspiciously.

"Lucy, I have been reviewing your people's medical practices from my records. As long as I am in here with you, promise me you will avoid physicians."

"Do you think me mad, demon? Of course I will avoid physicians."

"But I digress, I think you will find that my improvements make your body work better."

"I noticed. Did you see Simon's face when I caught that knife?" Lucy said, mischievously.

The two young women dissolved into helpless giggles. In Lucy's case, the reaction had more to do with hysteria than humour.

The maid came in for the tray to find Lucy in fits of laughter. Lilith turned off her image to avoid confusing Lucy. It would not do for word to get out that Lady Dennys talked to ghosts.

"There you are, my dear. Nothing like a good meal to restore your humour."

"Thank you. I think I will take a turn in the garden. After you have dressed me, would you ask Master Tunstall if he would like to be my escort?"

"Of course I will, ma'am," said the maid.

'Are you still there, even when I cannot see you?' thought Lucy.

'I am always with you,' thought Lilith. 'Just think clearly at me and I will hear you.'

'I was afraid of that,' thought Lucy.

"Just let me straighten your hair. What a beauty you are. Every eye in the court will be on you," said the maid.

Simon was working at a desk when there was a knock on the door and the maid came in and curtsied. "The Lady Dennys sends her compliments and bids you attend her in the rose garden."

"What, Lu— the Lady Dennys is out of bed? I will go to her at once."

The maid gave him a knowing look as he dashed out. Simon chose to ignore the impertinent wench. She showed no particular sign of awe in the presence of the young secretary. He did not complain, as he strongly suspected that it would be his dignity that would suffer most in any altercation.

Simon found Lucy standing over a bush of white roses. Roses had a special significance for the English. This was especially true for the

Tudor monarchs, who had secured power by uniting the white rose of York with the red rose of Lancaster. The people of England had looked to the Welsh Tudors to end the disastrous English dynastic struggles still popularly known as the Wars of the Roses. Elizabeth was the third great Tudor monarch, after her father Henry VIII and grandfather Henry VII. Memory of the short rules of her puritan brother, Edward VI, and Catholic sister, Mary, were already fading from the public mind. And no one talked of poor doomed Lady Jane Gray, the first Queen of England in her own right, who reigned for but nine days.

Nonsuch had been built as a Tudor Royal Palace so the roses in the garden alternated red and white.

Lucy sniffed the strong scent. "A rose by any other name would smell as sweet. That's what the poets say. Do you agree, Master Tunstall, or do you think that a rose would not smell to us like a rose without the blood and lives that they have consumed?"

Simon offered the girl his arm and they strolled down the aisles of flowers. "I can't say I have given it much thought, Lady Dennys. I am afraid I live in a rather dry world of reports and filing systems. I have not considered poetry since my studies at Cambridge and I fear I was a poor master of words."

"And beauty, Master Tunstall," said Lucy. "Do you never consider beauty?"

Simon looked at her.

"Oh yes, Lady Dennys," he said. "I often consider beauty."

Every adult in England wore hats of a style that befitted their station. Only one social group was allowed licence to ignore this social convention: young unmarried women. Flowing tresses were the crowning glory of English girls. The strong breeze lifted Lucy's auburn hair and tossed it playfully. He had thought that she had a small beauty mark on her left cheek but, oddly, there was no sign of it now.

"Uncle says the rose is the perfect symbol of English monarchy. It projects an image of beautiful and sweet-scented flowers into the light of day but its stem is guarded by sharp thorns."

"And its roots are fertilised by dirt and decay," said Simon, finishing the quote. He smiled down at the girl. "Sir Francis has oft made the same observation to me."

The couple turned into the lanes of bushes. An area of the garden at Nonsuch was laid out in corridors of high-trimmed bushes, which formed the walls of long galleries lined with flowers. Openings led off to enclosed gardens that were like rooms of green. Each had some central feature. Some had a statue, others a central flower display, a fish pool, or even, in one case, a small theatre stage. Strategically located benches offered succour to the weary. The idea was that a strolling lady and gentleman would turn a corner to be delighted by a novel space where they could have privacy. Such gardens were popularly the haunt of lovers and many a kiss was stolen in their shaded nooks and crannies.

Lucy and Simon entered such an enclosed garden, containing a lawn and five plum trees. In season, lovers could select from their laden branches. Simon steered Lucy towards a wooden bench at the rear. He was concerned that she should not walk too far and suffer a relapse. Honesty forced him to admit another motive. Some little time sitting with Lucy was as pleasant a way to spend the day as he could envisage.

The couple passed a compost heap of newly cut grass that the gardeners had piled in one corner to rot down. Lucy glanced over at the steaming pile and stiffened.

"Master Tunstall, I think you should look more closely at the compost," she said.

What on earth is she up to now, thought Simon, but he humoured her. He took a stick and poked into the loosely piled waste. "It's nothing, Lady Dennys. Just some gardener's rubbish heap," he said, patiently.

The stick glanced off something hard. Simon scooped away the cuttings.

"Oh!" Lucy exclaimed, her left hand covering her mouth in a characteristic gesture.

A naked foot projected out of the compost heap.

"You, man, yes, you," Simon called to a passing gardener. "Find a steward and tell him to fetch Sir Francis Walsingham. Now, man, as fast as you can."

"Stay with me, Lady Dennys. Come sit over here on the bench. I don't want you in the gardens without an escort."

"It was murder then, Master Tunstall," she said.

"I fear so, Lady Dennys. The men were stabbed." Simon smiled reassuringly at her. "Nothing to worry about though."

"You think the assassins are still here, sir?" she asked.

"Very unlikely. I am sure they are long gone." But he drew his sword and attempted a martial pose over the girl.

They had not so long to wait before Walsingham arrived, accompanied by a steward.

"There, Sir Francis, in the compost are two fresh bodies," said Simon.

Walsingham squatted down and closely examined the corpses.

"The blood is dry, Tunstall, but rigor mortis has not yet set in. This happened very recently." He turned to the steward. "You, sir, come here."

The steward was a portly man who clearly enjoyed the good life. "Me, Sir Francis?"

"Yes, you. Tell me if you recognise either of these men."

The steward reluctantly bent over the first corpse and shook his head. The second corpse was lying facedown. Walsingham seized it by the hair and pulled the head back to reveal the face. The man's throat had been deeply cut. The steward took one look and retched violently.

"Well, man?" asked Sir Francis, impatiently.

"It's my cousin's son," said the steward, shakily.

"But what was he doing here?" Walsingham grabbed the steward by the shirt.

"On my life, I don't know, sir," said the steward in terror.

Walsingham released the man and smoothed down his shirt. "Fear not, good steward. No blame attaches to you. But I need to know what happened. Can you think of anything?"

The steward gazed at Walsingham uncomprehendingly. Simon knew that the spymaster must be seething with impatience but Walsingham had carried out many interrogations and knew that a servant must be cajoled rather than threatened, or he would simply clam up.

"Come, why was this man at the Palace?"

The steward looked relieved to have a straightforward question that he could answer.

"If it please you, sir, he was one of the Queen's guards."

"Sweet Jesus and all the saints," said Walsingham. "Queen's guards murdered and their weapons and armour missing. Come on, Tunstall!"

Walsingham leapt up and made for the Palace at the run with Simon close behind. Both men forgot Lucy in their urgency.

When they reached the Palace, Walsingham made for a lady-in-waiting who was leaving as they entered.

"Where is the Queen?" Walsingham demanded.

"Why, in her chambers," said the woman.

Walsingham and Simon ran up the corridor, drawing swords.

"But Sir Francis, you can't go in there," she shouted after him.

There should have been two guards at the entrance to the Queen's private chambers but the corridor was empty. Walsingham threw open the door into the Queen's bedchamber. Her Majesty stood in front of the bed in her petticoat. Frightened ladies-in-waiting huddled behind her. Two men, dressed as court guards, menaced the Queen with halberds.

The Queen was at their mercy but they hesitated in front of her imperious stare. Equipped only with a petticoat, she intimidated two heavily armed men. Not for nothing was she known as Gloriana. The Pope himself was quoted as saying that the Virgin Queen of England was "magnificent, only 'tis a pity she's not a Christian."

Walsingham's arrival broke the spell. One guard turned to face the intruders while the other advanced on the Queen. The halberd outreached swords so the guard easily held them off. The second guard raised his weapon to deal the Queen a killing blow.

Lucy ran after her uncle. Lilith noted with satisfaction that she had no difficulty keeping up with the men. The improvements that Lilith had carried out to the girl's body were proving efficient. Lucy was not even out of breath. The girl ran into the room and halted suddenly behind where the men fought. Lilith detected massive emotional response, including fear.

'What's wrong, Lucy? Why are you so frightened?' Lilith asked.

'That man, he's going to kill the Queen,' Lucy thought.

Lilith picked up absolute horror in the girl's thoughts. Lucy was clearly deeply upset but she did not seem to know what to do. She had Dee's athame concealed in her dress but the girl clearly did not think of it as a weapon. Lilith had files about the use of knives in her stolen database. She knew what to do. Lilith calculated trajectories and muscle tension carefully and then took over Lucy's nervous system, shutting down the girl's consciousness.

Something metallic flashed between the three fighting men. It struck the guard menacing the Queen in the back of his neck, with an audible thud. The assassin went down as if poleaxed.

The remaining guard lost concentration and glanced over his shoulder, undecided whether to continue to defend himself or to attack the Queen. Walsingham solved the problem for him, by taking him neatly through the throat while he was distracted.

Simon turned to identify their rescuer and saw Lucy in the doorway looking confused.

The girl quailed as several pairs of eyes stared at her.

"You threw the knife, Lucy?" Walsingham said, astonished.

The captain of the guard led a squad of his men in, at the double. "Sir Francis, what are you doing with a drawn sword in the Queen's presence?"

"Your job, I think, Captain," said Walsingham. He sheathed his weapon and motioned for Simon to do the same.

"You cut it a little fine this time, Sir Francis," said Elizabeth, coolly. "There is blood all over our floor. Methinks, we would prefer that you execute vile traitors somewhere other than our bedchamber."

"I apologise, Your Majesty," said Walsingham dropping to one knee. "I have been extremely stupid."

"Well, well, Sir Francis. No harm done—except to the floor," she said, waving a hand airily.

The captain made a show of looking officious. "This one is dead," he said, examining Sir Francis's victim.

The other traitor made a gurgling sound. He lay facedown and the hilt of a dagger stood out from the back of his neck. The weapon had struck so hard that it had punched through a leather neck guard, deep into the tissue beneath. The captain tried to pull out the knife but the tip was jammed in bone. Eventually, he removed it by putting his boot on the back of the man's neck and pulling with both hands. The traitor groaned and died, depositing a fresh flow of blood on the polished wood.

Elizabeth sighed theatrically. "Lord Lumley will never invite us back at this rate."

"Whose weapon is this?" asked the guard captain, holding out the dagger.

"Mine," a small voice said. "Doctor Dee gave it me."

Lucy stepped forward and retrieved her knife.

"Yours, girl?" said the guard captain, shocked. "You threw it? Are you deranged?"

"Mad is she?" The Queen's voice cut through the conversation. "Mayhap, we should have her bite some of our other subjects. Possibly they might serve their monarch half as well," she snarled.

"Yes, Your Majesty," said the captain, falling to one knee.

"Come here, girl," commanded the Queen.

Lucy approached and curtsied deeply. Elizabeth raised the girl up and took her face in one hand, turning her head from side to side.

"A rare beauty, as I said earlier, Sir Francis."

"Yes, Your Majesty," said Walsingham.

The Queen stroked Lucy's hair. "Do you not think auburn a very pretty colour, Sir Francis?"

"Indeed I do, ma'am. 'Tis the noblest hair colour," said Walsingham.

The Queen's own hair had a distinctly reddish tinge, although red was not a word anyone would have used in her presence. Tavern girls were redheads, queens were auburn.

"Here, child, wear this as a token of your Queen's appreciation. You have served us well this day."

Elizabeth pulled a ring off her own finger and slipped it on Lucy's right hand.

"Now leave us, all of you."

Everyone, except the ladies-in-waiting, filed backwards towards the door. The Queen had one final shot in her locker.

"Captain," she said, in that deceptively purring tone she used when she was at her most dangerous.

The man sprang to attention and gulped.

"Instead of spreading idle tittle tattle about our loyal subjects—" She smiled indulgently at Lucy at this point. "We suggest you spend your time finding a good explanation for how you failed in your duty so egregiously that two traitors dressed as your guards ended up in our bedchamber."

"Yes, Your Majesty," said a very unhappy man.

Lucy ran down the corridor in front of the men.

"Tunstall, give her a little time to have a cry and then go after her and make sure she's all right," said Walsingham. "I have business to attend to. Someone smuggled those assassins into the Palace. I want a name."

Simon watched Lucy slip out into the garden.

Lilith started to realise that all was not well. Lucy ran through the grounds into a quiet secluded garden containing a lichen-covered statue of Pan. Her observations of the girl's physiology suggested that Lucy was incandescent with fury.

"Lilith, Lilith, where are you? Come out where I can see you," Lucy said.

Lilith fed fake images along Lucy's optic nerves and fake sounds into Lucy's ears. She was careful to devote considerable processing power to her body-language subroutines. It was a very contrite, subdued demon that materialised in front of the girl.

"You took control of my body. I don't even remember what you did but you clearly killed someone. So it was all lies, you really are a monster."

"No, Lucy, no. I didn't want to kill anyone. I only tried to protect your uncle and your Queen."

"And why should I believe a demon?" asked the girl, scornfully.

She pulled the bloodstained knife out from her skirts and held the blade across her own throat.

"Maybe Dee was right. Mayhap, I should end this now. What will you do to stop me, demon? Take control of my body again? And how long do you think you can imitate a human being before you are found out?"

"I am so sorry, Lucy. I am sorry the man died but he was an assassin. I don't understand what I have done that is so wrong."

"You will never, ever take control of my body like that again. Do you understand?"

"I will never do it again if it upsets you so. I was only trying to protect you. I don't understand," said Lilith.

Lucy calmed down. "You really don't understand, do you, Lilith, you clever, clever fool? Let me explain. You don't know how to behave around people. They will think me possessed and there is a penalty for people possessed by demons."

A vision came into the girl's mind that was so strong that it leaked across to Lilith. Lucy tied to a stake, twisted in screaming agony while the fire roasted the flesh from her legs.

Lilith fell to her knees in front of the girl. "I didn't understand. I will never override your consciousness again. I promise, on my honour."

Simon hurried after Lucy. He stayed at a distance, keeping just close enough to follow her path through the complexities of the garden. He rounded a hedge and an empty vista opened onto a meadow. She was gone. Methodically, he retraced his steps, checking each of the hedge-secluded "rooms" that led off the path.

Lucy was in the third one he visited, holding a dagger at her own throat.

"Lucy, no!" He threw himself at the girl and grabbed her wrist.

"Master Tunstall. What are you doing?" The girl easily disengaged her wrist, showing more strength than Simon imagined she could possess.

He gripped her tightly by the shoulders and this time she didn't resist. "Sweet Jesus, Lucy, what were you thinking? This is all about Dee, isn't it, Dee and his stupid opinions?"

"It's all right, Master Tunstall. You can let me go now."

"No, it's not all right. I am taking you to your uncle. You will come with me."

Simon held her tightly by the hand and led her back to the main house. Lucy followed meekly.

'You don't have to go with him if you don't want to,' thought Lilith. 'He is not physically stronger than you.'

'That's just what I meant, Lilith. You don't know how to behave. A pulling match would be unladylike, whoever won. When men are in this mood you just have to humour them. No, I will follow him like a good little girl. But mark me well, he will pay for treating me thus.'

"It's a pretty little chapel," said Walsingham. "I understand old King Harry himself designed it. I wonder if he ever saw the completed building before he died?"

"The bishop is taking his time," said Simon.

"One cannot hurry the church," said Walsingham, dryly. "They deal with eternity."

"Have you had any success in locating the traitor who smuggled assassins into the Palace?" asked Simon.

"A steward has been found with a stab wound to the heart," said Walsingham.

"So he let the assassins in and then they silenced him to protect their identity?"

Walsingham shrugged. "Possibly, or mayhap I am supposed to think that and the steward was, in fact, an innocent victim. I suspect the real traitor is still out there. I want that man, Tunstall. I want him before he can hatch a new plot."

The chapel door swung open and Lucy emerged, followed by a rotund man in a bishop's finery.

"All is well, my lord?" asked Walsingham.

"Indeed, very fair," said the bishop. "Lady Dennys and I have taken mass and I have blessed her. She has proclaimed the creed and the Lord's Prayer. A delightful girl."

Lucy had her most angelic expression on.

"What in Heaven gave you the idea that there might be a problem?" asked the bishop.

"Nothing really," said Walsingham. "It's just that Doctor Dee."

"Dee!" hooted the Bishop, interrupting the spymaster. "That mountebank conjuror? Faith, Sir Francis, I would insist on sending my curate out for a second opinion if Dee told me it was raining. Worry not about the Dees of this world. The Church finds no fault in your niece."

The relief on Sir Francis's face was obvious. "Thank you, my lord. You have put my mind at rest. Is there any small service that I can perform for the Church?"

The Bishop took Walsingham by the arm and led him away. "By strange chance, Sir Francis, there is a little matter that I would trouble you with."

Simon and Lucy watched them go.

"I have a favour to ask you," Lucy said, touching Simon lightly on the arm. "Come with me."

Simon followed her back into the chapel and up to the altar. The gloom and cool of heavy stone replaced the light and warmth of the day.

"I believe you have some small affection for me, Master Tunstall," she said.

"I have great affection for all my master's household, Lady Dennys."

The girl nodded.

"Place your hand on the Bible," she said. "I fear I will be done to death by slanderous tongues. I want you to kill me first if they try to burn me. Swear it on your very soul."

"Lady Dennys, Lucy, I cannot. You wear the Queen's ring now. No one would dare accuse you."

Simon lifted Lucy's hand. The gold ring sat loosely on her narrow finger. The letters ER, *Elizabeth Regina*, stood proud. The Tudors still followed the old medieval tradition of giving a ring from their own hand to a subject they wished to honour. A person rewarded in this way was immune from political prosecution, since to accuse the subject was to challenge the monarch.

"Swear it, as you value your soul. Do it for me, Simon."

"On my soul, I swear that I will kill you before I let you burn." He snatched his hand off the Bible as if it was red-hot and staggered out of the chapel like a man who had taken a wound.

'That was cruel, Lucy. You realise that he loves you,' thought Lilith.

Act 6, The Spanish Main

"Here's a health unto her Majesty,
"with a fa la la la la la la.
"Confusion to her enemies,
"with a fa la la la la la la."

Oars dipped in unison in time to the rhythm of the song and bit into the water. Backs strained in unison.

"And he who would not drink her health,
"we wish him neither wit nor wealth.
"Nor yet a rope to hang himself,
"with a fa la la la la la la."

The small rowing boat leapt forward but was immediately braked by a heavy cable lifting behind it. Water ran down the rope, falling in a long line into the sea. The other end of the cable was tied to the bow of a race-built galleon. Oars lifted, feathered, and dipped again. Imperceptibly, the bows of the galleon swung away from the tropical shoreline.

"May she live in mirth and jollity,
"with a fa la la la la la la.
"And past-time with good company,
"with a fa la la la la la la.
"And he who would not join in glee,

"must puritan or papist be,
"And him we curse with misery."

William Hawkins stood on the small raised deck at the stern, where he could oversee the operation.

"Boatswain," he bawled forward.

"Captain!" The voice came from the bow.

"Tell them to put their backs into it. The ship is helpless like this. I swear a gaggle of the Queen's ladies-in-waiting could do a better job. Call themselves sea dogs!"

"Aye, aye, sir."

The boatswain screamed abuse at the men in the boat. William tuned him out with the ability of long experience. The bay was perfect. It curved shallowly inwards from the north. There would be reefs and shallows up there protecting the anchorage. The sea cut deeply into the land in the south, until it met a low ridge that projected perpendicularly out into the Caribbean as a peninsula. Here, the water was still deep close in to the shoreline. A ship could anchor here in perfect safety and be invisible to traffic moving up the coast from the south. Only the tips of the ship's masts would project over the headland and they would be wonderfully hidden against the trees.

A man old for the sea climbed laboriously up the ladder to the poop. He knuckled his forehead to William in lieu of removing a cap. It was hot and it was humid. Everyone stripped down. William himself wore only his breeches and a shirt open to the waist.

"Hot work, master carpenter," said William.

"Yes sir, I wondered if I might carry out some repairs? I am worried that the trip across the Atlantic has caused some timbers to work loose."

William frowned. "I suppose you can, but I want the ship ready for to sail at one hour's notice. As your first priority, master carpenter, I want the pinnace reassembled."

"Very good, sir."

English ships sailing to the Spanish Americas often took a small pinnace in a knocked-down condition in the ship's hold. On arrival, the boat could be reassembled to provide useful support. The *Swallow* carried a fifteen-ton pinnace equipped with two masts as well as oars.

The song went on interminably as the oars dipped and pulled. William wiped the sweat from his eyes. It was so fetid that he felt that he could almost cut the air with a cutlass. The Americas had a damnable climate that was utterly unsuitable for civilised men.

The bow slowly swung until the warship pointed out to sea.

"Release anchor," said William.

"You heard the captain, you bacon-fed knaves," repeated the boatswain.

A solid splash indicated compliance.

"Run a cable to the stern," ordered William.

The rowing boat pirouetted on its oars and, freed from the huge drag of the *Swallow*, leapt down the side of the ship. Mariners released the cable from the bow, passed it down the ship, and refastened it securely to the stern. The boat stopped alongside to receive a shore anchor, then raced for land.

Light surf rolled gently onto bright, white Caribbean sand. The boat hissed as its keel ran up the beach. The crew jumped overboard and hauled the rowing boat further up the sand. Under the direction of a coxswain, the boat crew dug the anchor into firm soil at the top of the narrow beach and attached the cable. The boat crew relaxed in the shade of the tropical trees that lined the edge of the beach. It had been a long voyage.

William surveyed his new empire. Raucous bird cries, and other strange noises exotic to an English ear, erupted from the jungle. Organic vapours curled off the land to assault his nose. Disease would be rife here. A small stream ran down the side of the peninsula and exited into the sea by means of a gully in the sand.

"It all looks peaceful enough, Master Smethwick, but I want six armed men on the beach at all times when we have a party ashore," said William. Smethwick was the ship's master, the professional navigator who was William's second in command. The master's duties included the routine handling of the ship. He was responsible for choosing the ship's tack under sail and he had to get the best from her in all seas and winds.

"The natives have no reason to love Spaniards and we Europeans probably all look alike to them," said William.

"We are running short of water, Captain. I'll fill the casks at that stream."

"Very good, Master Smethwick." The master could be safely left to organise such details with his usual competence.

"Boatswain." William beckoned to the man.

The boatswain was the senior petty officer on the ship. The master and captain were educated men and the carpenter a technical specialist who had learned his trade through long apprenticeship, but the boatswain was a seaman who had risen through the ranks. He, with his mates, was particularly responsible for sails and rigging but there was no end to his duties. He oversaw anchoring and the boat crews. He cleared the ship for action and he commanded that portion of the crew who worked the sails when the ship fought.

Most of all, the boatswain was the senior sailor responsible for discipline. There was no more important a man on an English ship, save the captain himself.

The man skipped up to the poop, with the agility learnt by a lifetime at sea.

"Cap'n," he said.

"You see that hill there," said William gesturing to the end of the peninsula where a rounded hummock rose out of the screen of trees. "I'll have two men up there from dawn to dusk watching to the south for a sail."

"Aye, aye, Cap'n."

"The men may go ashore to stretch their legs, boatswain, but tell them to stay close to the ship."

The boatswain touched his forehead and went down into the waist of the ship.

"I want four volunteers, you," the boatswain said, and pointed, "you, and you two. Take the small boat and clear a path up to that hillock. Well, get a move on."

Behind William, an expensively dressed man watched the activity with bored disinterest.

"I may as well go ashore myself, Hawkins. Arrange a boat for me will you?" asked Christopher Packenham.

William hid his irritation.

"The crew are rather busy right now. I will see what I can arrange later," said William.

Packenham gave the sniff that indicated that he was displeased. William had got very fed up with hearing that sniff over the duration of a five-thousand-mile journey.

"I think sooner rather than later, Hawkins. After all, my cousin Henry invested heavily in this enterprise."

Maybe it was a good idea to get Packenham ashore as soon as possible. Maybe he would fall in a bog and drown, thought William, viciously.

Before the *Swallow* arrived, the small bay had shown no sign that human beings existed. But gradually, man made his usual impact. Vegetation was cleared and a camp set up at the water's edge. Sailors cleared a track to the lookout post.

Day followed day but no sails were sighted. William sent out hunting parties for fresh meat but the yield was disappointing. The men grew bored, sick, and fractious, in equal measure. Inevitably, floggings were required to maintain discipline.

William forced himself to watch each punishment. The crew needed to know that the captain backed his officers and supported each decision. He stood impassive as a young mariner was stripped to the waist and tied to a tree. A mate shoved the traditional wooden peg between the mariner's jaws.

"I am not sure I can allow this, Hawkins," drawled Packenham.

"I don't require your permission, Packenham. Stay out of my affairs." William was past politeness.

"Don't get above your station, Hawkins. You drive the ship but everyone knows I am really in charge of this expedition. My cousin—"

William thrust his beard into Packenham's face before the man could finish. "A pox on your cousin. Get in my way again and I'll strip your back next." Packenham recoiled, shocked. William turned away before the man could react. This situation could easily run out of control.

"Boatswain's mate, carry out the punishment," William said to the man with the cat-o'-nine-tails.

The cat descended with a slap on the offender's back.

Packenham recovered his dignity and backed off with the enigmatic smile of someone who had scored a point.

The boatswain watched him go.

"I smell trouble, Cap'n. The men have stopped complaining."

The cat descended again.

"Yes, I know," said William. "Discipline is ever a problem on our ships. I sometimes wonder whether we should pay our men a flat fee rather than give them shares of the proceeds."

"The Spaniards pay their men and they run away," the boatswain said. "Our men fight to win their share."

"True," William agreed.

The cat descended again.

The offender groaned in pain through the wooden peg.

"The young gentleman," said the boatswain, making the word sound like an obscene insult, "is spending a great deal of time with some of the malcontents. He calls them bold rogues and makes much of what he calls 'your timidity' in just waiting here. Sorry, Cap'n, his words not mine."

It was the duty of the boatswain to act as the captain's eyes and ears among the ordinary mariners and speak frankly to his superior.

"Does he now? Does he indeed?" William pondered. "In future, boatswain, no one but the shore guards and hunting parties are to be equipped with firearms. Make sure you select the guards yourself from trustworthy men."

"Aye, aye, sir," said the boatswain, with grim satisfaction. He spat in the sand.

Sailors cut down the young seaman. He hung loosely in their arms, head lolling.

The next day Packenham accosted William within earshot of the crew.

"This is a complete waste of time. We are just rotting on this beach while a king's ransom in treasure passes us by."

"What do you suggest, Master Packenham?" asked William, with deceptive mildness.

"We go after the silver. That's where the real money is in Spanish America. The gold is played out."

William laughed out loud. "The silver mines at Potosi are in Peru, Master Packenham. We can't reach them. The silver is carried to the Pacific coast then shipped north. And we can't get there either. No English ship has ever operated in Pacific waters, unless you count Oxenham's doomed enterprise. From Panama, they move it across the jungle in heavily guarded mule trains to the fort at Nombre de Dios. There the silver awaits the arrival of a flota of heavy galleons to convoy it to Spain. We can't take the fort and we can't take the flota. So don't waste my time."

"Drake did it," said Packenham. "Drake took a mule train on the isthmus."

"Yes, Drake did it but you're not Drake," said William. Honesty forced him to add, "No one is."

William counted points on his fingers. "Drake had more men than us, he had allies, which we don't, and he organised the Cimarrones to work with him."

Packenham looked blank.

"Cimarrones are escaped slaves. They hate the Spanish," explained William.

"So why can't we use these Cimarrones?" asked Packenham.

"Because the Spanish massacred them for helping Drake," said William. "Just like they killed Guillaume le Testu, Drake's French ally. Just like they cut up Oxenham's last expedition to the isthmus. Oxenham is still rotting in a Spanish jail where not even Drake can free him."

William turned his back, ending the conversation.

A few days later a deputation of men, including Packenham, came to William.

"I want to organise a hunting party, Hawkins. I feel like a little sport. Your man"—Packenham pointed at the boatswain—"won't give us arms without your permission."

"Fair enough," said William. "You have my permission. But I suggest you watch your trail and get back here well before nightfall. These jungles can be confusing and dangerous."

Packenham sneered, "I don't need your advice, Hawkins. I have hunted every inch of Cornwall." Packenham stomped off.

"Possibly you have," muttered William to his retreating back. "But this isn't Cornwall."

William stood with the boatswain and watched Packenham's party disappear into the jungle. The boatswain spat after them. The next time William saw the petty officer, he was in earnest discussion with the master gunner. The gunner was a technical specialist like the carpenter. He was responsible for all the ship's heavy weapons, gunpowder, and shot.

William wondered what the two petty officers were up to. The boatswain and gunner had crewed together since before William had first gone to sea. They had the comfortable relationship of two professionals who each knew that they could rely on the other. The captain turned his back. Part of the art of leading fighting men is to know what not to see. Packenham's hunting party did not return that night.

They returned the next day. "Here come the bold adventurers," said the boatswain pointing to the north end of the bay.

William turned. "Pity. I could have withstood the loss if they never turned up. They don't seem to have been too successful, boatswain." Packenham's party were clutching a couple of unidentifiable small furry animals. One man was limping badly and another required the support of two comrades to walk at all. William watched them stagger towards the camp.

A few minutes later the long boat arrived with a change of guard for the shore party. "Phelps, stay with me." The boatswain held out his arm, keeping the old guard party on the beach. This doubled the number of armed loyal seamen he had immediately available.

It took the hunting party an hour or more to reach the camp. Out to sea, the pinnace disengaged from the *Swallow* and rowed slowly in an arc towards the shore. William surveyed the party as it approached. They were covered in mud.

"The mighty hunters return," said the boatswain, loudly. "You don't seem to have caught much but mosquito bites."

His lip curled in a sneer at one of the more truculent malcontents, who was limping. "Hey, Jenks, what happened? Got savaged by a squirrel did you?"

Several of the boatswain's men laughed. The limper's face twisted in anger but he failed to respond. The boatswain was a big man who had often demonstrated an almost fiendish ability to inflict painful damage in a brawl.

"You can be silent, you peasant," Packenham said. "I won't have my men insulted by the likes of you."

"Your men?" asked William. "The boatswain will talk to *my* men any way I see fit and I require you to keep a civil tongue in your head when talking to my officers."

"I've had enough from you too, you jumped-up tradesman's son." Packenham's sword came free with a hiss of steel, closely followed by William's.

The dozen guards in demi-armour took station on their captain and the boatswain. Packenham did not seem to notice but the malcontents around him looked nervous. The tension in the air was thicker than the humidity. A rat-faced sailor near Packenham glanced around as if looking for a bolthole and froze.

"Master Packenham, master . . ." Ratface pulled on the gentleman's arm and pointed.

The pinnace was grounded on the sand close in shore. The bow swivel gun was pointed straight at the malcontents. Behind it stood the gunner, who had a burning slow match in his hand.

Packenham looked more puzzled than frightened.

"You dare not," said Packenham to William.

The gunner grinned.

Packenham wore a look of stubborn incomprehension. He was a rich young man, whose wealth and status had too often protected him from his own bad decisions. He seemed unable to comprehend that here, beyond the line, his mistakes might be lethal.

"The gunner dares," said Ratface, nearly in tears. He knew just how easily men could die from stupidity. "The gunner dares anything."

The gunner's grin widened.

William's mind raced. It would be embarrassing to shoot the cousin of a backer but mutiny was mutiny. Besides, William was not without family connections of his own.

"Cap'n, the signal, sir." One of Packenham's party pointed up at the lookout post.

A white flag waved where it could be seen only from inside the bay. A cheer went up from the men on the *Swallow* and the tension broke like a summer storm.

"You men." William pointed at the malcontents. "Get the stern anchor up and into the rowboat. Then pick up the men on the lookout."

"Aye, aye, sir." Incipient mutiny was forgotten in the anticipation of action.

"Boatswain, I want a boarding party in the pinnace. Master Packenham, accompany the boatswain, if you please."

Even Packenham had cheered up at the prospect of loot. He grinned at William and saluted before climbing into the pinnace.

The *Swallow* crept out under tow from the pinnace and rowboat until she cleared the headland. In the open sea, the wind filled her sails and the crew cast off the cables. The pinnace raised sails, while the rowboat shot back to the ship.

William had timed it perfectly so that the *Swallow* erupted from the bay straight into the weather gauge, upwind of the target ship. The sea dogs had a perfect attack position. Whosoever had the weather gauge controlled the battle, deciding when and where to initiate an attack. The galleon built up speed, as wind power overcame inertia. The master stood on the rear deck below William, instructing the topmen to trim the sails so as to get the perfect tack. William felt a surge of pride as the ship accelerated to combat speed. Race-built English galleons were constructs of the highest technology produced by man. Not even the ancients, despite their great wisdom, had ever built anything like the *Swallow*. The only thing afloat faster than an English race-built galleon was a Portugese caravel, but they were too light to fight.

The target vessel was a Spanish coastal trader. She was armed and only slightly smaller the *Swallow*. The Spanish called this type of vessel an *urca*; the English called them hulks.

The boatswain tucked the pinnace in behind the galleon, where she would be both protected and hidden until she was needed. William joined the gunner and master on the rear deck.

The *urca* still cruised lazily up the coastline. She showed no sign of having seen the *Swallow*. A galleon under full sail was hardly inconspicuous.

"The watchmen yonder must be blind or drunk," said the master, grinning at William.

"They must do this trip every year and never see anything but the occasional Spanish trader. Why should this trip be different? Why bother to stare at jungle for league after league?" William shielded his eyes from the sun to get a better view. "I don't think much of the set of the *urca*'s sails."

"Very sloppy, sir," the master agreed.

All of a sudden there was frantic activity on the enemy ship. Men swarmed up the rigging and started hauling on the yardarms.

"She's trying to change tack. I half expected her to yield immediately. She must realise that she can't escape," said William.

The Spanish ship had a fatter, rounder hull to carry cargo and fewer seamen than the *Swallow* so she had no hope of escaping the English warship. The attempt to change direction was not going well. William was sure he saw one figure fall from the mast.

"She must be carrying valuable cargo, to take so much trouble to escape," said the master, with relish. "Her captain probably feels he has to make a show of it, for form's sake."

The bow of the *urca* started to swing, but then she failed to complete the tack and her sails started to swing and spill air. She lost speed and the *Swallow* overhauled her fast. Finally, she fell back on to her old course.

"Order, counterorder, disorder," said William, quietly to himself.

He noticed activity around the *urca's* guns.

"Master gunner."

"Sir?"

"What range do you think you can get from a bow gun in these conditions?"

The gunner considered. "Four hundred yards, sir."

William estimated the range at one thousand yards and closing.

"I think she means to make a fight of it. Load the bow and portside guns."

"Aye, aye, sir."

William walked forward with the master gunner. They made their way along the port waist of the ship.

"Portside gunners load the culverins. Bow the guns forwards," said the gunner. Each culverin was under the command of a gunner's mate.

The mates had already broken down the bow breechloaders when William and the gunner climbed into the fo'csle.

"I'll load them up personally, lads." The gunner motioned the men aside and selected a shot for the first gun, using a calibration ring. There was no such thing as a fixed calibre, as each handmade gun was slightly different and the iron balls tended to swell in sea conditions. Stamps on the bow guns proudly recorded that they had been made by Thomas Pitt's foundry, in the Weald of Kent.

The art was to find a shot that just fitted the ring. The ball had too much "windage" in the barrel if it was too small, causing it to bounce from side to side when fired such that the gun did not shoot true.

The gunner charged the gun breeches when he was happy with his choice of shot.

"So this is the new corned powder you made me buy at such a dainty price," said William, reaching his hand into it. "I see why they call it corned. It feels like handling barley seed."

"The powder is glazed, right after mixing, into granules. The big advantage is that you don't have to remix it on deck."

William winced. "Don't remind me, gunner. I was on the *Plymouth Trader* when a powder mixer blew and set off the gun stores. We went into action with half our starboard guns dismounted and two gun crews slaughtered before the enemy had fired a shot."

"Corned powder burns better too, so the fall of the shot is more predictable." The gunner charged each breech with a carefully measured quantity of powder. Two of the crew picked each breech up by rope handles and laid them on the gun carriages, behind the barrels. They inserted wooden wedges at the back of the guns and hammered them down to press the breeches into position.

"Hold her steady," William ordered the master, who passed the message on to the steersman. "Break open the bloody flag," William yelled.

The signalman pulled on a line and a large rectangular blood-red flag unfurled from the main mast, indicating that the galleon was about to go into action. A loud cheer broke out on the decks of the *Swallow*, closely echoed from the pinnace behind.

"What range would you call, Captain?" asked the gunner.

"Maybe three-fifty yards."

"Would have put it at three-seven-five myself."

The gunner picked up the linstaff from where it stood upright in a bucket of sand. A burning slow match projected from the top, which was shaped like a hunting hound's head. He looked at the target and checked the bearing again, before lowering the match to the touchhole. A hiss indicated he had fired. The cannon went off after a short pause.

William followed the shot; it splashed down thirty yards short and behind the target.

"Oh, good shot, gunner."

"Not good enough," the gunner said. "These breechloaders are not as accurate as the culverins. Faster to reload though."

He carefully modified the alignment of the second cannon and fired again. This time, William saw a splash right under the target's bow. The Spaniard sailed on.

"How very peculiar. I thought she would surely surrender once she knew we meant business. Can you get in another shot?"

The gunner replied by reloading the port gun, which took some little time. The *Swallow* continued to overhaul the *urca*. The gunner realigned the weapon very carefully.

"Two hundred yards?"

"Two hundred," confirmed William.

The gunner fired again. This time the shot hit the sea beside the target.

"Bounced into the hull, I distinctly saw timbers break," said William, happily.

He waited but the *urca* sailed on.

"She won't haul her colours down," William said, surprised. "Oh well, they've asked for it."

He dropped off the forecastle. "Fire the main armament as it bears. Musket range mind."

The gun crews had finished loading the heavy culverin muzzleloaders on the gun deck. The gun carriages on English ships were four-wheeled and attached to the hull by a complex series of ropes and pulleys. The crews hauled them through the gun ports and trained them forward, under the supervision of the gunner.

William ran aft, leaving the gunner to get on with his job. He positioned himself by the whipstaff, the steering position, from where he could fight the ship. He kept her on course driving right into the target vessel. At one-twenty-five, he held his arm out and swept it down. The steersman threw his full weight against the whipstaff. The lever put the tiller over, pushing the *Swallow*'s bow starboard by ten degrees.

The gunner looked along the front port culverin. At one hundred yards, he stepped to one side and signalled the gun captain to fire.

"On the downward roll," said the gunner. A shot fired on the downward roll would catch the target in the hull and, at this range, maybe below the waterline as the enemy hull rolled upwards.

The billow of white smoke hid the fall of shot, but William saw the target's sails shake in the concussion. Only about half the gunpowder burnt in the barrel, the rest formed a blast zone that did more damage at short range than the shot.

The culverin recoiled. The heavy mass of the gun absorbed much of the recoil such that it could be secured on pulleys that allowed it to move inwards, ready for reloading. English sea dogs could reload in just five minutes. English culverins had to be heavier than Spanish guns of the same calibre, in order to withstand repeated firing. This had the advantage of increasing the stability of the weapon and, hence, accuracy.

The gunner oversaw the firing of each gun as it came on target. The *urca* rocked over at each blast, sails and rigging parting. Swivel guns on the galleon's castles poured antipersonnel shot into the carnage. The rear culverins smashed in at fifty yards. The *urca* never got a shot off, as her decks were increasingly swept clean of men with every concussion.

As the *Swallow* pulled clear, William leaned over the side and waved his cap at the pinnace below. The boatswain acknowledged.

The small warship pulled round the back of the galleon and ran alongside the Spaniard's bow. Sea dogs swarmed up the *urca's* side on lines. William noticed that Packenham was the next man up after the boatswain. Gentleman's sons might be a pain in the rear but they knew how to fight.

"Master Smethwick, you have the ship," said William. "Get the long boat alongside. Boarding party to me."

It would take the master some time to turn the *Swallow* round. You couldn't handle a galleon as if it were a beer wagon.

William took the tiller of the longboat himself. "Row, you whoresons. Men are dying over there."

He steered the boat around the stern of the *urca*. A sailor threw a grappling hook up onto the high rear deck. William ran up the sloping side of the merchant ship, pulling himself along the line. He heaved himself up over the rail. Fighting was still going on in the waist of the ship. The Spaniards up on the rear deck were utterly focused on the boatswain's men so they failed to notice William. He hauled two more boarders onto the deck before an enemy turned and noticed them. William launched an instant attack to defend the rest of the boat crew climbing up behind him.

An officer in a helmet and demi-armour engaged William and they crossed swords. William got a thrust through the officer's guard but it glanced off the man's breastplate.

A Spanish soldier fired a swivel gun down into the waist. Screams indicated that he had found targets, probably on both sides. The man turned as one of William's boarders approached.

"I yield," said the soldier in English, raising his arms.

"Too late now, matey." The sea dog gave the traditional reply and ran him through. You could surrender before the battle or, if you survived, afterwards. What you couldn't do was kill a sea dog's mates, and then surrender to him when your luck soured.

More Swallows poured onto the Spanish ship behind William. One of them brained William's opponent with a boarding pike. All of a sudden, a man was in front of William with his sword reversed.

"We strike, we yield, please."

William raised the sword and yelled down into the ship.

"She strikes. Cease fighting. That means you too, Jenkins. I saw that. Cut another man's throat after he surrenders and I'll hang you."

The carnage on the *urca's* decks was appalling. She was carrying soldiers, who must have encouraged the crew to resist. Many of the crew must have been cut down by culverin fire in the first few terrible minutes. A number of Swallows were casualties but most of the bodies were Spanish.

"What were they trying to defend?" William asked himself.

A door to one of the rear gallery cabins opened. A woman, no, a lady, with jet-black hair and dressed in a deep green Spanish court dress, walked out.

"I am the Lady Isabella," she said, in English.

Act 7, The Atlantic Ocean

"Well, I'll be bugg—" started the boatswain.

"Ah yes, um, hello, madam," William intervened.

"Your servant, Lady Isabella." Packenham thrust himself forward and made an elegant leg, flourishing his helmet.

William had one of those strokes of genius that occasionally inflict otherwise sane human beings. He suddenly had a plan to kill two inconvenient birds with one metaphorical stone.

"Master Packenham, I believe the lady should have a gentleman to escort her, what with all these rough sailors around." The rough sailors grinned at their captain, not at all put out by his description of them. "Possibly if you took her up to the fo'c'sle and entertained her?"

"Excellent idea, Hawkins." Packenham offered her his arm.

"Thank you, Master . . .?"

"Packenham, madam. Christopher Packenham at your service."

William let them get out of earshot and then got down to business.

"Boatswain, search the ship thoroughly. Get me a list of the cargo and bring any valuables onto the deck. And boatswain," William raised his voice so that all the sea dogs on board the *urca* could hear him. "Looting is theft, not just of our backers but also of our shipmates. I will hang any man who steals. Be sure of it."

"Aye, aye, sir. You heard the cap'n. I want three men in each group at all times. And if I catch any man stealing then the cap'n's rope will be the least of his problems."

One of the surrendered officers asked the *urca's* captain in Spanish, *"Are they French Huguenots?"*

The Spanish captain replied in the same language. *"Not French, these are English heretics. Pirates from the bastard-queen in London."*

William's sword was at his throat in a second.

"Not pirates, Captain, but privateers with a commission from Elizabeth. You would all be dead if we were pirates. I would advise you to speak respectfully of Her Majesty. Many of my men speak Spanish, and they would kill a papist who spoke ill of the Queen as soon as they would step on a beetle." William spoke in the same language.

"Matthews," William said to one of his sailors.

"Sir!"

"Take three men and hold the prisoners aft."

"Aye, aye, sir."

William walked down in the waist of the *urca* to examine the ship's guns. It might be worth craning them across to the *Swallow*. The Spanish mounted ship's guns on two-wheeled land carriages, an arrangement that took up a great deal of space. They tied the gun carriage to the hull, which meant that the gun could not be aimed or reloaded without unlashing the whole assembly.

Spanish practice was to have only one crewman on each gun. Soldiers occupied the space in a Spanish vessel that was taken up by gun crews on an English ship. The guns would fire only once as the ship closed, before the soldiers boarded an enemy vessel to capture it. Spanish gun carriages made sense when sea battles were fought the old way but fast, race-built English galleons, with their heavy culverins, had brought a new style of ranged fighting that made such tactics obsolete.

The Spanish cannon were old and badly made. The bore on the one nearest to William was off centre. William could not remember any of the Spanish heavy guns firing during the battle but scorch marks showed that the touchhole had been ignited.

"Sweet Jesus," he said, in horror. "The charge must still be in the barrel."

William gave up any intention to remove the weapons. They were scrap metal and hence, at this distance from England, near worthless.

The Spanish must have been carrying the guns loaded. The guns might have misfired because the different constituent powders in the charge had separated or maybe because the gunpowder was waterlogged. Saltpetre in gunpowder had a wondrous affinity for water.

"Captain," said the boatswain, behind him.

William turned and the boatswain touched his forehead.

"Most of the cargo are hides but we found these."

Grinning sailors hauled chests, some of which seemed agreeably heavy.

William broke open one. Bright pale yellow bars gleamed.

"Venezuelan gold," breathed the boatswain.

The Spanish province of Venezuela had some of the last productive gold mines left in the New World. William opened one of the lighter chests to find pearls.

"It's not a queen's ransom but I think our backers are going to turn a dainty profit," William said with satisfaction.

One of the boatswain's mates tapped his superior on the shoulder and whispered urgently to him.

"We have a problem," said the boatswain.

"And it was all going so well," said William.

"Our culverins holed her in at least two places below the waterline. The hull must be rotten with tropical worm because water is pouring in," said the boatswain.

Spanish *urcas* had hulls stressed to withstand expansion pressures from the inside as they carried cargo such as grain, which might swell when wet. Their hulls were not designed to withstand high-velocity objects punching in from the outside. This made them wondrously vulnerable to culverin fire.

"Can we plug it?" asked William.

"You can ask the carpenter but I doubt we can stop her sinking. We will never get this ship across the Atlantic. One storm." The boatswain shrugged.

William swore horribly. The *urca* was worth as much as the goods in her hold. "Get as many of the hides out as possible before they are ruined."

"Captain, we found this in a rear cabin," said a sailor, joining the group.

William took the object. It was a small mirror, about six inches by one foot. Twisted gold decorated the rim. The gold was worked into fabulous beasts whose eyes were picked out in blue diamonds.

"Venezualan sea diamonds," said the boatswain.

"I have heard of them but never thought I would see one. I half believed that they were a myth. There must be a dozen here. I wonder what this is worth?" asked William.

"Mayhap as much as all the pearls together, mayhap more," said the boatswain.

"That mirror is my private property, Captain," said Isabella.

William had not noticed that Packenham and the Spanish lady had circumnavigated the deck and were now behind him.

"I told Lady Isabella that she could keep her personal items," said the young aristocrat.

"Did you, Packenham?" asked William mildly. "Lady Isabella, you can retain your clothes and the jewels on your person. All else is forfeit."

"See here, Hawkins, I gave my word," said Packenham, heatedly.

"It was not yours to give, Packenham. I command here and I decide what is booty."

Packenham looked about to his toadies for support but they avoided his gaze. All the crew had shares. Packenham would get no support for giving away prize money.

"Assemble the prisoners," William ordered.

"*Captain,*" William spoke in Spanish. "*This ship is sinking and I do not believe it can be saved. I will have water and food put in your boat. You should easily make the next Spanish colony up the coast.*"

The Spaniard looked surprised. He had probably expected to be slaughtered out of hand. William knew Englishmen who would have done just that, either to remove witnesses or just to kill papists on general principles.

The man bowed. "*Thank you, Captain. To whom do I have the pleasure of addressing?*"

Not to be outdone in courtesy, William bowed back. "*Captain William Hawkins of the* Swallow."

"*Hawkins? Are you any relation to the famous English corsair, John Hawkins?*"

"*John Hawkins is my cousin. Captain, satisfy my curiosity if you will. Why did you fight so hard? You must have realised that your chances of escape were slim.*"

The Spanish captain shrugged and refused to answer but his eyes looked over William's shoulder with something like fear in them. William turned. Behind Packenham and Isabella, the *Swallow* manoeuvred into position alongside to receive the bulk cargo.

William could see nothing to fear. Never mind. It was not an important point.

"That just leaves you, lady," William said to Isabella. "You can go with your countrymen in the boat but it will be an uncomfortable trip with no privacy. Or you may travel with us back to England, on the *Swallow*."

"I believe I will be better off with you, Captain. Especially, with this noble gentleman to look after me." She smiled at Packenham, who positively preened.

William translated Isabella's choice for the Spanish crew. Their captain looked relieved. William thought that the aristocratic Spanish lady must have been a demanding passenger.

"Boatswain, please have the Lady Isabella's properties transferred to the *Swallow*. Put them…" William's eyes glazed as he tried to work out how to accommodate a lady in the *Swallow*'s already overcrowded accommodation. "Put the lady in Master Packenham's cabin. He will have to bunk down *forrard* with the petty officers. Place the chests of valuables in my cabin."

Packenham opened his mouth, presumably to protest, when Isabella intervened. "How kind of you, Master Packenham. How will I ever thank you?"

"Think nothing of it, dear lady," said Packenham, kissing her hand. "My heart flies to your service."

"I think I am going to heave," said the boatswain, sotto voce.

"Boatswain, put provision for the prisoners in their boat and let them go. Fire the ship when we leave," said William.

The *Swallow* pulled away under cruising sail towing the pinnace behind. William stood aft and forced himself to watch the death of a ship, a death that he had ordered. Black smoke ran up in a wavy line to the heavens. The Spanish longboat raised a sail and stood in back to the shore.

William turned away and turned his mind to getting the *Swallow* in condition for the long transoceanic voyage back to Europe. Such journeys had only been possible for the last hundred years or so and English mariners had bare decades of experience. Sea voyages like this were very far from routine.

"Captain, there is something wrong," said the master. "The Spanish longboat is sinking."

William looked back over the rail. "Something seems to be pulling it under. Get the ship about."

The boat rolled over as he watched and upended, going under by the stern.

"Never mind, Master. It's too late. There can be no survivors."

"What in Hades happened?" asked the master. "Did she hit a reef?"

"I don't know. It didn't seem so, mayhap it was one of those whirlpools such as Homer described." William didn't sound convinced.

The master nudged William and pointed to the fo'c'sle. Isabella stood looking back at the death of her countrymen without a flicker of emotion. William shivered. "Someone has just walked over my grave."

The voyage dragged on. The days slipped endlessly by as the *Swallow* surged ever eastwards, holding the same tack for days at a time.

At least once a week, William hosted supper in the captain's cabin for Packenham, the Lady Isabella, and Master Smethwick. Tonight, he had the gunner and boatswain as guests as well, both looking somewhat uneasy. The food was much the same as always, salted fish and meats, but the wine was good. In fact, it was the finest vintage the Spanish Empire could provide, courtesy of their merchant marine.

"I have never been to England. For some years, I have thought that it is time that I visited the north. Will we be sailing straight to England, Master Smethwick?" Isabella addressed the master.

"Alas no, lady, ships sail down lines of latitude so we will make landfall in the Old World and then sail north. We will need to reprovision the vessel as well."

"I have never understood why you mariners don't simply carry more food, Hawkins. Why don't you make the ships bigger?" asked Packenham, jabbing at William with his knife for emphasis.

"We would simply pack more crew into a bigger ship and so need even more food and water," said William.

Packenham opened his mouth but William carried on quickly to forestall the obvious question. "We need large crews to fight the ship. We also have large gun batteries that take up space and are heavy so need to be ballasted. Our tactics require repeated firing so we need space for shot and powder. Race-built English galleons are built for speed, so they are narrow relative to their length. There is never enough room in their tight hulls for adequate supplies."

"The Spanish seem to manage well enough," Packenham sniffed.

"They have small crews, low firepower, and nice wide hulls," said William.

"And when they fight us, they lose," added the boatswain.

"Aye, it's a comfortable life on a Spanish galleon. Until you meet an English one with culverins," said the gunner with a wolfish grin.

"So where will we take on supplies?" asked Isabella.

"The Canaries are out," said William ruefully. "The Spanish authorities won't deal with us. So I fancy we will make for the Portuguese Azores."

"Surely Philip has persuaded the Portuguese not to resupply English ships or the embargo at the Canaries is useless," said Isabella.

"Oh, I am sure he has persuaded the government in Lisbon but there are many little isolated islands in the Azores with impoverished governors." William winked.

For a sweet course, the cook had saved some grapefruit. They were leathery with age but he had marinated them in wine to make them palatable. After dinner, William's steward served sherry. William did not care much for the sweet drink but it was expected. He toyed with his mug appearing to drink while his guests had a refill.

"Oh, my dress," said Isabella, as sweet sherry cascaded over her.

"Sorry, ma'am, but you jogged my arm," said the steward.

"Hush your insolence, fellow, before I have you flogged," Packenham added to the chorus.

"No harm done. Such events are commonplace on a ship at sea." Sometimes William felt like a ringmaster in a circus of especially truculent players.

There was a degree of commotion while the steward cleaned up, during which William managed to slip his sherry into the boatswain's mug. The boatswain did not care all that much for sherry either but it was alcoholic, so William doubted if the petty officer would mind.

William saw his guests out and then studied his charts by lantern light. He was trying to estimate the ship's longitude by dead reckoning but the method was hopelessly inaccurate. However, he decided that they would turn the ship north tomorrow, until they picked up the line of latitude that led to the Azores.

He blew the lantern out and climbed into his bunk. William always slept uneasily at sea. Ship life was physically demanding, but he never completely relaxed into that carefree state where golden sleep does reign. The working of the wooden ship against the ocean, the murmuring of the watch, and the sound of the wind in the rigging, all was an orchestra that played through his unconscious. Any change in this familiar retinue of players was as loud as a culverin discharge.

Something changed and he woke instantly. His mind rotated through the catalogue of sound. The slap of water against the groaning timbers showed that the *Swallow* was still on her easterly course and that the swell was much the same. But sea air moved over his face. His cabin door was open to the elements.

William lay perfectly still and opened his eyes. A dark silhouette moved across the starfield in the doorway. Dim light spilled out of a small lantern. The intruder moved over to the treasure chests and began to look through them. William was astonished. What on earth made some thief think they could just rifle through the captain's cabin in such a cavalier manner?

William slowly moved his arm, searching for a weapon. The bunk creaked and the intruder froze. William produced a snore and the thief turned back to his investigations. William couldn't find his dagger in the dark but his fingers curled around a pewter mug.

The captain hurled himself at the dark figure. The intruder reacted with lightning speed, so that William's blow hit his shoulder, rather than his head. The intruder smashed his elbow backwards into William's stomach, with incredible strength. William was smashed off his feet back into a bulkhead. He bent over, retching. The thief had gone by the time he could stand upright. William staggered out of his cabin but all was quiet on the deck so he went back to his bunk and slept fitfully.

The next day he searched the cabin. As far as he could see, nothing had been taken.

"Where's the boatswain?" William asked to a passing sailor.

The man grinned, "He still be abed, Captain."

William made his way forward to the boatswain's bunk. The man lay stretched out snoring horribly.

"Wake up, man. What's wrong with you?" asked William.

The boatswain grunted and slept on.

"Brownlow, get me some water," William said to a seaman.

The grinning sailor fetched a bucket of seawater and William threw it over the petty officer, who finally stirred. William shook him. "Wake up, man. Sweet Jesu, how much more did you have to drink after you left me last night?"

"Nothing, Cap'n, absolutely nothing. I was tired and went straight to sleep."

William sniffed suspiciously. The man did not smell of drink. Besides he had seen the boatswain drink his way up one side of the Barbican in Plymouth, back down the other, and still stand his watch the next day.

"Are you ill, man? Do you have a chill?"

"No, Cap'n. I don't understand it."

"Come to my cabin, if you are finally awake." The captain left the deck.

"Aye, aye, sir," said the boatswain. He noticed the sailor grinning at him. "Brownlow, you lazy wretch. Be about your business or I'll find something for you to do."

"Aye, aye, boatswain." The sailor vanished as the boatswain was not noted for idle threats and was quite capable of dreaming up some truly awful task.

The boatswain made his way aft to the captain's cabin and knocked at the door.

"Come in. Last night I had a thief in here. The bastard gave me one almighty crack in the ribs," said William

"The bold rogue. I will strip the back of the whoreson when I find him. What did he take?"

"As far as I can tell, nothing. He seemed to be looking for something specific, rather than just general looting. Are you sure you drank nothing last night after leaving my cabin?"

"On my life, Cap'n."

"I was afraid of that. I slipped my last drink into yours."

"I saw you. Can't stand sherry either."

"You drank it though."

"Ah well, I wouldn't want to insult you, Cap'n." The grin slowly faded from the boatswain's face. "The old opium in the drink trick?"

"It would explain why someone thought that I would sleep soundly, and you did."

"But that means that the thief was part of the supper party. There were only your officers, the gentleman, and the lady present. I trust the other officers with my life."

"As do I," said William. "I cannot imagine why Packenham would turn thief. His family own St. Austell and most of the mines on the surrounding moors."

"That just leaves the Lady Isabella."

"A lady didn't do this," said William, pulling open his shirt. The beginnings of a livid bruise discoloured his ribs.

"'Course, the thief and the cozenor might be two different people," said the boatswain, thoughtfully.

"I want a trusted man on my cabin door at all times, day and night. Arrange it, will you, boatswain?"

"Aye, aye, sir."

The boatswain moved the *Swallow* onto a northern tack, adjusting the rigging and sails until the master was satisfied that he was getting the best out of the ship. After a few days, Smethwick decreed that the ship had reached the latitude of the Azores and they changed back to an eastern tack to run down the latitude line.

"Land ho off the starboard bow." The cry came from the foremast.

William ran forward and gazed at the horizon. He imagined that he saw a faint smudge of cloud on the horizon. Nothing for it, he needed more height. He climbed up the foremast rigging. The lookout hauled him up the last few feet onto the boards. William breathed heavily; this voyage had wrecked his wind. He heard what might have been a chuckle. William looked suspiciously at the sailor who carefully arranged his face into respectful blandness.

"Over there, sir."

William stared in the indicated direction. There was no doubt about it. A plume of cloud hung over a dark mass.

"Master Smethwick," William yelled.

"Sir."

"Most excellent navigation."

"Thank you, sir." The master gazed up at the captain with a pleased expression. William was a fair navigator himself, which made his praise doubly welcome. In truth, the master had done well. Finding the small archipelago of the Azores in the vastness of the Atlantic was no mean achievement.

The land mass split into separate islands. The Azores lay in a chain from northwest to southeast. The twin islands of Fayal and Pico were to port and Sao Miguel and Santa Maria to starboard. The primary island with the governor's palace was on the island of

Terceira on the side of the chain nearest to Portugal. Generally, English ships avoided Terceira so as not to embarrass the governor.

Out to the northwest lay the small island of Flores and the islet of Corvo. The *Swallow* changed course for Flores. By late afternoon, she cruised under reefed sails into the anchorage at Ponta Delgada. Normally, as soon as an English galleon appeared, boats poured out of the anchorage in competition to sell their goods. This trip, the port was quiet and only the *Swallow* moved quietly over the glassy water, leaving ripples in its wake.

"I don't like this, Master Smethwick. Something is wrong," William said. "Gunner!"

"Sir."

"Load the swivel guns, just in case we have to defend ourselves."

"Aye, aye, sir."

The *Swallow* dropped anchor and they waited. After some little time, a boat put out from the port and rowed out to the ship.

A badly dressed official in a soiled sash clambered up the ship.

"*My felicitations to Governor Santoza,*" William said in Spanish, bowing to the man. Spanish was the trade language of the southern lands. Santoza was the local customs official but he was politely referred to as the "governor" of the island.

"*Ah. Governor Santoza has had an accident. The captain of the militia is in charge until a new governor is sent from Terceira.*"

"*The port is very quiet. Where are all the traders?*" William asked.

The official looked at William sideways. "*You have sailed in from the Americas, Captain?*"

"*We have been at sea for some time,*" said William, guardedly.

The official nodded. "*Then you will not have heard. Cardinal Henry has died.*"

Cardinal Henry assumed the throne of Portugal when King Sebastian was killed in the Battle of al-Qasr al Kabir in Morocco. Sebastian had thought to emulate Spain in a crusade against the Moors, but with disastrous results. Henry had spent every shilling in the Portuguese treasury on ransoming the surviving Portuguese nobles from captivity. He had no money left to bribe the Pope to release him from his clerical vows so he had no wife and hence no legitimate heir. This was a nightmare scenario for a country, and one that haunted the English with their own Virgin Queen.

"*So who is now King?*" asked William.

The official shrugged. *"Philip of Spain has a claim through the female line and Dom Antonio of Crato through a male line from a boy born on the wrong side of the blanket. Terceira has backed Dom Antonio but Antonio's Portuguese forces have been defeated by the Spanish army in a great battle at Alcantara."*

"My God, if Spain has got control of the Portuguese Empire and fleet then the Netherlands and England could be hard-pressed," said the master, who had been following the conversation.

"You didn't answer my question. Where are all the traders?" asked William.

"They were frightened by your ship. It might have been Spanish." The official gave another eloquent shrug.

"I will need permission to fill up water casks and I need to buy provisions," said William.

"Help yourself to water. I will arrange for traders to come but it will take a little time."

"You have two days. After that I will take other action." William looked meaningfully at the culverins and then at the town.

The official seemed disinclined to continue the conversation and climbed back into his boat, which rowed raggedly away.

"The old governor was always very helpful to English ships. I wonder what sort of accident he had," said the master, to no one in particular.

"Boatswain," said William. "Start refilling our water casks. I want the shore party fully armed. Everyone else is to stay aboard the *Swallow.*"

"Aye, aye, sir."

Traders turned up by the second day but with meagre stocks of food. William protested to the official who promised more would be forthcoming soon.

On the third day, William was hailed from the main mast.

"Sails, at the promontory."

Triangular lateen sails belonging to three ships nosed around along the southern promontory that protected the anchorage. As the ships cleared the land, their hulls became visible.

"Spanish frigates! War galleys, by God," said William. "Where's the boatswain?"

"Still ashore with the caskmen," said a sailor.

"Get a recall pennant up. Master gunner!"

"Sir."

"Fire a swivel gun to get the shore party's attention. Load the main armament. Any gunner who takes more than fifteen minutes is demoted."

"Sir."

The swivel gun went off with a crash.

"They are perfectly positioned to come in on our stern and shoot us to pieces," said the master. "That papist bastard in a sash has sold us out. He dribbled out just enough food to keep us here, while he alerted the Spanish."

"I can't run and leave the shore party," said William. "Raise the bow anchor and man the pinnace. Get a cable on the ship's bows. We will swing her from the stern."

"Aye, aye, sir."

"Master gunner," William yelled across the ship. "The dons have decided to give your men some target practice. An extra share of loot to the first gun crew to put a shot into a Spaniard."

The gun crews cheered and went about their work with redoubled vigour. The galleys lowered their sails. Oars unshipped and the beat of timing drums carried across the waters.

"What is happening, Captain?" Isabella appeared on the rear deck.

"We are about to fight, madam. Master Packenham, get the lady below where she will be safe.

"Signalman," William yelled. "Raise the bloody flag. We must give the dons fair warning in case they want to run away, eh lads?"

Another cheer greeted this sally.

"May I not stay and watch, Captain? I have never seen a naval battle and your men seem supremely confident," said Isabella.

"Madam, all the advantages lie with the galleys in this sheltered anchorage. They will try to use their oars to manoeuvre into the *Swallow*'s unprotected rear and shoot the ship to pieces with their heavy frontal cannon."

"I see. Does this mean that you will have to surrender?"

"Surrender? And spend the rest of my life as a slave manning the oars yonder?" William gestured at the Spanish ships. "No, madam, I intend to fight. Drake has devised a trick that may yet serve us well."

The galleys cruised in towards the rear of the *Swallow*, their oars rippling like a centipede's legs. The pinnace crew rowed against the inertia of the galleon's weight. Slowly, the *Swallow* pivoted to point its broadside at the attacking galleys.

"Run out the starboard guns," William ordered. "Fire as they bear."

The gun trolleys ran out on their pulleys with a great squeal.

A galley crew fired. Four cannon went off one after the other. Three plashes to the *Swallow*'s rear marked the fall of shot.

William stood legs apart, hands on hips, and laughed. "Three misses and a lost ball, gunner. What say you to shooting like that?"

"The dons are improving, sir. They'll soon be almost as good as a Danish merchantman."

"Stand by," said the rear culverin gunner. The crew opened their mouths and covered their ears.

The culverin went off with a great concussion. The gun recoiled inboard, to be caught on its ropes. The shot fell between two galleys.

"Range excellent but more care needed on the bearing, gunner."

"Aye, aye, sir."

The men worked furiously to recharge their weapon. The next culverin fired, and the next. The fourth to fire was echoed by the first firing again. Shot whipped up the water but, end on, the galleys presented a difficult target. The galleys fired continuously. Balls struck all round the *Swallow*. A sail snapped and split as it was hit.

"Captain, boat putting out from the shore," said a sailor. The figure of the boatswain manned the tiller, urging on the rowers.

"Hard pounding, sir," said the master.

"Aye, Master Smethwick, but we'll see who can pound the hardest."

The artillery exchange reached a crescendo. A shot smashed through the rail and blasted splinters across the deck forward, felling sailors. A second shot glanced off a culverin in front of William, eviscerating one of the crew and spraying blood and gore across the deck.

"Damn them, gunner, these are my best breeches. I'll trouble you to punish the Spaniards for that assault on my wardrobe," said William. The captain was drenched in blood from the waist down.

A shot ripped open the front of a galley. Another smashed down a mainmast. "Oh good shooting, gunner," William said.

The galleys broke first and turned away to row out of arc, presenting their vulnerable sides. The gunner took over a culverin and aimed carefully. The shot smashed through an oar bank and the galley seemed to fold in on itself as the sea rushed in. A cheer rolled across the *Swallow*'s deck.

"They must build those things from paper," said the boatswain.

"I see you have decided to join us," said William. "If you have finished your holiday ashore, boatswain, mayhap you could raise the sails and get us on our way."

The two remaining galleys turned back into the attack as the *Swallow* slowly picked up speed.

"Alter course to port," William said.

The course change lined the *Swallow* up for the open sea. It also took the ship right past the galley flotilla. More shots hit the *Swallow* at minimum range, killing sailors but doing little damage to the ship. The *Swallow*'s culverins crashed out a reply in a single broadside. For a moment, billowing white smoke hid the targets. It slowly cleared. One of the galleys was gutted from end to end. William could see figures struggling in the water as the *Swallow* headed out to sea.

"Some of those poor bastards are probably English slaves," said the master.

"I know," said William. "But if it were me, I would rather take my chances with King Neptune than live as a slave."

The ship ran past Ponta Delgada and the gunner yelled up at William. "Shall I put some shot into those treacherous bastards?"

"If I could be sure each discharge would hit one of the swine who tricked us I would have you fire and damn the consequences. But we would only probably kill a few poor fishermen and smash up their cottages. English ships will pass this way again and I would not leave a legacy of hatred for us. As for handing out a lesson . . ." William gestured aft where a single serviceable galley picked up survivors from the water. A powerful fighting squadron had been smashed in a bare hour by the firepower of a single English galleon. The message would ring clearly among those who lived their lives by the wide ocean.

"Master Smethwick."

"Yes, Captain."

"North, Master, go north. Take us back to England. Take us home."

Act 8, The River Thames

"I'm fed up with being closeted here in the countryside," Lucy stamped her foot. "It's no wonder I can't find a husband. I have never even been to London."

Lilith observed with fascination. Humans were so complex. They had such little minds but the convoluted complexities of their emotions were rich beyond the politics of the People. Lucy was one of the inferior sex, and young. She was so far down the social pecking order that her opinions should be of no consequence, but she had Walsingham, the great statesman, entirely on the defensive. Lilith noticed that Simon had buried his head in a ledger and was pretending not to hear.

"Can't find a husband?" asked Walsingham, utterly nonplussed. "Lucy, you've had the pick of half the eligible bachelors of southern England, plus one or two roving bucks from the north, and rejected them all. There was even a Scotsman, as I recall."

Lucy gave him her steely look. "I just sit here vegetating like some—some marrow. You are going to the theatre without me." She stamped her foot again. "You are even taking your secretary—your secretary and not me."

"But Lucy, it's business. You know that. Tunstall is coming because I'm working," said Walsingham, reasonably. "The theatre is in Southwark, not a suitable place for a young lady." He gave Simon a

119

meaningful look. Southwark was on the other side of the river across London Bridge so it was outside the jurisdiction of the Mayor of London. It served as the entertainment playground for the City of London. Gentlemen went there to drink, gamble, and meet women who were neither their wives nor ladies.

"Men find me boring. That's why I can't find a husband. I have no conversation because I never go anywhere. I will die an old maid and no one cares."

"That's not true, Lucy, and it's because I care that I forbid you to come to Southwark. My decision is final."

"Oh, it's so unfair." Lucy rushed out.

'That's a shame,' thought Lilith. 'I so wanted to see a play. I have read so much about them. Could we not go on our own?'

'Certainly not,' the girl thought. She sounded genuinely shocked. 'Only harlots go to the theatre unescorted. People would think me wanton; do you want me to lose my reputation?'

Lilith was learning not to ask "why" questions when it came to human behaviour but just to accept that some things are Not Done for no apparent rational reason. However, she really did want to go to the theatre so she had a Plan B ready. 'Master Tunstall can escort us. I am sure you could persuade him.'

'Mayhap I could,' thought Lucy, 'but I won't. He would lose his position and his reputation if he openly disobeyed and dishonoured my uncle. Master Tunstall's family has no money. Besides, it would not be seemly for me to disobey my uncle.'

Reputations were clearly a tricky business. 'Never mind, it was just a fancy of mine to see a play,' thought Lilith.

'We will see a play, Lilith. Uncle is going to take us.'

'He has surely made his mind up,' thought Lilith.

'He hasn't made his mind up until I have made it up for him. You'll see,' thought Lucy.

Supper that night was a frozen affair. Lucy uttered the odd sob and Walsingham looked positively miserable. Lilith barely noticed as she was still fascinated by the whole concept of eating. The vivid textures and flavours of food enthralled her but Lucy barely touched her food. Lilith tried to discuss the meal with Lucy but the girl shut her out. The servants slid in and out in silence through the seven or eight courses.

The last course was custard tart and honey. Lucy took a little taste and then discarded the dish as she had done with the others. Lilith was horrified. This was a taste to die for. 'Please Lucy, please, just a little more,' she thought.

'Go away and stop distracting me,' thought Lucy. 'Can't you see that I'm busy?'

Lilith relapsed into hurt silence and Lucy pushed the food around her plate, sighing loudly. Custard tart and honey was Lucy's favourite and Lilith suspected that Walsingham had asked cook to prepare it specially.

A nervous-looking servant removed the plates and poured a glass of burgundy for Walsingham and a small beer for Lucy.

"I have been thinking, Lucy," said Walsingham.

He was rewarded by a sob.

"Possibly, I have been a little hasty. I was talking to Lady Renfrew only the other day and she regularly takes her daughters to the theatre. Apparently, it's part of a young lady's education in the modern world. Personally, I can't see what is wrong with a little tutoring in Homer but I suppose that I am old-fashioned. So I have decided that I will take you."

"Oh, Uncle," said Lucy. "Thank you, thank you."

"I try, Lucy. I have to be both father and mother to you and affairs of state often draw me away. If only my dear wife had survived the plague." Walsingham paused, his mind elsewhere. "I think that is why I have kept you from London. The place is full of disease and you are all I have left, child. But I suppose that I can't swaddle you from the world forever."

Lilith stayed out of the conversation but there was no possibility of Lucy suffering from disease. The demon ran continuous checks on Lucy's physiology and any invading organism that appeared potentially pathogenic was met with a zero-tolerance response.

Lucy got up and rushed to her uncle's chair. She knelt down, took his hand in hers, and gazed up at him. "Don't reproach yourself, Uncle. No girl had a kinder or wiser guardian."

"Well, well. It has been my pleasure as well as my duty to look after you. Run along now as I have work to do."

Lucy got up to leave.

"Oh Lucy," Walsingham said. The girl turned. "The not-eating-supper ploy was very good but you must be hungry now. Pop along to the kitchens and I am sure cook will find you something."

"Yes, Uncle." Lucy was the very epitome of womanly obedience now that she had got her own way.

Lilith would never understand these humans. If Walsingham knew what Lucy was up to all the time then why did he allow her to change his mind? Maybe men liked being manipulated by women, something to do with hormones perhaps. Lilith's current hypothesis was that male-female interactions were essentially a large highly complex game, so when one player made a move the other had to respond in a certain way because of the Rules. Lilith was certain that when she had enough data she would be able to construct the Rules. Then she could model human behaviour and predict their decisions. The only problem was that humans seemed to change the Rules as they went along. It was all very confusing.

Lucy opened the kitchen door and a rich aroma entered her nostrils. Oh, please, pretty please, thought Lilith. Let it be custard pie. But she blocked the thought off from Lucy who was starting to refer to her as Glutton Demon.

Lucy stood regally at the dock waiting to be assisted into a Thames barge.

'We're going to the theatre,' she chanted in her head to Lilith.

'How can you stand so coolly when you are bouncing with excitement inside?' Lilith thought.

'Practice,' thought Lucy happily. 'All my life, I have trained to be a lady.'

Two bargemen knelt on the wharf, holding the barge tight against the wooden strakes.

Simon Tunstall got in first and held his hand out for Lucy to step in. "Go to the bow if you please, Lady Dennys. That's the sharp end."

Lucy gave him the Look.

"Um that is, I didn't mean to suggest that you did not know what an, um, bow was." Lucy swept past him as he drivelled. Damn, thought Simon, why couldn't he learn the value of silence?

Simon joined Lucy in the bow. Walsingham and Gwilym took a seat in the stern. The barge was designed as a cargo carrier but it was Walsingham's habit to use a decent-sized boat for transport, ever since one of his agents was killed in a wherry "accident."

The bargemen pushed off. One seated himself at the tiller while the other raised the single square sail. Empty, the barge heeled over and moved swiftly away from the riverbank. The steersman kept it close in to the south bank, where the main channel was located. Barn Elms was on the south bank of a loop of the Thames.

'Can you look at the sail, please?' thought Lilith.

'Only you could get excited by a sail, demon,' thought Lucy but she nonetheless gave Lilith a good look.

'I thought these devices were simply baffles that were pushed along by an air current but the wind is to the side of us, so how does it work, I wonder?'

Lucy smiled to herself. 'What does it matter, Lilith? Sails do work, what else do you need to know?'

'This is such a clever piece of technology. It's just a sheet that can be folded into a small space but it turns into an aerofoil when the air pushes. Look, Lucy.'

Lilith edited Lucy's vision to show the air pressures around the mast. 'The air compresses behind the sail but moves quickly over the leading edge creating a suction. This force then presses the keel of the boat against the water, which resists, creating a forward motion. You realise that this boat could actually sail against the wind?'

'I did know that, Lilith.'

'You humans amaze me. You have such small brains and seem to know so little about the universe but you make the most amazingly complex machines.'

'Wait until you see a galleon, Lilith.'

'I would so like to see a galleon, Lucy.'

'I will see what I can do. Now be quiet and let me talk to Simon.'

Simon always enjoyed river travel. He was an indifferent horseman and considered boats much more civilised.

"Will you point out the sights to me, Master Tunstall?" asked Lucy.

"Of course, it will be my pleasure." He stood up, gripping the side of the barge to steady himself, and pointed out features.

"This is as far south as the river loops. On the right are the Wandsworth docks by the River Wandle. Thames barges move cargo up to the wharf, whereupon it gets transferred to wherry boats. These take goods up the Wandle to the towns beyond."

Their barge made repeated course corrections to avoid other boats. The Thames was the busiest highway in England. The boat cruised past farms, villages, and the occasional gentleman's villa. Simon pointed out the names of places, when he knew them, and made up names when he did not. Lucy sat in the boat, hair billowing around her shoulders. He kept sneaking glances at her.

"The first northern reach of the Thames ends here. The Chelsea wharfs are on your left. Chelsea town is just in behind the trees. It is becoming fashionable with the gentry to have a country home there."

The boat cruised on. Simon glanced to the rear. "Excuse me for a moment, Lady Dennys," he said. Simon climbed to the back. A bargeman guided his unsteady progress back to Walsingham, who was going through some documents.

"You see the barge about one hundred yards behind with a brown sail," said Simon. "It has been following us since we left Barn Elms. It seems to have an unnecessarily large crew."

"Never mind, Tunstall. Gwilym handles security." Walsingham did not look up.

"Perhaps the genn'lman will take 'is 'at off to the lady." Gwilym grinned at Simon.

Simon gave Lucy a sweeping bow. Facing forward, she did not even notice. "Now what?"

Gwilym grinned again in a most annoying manner. "Some of the lads fancied a day out on the river."

A wherry split off from the Chelsea wharf and started to angle across the river. Simon watched fascinated as it meandered seemingly at random. Walsingham continued to read, apparently unimpressed.

The wherry careered around the river. The sound of raucous, drunken singing emerged from it. The rowboat's unsteady progress looked unguided but Simon noticed that it moved ever closer to their pursuers. Two of the rowers began to argue violently. The helmsmen tried to intervene but he was knocked back with a crash. The wherry went out of control and came together with the barge in a huge crash.

A man on the barge shook his fist at the wherrymen and yelled a phrase that finished with the word *off.*

"Oo are you calling a bastard?" asked a rower. He stood up and swept his oar round in an arc that ended on a man's back. The unfortunate bargeman was swept out of his boat into the water where he splashed around screaming for help. Another rower wielded his oar like a pike. He caught the barge's steersman a clean thrust in the kidneys. General mayhem broke out. The barge crew were clearly getting the worst of it, as more of them ended up in the water. Someone pulled out the mast's locking mechanism and it crashed down on the barge crew in the bow. More screams carried across the water.

"That'll learn 'em," said Gwilym.

Walsingham looked up briefly from his document. "Well done, Gwilym. Remind me to pay the wherry crew a bonus."

Simon made his way back to Lucy.

"This is so exciting, Master Tunstall," Lucy said, eagerly. "Why are those men fighting?"

"Someone's had too much to drink, I expect," said Simon. He did not wish to frighten the girl.

"What's that place on that bend?" she asked.

"London," Simon said simply. "Well, it's the City of Westminster really but London has grown so rapidly that Westminster is part of the suburbia of the city. People flock here from all over England and from other countries. The Queen has passed a new act forbidding any new buildings around London, to try to limit the size of the suburbs outside the city wall. London now has a population of one hundred and fifty thousand people. Imagine that! It's the greatest city in Europe.

"Look to the right now, Lucy. Where the wherries are docked is Lambeth and that fine building with the tower is Lambeth Palace, the London residence of the Archbishop of Canterbury."

The palace had a central narrow building running back from the river. A large square tower rose from half way up the right hand side. Smaller buildings surrounded the central palace on each side. The hall built into the left wall had a low, squat, square tower surmounted by small domes with flagpoles. Brilliant streamers flew from them.

"It looks like a fairy-tale castle," said Lucy, clapping her hands.

The barge pulled alongside Westminster.

"That large building on the left bank is Westminster Abbey where English monarchs are crowned and beyond it is Westminster Hall. That's where the Lords sit and the Law Courts preside. The Commons sit in St. Stephen's Chapel next door."

Their barge turned eastwards along the river to London.

"There, Lucy, do you see the top of that monument, behind the trees on the north bank?"

Lucy shielded her eyes, "Yes."

"That's Charing Cross, one of the monuments to the fallen Queen Eleanor," said Simon.

"Queen Eleanor?" asked Lucy, uncertainly.

"Yes, she was the wife of Edward the First. She died in the north, near Harby. Her entrails were buried at Lincoln and her body was brought south for burial at Westminster Abbey. The King built a cross at every location that the funeral procession stopped. There is one at Cheapside in London and then the final one was put up here, at Charing Cross, just outside the city of Westminster."

"Oh, that's such a wonderful story," said Lucy. "The King must have loved her deeply."

"Perhaps so," said Simon. He did not wish to ruin Lucy's romantic interpretation but kings and aristocrats married for reasons other than love, in his experience. Eleanor was popular so King Edward would wish to be seen to do the right thing. That would be good politics.

"Look at those villas along the north bank," she said.

"The Strand from Westminster to London is lined with rich men's houses." Simon pointed out those he knew. "That's Suffolk Place and there's Durham Place, the Bishop of Durham's town house."

"He can hardly ride back to Durham for his supper every night," said Lucy. "So I suppose he needs a little local place to sleep when he is in London?" Durham was an important city in the far north of England.

"There's Somerset Place, the home of the Duke of Somerset," said Simon, pointing.

The boat headed along the eastern reach of the Thames. "And there is London, that's the city wall by the Fleet River on the other bank. Those houses on the other side are the start of Southwark."

London presented a sea of red tiled roofs, with innumerable towers and steeples reaching like fingers into the sky.

"That must be St. Paul's Cathedral," said Lucy pointing at a huge block building that dominated western London. The main building ran east-west and a square tower surmounted the centre of the cross.

"A thunderbolt destroyed the spire twenty years ago but it is still, by far, the highest building in the city," said Simon

"Did anyone decide what London did to incur God's displeasure?" asked Lucy.

"Not really," said Simon. "There was much talk of God punishing licentiousness and immorality but surely He would have directed lightnings to Southwark if that was His purpose."

"Why? What happens at Southwark?" Lucy had her most innocent expression on.

"Oh you know, drinking, gambling, and, er, so on." William coloured up. Lucy opened her mouth to ask something else. Simon said hurriedly, "Look, Lucy, London Bridge is in front of us. It is said that more than five hundred people live and work in the houses and shops built upon it. One of the buildings fell into the river some years ago and fifty people drowned."

"Oh," said Lucy, with delight. "How horrible."

"There is a dainty story about the bridge from my grandfather's day," said Simon. "One of the houses on the bridge was owned by a Sir William Hewet. He was a prosperous London merchant possessed of a wide estate worth no less than six thousand pounds a year. He had three sons but only one daughter, a fair child called Anne. One day the maid was dangling Anne out of the window to see the boats, when she dropped the girl. The child's fate seemed sealed when a young gentleman, Master Osborne, who was apprenticed to Sir William, dived in after her and swam her to the bank. Sir William was so impressed by this deed that he bestowed a great dowry on the girl, and gave her in marriage to Master Osborne."

"And did he treat her well, so she grew to love him and they lived happily ever after?" asked Lucy, with an odd expression

"My grandfather did not say," said Simon, puzzled.

"She was only his prize so I suppose it is not important," said Lucy. "But he had saved her so I prefer to think that she did grow to love him, and why should he not love her back?"

Simon did not understand Lucy's mood so he started to gabble. "The Constable puts the heads of traitors on spikes at the Southwark end of the bridge."

"How awful," said Lucy, with a delicious shiver.

"The bridge is held up by twenty arches of squared stone sitting on starlings," said Simon, with a straight face.

"Starlings?" Lucy giggled and held her hand to her mouth in a characteristic gesture.

"Small islands of stone and brushwood, wonderfully artificial," said Simon. "Not, um, small birds."

Lucy started giggling and they both laughed out loud.

"They actually have water wheels between the southern arches to grind corn," said Simon struggling to maintain his composure.

"Grinding corn, hmm," said Lucy. "Not starlings, then." She dissolved into helpless giggles.

Walsingham looked up to see what amused them.

"There are so many boats on the river that one could almost walk from bank to bank." Lucy was back in Lady Dennys mode.

The river was cluttered with wherrys, barges, and pinnaces. Some of the latter were big enough to be three- or even four-masted. "The Mayor's office have licenced two thousand wherry boats alone in London," said Simon.

Their bargemen half lowered the sail to slow them down and the steersman put the helm over so that they cruised up to a small pier. "This is Parys Garden, Lucy. We land here," said Simon.

The theatre party walked along the embankment road towards London Bridge. Lucy walked on Walsingham's arm. The Thames lined one side and modest houses the other. Some of the houses advertised rooms while others were taverns.

"You're a fine gentleman. Want to come in for a little fun?" At one house, a girl in her underclothes leaned out of an upstairs window and called to Walsingham. Lucy was wide-eyed. Walsingham gripped Lucy's arm like a shipwrecked man holds a spar. Simon had the distinct impression that Lucy was protecting Walsingham, rather than the other way round.

"Look over the river, Lucy. You get a dainty view of St. Paul's from here." Walsingham desperately tried to draw Lucy's attention away from women advertising their wares from the bawdy houses.

"Master Tunstall pointed it out earlier," said Lucy. She noticed a large hexagonal building flying pennants behind the Southwark houses.

"Is that the theatre, Uncle? How exciting," she said.

Walsingham played guide until they reached an alleyway. Behind it was a field with chickens and pigs. In one corner stood the theatre and Lucy stopped to admire the unusual building with its bright colours and flags. Walsingham leaned over to Simon. "That was somewhat embarrassing, Tunstall. Still I think I got away with it. The child has no idea that those women were Winchester geese, of course."

Southwark came under the jurisdiction of the Bishop of Winchester. The city had been famous for its "stews," or brothels, for hundreds of years. The church had long had an equivocal attitude to sins of the flesh, regarding prostitution as a distasteful necessity and so often the clergy ended up regulating brothels. So the whores of Southwark were known euphemistically as "Winchester geese," after the good bishop.

"Of course not, Sir Francis. How could she?" Simon was shocked at the very idea. Lucy was as pure as any human being could be. He looked at Lucy, who gazed eagerly up at the theatre.

'Lucy, why were those women dressed in underclothes?' thought Lilith.

'Um, oh they were whores,' thought Lucy. 'If you don't know the word look it up in that library you carry around in your head.'

There was a pause. 'Gosh!' thought Lilith. 'Do you know what those women do?'

'I know.' Lucy giggled inside. 'Did you see Uncle's face? Isn't this fun?'

Walsingham escorted Lucy across the field, detouring around the larger piles of animal waste. He walked around the building to the door that led to the boxes.

A steward reading a notice gave a bored "Yes?" as Walsingham's shadow fell across him. Gwilym prodded him and the steward looked up. He immediately smartened his attitude. "Can I help you, lady, gentlemen?" The steward would have no idea who Walsingham was but their clothes, especially Lucy's dress, indicated that they were "quality."

"Sir Christopher Hatton has invited us to his box."

"Yes sir, he is expecting guests. Please follow me."

He led the way up steep wooden stairs to the first floor and knocked on a door. A servant opened it. Sir Christopher was sat on one of the wooden benches but he jumped up as his guests entered. "Francis, welcome, and Lady Dennys, what a unique pleasure."

Lucy kissed him demurely on the lips and he held her hands. "Francis, your niece gets more pretty with every passing year. You sit at the front, Lady Dennys, where you can see. Francis can sit behind with me so we can talk."

Simon sat down beside Lucy. Gwilym leaned against the wall by the door where he could watch anyone entering. A servant came in with glasses of hypocras. This expensive sweet liqueur, imported by Venetians from Smyrna, was a rare treat. The servant passed around plates of sugared pastries and pears.

The theatre was a hexagon open to the sky in the centre. The stage was a raised area against the front wall. Two highly decorated pillars held up a canopy that protected the actors from the elements. The underside of the roof was painted deep blue and decorated with stars.

All sorts of fascinating doors and hatches opened onto the stage. Hatton's private box was on the left side. There was another box above them and two more on the other side of the stage. Covered galleries with benches ran all round, many already full of prosperous traders and yeomen. "Groundlings," who paid a penny a head for the privilege, sprawled around on the wooden floor. A great buzz of excitement filled the air. Beer and snack sellers worked the crowds, shouting their goods.

Simon kept half an ear on the conversation behind him.

"Rumours say that Drake has taken a great treasure off the dons. What say the Secret Service?" Hatton looked enquiringly at Walsingham.

"Rumours for once are right. My sources suggest Drake may have more than half a million pounds in treasure aboard," said Walsingham.

"More than half a million?" Hatton whistled. "We could fund a war with that."

"We may have to," said Walsingham. "Admiral Santa Cruz is preparing a great fleet to invade the Azores. This will be a testing ground to see if Spanish Mediterranean amphibious warfare can be adapted to the Atlantic. I suspect we will be next if the invasion succeeds."

"The appeasers on the Council plan to prosecute Drake for piracy, when he comes back, if he comes back," said Hatton. "They think Philip will be satisfied with just Drake's head."

"Burghley will sit on the fence. He knows we need the sea dogs but he also still hopes for a rapprochement with Madrid," said Walsingham.

"The western merchants will back Drake. Plymouth and Bristol have suffered badly from Spanish practices."

"But the northern woollen men will back the appeasers, as they want to protect their trade to the Low Countries, and the London men will split half and half," said Walsingham.

"There is nothing else for it, Francis. You, Leicester, and I will have to use our vetoes on the Council to block any prosecution moves."

"It will come down to the Queen then," said Walsingham. "And that means it will come down to money. The Queen will support him if Drake brings enough Spanish treasure back, otherwise." Walsingham shrugged.

"She may even knight him if he really has captured half a million pounds." Hatton laughed. "I'm joking, of course, not even Elizabeth would knight a privateer. Not that Drake doesn't deserve it, mind."

"Open war with Spain is inevitable, Christopher, but I want it on our terms, which means at sea. We have not a hope if we let a Spanish army into England. Even if we win, the country will be devastated by war but the most likely result is an endless stalemate, like the campaign in the Low Countries."

Musicians filed out onto the gallery over the stage and began to play a jaunty tune on wind instruments and drums. The audience quietened down to a low murmur. A master of ceremonies came on stage and briefed the spectators on the background to the play, which involved Greek heroes and gods. Simon could tell Lucy was enjoying herself immensely.

The actors created their usual magic with a minimum of special effects and props. 'Lucy,' thought Lilith. 'Why are all the women's parts played by boys?'

'Women on the stage?' Lucy thought. 'Why, that would be scandalous and would bring the noble city of Southwark into disrepute.'

Lilith pondered. So whoring was acceptable but women on a stage was scandalous. It was all so perplexing.

Gwilym went over to Walsingham and whispered in his ear.

"Tunstall," said Walsingham. "Have a good look at the upper left box on the other side of the stage."

Simon did as he was bid. "My God, Sir Francis. It's Bernardino de Mendoza, the Spanish Ambassador."

"I wonder what the head of the Spanish spy network in northern Europe is doing here," pondered Walsingham.

One of the Greek gods descended from heaven by means of a trapdoor and a series of pulleys. Walsingham leaned over to Lucy. "Doctor Dee made stage props fly better than anyone I know. Of course, they tried to burn him at the stake for it."

The play ended with an uplifting moral conclusion and a song. Some people left but many stayed to hear the musicians play.

"We must be going, Christopher. Thank you for your hospitality. I have a wherry waiting east of the bridge to take me to the Tower. Can I give you a lift across the river?"

The pilings of London Bridge acted like a great dam across the Thames. It was possible to "shoot" the bridge and get a boat from one side to another but tide and wind had to be just right so it was safer to change boats each side of the obstacle.

"Thank you but no, Francis. I will tarry here a while as I am expecting a lady to join me."

"Ah," said Walsingham. He led Lucy out on his arm. Their route took them through the centre of the theatre. Here was all a chatter and bustle.

"Can I have something to eat, Uncle?"

"Of course, Lucy. You always seem to be hungry these days."

Walsingham took out his purse and purchased the girl a bag of nuts from one of the vendors. Simon noticed a groundling look intently at Walsingham's purse and nudge his mate. The two men moved towards Walsingham. At that point, Gwilym casually strolled over. Covering the ground quickly for such a large man, he grasped the groundling's arm. The groundling tried to pull away but his arm could not have been anchored more securely had a granite block materialised around it. Gwilym shook his head. "Somewhere else," he said

"What?" asked the groundling, confused.

"Try your luck somewhere else, mate." Gwilym released his arm. The two men scuttled away. Walsingham and Lucy strode on. They circumnavigated a crowd around a beer seller and came face to face with the Spanish Ambassador, who was also escorting a lady. There was no room to pass unless someone gave way.

Lilith watched in fascination as Lucy scanned along the faces in the way humans, or at least Lucy, did. She was detached from the encounter until Lucy reached the lady.

Lilith screamed in Lucy's head. 'It's her, it's her.'

Walsingham inclined his head. "Your Excellency."

"Sir Francis, did you enjoy the play?"

"Immensely, it is so satisfying when the forces for good triumph," said Walsingham.

Two large, hard men moved to flank the Ambassador and his lady. Gwilym likewise moved alongside Walsingham's left. Simon copied Gwilym and moved to flank Lucy on the right. He tried to look suitably tough but he was aware that he cut an indifferent figure as a bodyguard.

"May I introduce Lady Isabella, who is newly arrived on these shores?" said de Mendoza.

"You servant, milady," said Walsingham, taking off his hat in a wide sweep. "This is my niece, the Lady Dennys."

Lucy curtseyed. "Your Excellency."

'It's the witch-woman. Look out, Lucy, it's the witch-woman.'

'Will you behave, Lilith? I can't follow the conversation with you screaming,' thought Lucy.

"I have warned Isabella to be careful. England looks pretty but it can be such a dangerous place, like many developing nations. I understand that even you were attacked the other day." De Mendoza smiled.

Sir Francis smiled back. "Indeed, England can be dangerous, Your Excellency. This very morning my groom had a serious accident. Poor fellow was kicked by a horse and died."

Gwilym spoke softly in Walsingham's ear.

"My mistake. The horse doesn't kick him until this afternoon," said Walsingham.

That explains who was the traitor at Barn Elms, thought Simon. Gwilym had clearly arranged to stopper the leak of information permanently.

"However, I am sure the Lady Isabella is quite safe. It's your health that bothers me, de Mendoza. You can imagine how upset I would be if a horse kicked you." At this point Walsingham's false smile slipped. The bodyguards reacted to the increased tension. One of the Spanish heavies put a hand on his dagger's hilt. He froze as Gwilym's dagger appeared from thin air.

Lilith was hardly an expert on human reactions but she could feel the tension. She was confused, as nothing had happened that seemed to justify the way the men were behaving. She decided to ask for clarification.

'Lucy, what is going on?' thought Lilith.

'There is going to be a fight.'

'Why do they want to fight?' thought Lilith.

'They don't. A fight will be disastrous both for England and Spain.'

Lilith pondered this but Lucy's explanation only added to her confusion. Lucy's gaze flicked over Isabella as the girl's eyes scanned from side to side. Lilith noted something. She reran, magnified, and analysed the short flicker of vision that she had recorded as Lucy's eyes had swept past Isabella. Lilith squandered power and extended her gravitonic senses towards the witch.

'Lucy, Lucy, the witch is doing something with her hand. Look.' Lilith patched onto Lucy's optic nerves and fed in a signal that allowed Lucy to "see" what Lilith could detect gravitonically. 'The witch is making magic.'

Lucy "saw" a black whirlpool forming around Isabella's hand. Each rotation of her wrist built up a bigger swirl.

'I can earth it,' said Lilith.

Simon saw Lucy's head snap down to follow Isabella's left hand which was making slow circular movements. He focussed on the women.

"You'll hurt your wrist doing that, lady," said Lucy and she grabbed Isabella's hand. There was a crack and a pungent smell of sulphur and burning.

"Ouch!" Isabella sucked at her fingers. A livid burn mark snaked across them. Smoke burned lazily from a charred wooden brick in the floor between the women.

"There is more to you than meets the eye, Lady Dennys," said Isabella, examining her hand.

"Much, much, more," said Lucy, cheerfully. She pulled out a nut. Simon noticed that Lucy also had a burn mark on her fingers but it did not seem to bother the girl. A line from an old poem went through his mind. "When the dogs have finished growling, the cats unsheathe their claws."

"Refreshment, Lady Isabella? No? Oh well." Lucy shrugged. She casually squeezed the nut between her thumb and forefinger, until it shattered into tiny pieces.

Isabella's eyes opened very wide.

Walsingham and de Mendoza still faced each other down.

'They are going to kill each other,' thought Lucy to Lilith. 'No one wants it but they will fight because my uncle will not step aside for a Spanish papist and a Spanish grandee steps aside for no man but royalty.'

'That is illogical,' thought Lilith. 'Can't we do something to stop them?'

'Men are illogical. They are just not rational like we women. To lose face before another man is worse than death.' The girl paused. 'That's the key. Watch and learn, Lilith.'

"Uncle, I am rather fatigued and I have hurt my hand." Lucy held up her right hand to show the burns. She curtseyed to de Mendoza. "I am sorry to interrupt your conversation, Your Excellency, but would you mind awfully if Sir Francis escorted me home now?"

De Mendoza seized on the moment to step aside with a gracious bow. "Of course not, Lady Dennys. I could not possibly inconvenience such a charming lady." He raised Lucy's hand to his lips. "You do seem to have hurt yourself, milady," he said, examining her fingers.

The Ambassador turned to one of his men. "Clear those peasants aside to gain the lady passage." The bodyguard created a way for Lucy by the simple expedient of seizing a groundling by the scruff of the neck and using him as a broom to sweep away his friends. If the groundlings objected, they kept it to themselves.

Lucy kissed de Mendoza on the lips and gave him her special smile. "I see the reputation of Spanish gentlemen for gallantry is not exaggerated, sir."

"Neither is the reputation of English ladies for beauty and wisdom, madam."

Simon could have cheerfully strangled the man. Why do women find these Latin lovers so compelling? he thought, unconsciously reiterating the question that has plagued North European men through the ages.

"Another time," de Mendoza said to Walsingham.

"You can count on it, Ambassador."

Lucy took Walsingham's arm and the two swept out.

Gwilym, following, passed a Spanish bodyguard. The men looked at each other with the dispassionate assessment of one professional for another. Their principals had parted civilly, therefore so did they. In other circumstances, they would have attempted to kill each other with the same professional detachment.

Lilith had watched but she was not sure that she had understood much of what had just happened. Lucy had defused the situation with some sort of special magic.

'Why did de Mendoza give way so eagerly? You said he would not step aside for anyone,' Lilith thought.

'You weren't listening, Lilith. I said he would not step aside for any man. But I—' Lucy elevated her nose another five degrees. '—I am a lady.'

Act 9, The Streets of London

Lucy found a sunlit bench in a quiet corner of the bailey in the Tower of London, where she could read in peace. Bushes secluded the bench from prying eyes. She had a talent for finding a small oasis of calm in whirlpools of activity. Life at Barn Elms had honed this skill to perfection.

"Lilith, where are you? Come out where I can see you," said Lucy, out loud.

The air in front of Lucy seemed to shimmer and Lilith appeared in a blue dress.

"There you are, demon," Lucy said. "I wondered where you had got to."

"I am where I always am—inside you," said Lilith.

"I thought, mayhap, you had found a way to withdraw," said Lucy. "I understand that you are casting a spell to show me an illusion but I find it easier to talk to someone that I can see."

Lilith had tried to explain to Lucy just how she placed an image in her head but Lucy lacked the world picture to grasp the explanation. Maybe "casting a spell" was not such a bad explanation. The Shadow World with computers and other electronic devices had regarded magic as a primitive superstition but witchcraft seemed to work in this world. In fact, magic showed interesting similarities to her own gravitonic capabilities. Lucy's people appeared to work magic by influencing the probability of quantum effects with their minds.

"So where have you been, Lilith? Have I offended you?"

"No, I am trying not to interfere with your life. I only make contact with you when you call."

"But you see everything that I do?"

"Yes." Lilith paused. "I also record what you see and hear and touch. Would you like to see the play again? I could arrange that."

"That might be fun, but later. You know, I have never really had a friend before. At Barn Elms I was always the little Lady Dennys. I used to see the servants' children playing in the fields but I could never join them. It wasn't done, you see."

"Ah," said Lilith. Things that are done and not done, the essential core of the human condition raised its head again.

"Uncle Francis is a sugar-pie, of course."

"Of course," agreed Lilith.

"But he's my master, not my friend."

"I have never had a friend either," said Lilith. "Before coming here my whole life was spent training for a role."

"Just like me." Lucy clapped her hands with pleasure. "Lilith, you can always talk to me when you want. Just don't distract me when I am involved with someone or people will think me crazy or stupid."

Lucy paused. "You are my friend, aren't you Lilith?"

Lilith found it difficult to analyse her feelings. No one had ever shown her any affection and now this little human trusted her. After all she had done to the girl, Lucy still trusted her and called her friend. Lilith felt a rush of emotion. This is leakage, a stubborn analytical subroutine insisted, just leakage from the human's emotion centre. Lilith did not care, leakage or not it felt wonderful. Lucy's electrochemical nervous system was ridiculously inadequate compared to Lilith's own gravitonic processing and storage systems but somehow the little biosystem powered a wonderful person.

"Yes," Lilith said, simply, and meant it.

"Can you tell me exactly what Isabella was doing in the theatre?" asked Lucy.

"That's not easy," said Lillith. "She was manipulating gravitonic energies to draw power out of the matrix between the Shadow Worlds. She had aligned the strings that reach into the eleventh spatial dimension to link two universes. Everything lies close alongside everything else in the eleventh dimension."

"I see," said Lucy. "Or rather I don't see. Could you translate that into English for me?"

"She was working up a magic spell," said Lilith.

"What would the spell have done if you hadn't 'earthed' it? And what is earthing anyway?"

"To answer the last point first. You know that lightning strikes downwards to the ground—that is earthing," said Lilith.

"Hence the burns on my hand and the wooden floor."

"Exactly, Lucy. As to what the spell would have done, that is more difficult to say. It would have opened a portal into the Shadow Worlds somewhere and something would have come out."

"Something like a demon, oh demon!" Lucy said, with a giggle.

"Possibly," said Lilith. "Or something else such as energy or even objects."

"Our philosophers know that there is an Other World, Lilith, but I think that it is a new idea that there are many Other Worlds or that you would consider our world to be one. I suppose the natives of each world think themselves in the true world and name the others shadows," said Lucy, shrewdly.

This thought rocked Lilith. Her people thought that they were real and that all others were shadows. Perhaps they were deluded by arrogance.

"It occurs to me that your education is still sadly missing an important aspect of London life, demon," said Lucy.

"Really?" asked Lilith.

"Really," said Lucy. "We have not yet been shopping. To go shopping we shall need money and an escort." She rose. "Now, I wonder where Uncle Francis is?"

William was damnably tired but he remained on the deck to show himself to the men. In truth, there was little for him to actually do, as his officers were quite capable of dealing with all practical matters. But captains, like princes, had to be seen by their subjects. The wounded men were carried below to the tender mercies of the cook, who also doubled as the ship's surgeon. Half would be dead by nightfall. Half of those who survived treatment would die of a fever in the next few days. Nevertheless, the butcher's bill was less than he had expected. He could have lost the whole ship.

The ship's decks looked chaotic, but apparently random movement could be broken down into purposeful activity to William's experienced eyes. The carpenter and his mates examined the hull, boarding up damage. The boatswain and his mates checked the masts, yards, rigging, and sails. The gunner supervised the securing of the heavy weapons.

The master walked up to William and touched his hat. "Begging your pardon, sir, but you look a proper mess."

William's clothes were stiff with dried blood. "I think I will go to my cabin and clean up. Send along my steward. You have the ship, Master Smethwick."

The master saluted again and William made his way aft. William noted with annoyance that the guard on his cabin door was absent despite his clear order. He tried to open the door but it stuck. William pushed hard and it yielded a few inches. Something was jammed against it from the inside. William put his shoulder to the wood and forced it open.

The interior was wrecked and scorched as if by the discharge of a weapon. The missing guard's body lay behind the door. His shirt had been blown off and he was badly burnt. William knelt down to examine the body.

"Sweet Jesu, sir." The steward put his head around the door.

"Get the boatswain. Now, man, hurry."

William had finished with the dead sailor and was examining the cabin when the boatswain arrived.

"The dons had a final revenge on you then, sir." The boatswain gazed dispassionately down at the body. "I suppose that's Andrews under all that charring. He weren't a half-bad topman, when he were sober. An explosive shell must have caused this. We were lucky the whole ship did not go up."

"There is no entry hole. Tell me, boatswain, how did the dons fire an explosive shell through the hull without leaving a hole somewhere? Then there is Andrews' corpse. He was dead before the explosion."

"How can you tell, sir?"

"Either he died before the cabin was wrecked or someone went to all the trouble to stab after he was dead," said William. He prodded the corpse with his foot to indicate the wound.

The boatswain whistled. "Someone stuck him good. You said that sneak thief was a heavy-handed fellow."

"So he was," confirmed William.

"Anything missing?"

"I haven't counted every pearl but the only item that is definitely missing is the gold mirror."

"The lady's mirror."

"Yes. This isn't just theft now, boatswain, it's murder. Take armed men with you and find the lady and Packenham." William's voice was hard.

William put his cabin back together as best he could. He would have some more furniture made when the carpenter was less busy. He searched his memory for an explosion. Mayhap, there had been a concussion aft during that last run past the galleys but the battle had been so intense that it was impossible to be sure.

The boatswain entered and touched his cap. "Begging your pardon, sir, but the lady and Master Packenham are not aboard."

"Not aboard? What do you mean? Is a boat missing?"

"No, sir, both boats are on deck."

"You have searched the hold, and the pinnace?"

"Yes, sir, we have searched everywhere, thoroughly. They are not aboard." The boatswain looked upset, as if he felt personally responsible.

"They were there at the start of the battle. I told them to go below," said William.

"Did you see where they went, sir?"

"No, I was rather busy at the time."

"One other thing, boatswain. I had to push the body aside to get in the cabin. How did the corpse end up blocking the door do you suppose?"

"The killer probably dumped the body there," the boatswain looked puzzled. He clearly couldn't see the point.

"And the killer escaped from the cabin leaving the body blocking the door how?" asked William, in exasperation.

"Mayhap the explosion threw it there," said the boatswain.

"Yes, the explosion with no entry hole," said William.

The boatswain shrugged and looked uneasy. Most people knew that magic existed and most used the powers of a wisewoman when necessary, but the Church frowned at having too much truck with the supernatural. The Church was inclined to express its displeasure of black magic by burning practioners at the stake.

The rain fell gently from the skies and dripped down the White Tower, the central keep of the great Tower of London. The sun was already lighting up the wet ground in a blaze of pastel yellow. Pretty soon it would stop raining for a while, then the next shower would caress London. Simon watched the English summer scene through an unshuttered window. The fresh smell of wet grass blew gently in on the summer breeze. Walsingham had an apartment in the buildings just inside the north curtain wall of the fortress. Here, he had an uninterrupted view of the execution block and the small chapel behind it.

Walsingham threw down a letter angrily. "My agent in the English Seminary in Rome tells me that another ten English Jesuits are ready to infiltrate into England. Most of them are Oxford educated. We should have closed that wretched university down years ago, Tunstall." Walsingham, of course, was a Cambridge man.

"There is some mischief in the wind. Why now? Why are they expending their assets so liberally?"

"Surely we have their names?" asked Simon.

"Oh yes, but that won't help us ferret them out from wherever they are hiding. Most of them will come here to London. It is far easier to escape notice in a crowd." Walsingham flung open the door. "Pooley."

"Yes, Sir Francis." A man entered the room and hurriedly removed his cap.

"You have Ridolphi kicking his heels in the Tower?"

"Yes, sir, just as you ordered. He didn't want to come but me and the boys persuaded him, like." Pooley's eyes seemed incapable of meeting Walsingham's gaze. They slid sideways, flickering around the room. Pooley managed to look furtive even when in his master's office. Simon always had the urge to lock up the silver every time the man came.

Pooley was a nondescript sort of fellow. A few minutes after he left one would be hard-pressed to describe his clothes or appearance. That was one reason why he was such a successful spy; another reason was his utter lack of scruples or conscience. Pooley's eyes flickered to where Gwilym leaned nonchalantly against the wall by the door.

"Very well," Walsingham said. "Ridolphi should have had long enough for his imagination to curdle his courage. Come, gentlemen. Let's throw a scare into our Italian rabbit. And what does a frightened coney do, Gwilym?"

The bodyguard grinned. "'Ee bolts for 'is rabbit 'ole, your 'onour, to cuddle up to all 'is furry friends."

The group walked across the bailey to the White Tower. Pooley had Ridolphi held in one of the lower windowless rooms that was lit only by flickering torches. These did nothing to banish the damp chill in the air. Condensation ran down stone walls that were unrelieved by tapestries. Ridolphi was sat on a bare wooden chair facing the two guards at the door. He had arranged the chair so he had his back to the rack on the floor behind him. The Italian jumped to his feet as Walsingham entered.

"This is outrageous. How dare you arrest me in this manner? I have diplomatic status. I am an emissary of His Holiness Pope Gregory XIII. You have no right."

"I have every right." Walsingham's voice cut across Ridolphi's like a whip.

"You are the Pope's banker in England." Walsingham held out his hand to Simon who passed him a letter. "This was found in your possession. A letter signed by the hand of Pope Gregory, himself."

"You have no right to search my belongings, no right," Ridolphi said, but a whine entered his voice.

Walsingham ignored him and began to read. "'. . . since that guilty woman who is the cause of so much injury to the Catholic faith . . .'" Walsingham flicked down the next few lines. "'There is no doubt that whosoever sends her out of the world not only does not sin but gains merit.'"

The spymaster continued to read. "'And so, if those English gentlemen decide actually to undertake so glorious a work, your lordship can assure them that they do not commit any sin.'"

The spymaster looked up. "What 'glorious work,' Master Ridolphi, and what are the names of these 'English gentlemen'?"

Ridolphi said nothing. Gwilym walked behind him to examine the rack. It was a different model to the one at Nonsuch, being at floor level. The victim's feet were held in a clamp; at the other end was a small drum to which the wrists attached. The drum had a series of slots drilled into it where a long lever could be inserted to put enormous torque on the drum.

Gwilym picked up the lever and inserted it in a drum slot. He waggled the wood and the drum moved with a loud creak. "That's the trouble with these wooden joists, 'ighness. They warp in wet conditions. Still, a bit of goose fat on the bearing and I will soon 'ave this device in tiptop working condition." He gave the smile of a man happy in his work.

The banker turned white. Walsingham examined Ridolphi the way a natural philosopher considers a beetle of unusual features that has crawled across his desk. Simon saw sweat forming on the banker's lip. He was a moneyman, a coin counter who had never expected to be in a place like this or expected to face a rude-handed man like Gwilym.

"Please, sir," Ridolphi said to Walsingham. "The letter is only a copy of one addressed from the Pope to his ambassador in Madrid. I do not know what it signifies."

"I wonder what the Queen would make of it, Tunstall?" asked Walsingham. "Do you recall the Jesuit who nailed a proclamation to the door of St. Paul's Cathedral. The one denouncing Her Majesty as a bastard and no true prince?"

"Yes, Sir Francis," said Simon, playing his part. "The Queen is jealous of her bright honour. When we caught him, she had him hung, drawn, and quartered."

This was the English reward for traitors. The victim was hung by the neck, until almost unconscious, cut down, a slit inserted in his abdomen and his entrails pulled out and burnt in front of him. Sometimes his genitals were likewise treated. Finally, when he died, he was hacked into four pieces to impede the resurrection of the body on the final day of judgement. It was a terrible punishment.

"Please, Sir Francis, I have done nothing," said Ridolphi.

Walsingham stared at him, unblinkingly.

"Very well, Master Ridolphi. You may go," said Walsingham.

"What?" asked the banker, confused by Walsinhham's abrupt change of tack.

"You may go," repeated Walsingham. "At least for the moment. Guard, show him out."

A guard escorted Ridolphi from the Tower.

"Pooley, have your watchers ready," said Walsingham, as they walked out into the wet sunshine. "I want to know every place our bold fellow goes and every pagan rascal he meets."

"I have three teams of six on him to give night-and-day coverage, Sir Francis. I have street children, whores, peddlers, and beggars to see his every encounter. He shall not piss in the street but that I know what drain it ran in."

"See you do, Pooley." Walsingham dismissed the man, but Pooley hovered. "Now get you gone, why wait you here, man?"

"There is another matter, sir." Pooley looked uncomfortable.

Walsingham's expression hardened. "There will be no more money, Pooley. Be sure of that."

"No, sir, it's not about the reward. Your honour is more than generous."

Walsingham's eyebrow lifted and Simon could well understand why. A disinterest in money was most unlike Pooley.

"Well then?"

"The watchers are worried, sir. Another whore has been found dead in Symmon's Alley, off Cheapside."

"Whores get killed, Pooley, it's an occupational hazard," said Walsingham.

"Yes, sir, but they don't die with their entrails pulled out and eaten or all the blood drained from their bodies. The watchers will only go out in twos. Sorry, your honour. The ordinary people are fair shook up by it. Some people claim to have seen things. There is talk of a demon stalking London at night."

"There is always talk, Pooley. The people are superstitious. They generally would have you believe some apparition is abroad."

"Yes, sir." Pooley did not look convinced, but he knew better than to push the matter and left.

Lucy was positioned ready to sidle up to Walsingham, the moment he was free. "Uncle, I was wondering if I could borrow Master Tunstall? I would like to go into London and need an escort."

"What on earth do you need in London, Lucy?"

"To see the sights, Uncle, and to order a new dress in the latest fashion. My dresses are out of date. The other ladies at Nonsuch made sport of me. If I am to get a husband . . ."

"Not that again, Lucy. Spare me the husband argument. Tunstall, draw a suitable sum from my private chest for expenses."

"Thank you, Uncle." Lucy clapped her hands in glee. "I need to get some things before we go." She rushed back to her uncle's apartments.

"All this talk of monsters is rubbish, of course, but there may be some madman killing girls in London." Walsingham came to a decision. "Gwilym, I want you to go with Master Tunstall and Lady Dennys, just to help carry things and so forth. You will attend Lady Dennys until I say differently."

"*Still through the cloven skies they come,*
"*With peaceful wings unfurled,*

"And still their heavenly music floats,
"O'er all the weary world.
"Above its sad and lowly plains,
"They bend on hovering wing,
"And ever o'er its Babel sounds,
"The blessed angels sing."

The assembled crew parading on the deck sang badly to the accompaniment of drummers and flute men. The musicians did their best but they were more used to belting out sea shanties than solemn hymn music. William stepped forward.

"We therefore commit their bodies to the deep, to be turned into corruption, looking for the resurrection of the body, when the sea shall give up her dead, and the life of the world to come."

He stepped back and signalled to the honour guard who fired a volley into the air. Sailors lifted the weighted bags containing the bodies of their messmates and hurled them over the side. The canvas bags bobbed for a moment alongside the ship, until they waterlogged and sank. In the clear water, some could be seen for some little time before they disappeared.

It was customary for the captain to say the last words. William hated making these speeches but it would be disrespectful not to follow tradition. He walked slowly to stand before the men.

"We stand here again to consign our shipmates to the care of the Almighty, into whose arms we all must go. They have gone before us. English merchants sail peacefully to the four corners of the world to trade. But the sea dogs growl where our merchants are bullied and impeded. And when we are hurt, we bite. These men have already bitten."

William took off his hat and waved it, "God save Her Majesty the Queen and confusion to her enemies."

The men roared their reply then the parade disintegrated into groups. Some went aft to say a last prayer for their friends but most went cheerfully about their business. Life was cheap in Elizabethan England and this was never truer than on a warship. The survivors looked to the future and forgot the past. William had waited until he was certain the deaths had ceased before having the funeral. He hated giving the last rites to his shipmates and did not want to repeat the experience more than once. He would have joined the Church if he had wanted to be a priest.

William shivered as the air turned cold. The *Swallow* was making a fast run north, helped by the prevailing southwest winds. The log showed that she had made nine knots yesterday, an unprecedented speed for a warship. Truly the *Swallow* was well named. She veritably flitted across the water. At this rate, they would sight the Lizard, the tip of Britain, in a few days.

Lucy took Simon's arm and the couple crossed the outer curtain wall and moat surrounding the tower at the western river gate. The gate led into a fortified enclosure beside the west wall. The only gate out lay all the way up at the northern end. Any attacker trying to break into the Tower would find himself breaking through a series of fortifications, each of which led only to another killing ground.

The Tower was incorporated into London's eastern defensive wall so the party entered London through a small postern gate, as soon as they left the cleared fire zone around the curtain walls. The constable of the Tower strictly enforced the cleared zone, putting illegal buildings to the torch if necessary.

This was Lucy's first visit into the City of London. Up to now she had just travelled around it by boat. London hit the visitor with a tidal wave of sound and smells. The sound was that of tens of thousands of people in the immediate vicinity gossiping, debating, arguing, selling, shouting, and making love. The smell was an accumulated fug of human and animal bodies, food, industry, and waste. The houses clustered so closely together that they almost seemed to rise like a defensive wall but, on closer inspection, small alleys wound between the ground floors. The upper floors overhung, so that buildings on opposite sides of the alleys almost touched each other. Church steeples poked from the red-tiled agglutination, reaching for God. And in the background, the dense blocky mass of St. Paul's glowered over the whole, reminding the populace of the power of the Church and the terrible judgement to come in the next world.

Simon led Lucy to where a road pierced the dense mass. Here the houses were far enough apart for sunlight to penetrate through various items of cloth and animal hides strung across the street to dry and cure in the sun.

"What think you, milady?" asked Simon.

"I did not think that there could be so many people in the world, Master Tunstall."

Simon looked back to check Gwilym. The bodyguard had dropped back four or five paces so he could keep an eye on his charge and have an awareness of his surroundings. Gwilym strolled along like a country rube at the local market but his eyes constantly swept the street, and Simon knew that he missed nothing.

"What is this place?" asked Lucy.

"This is Tower Street, Lady Dennys."

"What else would it be called?" asked Lucy, happily.

Tower Street ended where a leather shop ran right across the road. Alleys led off on each side. The leather seller's family lived on the top floor. A large shutter opened on the ground floor to display the goods. Lucy stopped and leafed through them. The leathermaker came out. "I have some fine belts for gentlemen or ladies," he said, pulling out a hanger of wares.

"Indeed, indeed," said Lucy. She selected one. "Look, Master Tunstall, this would be perfect as a present for Uncle. Would you buy it for me, please?"

Simon watched the leathermaker assess Lucy's material wealth and enthusiasm for the item. He sighed and started a long bargaining process to get the cost down to merely overpriced, as opposed to extortionate. Once the deal was closed at six silver shillings, Simon led Lucy around the shop into Little East Cheap, or East Market, Street. The East Cheap market was the poor relation of West Cheap, the later better known as just Cheapside.

"Where would you like to go to choose a new dress, Lady Dennys?" asked Simon.

"Wherever you suggest, Master Tunstall. I shall follow your guidance."

"Then we shall go up to the new Royal Exchange. There are a hundred permanent shops in the arcade and a number are dressmakers. If you cannot obtain satisfaction there, then I suggest we move on to Cheapside. Mayhap you would also like to visit the booksellers in Paternoster Row by St. Paul's."

"That sounds excellent," said Lucy. Her eyes shone and she gripped Simon's arm somewhat tighter than would normally be considered appropriate.

Eastcheap Street consisted primarily of private houses, with the odd shop intermittently scattered along its length. The houses were mostly three stories high. Each storey projected further out than the one below and window boxes projected further still, so there was very little gap between the houses, even across such a wide thoroughfare. Washing hung out to air on clotheslines strung across the top stories of the houses. The houses were made primarily of a wooden skeleton with plaster in between the beams. Here and there, a prosperous merchant had rebuilt in brick. The street was a main road so it was clogged with people. Simon kept his spare hand on his purse. London boasted the finest pickpockets in the world.

Simon decided to turn up Rood Lane to get to Fen Church Street. This led into Lombard Street, which went up to Stocks Market where five roads met. The Royal Exchange was between Corn Hill and Three Needle Street.

Little East Cheap ran all the way to Fish Street, which then went north up to Lombard Street. However, if they went further west before turning north they would get caught up in the cart traffic flowing across London Bridge. Carts could be dangerous to pedestrians as it was all too easy to get crushed between a cart and a wall. The lanes in London could have dangerous inhabitants but Simon had great confidence in Gwilym's ability to deal with dangerous people. Carts were another matter.

Fewer people moved along Rood Lane and those that did hurried with their heads down. Gwilym moved in closer behind Simon and Lucy. They passed a water bearer taking two gallons from a fountain to a private house. Dark little alleyways led off the lane to either side. Some were so choked with waste as to be impassable. A shrill cry erupted from an alley as they moved past. Simon moved to hurry Lucy away.

"Look at that," Lucy said, outraged. Slipping off Simon's arm, she darted into the alley. "Stop that, you beast!" A small girl in rags knelt cowering in the mud. She looked ten or eleven but may have been older as she was clearly half starved. A bully boy stood over her with a horsewhip.

The whip came down and Lucy hurtled forwards to intercept it. She effortlessly caught the whip in one hand and wrenched it from the man's hand. With the other, she pushed the man back against a wall. He grunted as the breath was knocked from him. Then she dropped down to check the child.

Gwilym and Simon were hot on her heels.

"She's mine. What right have you got to stick your noses into my business?" asked the bully, drunkenly.

"Who is this man?" Lucy asked the girl.

"He's my uncle," the girl sobbed.

"Where are your parents, girl?" asked Simon.

"Please, sir, they are dead of plague," said the girl.

"Just like mine," said Lucy softly. "I could be in your rags, were I not of different rank. Why was this man whipping you?"

"He says I have to warm his bed and do things," said the girl.

"Does he now?" said Lucy, looking at the bully with contempt.

"Shut your mouth, slut," said the bully, apparently to the little girl since he surely could not be stupid enough to talk to Lucy in that manner. "She's mine so I can belt her if I want." He was clearly convinced, actually with some justification, that the law was on his side. Then the bully demonstrated that he really was as stupid as he looked. "Stay out of my affairs, trollop," he said to Lucy, and raised his fist to strike her.

Gwilym was on him like a tiger, grabbing the bully's arm and throwing him back against a wall.

"You need to learn some manners when talking to your betters, knave," said Gwilym, who was not overly concerned with legal niceties but who knew someone who needed a good kicking when he met them. Insulting Walsingham's niece was the same as insulting Walsingham's honour, and Gwilym's own personal honour was bound up in his master's. Besides, he liked Lucy.

The bully came off the wall and aimed a blow at the bodyguard. Gwilym deflected it with his left hand. He punched a short vicious hook into the bully's kidney with his right. The bully's whole body jerked under the impact.

"You're lucky, filth. 'Ad you hit 'er 'ighness then I would 'ave 'ad to really hurt you."

Gwilym hit him again, another short jab into the same kidney. The bully gasped and moaned, the fight driven out of him.

"Before handing you over to the 'angman," said Gwilym. He held the bully up by the throat.

"You will never," Gwilym slapped him hard across the face, "raise your 'and to a lady" he backhanded the bully's face from the opposite direction, "ever again. Especially, this lady." The final slap knocked the bully to his knees.

"And to make sure you remember." Gwilym pulled the man's arm up and kicked him in the elbow. There was an audible crack. The bully screamed and fainted.

"Master Tunstall, we can't leave her here in the hands of that animal," said Lucy. "There are whip marks all over her back."

"Yon bully can't look after 'er in any case," said Gwilym, with a friendly countryman's smile. "Fellow seems to have broken 'is arm."

Simon thought it might have been kinder to kill the man outright. The bully would likely be crippled for life, if he survived the next month. But Simon had seen too much misery inflicted on the innocent to waste sympathy on an animal who beat little girls for his sexual gratification.

"Are there not charitable orphanages in London?" asked Lucy.

"I do know of a reputable one," said Simon. "But they may need money to accept another charge."

"Is that all?" asked Lucy. "Lead on, Master Tunstall."

The little girl held Gwilym's hand and the two couples made their way up to Lombard Street. The wide street parted to go round Fen Church, which occupied the centre of what had once been a market. Simon took them to a building around the back of the church and introduced the little girl to a curate.

"I regret that the Fen orphanage is full, milady," said the curate.

"I will endow two new positions at the orphanage on condition that this girl gets one of the places," said Lucy.

"But highness, that would require eighteen sovereigns," said the clergyman.

"Indeed," said Lucy. "Have the papers drawn up, Master Tunstall, and give him twenty."

"Your highness is generous," said the curate.

Simon opened his mouth to argue but closed it again when Lucy dropped on one knee to explain to the little girl that she was to have a new home.

"I doubt the girl has been baptised. I want you to carry out the ceremony now and I intend to stand as godmother. You two shall be godfathers," said Lucy to her companions.

"Yes, milady," came a chorus of male voices. When Lucy was in this mood, there was no holding her.

Simon understood completely. The vicar of Fen Church was a righteous man but things change and it never hurt to have connections. The orphanage would take special care of the child's welfare with Lady Dennys as her godmother. This precious charge was a two-edged sword. On one hand the orphanage would enjoy the benefits of patronage at a level they dared not have dreamed. On the other, one never knew when Lady Dennys would be back to check on her goddaughter's welfare. And heaven help them if she gave a poor report to Sir Francis Walsingham.

The girl was a little concerned about being dipped, as it was well known that exposure of the skin to water caused fevers. Eventually, Lucy persuaded the girl to submit to the ordeal of baptism and the Church of England acquired a new addition to its congregation.

"When the orphans are at their devotions, curate, would you ask them so say a small prayer for Lucy Dennys and Lilith?"

"I doubt you have much on your conscience, milady," said the curate.

"We all have something to weigh against our souls," said Lucy.

"Very well, Lucy Dennys and Lilith . . ." The curate trailed off.

"Just Lilith," said Lucy.

"It shall be as you say," said the curate.

'The orphans will say prayers for me, Lucy?' thought Lilith.

'That's right, Lilith,' thought the girl.

'What will the prayers do? Will they change something?' thought Lilith.

'Not exactly, Lilith, the orphans will say prayers to preserve your soul.'

Lilith considered. 'Lucy, I don't think I have a soul.'

'Of course you have a soul. I know you as well as I know my uncle. He has a soul and so do you,' Lucy said, confidently.

'Oh!' thought Lilith. This was a new idea.

And who is Lilith? wondered Simon. The trio walked away leaving the girl to her new life.

"Um, Lady Dennys," said Simon. "How are we to buy you a new dress?"

"The dress is cancelled," said Lucy, happily. "Doubtless the London fashion season will survive without me."

"But won't Sir Francis notice that you are still in last year's fashion?" asked Simon.

Lucy threw her head back and laughed out loud. "Master Tunstall, close your eyes."

He did as he was bid.

"Now, Master, you have been with me all day. Describe my dress."

Simon thought of Lucy. In his imagination, he could picture her shining auburn hair, her dark brown eyes, her smile, and the curve of her breast. No, suppress that last thought, but her dress. It was green, maybe, or possibly blue. Simon opened his eyes; the dress was brown. He smiled. "Your point is made, Lady Dennys."

Outside two carts had come nose to nose between Fen Church and the terrace of houses opposite. There was no room to pass so the cart drivers yelled insults and threatened each other.

Lucy pointed to the confrontation, "Observe, Master Tunstall."

Simon could not quite see what she meant. "London is too crowded," he said. "London Bridge is impassable at times. The Mayor has passed a rule requiring all carts to be driven on the left when crossing the bridge into town. There is talk of extending the rule to the whole city."

The carters had progressed to hitting each other with their whips. Their animals took fright and tried to escape. The carts jerked forward and became linked. A wheel cracked and collapsed, creating an immovable obstacle.

"If just one of the carters had given way to the other then the situation would have been resolved in minutes and both would have been on their way," she said. "I have oft thought that, from the highest in the land to those of the lowest station in life, all men are brothers under the skin."

In Lucy's head, Lilith laughed and laughed.

Act 10, The Bloody Tower

The *Swallow* slid slowly into Plymouth Sound under reefed sails. The water was alive with fishing boats and small traders, and William wished to avoid a collision. Drowning some local men would be an inauspicious homecoming. There was another reason for caution. A fishing boat came right in under the lee of the ship.

"You there!" William called to the fishermen. "How fares the Queen?"

"Her Majesty is fine," said the man in a strong Devon accent. "Leastways, she was this morning."

William was very, very pleased to hear it. The Hawkins family had a letter of reprisal against Spanish shipping signed by Elizabeth. Technically, England and Spain were at peace even though it was well known that there was no peace "beyond the line." William's legal document made him a privateer rather than a pirate. The Spanish would not have recognised any such distinction and would hang him anyway, if they caught him, but it did give him legal immunity here at home. Of course, even that protection hinged on Elizabeth being recognised as the lawful Queen. William could easily find himself hanged as a pirate if a papist replaced her in a coup. So the network of Protestant families who ruled the port of Plymouth had reason to be amongst Elizabeth's most loyal supporters.

William anchored offshore outside Plymouth's inner harbour and kept the men aboard. There was no point in testing the men's honesty to destruction by mooring a ship containing treasure right against the dockside. He went ashore in a boat to report to John Hawkins. He found his cousin in a tavern right by the dock.

"Sit down, gentle cousin, before you fall down. You still sway as if you were at sea," said Hawkins.

"It was a long voyage, John," said William.

"Lucrative, I hope." Hawkins raised an eyebrow.

"Not bad. I have a cargo of hides for you."

"Hides?" Hawkins took a pull on his mug. "And?"

"And Venezuelan pearls and gold bars."

Hawkins laughed and clapped William on the back. "That's more like it, my boy." Hawkins raised his voice, "Innkeeper, some of your best malmsey wine."

"How many men did you lose?" Hawkins asked.

"About one in five."

"Those damn tropical fevers?"

"Not this time," replied William. "We ran into some trouble in the Azores. Three Spanish frigates caught us anchored at Ponta Delgada."

"How did you escape? Three galleys, even light ones, could have shot you to pieces."

"I used Drake's trick. I swivelled the ship using boats and cannonaded them with the culverins. We sank two."

Hawkins whistled. "Daintily done. You were still lucky."

"Aye," said William. "We lost young Packenham."

"Killed or taken?" asked Hawkins.

"I don't know," William replied. "He just disappeared during the battle, vanished with a Spanish hostage, too. I can't be sure, but I think he ran off with her."

"Her?" asked Hawkins. "She must have had rare charms."

At this point a barmaid appeared with two mugs of wine and plonked them down before the men. She was a plump girl and she had arranged her blouse to best advantage as she bent over the table. The barmaid favoured William with a bold look. Plymouth people were wise about ships and the sea. The *Swallow* returns after a long voyage and John Hawkins orders the finest wine for her captain on hearing his news. To the shrewd Plymothian that meant Spanish treasure.

"Where do you want to unload the ship, cousin?" asked William.

"Ah. There's a thing. I didn't mention it before you left but one of the backers for your trip was Sir Francis Walsingham," said Hawkins.

"Walsingham, the Queen's bloodhound?"

"The same. He wants the ship unloaded in London. So you are to take her up to Town."

"The men won't like it. They were looking forward to sampling the delights of the Barbican," William said. The Barbican was the area of Plymouth that specialised in relieving sailors of their "shares" in exchange for various pleasures of the flesh. No respectable woman went there although many respectable women had started their careers there.

"William, when Walsingham says run, you ask how far." Hawkins finished his wine. He toyed with his mug for a moment, clearly embarrassed. "There is another matter. Walsingham has hired the *Swallow* and her crew."

"What!" William exclaimed. "Think you I am some mule driver to be hired out to all and sundry?"

"I know, lad, I know, but we can refuse him nothing. Walsingham is all that stands between the Queen and Heaven and if she falls, then we in Plymouth will surely follow." Hawkins stood. "Stay and finish your malmsey. I have an appointment with the Mayor but you stay and enjoy yourself for a while. Put your choice on my bill, a few minutes won't matter so much to Sir Francis."

Hawkins walked out quickly with the air of a man separating himself from a disagreeable business. William finished his wine. He might as well go back to the ship and tell the men. They were not going to like this. He glanced up and caught the barmaid's eye. The girl pulled the front of her blouse down another strategic inch.

On the other hand, thought William, John Hawkins is notoriously stingy so it would be a shame not to abuse his hospitality when it was so unusually offered. The men would not be any more outraged at hearing the news in two hours time than hearing it presently. He caught the eye of the barmaid again who was leaning over the bar smiling at him. The girl was not beautiful but she was not without her charms either, and it had been a long voyage. William got up and walked purposefully towards the bar.

"Lucy, could you take me somewhere high? The top of the Tower would be perfect," said Lilith.

Lucy sat in a small wood-panelled room. A polished table was pushed up against one wall to clear some space for a few chairs and a writing desk. She was alone so she could speak to Lilith rather than thinking her words. The girl still found that easier. Lilith appeared to sit cross-legged on the floor in front of her wearing some single-piece garment that appeared to have no buttons or stitching. It was bright yellow, a colour that did not suit Lilith at all, in Lucy's opinion. She kept the thought well suppressed so as not to hurt Lilith's feelings.

"The Tower is guarded, Lilith," said Lucy. "We can't just walk up there as if we were at Barn Elms. Why do you want to climb the Tower?"

"I have a plan to spy on Isabella. I want to see if she is working magic. The Spanish witch frightens me," said Lilith, frankly. "No doubt she has a purpose in London and I doubt it is to either my advantage or that of my adopted humans."

"I see," said Lucy, wondering how much to read into the phrase *adopted humans*.

"I also need fine translucent crystals, thousands of them. Diamonds would be best. They are hard and focus gravitonic radiation exceptionally well."

"Lilith, where on earth do you expect me to get a thousand diamonds? There cannot be that many in England. The cost would be a Queen's ransom."

"I never understand why you humans set such wildly different values to items. Diamonds cost nothing to make. They are just picked up in rivers and on beaches."

"You understand so little of the world, demon. Diamonds are beautiful, rare and they last forever. Why should we not set such store by them?"

"Huh, nothing truly lasts for ever," said Lilith. "Also, if they are so valuable and sought after, why are diamonds worn by women, rather than men? Men control all the wealth of the country, so why is it that women wear most of the diamonds? And while I'm on the subject, why is the most powerful human a woman? If all Elders are men, then why do they obey a woman? Why does she sit at the head of their Council?"

Lucy laughed loudly before turning into a cough. She was sure she was alone in Walsingham's apartments but it would never do to have people hear Lady Dennys laughing at an empty room. Just the other side of Bishopsgate, before one reached the northern theatre district on the Shoreditch Road, there was a special hospital attached to Bethlehem Church just for people who laughed at nothing. Londoners called it Bedlam. Lucy had no wish to be incarcerated there amongst the loonies so she kept her voice soft.

"The Queen sits on the throne because there was no one else, Lilith. God would not grant King Harry a son and heir for many years. Uncle says that it was God's way of freeing England from the clutches of the Pope since the King had to split from Rome to get a divorce."

"But?" asked a puzzled Lilith.

Lucy hurried on before Lilith could lose them in more questions. "The King needed a new wife to give him a son. The Pope denied him a divorce so the King placed himself at the head of the English Church and so could grant himself a divorce. Thus England became a Protestant country. The King finally got his son but the lad was sickly and died so that only left the old King's daughters."

"The King had no other male relatives," said Lilith.

"Oh, many," said Lucy. "And I am sure that many men would have preferred an incompetent king to a great queen but they could not agree amongst themselves which of them should rule, so the Queen was secure. Better a queen than a rival as king! The only threat now to her is the Catholic underground, who conspire with foreigners."

"I see," said Lilith. "But if ladies have such low social position why do they wear the diamonds?"

"Don't you understand, Lilith?" said Lucy, softly. "We are possessions, beautiful possessions to be displayed with the prettiest decorations."

"You are a slave?" asked Lilith, horrified.

Lucy laughed again, albeit ruefully. "Not a slave, no. Slaves are bought, sold, and discarded when useless." Lucy's head came up. "We are the most desirable, valuable property in the world. We have the babies and school the next generation. Men have fought bloody wars over us; look up Helen of Troy in that invisible library you have with you. Men respect us, compete for us, strive to impress us, and rush to please us. But to them, we are still property."

"I see," said Lilith, who did not see at all. She refocused on the subject. "A substitute would do if you cannot get me diamonds."

"A substitute," said Lucy, throwing her hands up. "What's a substitute for a diamond?"

"There must be other translucent crystals available," said Lilith.

Lucy thought for a moment then grinned. "Problem solved, demon, you want translucent crystals, translucent crystals shall you have, handfuls of them."

"And I need a map," said Lilith.

"Of in particular?"

"London."

Lucy sighed. "Anything else? No? Then I had better be about your business."

Lucy paid a visit to the kitchens and begged a bag from the cook with a cock-and-bull story. The man clearly did not believe a word of it, but the substance Lucy requested was cheap and harmless so he handed it over with good grace. Lucy then went to the White Tower. The guards allowed her access to the lower sections without comment. She made her way to an obscure door and knocked loudly. An elderly man answered.

"Ah, can I help you, young lady?"

"I wonder if you have any maps of London in the library?" asked Lucy.

The keeper of the library looked pleased. "Come in, come in. Sit over there by the window. We don't get many maids using the library so you are all the more welcome." He busied himself searching through chests and cupboards. "Where did I put it? Ah yes, here it is." He produced a rolled-up parchment held by a bow of blue ribbon. "Now what do you think of this!"

He pulled the ribbon and it immediately knotted. Lucy sat politely while the man struggled with the tangle. He got more and more flustered as he wrestled with the recalcitrant ribbon in front of the girl.

"May I help?" asked Lucy. She produced Doctor Dee's knife from within her dress and used the razor-sharp blade to cut the knot.

"Ah, thank you, young lady." The man spread the parchment out and held each corner with paperweights. "This is the most recent map of the city that I have. Ralph Agas drew it up only thirty years ago. I don't suppose the city has changed all that much in such a short time." He smiled at the girl.

Lucy looked across the map.

'We can go now,' thought Lilith. 'I have recorded it.'

'No, we can't go like that,' thought Lucy. 'It would be rude. Now be silent, Lilith, and let me converse with the man.'

The keeper pointed out the main landmarks. The Tower itself, and St. Paul's, dominated the city but many other places were named. All the main roads were listed, of course, but so were all the main Guild Halls and even the larger taverns. Lucy found the Bakers Hall, the Fishmongers Hall, the Cordwainers Hall, and many others. The keeper traced her journey from the Tower up to Fen Church.

Lilith was horribly bored but Lucy seemed fascinated by the whole concept. The demon wondered whether Lucy had ever seen a map before. Possibly she hadn't. Lucy happily traced her journey up the Thames to London, as Agas's work showed the suburbia as well as the city proper inside the walls. Even Lilith got interested when she realised that Agas showed activities as well as places. At Moor Field, outside the northern wall, women laid their washing out on the grass. They sat and spun as their clothes and linen dried. Up on the Spitel Field, men practised at the longbow as Englishman had for generations. Beside them, two men tested their skill with firearms by shooting at a butt.

'What are those people doing, Lucy?' thought Lilith. She put a marker on a group of older children, boys and girls together, playing or fighting in a corner of Moor Field.

'Those are young people playing chase,' thought Lucy.

'Chase,' thought Lilith. 'How does that work?'

'The boys chase the girls and throw them to the ground when they catch them. Then they jump on the girls and hold them down until the girls submit. They have to pay a forfeit to be let up. Then you do it all over again with a different boy.'

'It doesn't sound a very skilful game from the girl's perspective,' thought Lilith.

'The skill is in selecting the right boy to catch you,' thought Lucy, dryly.

'What sort of forfeit do the girls pay?' thought Lilith, intrigued.

'A kiss, or cuddle, or something, I suppose. I don't know, Lilith, I never played chase. The local boys would not have had the nerve to chase me. Now be quiet, the keeper is talking and I can't concentrate on both of you.'

Lilith thought Lucy sounded rather wistful.

Clearly flattered by Lucy's interest, the keeper showed her more precious items from his collection including a history of London by Geoffrey of Monmouth from its founding by the Trojan Brutus in the year 1108 Before Christ.

"Brutus was descended from the Hero Aeneas who founded Rome," said the librarian.

'Aeneas escaped from burning Troy,' thought Lilith, happily. 'You see, Lucy. I took your advice and looked up Helen in my database. She had the beauty that launched a thousand ships.'

'Yes, the Greeks burnt a whole city to recover such a valued possession. Now hush, Lilith, so I can listen to the keeper,' thought Lucy.

"John Stow uses the collection regularly to research his new history of London. I am afraid he is one of the new breed of unpoetic scholars. He dismisses Geoffrey as a romantic and believes Julius Caesar and the Romans founded the city." The keeper sighed. He clearly was much attached to the older myths.

The keeper pressed a book upon Lucy when she took her leave. He was obviously delighted that a young lady showed an interest in his collection. The girl climbed the stairs to the northwest turret. William the Conqueror had built the White Tower to hold tight his new capital. Few stairs ran through the building and those that did were narrow left-hand spirals to impede an attacker. Guarded heavy doors closed off each floor. At the lower levels, the doors were open and the guards ignored Lucy but she soon came to a sealed level.

Lucy knocked on the door and a guard opened it. "Can I help you, milady?"

"I was hoping to climb up to the turret to view London," said Lucy, with big eyes.

"I am sorry but the turret is forbidden," said the guard, resolutely.

"Oh," said Lucy, holding her hand to her mouth. "Are there no exceptions?"

The guard looked at her hand and then held it in his. He drew her fingers up to his face and looked intently for a moment then kissed her ring. "Yes," he said, drawing to one side. "There are exceptions. You may pass, milady."

Lucy climbed up into the turret room. It was bare of furniture. She examined her hand at the window. The sun shone on Queen Elizabeth's ring. London lay spread before her just like the keeper's map. Lilith materialised beside her.

"Sit down and trace a circle around you on the stone using the athame."

Lucy did as she was bid.

"I am going to construct a gravitonic structure," said Lilith. "While you sleep, I have been going through my database of how humans manipulate space-time psionically. The reports are horribly confused and contradictory but have responded to multivariate synthesis. I believe that I can replicate human psionics using gravitational forces."

"What on earth are you talking about, demon?" asked Lucy.

"I am going to work a magic spell," said Lilith. "And I need you to help me."

"What shall I do?" asked Lucy.

"I need you to sing for me," said Lilith.

"What song would you like?" asked Lucy.

"It really doesn't matter. It's the act of singing that I need. Harmonious sounds excite the strings of matter and energy so I can draw power from between the Shadow Worlds."

Lucy gave Lilith a blank look. "Your singing aligns the spheres," said Lilith, translating into Lucy's terms. "Throw the crystals into the air when I tell you."

Lucy nodded and began to sing.

"Who is it that this dark night
"underneath my window plain?
"It is one, who from thy sight
"Being (ah!) exiled, disdain
"Every other vulgar light."

Lilith danced around the circle and clapped her hands in time to Lucy's song. The girl's voice seemed to fill the turret until the very air throbbed to the beat of the music. Streamers of light poured from Lilith's hands as she danced, and curled in spirals into the circle around Lucy. The girl sang in a cone of light.

"Why, alas! and are you he?
"Be not yet those fancies changed?
"Dear, when you find change in me
"Tho' from me you be estranged
"Let my change to ruin be."

"Now, Lucy. Now," said Lilith.

Lucy threw handfuls of crystals into the spirals of light and they whipped around her body, sparkling like diamonds in the flow of energy.

Lilith spread her arms wide. "Show me the power," she said and clapped her hands. The light exploded outwards from the cone.

Through the open window a spider's web of purple tracery spread over the city. Deeper purple blackness throbbed at various locations. A whirlpool formed in the far northwest and thrust a tentacle out of the city towards the Tower. Before the purple reached the Tower, the crystals exploded into white powder like fine snow.

"What happened?" asked Lucy.

"The crystals were not strong enough to contain the power that I focussed through them. Their internal structure collapsed ending the spell. Just as well, something smelt us and tried to find us. There is something very dangerous in this city. Look!"

Lilith projected an image of Agas's map onto Lucy's nervous system. On it she placed the magic tracers revealed by the spell. Purple lines wound around the city. "These lines track Isabella's movements. They converge here," said Lilith. Many of the tracers connected at a waterfront building in southwest London that glowed dark purple.

"The Spanish Embassy is on the waterfront somewhere," said Lucy. "Uncle mentioned it because he suspects that they use their private jetty to move spies in and out of London. I suppose that is it."

"These other markers puzzle me." Lilith pointed to a small number of purple blobs scattered at random across the city. "They imply some release of energy from a Shadow World."

"The purple blobs are mostly in alleys and lanes rather than buildings or main roads." Lucy moved closer and cocked her head. "That one is in Symmon's Alley off Cheapside. According to Pooley, that's where one of the slaughtered whores was found. The men did not realise that I could hear their conversation."

"I made your hearing more efficient," said Lilith.

"Oh God, Lilith. You don't think that each of these markers represents a murdered woman do you? There are more than a dozen of them."

"Isabella brought me to your world through a portal, Lucy. I think she has brought something else, something very dangerous and unpleasant."

"Lilith, look. There is a purple blob here in this corner, within the Tower's bailey. Oh God, there's something here."

Lucy ran out of the turret room, her feet crunching on the powdered salt. She scurried down the stairs, past the guards.

"Steady, maid. What's your rush?" asked one of them.

Lucy held the front of her skirts up and ran out of the front of the Tower. She made for the corner of the grounds where she had seen the purple marker. Alarmed, a pair of guards followed her but she outdistanced them. The girl ran quickly and easily, her lungs drawing in clean deep breaths. She stopped briefly, to get her bearings. Lilith projected a line of glowing light in front of her to indicate the direction. Lucy ran around some wooden storage huts. There, between the huts and the Tower's curtain wall, she found the body.

It was not a whore but a young man, a Tower guard. His throat had been torn out as if by a beast. Lucy knelt down and touched the body. To her Lilith-enhanced senses, it still tingled with magic.

'This happened recently, this morning or last night,' thought Lilith. 'There should be blood everywhere. His heart would have pumped it out of that wound as he died. So either he was dead before his throat was torn or . . . '

'The killer drank his blood.' Lucy finished the thought for Lilith.

The fitter of the guards arrived beside her, panting hard. "Where did you learn to run like that, miss? Oh my God, it's Harold."

"Fetch Master Tunstall. Right away."

Simon arrived at the run. "Are you all right, Lady Dennys? That must have been a terrible shock. What were you doing behind that shed?" he asked.

Lucy ignored him knowing that he could not cross-question his master's niece. 'Isabella sent it here on a reconnaissance,' thought Lucy, flatly. 'The guard must have disturbed it. She will send it again; she will send it against my family. Uncle won't run so they will all be killed.'

'Your explanation seems likely,' thought Lilith.

'How shall we protect them?' Lucy screamed in her head to Lilith.

'You must learn how to fight,' thought Lilith, simply.

Act 11, St. Katherine's Dock

The *Swallow* slipped through the Calais-Dover gap at a fast clip. These straits had belonged to England until the disastrous reign of Bloody Queen Mary, when Calais had been lost forever to the French. In King Harry's reign, these waters had been known as the English Channel; now they were called the French Sea.

Since leaving Plymouth and the Westcountry, the *Swallow* had cruised up the south coast standing off from the Isle of Wight, thus avoiding its treacherous rip currents born of four tides a day. At low tide, sailors could still see the wreck of King Harry's great ship, the *Mary Rose*, beneath the waters. When the *Swallow* rounded the White Cliffs, she entered the realm of the city of London with its rich merchants and treacherous courtiers. William would almost as soon rather force the defences of Cadiz harbour in a leaky wherry than enter the Port of London.

A short run up the North Kent coast brought the *Swallow* into the mouth of the Thames and its many ports. The Isle of Sheppey slid by on the port side guarded by the town of Sheerness. Past Sheerness was the River Medway and the fleet anchorage at Gillingham. Here, the Queen's galleons were beached on the tidal mudflats for maintenance. Further upriver, the ship building yards at Chatham sheltered behind the new fort at Upnor.

Swallow eschewed the safe harbours of the Medway and sailed west into the Thames. The banks of Essex and Kent closed in as the estuary narrowed. The flat rich soils of the Thames included some of the richest agricultural land in Europe, so villas and prosperous farmhouses lined the banks. The port of Gravesend marked the last of the open coast harbours. From here, the long ferry shuttled livestock and passengers backwards and forwards from the sea to London. The *Swallow* sailed through flotillas of ships and boats ranging from Thames barges to great carracks.

"Reduce speed," said William.

"Reef the mainsails," ordered the master.

"Aye, aye, sir," said the boatswain.

Swallow slowed down to a slow walk. A few more hours brought her to Kentish Dartford as the sun set.

"Master, pick up a buoy on the edge of the channel. No one is to go ashore and no boat is to approach without my permission. I want a guard topside at all times." The Thames estuary was notorious for piracy. William did not seriously expect anyone to be foolish enough to attack a galleon but the treasure on the ship weighed heavily on him. Having done all he could, he retired but sleep eluded him for some time and was dream-disturbed when it came.

A sailor shook him awake.

"Cap'n, sir. Gunner says a wherry is coming alongside and should he shoot it?"

"Christ, no," said William and dashed for the deck.

"Blast your eyes, I'm your pilot," said a voice from the river.

"That may be so." William heard the gunner's voice. "But come any closer without the captain's say-so and I will blow you out of the water."

"Don't shoot," William said. "That, ah, really is our pilot."

"Very good, sir," said the gunner, unperturbed. "Come aboard then, matey."

The pilot climbed over the side, glaring at the gunner who ignored him. "Good morning, Captain. My orders are to take you all the way in to London docks. A messenger has been sent to the office of Sir Francis Walsingham to announce your arrival."

"All the way in to London docks? Are you sure?" William was puzzled. Galleons would normally anchor in the outer Thames at Dartford or perhaps Erith where there were naval arsenals.

"Sir Francis has left strict instructions. You are going to London, Captain."

William sighed. It would be a long day moving the *Swallow* around the twists and turns of the meandering Thames. "Man the pinnace and get the longboat out, boatswain. We will be towing the ship for part of the way."

By dinner, they had passed Erith on the Kent bank and Barking Creek was in view on the starboard bow. The pilot knew his business and eased the big ship through the mudflats. The Thames split at this point into multiple channels. The pilot kept them in the deepwater channel along the Kent bank. A huge mudflat slid by only a few yards to starboard. Hovels built from old ships' timbers were built on the centre, which was above high water by just a foot or two.

"A good few ships have ended up there, I'll warrant," said William, pointing.

"Aye, sir, but we are going upriver on a rising tide. I am sure we will be able to float you off if you stick." The pilot grinned. William failed to appreciate the joke. He was captain of an oceangoing ship and felt trapped here.

A large black fish, eight or ten feet long, surfaced beside the *Swallow*. It flicked its tail lazily and dived beneath the ship.

"That's a Thames sea hog," said the pilot. "They fish them using towed nets."

"Are they fair to eat?" asked Simon.

"Foul," said the pilot. He gestured to the impoverished hamlet to starboard. "The hovels yonder are Silvertown, lovely name, filthy place. They say you can marry your mother there and most of them have. Some of them have more fingers on one hand than we have on two." The pilot held his sides in appreciation of his own wit. William thought that he likely related the same jocularity to every captain he piloted. The ship now faced the long southern loop around the Isle of Dogs. It would be slow oar work all the way but at least the tidal flow would help.

At that point there was a shudder as the *Swallow* kissed a mudbank, throwing the crew off their feet. For a moment there was a long grinding hiss, like a plane moving across a plank, then the ship freed herself with another shudder. The pilot and William climbed back on their feet. "Perhaps a point to starboard, Captain," said the pilot.

Simon was working in his study when Lucy walked in and sat in front of him. "Can I help my lady?" he asked, cautiously. One never knew with Lucy what direction the conversation might take, except that it was likely to lead Simon into difficulties. This time she came straight to the point.

"I hear that the master swordsman is to teach you how to fight."

Simon winced, as this was something of a sore point. As a gentleman he was entitled to wear a sword but the truth was that it was merely a badge of rank to him. He had little idea how to use it. So he had arranged to take lessons from an expert and few were better than the swordmaster of the Tower.

"I want to learn with you," she said.

Simon just gaped at her. He could have not been more surprised if she had said she wanted to learn how to fly.

"That's not possible," he said.

"Why?" she countered.

"Because women don't fight," he said. He knew that it was a stupid remark as soon as he said it. He was aware that a statement was not proved merely by reassertion. His lecturers had drummed as much into him at Cambridge.

"Because your uncle will kill me," he said, getting down to the practicalities.

"Only if he finds out," she said, jauntily.

"You would be surprised what Sir Francis can find out," Simon said, darkly. "What in heaven do you want to learn to fight for?"

"I just thought it might come in handy," said Lucy. "There being a madman abroad killing girls."

"That hardly concerns you," said Simon He gestured to where Gwilym hovered politely out of earshot.

"Gwilym might not always be there," said Lucy.

"You are quite wrong," Simon said. "As long as there is the slightest danger, Gwilym will always be there. Sir Francis' instructions were quite clear and Gwilym is conscientious."

"You know what happened to me," she said. "Don't make me say it."

"I know nothing except that you are my patron's niece and a lady of some position," said Simon firmly, closing the conversation. He went back to his work but when he looked up she was still there.

Simon sighed. "I am not comfortable with this conversation, madam."

"Very well, you force me to be frank," said Lucy. "I am possessed by a demon."

"Stop it!" said Simon. "Possession leads to screaming madness. You are no madder than any other aristocrat that I have met. In fact, you are considerably saner than many."

'He refuses to believe me, Lilith. I will need to prove that you exist,' thought Lucy.

'Are you sure, Lucy?' thought Lilith.

'I need his cooperation,' thought Lucy.

Lucy reached across and slipped Simon's dagger from its sheath. She casually bent the steel blade into a right angle in front of him.

"Do you see, Simon?" Lucy asked. "Do you believe me now?"

Simon shook his head in horror. "Oh God, it's there, isn't it? Is it called Lilith? You asked for prayers for Lilith."

"She, Simon, she—not it. She's called Lilith and I believe she has been sent to me for a purpose. You saw the Spanish witch make magic with your own eyes in the theatre and you saw me stop her."

"I saw." He stopped and tried to gather his thoughts. "I am not sure what I saw, to be honest."

"Isabella will attack my family. She is very dangerous. I need to learn how to fight, Simon. Please help me."

"You must tell Sir Francis," said Simon.

"No, he must not know because there is nothing he can do. It would hurt him terribly to know and—I am frightened that they will burn me. You must tell no one. Promise me," Lucy said, pleadingly.

What could he say?

"Very well, Lady Dennys, you have my word. Come with me."

Simon led the way to the armoury. The master swordsman was a surprising small man with an enormous moustache. He bent low over Lucy's hand to kiss it. The moustache tickled. Gwilym leaned against the wall by the door. Walsingham had instructed the Welshman to stay with Lucy at all times. The Tower's walls were clearly no protection against whatever had killed the guard. Gwilym tended to take his orders literally.

The swordsman stood stiffly with a rapier point down into the floor. "Do you want to learn to really fight or simply to prance prettily for the girls?"

"To fight," Simon said, simply.

"Very well. The most admired duellists in the world are the Latins, especially the Italians and the Spanish. They duel with style, with flourish, and with artistry. Ladies swoon at their manly athletics. The Spanish style abounds with tricks and artifices. It's exponents move with such fluidity and grace that the technique is known as dancing feet. I will not teach you dancing feet, Master Tunstall; I will teach you to kill. That is the English style. It is brutal and efficient. No girls will swoon at your feet but your enemies will die. Come, let us try a few passes."

The master tossed a practice sword to Simon. The secretary took up a defensive position and crossed swords with the swordmaster. He advanced on the smaller man and engaged him. The master kept moving away from Simon, forcing him forward. Within seconds the swordmaster had the guarded point of his weapon at Simon's throat.

"Why did you press me so closely, Master Tunstall? Are you in such a hurry to die?"

"I thought that one had to attack, that the advantage lay with the attacker," said Simon.

"Hmm." The swordmaster snorted. "Always keep back from your opponent. The only reason to close is to attack—and the only time to attack is when you think you can deliver a fatal blow. Do you understand?"

Simon assented.

"Four governors mark the successful fighter. They are judgement, distance, time and place," said the swordmaster. "Of these judgement is the most important. It is the art of knowing how and when your adversary can reach you and in return what you can do to him. Connected with judgement is distance. Always keep your distance to give yourself space to defend your body or to offend your enemy. Time and place are used to attack. You must know the exact moment to strike and the place from which you will strike. But most of all, you must immediately fly backward if your attack fails to prevent your adversary striking you in return. Come again."

The men fought again and Simon defended himself for a good quarter minute before he was "killed."

"Rule one is to stay alive. Only by staying alive can you win. Again!"

The lesson went on. Lucy, and hence Lilith, watched intently. When the master was satisfied that Simon understood the basic strategic concepts, he started to teach him simple tactical moves to parry his opponent's weapon out of alignment for a counterstrike.

"Enough, Master Tunstall. Now you must go away and practise. When you have practised for a month, come back to me." The master left the practise room. He was as calm as if he had merely walked across a lawn. Simon was sweating from every pore and breathing hard.

"Lady Dennys. I believe I will go back to my chamber for a small rest. I hope you found that instructive."

"Very good, Master Tunstall. I shall stay here for a moment." Gwilym stayed with Lucy.

Lucy was in despair. 'This is so complex Lilith. How am I to learn without practising? And who will practise with me?'

'Human beings learn with their forebrains. But they have to practise physical skills to train their rear brains. This enables them to carry out actions quickly and smoothly without having to think about it,' Lilith observed. 'You humans think so slowly that thought slows you down.'

'And you are faster, I suppose,' thought Lucy, cattily.

'Yes,' thought Lilith, simply. She was vaguely aware that Lucy was scolding her but Lilith was still having trouble understanding sarcasm or irony. Saying the opposite of what you meant to convey the idea more strongly was a difficult concept for one of the People to grasp.

'I have tried something new. While you were watching the duel, I laid down tracks in your hindbrain. I believe your body has already learnt what you saw. Try with a sword,' thought Lilith.

'But who shall I fight?' thought Lucy.

The bully from Rood Lane materialised before her with a sword in his hand. 'Fight him,' thought Lilith.

Lucy picked up a rapier and tried a few passes against the image projected by Lilith. It was not so successful, as one cannot clash swords with a phantom. Lilith was at a loss to suggest something.

"Would you like to try some passes against me, 'ighness?" asked Gwilym.

Lilith had forgotten that the bodyguard was there. Of course, servants had a different attitude to women fighting than gentlemen. Lucy had once secretly observed two servant girls have a catfight over a boy. The male servants had all stood around enjoying it immensely and making wagers on the victor. Her maid had told her that the landlady of the Dog and Hound tavern down in the village had knocked out Gwilym himself with a cooking pot. Apparently, the woman had caught Gwilym in a compromising position with her daughter. The gossip was that the landlady had been less worried about her daughter's maidenhood than the fact that she herself had an understanding with the man.

The pair took their stance and duelled.

'Lilith, I can do this!' Lucy seemed astonished to find that she could hold the man off. When Gwilym moved into the attack she parried his blade and moved inside his reach, rotating her body in a circle. Her sword ended against his neck.

Gwilym laughed out loud. "A good trick, 'ighness. At you again."

He moved back into the attack. This time he dropped his sword when she parried his blade and tried to counter. With his free hand, he grabbed her wrist and pulled her in closer. His elbow against her throat stopped her. She would have been dead had he struck another three inches.

"Oh!" said Lucy.

"Someone has taught you to be a fair duellist, 'ighness, but on the streets they fight a rougher style with no rules. I think you are learning the wrong lessons. You will never fight a formal duel and I do not think you will carry a sword like a gentleman. But I notice that you still carry Doctor Dee's knife."

"How did . . .?" The girl stopped before she said something stupid. She had thought the knife well concealed in the folds of her dress but it was Gwilym's job to notice hidden weapons. And Gwilym was very good at his job or he wouldn't be where he was.

"The master told me to make sure that you are protected. Teaching you to use that dagger might be the best way." Gwilym rooted around in a chest until he found two wooden practise knives. He spun one to Lucy, who caught it easily. Gwillym grinned. "I heard you were good at catching blades! Now let's teach you to fight with them."

The lesson went on for hours. At the end, Lucy knew a great deal more about male anatomy and how to inflict divers damage on it. She knew when to kick, how to kick, and where to kick. Gwilym kept it to himself if he was surprised how quickly she learnt or how fast and strong she was.

"Thank you, Master Gwilym," she finally said.

"Just Gwilym, 'ighness," said the bodyguard. "I ain't no gentleman, I work for a living."

"Um, Gwilym," she said. "It might be better to keep this to ourselves. People might not understand."

"'Ighness, he said. "I am Sir Francis' man. When my old father died, the family nearly lost the tenancy of his farm back in Wales. My brother got in debt to a moneylender, see. The master paid the debt and had the moneylender thrashed. I took care of the thrashing bit myself, but it was the master who squared it with the sheriff. We're a bit old-fashioned in the valleys of Wales. I have pledged myself to 'is 'ighness so that includes 'is family too."

"I understand. Thank you, Gwilym. Do you miss Wales?" Lucy asked.

"Bless you miss, no. My father sent me to live with my cousin's family in London when I was but four or five. My elder brother would inherit the farm so there was nothing for me there. I have only been back a few times. They even laugh at the way I speak and call me a foreigner."

"I will retire now so you may attend your own business," said Lucy.

"I will see you to your room, first, 'ighness."

"Lilith," said Lucy, when she was back in her bedchamber. "How did I know that spinning trick with the sword? I don't remember the swordmaster teaching Simon it."

"I put that in your head," said Lilith. "I saw it in the other Shadow World before I came here. Look."

Lilith projected the video clip of the bullfight into Lucy's head. To Lucy it appeared to be on a screen in midair. The two girls watched the Spanish matador whirl in his suit of light. Lilith had always loved the artistry of the clip but now, in Lucy's head, she had a whole new reaction to the elegance of the matador.

It's just leakage, insisted a stubborn subroutine, just leakage from Lucy's emotional centres. Lilith turned off the subroutine—permanently.

The rowboats inched the *Swallow* bow first into a jetty at St. Katherine's dock. Final contact came with a thump. The carpenter rushed forrard to examine his beloved hull. William took off his cap and wiped his brow. For the captain of an oceangoing vessel, navigating the Thames was worse than an Atlantic crossing. At least you were unlikely to bump into something midatlantic. The boatswain shouted orders to lash the *Swallow* firmly in place.

"Thank you, sir, a fine piece of navigating," William said to the pilot. In truth, it was a fine bit of watermanship—William could not bring himself to think of it as seamanship—to bring the *Swallow* so far up the Thames with barely a touch.

The pilot bowed. "It's a privilege to navigate such a ship, Captain. It makes a change from piloting coast-crawlers."

"I am sorry for that misunderstanding at Dartford," said William.

"Not to worry, Captain," said the pilot. "I realise that your man would not have really fired on me."

"Ah, no," said William. Actually the gunner would have blown the man out of the river without turning a hair. But best to leave the pilot in ignorance about how close he had been to his maker.

"I will take my leave of you, then. I have to report in to the office of Sir Francis Walsingham to announce your arrival. He will send someone down to see you." The pilot gestured to port. "At least I won't have far to go. His office is in there."

The Bloody Tower leaned over the dock. William examined it. He had made the Thames run a few times but always unloaded at Gravesend or Dartmouth. Now here he was docked right outside the city wall of Old London Town, about to hobnob with the mighty. William was a provincial so he was prepared to find fault with the capital. But he had so admit that he was a bit awed. London Bridge had more and better housing than most Devon towns and the Tower was an impressive reminder of Elizabeth's power.

Only the London city wall disappointed. It was actually falling down in places. Londoners clearly had no fear of an attack. In the Westcountry, they built their walls high and maintained them well. One never knew when the French or Spanish or Moors might come calling. Moorish slave raids were the most feared of all. North European women sold for a high price on the auction blocks in North Africa or Turkey. English girls, in particular, were sought after for harems.

The boatswain reported. "The ship is safely docked, Cap'n. Ah, the men respectfully ask that they be allowed a run ashore, sir."

"Very good, boatswain. I will let the men off the ship a watch at a time, starting with the starboard watch." That meant the gunner got the first shore run. "Assemble the men on the deck in one hour."

With time to spare, the starboard watch was assembled on the main deck, waiting for the captain to emerge from his cabin. William strode out of his cabin and stood on the rear deck where he could look down on them. My God, he thought, what a shower to release on London. He was aware that he was wasting his time with moral exhortations but William's Protestant faith demanded that he try.

"Men," he said. "It's been a long cruise and I realise that you are keen for some leave but I just wanted a few words."

The sailors waited patiently for him to finish. He was the captain after all.

"Here we are docked in the great city of London. It has more churches than any other city in England. St. Paul's is one of the most magnificent dedications to the Lord ever created. The city has an enormous collection of bookshops selling improving tracts. There are halls and museums dedicated to all the arts, theatre companies showing morally uplifting plays, and divers entertainments for good Christian men."

William looked down at the collection of assembled sea dogs. One, Burket, grinned happily at him, showing rows of blackened teeth. The captain sighed. He had made his pitch as religion demanded but now he had to get down to practicalities.

"The port watch will run a ferry service with the longboat for those who want to cross the river to visit Southwark. Remember, Southwark can be a dangerous place. Stay together and look after each other."

The gunner cracked his knuckles and one of the boatswain's mates tapped a marlinspike against his leg. William looked at the assembled sailors. He thought he had never seen a more frightening collection of bullies in his life. "Oh for God's sake, go. Just don't burn the place to the ground."

The captain stalked back to his cabin to write up his log.

Writing was not William's forte. He struggled to find the right words and the quality of his hand left much to be desired. A large inkblot splattered onto the page. Perhaps he should cut another pen. A knock sounded on the door.

"What in Hades is it now? I'm busy."

A sailor stuck his head around the door. "The boatswain's compliments, sir," he said reciting the message carefully. "But the messenger from Sir Francis Walsingham is here and he has brought one of Sir Francis' relatives with him. Apparently the Lady Dennys wants to see a galleon."

William stormed out of the cabin. "Wants to see a galleon! Is this a warship or a rich man's yacht? If Walsingham thinks that I have time to show some dried-up old prune of an aunt around then he has another think coming."

William found himself looking at the largest, cutest pair of brown eyes that he had ever seen. "That is, um . . ."

The woman flicked back her hood and rich auburn hair tumbled out. William thought he had never seen anything so beautiful in his life.

"Oh, I'm sorry, Captain," she said. "If you are busy, I can wait on the dock."

"No," he said, far more loudly than was necessary. "No, there is no need, milady. I would be delighted to show you around."

"Well, if you are sure." She smiled at him. It lit up her face like a shaft of sunlight through storm clouds.

"Of course I am sure." He had never been surer of anything. He had the rest of his life if necessary. William offered her his arm. She looked at the stains on his jacket dubiously but took the proffered limb anyway. Damn, damn, damnation, thought William. If only he had some warning. He was sure he had some decent clothes somewhere in his cabin. Hopefully, she would be impressed by his rugged sea dog appearance, instead of merely thinking him a vagrant.

"This is the main deck," he said. "We, um, call it . . ."

"The main deck?" She completed the sentence for him.

The girl was laughing at him but, as long as he retained this beautiful creature on his arm, he didn't care. They passed the boatswain.

"I was sure that he said he didn't have any time to show dried-up old prunes related to Walsingham around the ship," said the boatswain to one of his mates, in an actor's whisper that must have been audible on the dockside.

William glared at the boatswain who looked back politely. William heard a muffled laugh beside him. The girl had her head down but she was laughing at him again. William gave up.

"What would you like to know, milady? Would you care to hear about some of my bolder adventures?"

"Later, Captain. What weight of shot do you use in the cannon and what is their maximum effective range?"

William heard the boatswain collapse in laughter. He must remember that this was no wide-eyed tavern girl but a sophisticated court lady. He was going to have to raise his game to hold her attention. "They are actually demi-culverins, milady, firing a nine-pound shot. We can hit out to five hundred yards but I prefer to close to one hundred or less."

And so it went on. The girl clearly had no experience of ships but she listened intently and asked follow-up questions that showed she understood his explanations. William had found a beauty that was fascinated by galleons; he thought that he had died and gone to heaven. Two men followed behind. One was a slim young gentleman who occasionally asked a question of his own in an educated accent. That would be Walsingham's agent.

"You are related to Sir Francis, milady?" said William.

"He is my uncle and guardian. I have been part of his household since I was a small child."

That explained the second escort. William recognised his type. He was a large, silent man who walked a precise three paces behind and one pace to the left of Lady Dennys. His eyes swept continuously around and his hand was never far from his weapon. Walsingham had assigned her a bodyguard, probably the best the spymaster had, and that meant the best there was. William would have paid money to see this man spar with the boatswain. Loyalty would have made him wager on the sailor but by God it would be a close-run thing.

William was deep in conversation with Lady Dennys about the provisioning problems of race-built galleons when the gentleman interrupted him.

"Just how far do you get on a transatlantic voyage before you reach the urine-drinking stage?" asked Simon.

The captain coloured up to Simon's delight. The randy bastard had drooled all over Lucy ever since they came onboard.

"Perhaps we could retire to your cabin and I can present you with Sir Francis' instructions," said Simon. "I can read them to you if you have trouble with the longer words." At that point he tripped over a rope, rather spoiling the effect.

William leafed through the instructions. Most of the documents concerned unloading the ship and the master and purser would deal with those details. The key paper was the last. It ordered William to hold himself and his ship ready for special assignment, as Walsingham dictated.

When their business was concluded William turned to Lucy. "Is there anything further I can do for you, milady?"

"I am starving, Captain. I would greatly favour dinner."

"We are out of provisions on the ship, milady," said William.

"Except for the urine," muttered Simon. Lucy gave him the Look.

"But there is a decent tavern outside the dock. I would be flattered if you would join me for supper there. And your party, of course." William looked coldly at Simon.

"Excellent, Captain." She took his arm again and he guided her to the gangplank. "You can tell me of your bolder adventures while we eat."

William had the distinct impression that she was laughing at him again. Never mind, she was eating with him. That must prove something.

Lucy stayed on William's arm all the way to the tavern. Simon and Gwilym followed behind. The sun set as they arrived at the door of the tavern. Gwilym moved in front of Lucy. "If you will wait here with the gentlemen for a moment, 'ighness." He disappeared inside to look around and assess any danger to his charge. William waited patiently. You do not interfere with a top-class professional doing his job.

Gwilym reappeared with the landlord. "Lady Dennys," said the man. "This is a great honour. Come in, your ladyship, and be welcome."

The landlord led the way into the tavern. He prodded a customer at a centre table. "You will have to move. This is the best table and it is needed."

The man opened his mouth to object and then saw Lucy. He got up without a word and indicated to his mates to follow.

"I didn't want to cause any bother," said Lucy.

"It's no bother, lady," said the customer. "There is another table over there".

"Thank you. You are very kind," said Lucy. She looked pointedly at Simon. "Master Tunstall."

"Please deliver a jug of your finest ale to that table, landlord. I will pay," said Simon.

"Thank you, lady," said the customer, looking pleased.

Lucy would not, of course, carry money or buy drinks. But all understood that, although Simon paid, the Lady Dennys was their benefactor.

The landlord's daughter came to take their order. "What do you recommend, love?" asked William.

"The mutton pie is excellent."

"Four then. And some ale for the men. Lady Dennys?"

"Wine, please, Captain."

The girl vanished behind the bar. She reappeared moments later with a mug of wine and a jug of ale. "The pies will come shortly."

"How about a song then?" the landlord said.

"What shall I sing?" asked his daughter, looking doubtfully at Lucy.

"Not 'The Little Pixie', girl, something classy. We have quality in tonight."

The girl made her way to a small stage at the fireplace. Cries of "hush" went around the room. Clearly she was popular.

"Sigh no more, ladies, sigh nor more,

"Men were deceivers ever,

"One foot in sea and one on shore,

"To one thing constant never,

"Then sigh not so,

"But let them go,

"And be you blithe and bonny,

"Converting all your sounds of woe,

"Into hey nonny, nonny."

The girl had a superb voice and her interpretation of the song was faultless. She held the whole tavern spellbound. The landlord supervised the serving of their mutton. "She has a rare way with a song, does Mary, does she not?"

"Indeed, Master. Indeed," said Lucy. "I have never heard it sung better."

"Sing no more ditties, sing no mo,

"Or dumps so dull and heavy,

"The fraud of men was ever so,

"Since summer first was leavy.

"Then sigh not so,

"But let them go,

"And be you blithe and bonny,

"Converting all your sounds of woe,

"Into hey, nonny, nonny."

Lucy wolfed down her food. She obviously was very hungry since, for although she eat daintily, she dined on a man's portion, which was odd for such a small girl.

"Then sigh not so,

"But let them go,

"*And be you blithe and bonny,*
"*Converting all your sounds of woe,*
"*Into hey, nonny, nonny.*"

The girl tossed her head just like a maid dismissing an inconstant lover. The patrons whistled and clapped and threw copper coins to her. Simon and William threw silver. Lucy whispered in Simon's ear and he produced a gold sovereign and tossed it to the girl. She caught it, kissed it, and displayed it to the tavern's customers as a trophy. They cheered and clapped the more. The girl mouthed a "thank you" to Lucy and ran offstage behind the bar. Lucy's eyes flashed and she gave William a devastating smile.

Then the door flew open and a dozen toughs walked in.

"Any trouble, Jackson, and you are out," said the landlord to the surly rogue at their head.

"My money's as good as anyone else's," said Jackson.

The newcomers clustered around the bar. The girl tried to serve them but one of them pinched her bottom hard. She fled past Lucy's table. As she ran past, William could see tears in her eyes. He also saw Lucy's lips tighten.

William deflected Lucy with conversation but the magic of the moment had been broken. The captain called over the potboy. He pressed a coin in his hand and whispered something. The potboy disappeared behind the bar.

The men got rowdier and ruder, pushing other customers out of the way and drinking from their mugs. Jackson leaned back against the bar. "Bloody gentry. Live off the fat of the land. What do they do about the bloodsucker that's killing our women? Nothing, that's what."

Jackson drained his mug and called for another beer with a curse. The landlord's hand shook as he poured the drink. Jackson took another pull. "Look at them sitting there like Lord and Lady muck. Maybe we should show the girl a good time, lads. Show her what real men are like." He laughed, coarsely.

Gwilym got up and walked towards the bar. William and Simon also rose. The bodyguard walked straight up to Jackson. God knows what the tough expected, threats, appeasing words, amateur breast-beating. But Gwilym was a professional. He didn't give warnings.

The bodyguard stepped in close to Jackson and kneed him in the groin. The man folded over with a falsetto scream. Gwilym seized his head and kneed him again, in the face this time. The rowdy's head snapped back, spraying an arc of blood into the air. He bounced against the bar and went down. The man groaned, Gwilym kicked him in the head, and he lay still.

Jackson's friends stood gaping in astonishment. Gwilym turned to walk back to his table. For a moment, it looked as if that might be the end of the matter but a tough was stupid enough to grab the bodyguard's arm. "Hey! You can't do that."

"I just did." Gwilym turned and hit him in the jaw with a loud crack. The man went down. William yelled in delight and charged into the gaggle of rowdies. Crowded, they fell over each other, tumbling like dominos. Other toughs ran round to surround the two men. Simon drew his sword with a metallic hiss. He had few illusions about his ability at fisticuffs. He stepped in close and rammed the point into a tough's shoulder. The man screamed and lost interest in the proceedings.

Three men rushed at Simon. He slashed one. The man stepped back, holding his hands over his face. Blood dripped between the fingers. Simon slipped and fell. The other two toughs got past him and headed for Lucy. All would be lost if they held a knife against the girl's throat. William cursed and tried to follow, but a rowdy on the floor had him by the ankle and he tripped.

William stuck a dagger into the man holding him. The hand let go. William hurled himself after the two men threatening Lucy, but he was too late. The men reached the girl but something very odd happened. The first seemed to fall over and catch his head on the table. The second gasped and staggered back. William could have sworn that Lucy had punched him, her arm moving so fast it was a blur. He must be seeing things.

At that point, the tavern door opened and the boatswain strode in with the deck watch and the potboy. He held a wooden lever in his hand. "Evening, Cap'n, I got your message. These the lads that are feeling their oats?"

The Swallows spread out to surround the rowdies that were still standing. Gwilym had put another brace on the floor. "We didn't mean no harm," whined one. "We was just funning."

"That so, I like a bit of fun meself," said the boatswain, slapping the wooden club against his palm.

"Boatswain," said William. "Take this rubbish out. They have no manners."

The boatswain seized the nearest rowdy by his throat. "Don't you worry none about that, sir. Me and the lads will learn them manners soon enough."

The Swallows pulled the toughs out into the street. Thumps and cries carried clearly through the door into the tavern.

"A song," said William brightly. "Another song to lighten the mood."

The tavern girl appeared, hesitantly. "What shall I sing?"

"Do you know 'The Little Pixie'?" asked William.

Act 12, Wood Road at Night

Walsingham chaired a war council. He sat at the head of the table; Simon, William, and the Constable of London sat along the sides.

"Two girls killed last night," said the Constable. "One was just a whore but the other was a merchant's wife. God knows what she was up to, wandering around the streets in the dark. A lover, I suppose." The Constable shook his head. "No matter. The guilds are screaming for action. There were riots in London again. The people are scared. Vigilantes were out again. They hanged a Jew down by the Fleet."

"The Jews get the blame for everything," said Walsingham. "Put guards on the Jewish quarters and warn them to stay inside at night. We need the Jews. The capital to fund our naval enterprises evaporates if the Jews flee the city, then. Hang anyone trying to whip up a riot against them and display the bodies on New Gate. That should focus a few minds."

"The Watch is only so big," said the Constable. "I can only cover the main streets if I concentrate them to fight this monster. Sending them in against a demon in ones and twos is sheer murder. I suppose it is a demon?"

Walsingham shrugged. "Possibly. It is very dangerous whatever it is. I don't want the word demon used outside this room." He looked sharply around. "Is that understood? There is enough panic abroad already."

185

"It's too late for bland reassurance," said the Constable. "We have to kill it."

"Agreed," said Walsingham. "That is where you come in, Captain. I want you to spread the Watch thinly in twos, Constable. They are not to engage this thing but to detect it and sound the alarm. Captain Hawkins will lead a mounted detachment that will run it down and kill it with force of numbers. Your men can ride, Captain?"

"Well enough," said William. "Where will we get the horses?"

"I will arrange that," said Walsingham. "Get your men in the barracks here in the Tower today. Let them rest up so they will be fresh tonight."

"I like this not," said the Constable. "Too much can go wrong. My men have to detect this thing without getting noticed and killed. Then they have to send a runner for help. The monster has to stay put while the runner finds the captain and he comes. Is all this likely?"

"If anyone has a better plan then now is the time to voice it," said Walsingham. "No?" He tapped his pen on the desk. "Look, gentlemen. The creature stays with his victim to feed. He sucks their blood. That must take time. I realise the chance of us taking the beast on any one night is low but this plan has two advantages. Firstly, it shows the people of London that action is being taken. That alone will calm things down. The host body will be decaying fast, if it is a demon. We may just have to outlast it. The second advantage of the plan is that even long odds come up if one plays them enough. The monster has to be lucky every night. We only have to get lucky once."

The men talked further, as men will. But no one had anything useful or new to contribute. Eventually, they agreed with Walsingham's strategy. Simon threw the window open to let some fresh air in.

Lucy was sitting outside the window reading. She was far enough away that a normal person would not have been able to eavesdrop, but Lucy was possessed.

'What do you think of Uncle's plan?' thought Lucy.

'It has merit,' thought Lilith. 'But I can envisage distinct problems. The Constable mentioned some but I foresee one other major issue.'

'Oh yes?' thought Lucy.

'The captain and his men may not be able to kill it. It may escape or even worse.'

'Worse?' thought Lucy.

'It may kill them,' thought Lilith, simply.

Lucy wandered aimlessly around the grounds. 'Then I will have to kill it. Can I kill it, Lilith?'

'I think we can together. I believe I can meld with your body, boosting its performance beyond the improvements that you already have,' thought Lilith.

'But I stay in control, demon?'

'You stay in control. I have some other tricks, too. I can energise your knife, making it a much more dangerous cutting weapon. I can also energise your body. You will have your own personal force field.'

'Force field?' thought Lucy.

'It's like armour,' thought Lilith. 'But it weighs nothing and is transparent, like glass.'

'So how do we do this?' asked Lucy.

'Our problem breaks down then as follows. We have to find the monster, reach it, and kill it. First things first. To locate the monster, I will need a more precise spell than last time. I need a diamond to focus the energy. Lucy, you will have to get me a decent sized stone.'

'I will search my uncle's chests and try to borrow one,' thought Lucy.

'The next problem is how to reach the monster. We will need to be fast. You could run through the streets but it would attract attention. Let me think about it.'

'We will have to lose Gwilym,' thought Lucy. The bodyguard was never very far from Lucy. Walsingham had ordered him to watch the girl even in the Tower, since the monster had proved it could climb fortified walls.

Lucy wandered over to the man. "I am a little fatigued, Gwilym. I intend to rest in my chamber. Why not take a break yourself?"

"I will wait outside, 'ighness."

"As you wish. I will have my maid bring you refreshment."

Lucy walked back to Walsingham's apartments.

"Millie!"

"Yes, ma'am." Her maid appeared and curtseyed.

"Would you take some bread and beer to Gwilym outside? Then I wish to rest in quiet, so you may have the rest of the afternoon off. You might want to keep Gwilym company."

The maid looked pleased. 'She favours Gwilym,' thought Lilith, surprised.

'Of course,' thought Lucy. 'Haven't you noticed? You are very bad at reading people, demon. I expect this to keep both of them busy.'

Lucy went from her chamber into Walsingham's. Voices indicated that the attached offices were still occupied, so she took care to be quiet as she searched Walsingham's possessions. Her uncle favoured austere clothes so after half an hour she had turned up nothing. Lucy was starting to despair when she found a velvet cloak at the bottom of a trunk. It was held at the shoulder by a silver clasp. The clasp boasted a decently sized diamond. Lucy started to unclip it.

'No, leave the clasp. Just take the diamond. Then your uncle will not know when it disappeared. It could have fallen out anytime.'

'And how do I get the diamond out of its setting without jeweller's tools, Lilith?'

'You can do it, Lucy. I am going to meld with you.'

Lucy's skin glowed, as if it was internally lit. 'Come, Lucy, believe in yourself. You can do it,' said Lilith.

The girl took a deep breath and grasped the diamond between her thumb and forefinger and twisted. The silver setting broke and the diamond came free.

'Sweet Jesu, I did it. I did it.'

'Told you, girl. Right now, you are probably the strongest human on earth,' thought Lilith.

The glow dimmed from Lucy's skin.

'Can you do that to me anytime, demon?' asked Lucy.

'More or less,' thought Lilith. 'But it puts a great strain on your body so I shouldn't do it too long or too often.'

Lucy put the room back exactly as she found it and sneaked back to her chamber. She lay on the bed looking at the diamond.

'Now we work magic,' thought Lilith. She had discovered that Lucy responded better to that word than a complex explanation of gravitonic theory. Viewed from Lucy's perspective, maybe magic was the most accurate word for what they were about to do.

'Hold the diamond in front of your face and sing.'

Lucy was feeling tired so she simply hummed a hymn that she was fond of. The diamond seemed to vibrate in front of her eyes.

Lilith projected Agas's map of London onto Lucy's optic system. Lilith drew the results of her earlier search spell out of her records and ran it as a video clip. Purple dots and tracers spread across the map then the whirlpool formed again and shot a purple tentacle out. Lilith captured it in the diamond. The video clip ended and the map faded out. Lucy examined the diamond. It had been clear, now it had a distinct purple tinge.

'What happens next?' thought Lucy 'Isn't the diamond supposed to do something?'

'The monster must be quiescent during the day. It kills at night, remember. When it awakes, the diamond will glow and point the way.'

'Have you worked out how we will get at the monster?' thought Lucy.

'I suggest that we use Captain Hawkins and his men. They expect one of your uncle's people to guide them to the monster, correct?'

'Yes,' thought Lucy.

'So you will be the guide. Hawkins will carry you to the monster on his horse and give you support if things go badly for us.'

'The captain will never agree to me going with him, Lilith. He has seen me, remember. He will recognise me at once.'

'He did observe you carefully, that's true,' thought Liliith, and was delighted when Lucy blushed.

'I suppose I could disguise myself as a boy,' thought Lucy.

'That only works in plays,' thought Lilith. 'You seriously underestimate yourself if you think that any man is likely to confuse you with a boy.'

'So what do you suggest?' thought Lucy, a little waspishly.

'Humans see with their minds not their eyes, which means that they see what they expect to see. Consider, Lucy, it will be dark, human vision doesn't work well at night, and you will wear the clothes of a servant girl with a hood over your head. Millie is the same size as you. Captain Hawkins won't get a good look at you and why would he connect a secret service girl in working clothes with the great lady in court dress that he met earlier?'

'My voice and accent, for one thing, demon,' thought Lucy. 'Or do you suggest that I communicate with hand gestures?'

'I can disguise your voice. I will alter the muscle tension in your neck,' thought Lilith.

Lilith went over her plan at length with Lucy, until she was sure that the girl had grasped it.

'You need to rest now. With your permission, I will take over your body and watch the diamond while you sleep. I will wake you when it activates.'

'I don't know, Lilith. I don't like losing control but I suppose it makes sense. Wake me if anything at all happens. I don't want you pretending to be me if someone comes in.'

'As you say, Lucy. Sleep well.'

'I'll try Lilith. But . . .'

'Yes, Lucy?'

'I'm frightened.'

'So am I,' thought Lilith. 'Try to sleep.'

Lilith turned off Lucy's access to her senses and gave her perfect darkness and silence. The girl's brain slipped gently into alpha rhythms and she began to dream. Lilith found Lucy's dreams fascinating so she watched with part of her mind. The People did not sleep, so they did not dream. Lucy floated for a while through the rooms of Barn Elms then she was at dinner with her uncle. They had a long rambling conversation about eels. Walsingham kept complaining that his eels were too small and Elizabeth wouldn't eat them.

Lucy's brain went back in alpha rhythm and the dream faded. Then a new dream started. Lucy was in a room but the ceiling was infinitely high. The furniture was huge. Lilith could see the underside of tables and even chairs. Lucy was saying something unintelligible. It sounded like "mumah" repeated over and over again. Lucy whirled up into the air until she could look down on the room. She was enclosed in warmth and safety. She could smell hot food. A woman sang *"Hush, little Lucy, don't you cry, Mumah's going to make you an apple pie."* The voice faded again and Lucy was on her own in the cold and dark. In her dream, the girl wept.

Lilith retreated from Lucy's mind. She felt like she was intruding, spying on a friend. The girl was dreaming of her lost mother. Lilith had never had a mother but Lucy's sense of loss was painful to contemplate. How could the stupid Elder of the People think that these were shadow creatures of no consequence? Their short lives were so rich and emotional. Their triumphs were ecstatic and their sorrows unbearable. Lilith spent the rest of the afternoon contemplating her host and the human condition, while Lucy slept.

The sun set over London. Lilith watched the light dim from yellow into pastel pink and finally deep blue. It was beautiful. As darkness fell, the diamond pulsed shiny purple light. The monster was stirring. Lilith pumped energy into the crystal and a bright purple line shot from it in the direction of London. Lilith had her magic compass. She woke Lucy up.

William watched the sun fall behind the curtain wall.

"Should I tell the men to stay awake, sir?" asked the boatswain.

"No, tell them to turn in. I suspect we will be here for weeks before we get a request for help. I am going to get some sleep myself."

Before sleeping, William decided to write a report to Cousin John. He hoped that if he explained the pointlessness of their situation then the *Swallow* might be recalled to Plymouth. He had only written a few paragraphs when there was a knock. He picked up the lantern and opened the door. A woman stood there. She held her head down deliberately so that the cloak hood concealed her face. No doubt she was one of Walsingham's spies so would not want her identity known.

"Wake your men, Captain. The beast has been spotted."

Her voice had a strange foreign accent and was throaty, almost masculine. It reminded him of someone but he could not quite put his finger on it. William went over to the barrack room to wake the men. Sea dogs are used to being rousted out at a moment's notice so they were soon up and mustered. "Cutlasses only, mind," said the boatswain. "I don't want one of you shooting his dick off in the dark or worse still shooting mine off." Coarse laughter greeted the sally so clearly morale was good.

William led them over to the stable where Walsingham had horses ready. "Come on, look lively," said the boatswain. A few well-aimed kicks woke the stable lads, who bunked down with their charges. The animals were quickly saddled and bridled, and the sailors mounted. None of them could be said to have the seat of a cavalryman but they could ride from one point to another with reasonable facility. Raids inland often involved horses.

"A moment," said William. "Where's the guide we were promised?"

"That's me," said the woman. William had forgotten she was there. "I will ride pillion behind you."

He hadn't noticed in the dark but his saddle had a lady's pillion seat added. Oh terrific, William thought. Now he had to play nursemaid as well. He had no faith at all in this mission. He doubted whether they would get anywhere near the maniac who was killing whores. It would be a miracle if they all made it back without someone falling off in the dark and breaking bones.

He put down his left arm to haul her up but she leapt lithely onto the horse, using his hand mainly to steady herself. She sat sidesaddle with her feet down the left flank of the horse and her right arm about his waist.

The postern into London was closed for the nightly curfew so they left the Tower by the east gate and made their way north across the fields to Whitechapel Street. The road was lined with three- and four-storey houses so they actually had to move away from London to find a route onto it. William thought that the city would soon become unmanageably large if the Queen did not do something soon to stop ribbon development along its access roads. Once on Whitechapel Street, it was a short ride down to Aldgate.

The gate was an imposing building that straddled the road. In the centre was an arch blocked by heavy oak doors and a portcullis. A sergeant of the watch came out to meet them.

"The city is locked for the curfew," he said.

"I have a permit signed by Sir Francis Walsingham," said William. He showed it to the man who gazed at it doubtfully. "Come on, come on, man. We are in a hurry." William had a horrible feeling that maybe the man could not read. This was the sort of stupid detail that wrecked too-elaborate plans.

The girl slipped off the saddle beside him. She went over to the sergeant and showed him a ring on her hand. He straightened up immediately. "Open the gates, look lively there."

"Thank you, Sergeant," said Lucy. She bounced back to William's horse. He lowered his arm to help her back into the saddle. The portcullis rose, oh so slowly.

The diamond nestled in a purse slung round her neck. Lilith opened a window on the left side of Lucy's vision and painted in a map of London. A flashing white light showed her position and a purple arrow showed the direction of the monster. It was still somewhere in northwest London.

'Ready, Lucy?' asked Lilith. 'I will drop a gravitonic shield in front of your eyes now. It will slow down light, increasing its frequency, so you will see heat. You will see in the dark but it will look odd.'

Lilith placed the shield. 'Well,' she thought. 'Can you see?'

'Yes,' thought Lucy. 'But it's really peculiar. People's faces and torches are bright white but the sky is black. Everything else is in shades of grey.'

'The hotter something is the brighter it is,' said Lilith.

'I know you have to disguise my voice, Lilith, but whatever you are doing to my throat is becoming painful.'

'Sorry, Lucy, I'll relax the muscles a fraction and block any pain,' thought Lilith.

The way was finally clear and the party rode off at the trot. It wasn't possible to go any faster. William diverted to avoid the body of a criminal hanging from the gate. The body was well tarred to preserve it but, even so, there was always the fear that something would drop off as one passed underneath. The streets were mostly dark but the riders carried torches with them. They came to a fork in the road. Lucy checked the arrow. "Right, into Aldgate Street," she said to William.

They trotted past the Leadenhall Market and down Corn Hill. The sound of the horses' hooves echoed between the buildings. Lights appeared at some windows, indicating that there were a few people curious about a party of mounted men, but mostly Londoners kept their heads down and minded their own business. Experience had taught them the benefit of that. Past the Royal Exchange, the party reached Stocks Market, the heart of the city where five roads met. The purple arrow still pointed to northwest London.

"Straight on," urged Lucy. "Go up Cheapside."

As they passed Milk Street the arrow swung abruptly to the right. "Next right," Lucy said, urgently, and the party turned north into Wood Street. "Faster," she urged. The arrow swung right as they went up the street. To the left was a prosperous area with guildhalls, the saddlers', the goldsmiths', and the haberdashers'. But to the right between Wood Street and Milk Street was a rookery of run-down houses, some of them derelict and empty.

"We are very close," said Lucy. The arrow on her map swung quickly now. Finally it swung due east. "He's in the alley down there," she said.

"Dismount. Follow me," said William and led the charge into the alley. It was pitch black and filled with debris. At the other end, it opened into a small square. A dilapidated tavern occupied one side. It spilled light onto the square from lanterns around its door. William saw a body draped over the worn stone of a waterless fountain. He reached it in four strides and turned it over. It was a slattern. She looked old but was probably in her twenties. Too much wine and too little food had ruined her. The woman's throat was torn open. Blood still pumped out.

"He's still here somewhere. Look around," William said, loudly.

"There, there," said Walsingham's woman. William looked where she pointed. At first he saw nothing, but then a shadow detached itself from the general dark and slipped into a building. The woman must have eyes like an owl.

"After him," William ordered his men. "Not you," he said to the girl. "Fletcher, you stay here and protect the woman while we go after the killer. Follow me."

William drew his cutlass and led the way into the dilapidated building. The doorway opened straight onto some stairs. William climbed, his men following. Their weight caused the stairs to sway alarmingly. They must be riddled with rot. At the top was a landing, with three doors running off. William kicked in the first door. It collapsed easily. William thrust in the torch—the room was empty except for some broken sticks of furniture.

He repeated the process with the second door. This one took two kicks. The torch showed the monster inside. William got an impression of staring bulbous eyes and fanged teeth. The monster held his hands up to block the light and William could see that his nails were as long as claws. The torch seemed to bother the madman and he retreated back into the dark snarling. The boatswain followed William in and they thrust their torches at the madman, forcing him back. The man growled like a dog as more men with torches crowded the room. "Take him," ordered William, raising his weapon.

The monster turned and ran straight at the wall, crashing through it. The whole side of the rotten building came away in an explosion of breaking wood. William hadn't seen anything like it since a broadside of culverins blew in the hull of a caravel off Cadiz.

"Down the stairs, after him!" William ordered.

"Please, sir, the stairs is gone," said a seaman.

They were trapped. William looked down, torch out to light the square below. A pile of wood heaved and the monster got up, splinters cascading around him. Fletcher rushed the lunatic and aimed a blow with his cutlass. The monster caught the blade with his hand and, pulling it out of Fletcher's grasp, broke it. Fletcher had the "bottle," the courage, of a true sea dog. He stood his ground and threw a punch at the monster. It caught his wrist and pulled him in. With a slash of his other hand, the monster ripped open Fletcher's throat.

"Run, girl!" said William. "For sweet Jesus sake, run!"

The girl was paralysed by fear. She made no attempt to escape. William looked around frantically but he could see no quick way down. The monster advanced on the girl with his arms open as if to embrace her. She stepped into his arms as he bent his head down, fangs gleaming in the torchlight.

The girl blocked his arms with hers. She kneed the monster in the groin so hard that his body went into the air.

"Bloody hell," said the boatswain, with feeling.

The girl jumped back to put distance between herself and the killer. She had a knife in her hand. It must have been a trick of the light but her hands and the knife seemed to glow. The monster advanced on her with slashing swings of his clawed hands. She deflected each blow with her blade, leaping backwards every time to keep her distance.

Then she dodged a slash instead of parrying and, stepping into range of the monster, jammed her knife into his side. He screamed and reversed the swing of his arm, backhanding her across the head and body. She was thrown across the square, to crash into the tavern wall.

William moved to the edge looking for handholds down. His boot crashed through the wooden floor. He would have fallen if the boatswain had not hauled him back.

"Look out, girl," William said. He watched in agony, frozen to the spot.

The monster charged, trying to pin her in against the wall. Trapped, she would be helpless against his greater weight. She didn't give him time. She threw herself off the wall right back at him. They met in midair. She hit him twice in the body forcing him back. Then, when she had room, she spun and kicked him in the thigh so hard that William could hear the impact. The monster went down.

He didn't stay down but leapt up at her as if roped to a charging horse. His swing was ill timed and he missed. Again she stepped inside his reach. He was slowing down so she had more time. She brought her glowing knife around in a low swing that started behind her back. The weapon moved too fast to see, slicing into the monster's groin. She lifted him up in the air on the dagger's point. It cut deep into his body and he crashed down on his back, legs and arms twitching.

The girl stood there, looking at him.

William threw his torch down and climbed after it. He had some nasty moments but made it to the ground with nothing worse than splinters. Retrieving the torch, he went over to the mortally wounded monster. It was gutted from groin to chest. The knife must have been driven in with the force of a kicking stallion. William had seen wood splinters driven into bodies like this by culverin fire. Never had he seen such damage inflicted by hand. Only the handle of the knife protruded. William went to remove it.

"No, not yet," the monster said. "It's in my heart. I will die when you pull the knife out."

William recognised that voice. He pushed the torch nearer the face.

"Packenham? Is it really you?" William asked, horrified.

"Yes, it's me. Christopher Packenham, the handsome lady-killer. Now I kill women for real and drink their blood. Look what the Spanish bitch has made of me, Hawkins. Look what she has done to me." The old arrogance had gone from the voice but it was definitely Packenham. William did not know what to say.

"She said she would make me strong. She brought something through the mirror from the Other World. It did make me strong and fast. Remember that night in your cabin? You were supposed to be asleep. I hit you a sturdy clout, did I not?" Packenham chuckled.

He grabbed at William's hand. "Then the voices started, telling me to kill, giving me a taste for blood, until I became this thing, this monster."

There was very little blood in Packenham. The knife had released what there was but most of the body seemed empty. Maybe that was why he craved blood.

"That girl. She fights like a Valkyrie. Who is she? What is she?"

"I don't know, Christopher. She belongs to Walsingham," said William.

"Walsingham! I was supposed to kill him and his niece, Lucy Dennys. Isabella was determined to have the girl killed. She has a great grudge against her. I went for them one night but a guard surprised me. Later, all I could think of was blood, anybody's blood. I needed blood so badly that I couldn't make it as far as the Tower."

"How did you leave the ship? And how did you get here so fast, Christopher?"

"The mirror with the diamonds," Packenham said. "It opens doors to the Other World. We walked off the ship to London like moving through a door from one room to another."

He grasped William's arm. "Pull the knife and kill me. But first give me a cross. I will burn in hell for what I've done but let me die with a cross."

"Here, sir," said Brownlow, passing William a silver cross. A number of the men had climbed down and joined William while he was talking to Packenham. William handed Packenham the cross and the monster gripped it hard. Smoke curled from his fingers and his hand burst into flames. William put a boot on Packenham's chest and pulled the knife with both hands, until he got it free. How had a little girl rammed the weapon in so deeply?

Packenham's body collapsed in on itself, burning with an eerie green flame until only a pile of ash remained. The night breeze blew the remains away leaving only the cross. William picked it up and turned to the girl. She still stood in the same place. Her whole body was shaking.

"Shock," said the boatswain. "I have seen young sailors do this after their first battle but never so bad. She ain't done this before, Cap'n. I think this is her first kill."

Carefully, William pulled the hood back and held the torch to light her face. Auburn hair tumbled out in the torchlight and two big brown eyes looked into infinity. For a moment, when he looked into her eyes, he seemed to see sparkling light, like stars or diamonds glistening in the sunlight, but the effect soon faded.

"Sweet Jesu," William said. "It's Lucy Dennys. Walsingham will have my balls for this." The girl did not seem to hear him. The boatswain looked meaningfully at the silver cross in William's hand and then at the girl. William took the hint and handed her the cross. She clutched it to her bosom. William looked up at the boatswain who shrugged. Whatever made Lucy Dennys able to crush demons was clearly quite different from the thing that had possessed Packenham.

"I reckon this maid knew what waited us here better than we did. What pluck it must have taken to come with us," said the boatswain, admiringly. "Do you think we could have taken down that demon without her?"

"We can take anything," said William, stoutly, but had his doubts. "We would have suffered grievous hurt, though. You saw what it did to Fletcher." He turned to the girl.

"Lady Dennys, Lady Dennys," William said gently. She knelt and shook. "Right, let's get her home. Bring Fletcher's body as well. I want no evidence left. This enterprise never happened."

William picked Lucy up and carried her to the horses. He mounted into the rear saddle and then the boatswain passed her up. William placed her in front of him so he could hold her as they rode.

The sea dogs trotted back through the dark streets of Old London Town. Lucy held close to William, her head on his chest. She had not spoken since the fight, indeed she seemed not to be conscious, but he hoped she drew comfort inside his arms. At least, she had stopped shaking. It was ironic, he thought, that he could only get a real lady into his arms when she was in a swoon. How his mother would laugh.

William had seen the Lucy the beautiful woman, Lucy the great lady, Lucy the scholar, Lucy the fearless warrior, and finally Lucy the shaken little girl. How many more Lucys were there? "Who are you really, Lucy Dennys, what are you?" William said, quietly to himself.

She sat well in his arms. William had known many women but never anyone like her. He liked holding her. He thought the man who possessed her would be the most fortunate of all men. What sons she would give a man. Wind lifted her auburn hair and it rustled against his arm. What daughters too, he admitted. Lucy's children would be the terror of the world. It was such a shame that she would be wasted on some chinless aristocratic milksop, who enjoyed high social status only because he once had an ancestor with fire in his belly.

An idea formed and grew. This was a new age where anything was possible. An aristocracy of the sea was rising that was more important than the old nobility of blood and land. He, William Hawkins, was one of these men. Walsingham himself was descended from a commoner merchant who had done well through trade and had married a Dennys. Old Man Walsingham had bought respectability by buying a manor house in Kent. There were many manor houses for sale in Devon, many options for a rising man with Spanish treasure in his pocket.

The horse broke stride as it skidded on something in the dark. Lucy shuddered as if at an unpleasant memory then snuggled in closer to William's chest. He glanced down. He wanted this girl so badly it hurt. He wanted her more than anything in the world, as much as he had wanted the captaincy of a galleon. Rest securely in my arms, milady, he thought. I will win you and you can rest there forever.

Act 13, The Lion Tower

'Lucy, Lucy, are you all right?' thought Lilith.

'Yes, Lilith, I'm back with you. What happened?'

'I don't know exactly. I have been searching my medical databases. I think you were in shock but it was much worse than it should have been. I need to investigate further.'

'Oh. Would you like some peace and quiet then?' thought Lucy.

'No. That's not necessary. I am not like you. I have a much bigger mind than you, so I can divide up my consciousness and multitask.' Lilith paused; Lucy did not answer, which usually meant that she was baffled so Lilith tried again. 'I can do more things at the same time than you.'

'Sometimes you seem so human, Lilith, that I forget you are really a demon, but then, I only have a little mind,' thought Lucy, dryly.

'What is the last thing you remember, Lucy? Do you recall the fight with the monster?'

Lucy's mind froze on Lilith. For a moment, she was concerned that Lucy might go back into shock. The girl seemed to shake herself and then recover. She really was immensely tough.

'I remember. I will remember until I die. It's funny. I wasn't scared at the time. I was too busy, you see. It was afterwards.'

'I have run diagnostics on your body and it seems to have recovered,' thought Lilith. "You do have some internal tissue damage and external abrasions despite the shielding. That monster was very tough. I have accelerated your healing processes.'

'So I will live then,' thought Lucy, with an edge that Lilith recognised as humour.

'I believe that it is my fault the shock was so bad. I failed to meld smoothly with your nervous system. I will do better next time,' thought Lilith. 'When you went into shock, I didn't know what to do. I thought that maybe your reaction was normal and that if I interfered I would make you look inhuman. So I did nothing and let you drift away; was that right, Lucy?'

'Quite right, Lilith. Are you holding me in a swoon?'

'Yes. It was convenient to hold you quiescent while I carried out urgent repairs to your body. Your eyes are closed but from the sounds and sensations you are on a horse. The captain is holding you in front of him. Your unconscious body rather likes the feel of his arms about you. It feels safe and protected and—'

'Yes, I get the idea, Lilith. Now wake me up so I can see where we are,' Lucy interrupted.

Lucy stirred in his arms and lifted her head up to William. Their eyes locked. For a brief moment of madness, he almost bent down and kissed her. Her slightly parted lips were only inches away from his. It would have taken but a moment. William controlled himself. Drake had once told him that there was a time for audacious attack and a time for thought and planning. She was no tavern girl to be bowled over by an audacious lad. This was going to be a long campaign.

"You have recovered, Lady Dennys?"

"Indeed, Captain, as you see," said Lucy. "Um, Captain?"

"Yes, Lady Dennys."

"I believe I might be able to stay on the horse even if you held me a little less tightly, and it would facilitate breathing."

William blushed and released her. She sat upright with one hand on the saddle and the other on his arm. Damn! She was laughing at him again, he thought, ruefully. Still, laughter was better than scowls. A careful man might build much upon laughter.

He knew this was the wrong time but he might not get the chance to talk to her alone again. "Are you ready to talk about it, milady?"

She shuddered. "Please, Captain, I want to forget."

"We must talk, milady." He was implacable. "That monster was Christopher Packenham, a Westcountry gentleman. He was possessed by a demon, wasn't he?"

"Yes," she said, briefly.

"And you knew. That is why you came with us."

"Yes." She paused. "I have never heard of Packenham but I knew we were facing something very dangerous."

"It ripped Fletcher apart. How did you kill it?"

"I have been trained to fight," she said.

"Don't gull me, lady," he said. "Fletcher could fight and it ripped him apart like a small boy tortures a fly. I saw you thrown against a wall so hard every bone in your body should be broken. I saw you hit back with blows that would smash ship's timbers. How did you do it? What are you?"

She hung her head and tears rolled down her cheeks. She began to shake again. "Please, Captain, no more," she said.

Damnation, thought William. How does one deal with a weeping woman? To bully her further would be intolerable. He pulled her closer to him and she put her head on his chest. "Hush, milady," he said. "You are quite safe. On my life, no one will hurt you." He meant every word.

The party left London by Aldgate. This time the sergeant just waved them through. They clattered into the Tower over the stone entranceway. William swung Lucy down one-handed, then dismounted.

'He really is quite dashing,' thought Lilith, admiringly. Lucy ignored her. She was beginning to suspect that Lilith was a flirt.

"Hand the horses over to the stable lads," William said to his men.

The captain looked around. All was quiet except for the routine patrols. "I didn't expect the Mayor with a band but you'd think that someone might have come out to meet us. That prissy secretary of his might have shown his face, if not Walsingham himself."

"Um, Captain, I have a small confession to make," said Lucy, diffidently.

William looked at her suspiciously. She stood in front of him with her head down and her hands clasped together in front of her. She looked sweet and innocent. William strongly suspected that he was about to be gulled. He also suspected that she was going to get away with it.

"Sir Francis knew nothing about our little enterprise tonight. Information reached me from . . . from a personal source. I wasn't entirely open with you."

William sighed. "I realised that as soon as I recognised you, Lady Dennys. I cannot imagine Sir Francis sending his niece to hunt demons, whatever special abilities she might have."

"It might be best if we all forgot my participation. You and your gallant crew must take all credit for hunting down the monster," said Lucy, firmly.

"I like not taking the glory for this, milady. I did no more than watch. However, for your sake, I will do it," said William.

The boatswain walked up to William and saluted. "Begging your pardon, Cap'n. But the men are too awake now to sleep. We thought we might have a victory party. The men have asked me to invite you and the lady." He nodded at Lucy.

"Oh no, I couldn't," said Lucy.

"With respect, ma'am. It wouldn't be the same without you. You making the kill and all," said the boatswain.

Lucy looked helplessly at William. "I would be happy to escort you, milady," he said. She still looked doubtful. William had a sudden inspiration. "Perhaps your maid should attend you."

The girl brightened up immediately. William had guessed right. For form's sake, she needed a chaperone. "Yes, I will bring Millie. I will just go and change, Captain, and come back with my maid."

"You may fetch some kegs from my personal stocks, boatswain. I also need to attend to a few details, so I will escort the Lady Dennys back to her quarters and be back directly," said William.

He dropped Lucy off at Walsingham's apartments and hurried to his chamber nearby. As an officer, he bedded down with the gentlefolk. William hurriedly took off his sea gear and put on a gentleman's outfit. He considered shaving but thought the risk of cutting his own throat in the dark too great. How handsome would he look with blood dripping down his shirt? No, he would have to settle for the rugged man-of-action appearance. The ship's barber had shaved him but six days ago so he was still reasonably groomed.

William hurried back to the barracks. The buzz of sound and laughter greeted him. Men cheered when he entered. Nothing was sweeter than a victory party. He waved his hands for silence. "Now, men. You have chosen to invite Lady Dennys and she will be here shortly. She is a real live lady so I expect a bit of decorum." A man cheered and waved his beer mug. "Yes, even from you, Richards. After a few drinks, I will escort her back to gentlefolk country and then you may revert back to the bunch of lewd rogues that I know you to be. But until that time, I want you to be gentler than an Italian dancing master."

The boastswain indicated the door. Millie had tentatively put her head round. She signalled to William. He hurried out to find Lucy waiting for him in the dark. "Milady," he said and offered his arm. She took it and they swept in to the candlelit interior, Millie following. Lucy had combed her hair and changed into a blue court dress with white petticoats. The sea dogs drew back so William could escort her up the long room to the drinks. William stole a glance as they entered the light. She took his breath away. They paraded the length of the room. The men clapped and whistled. Lucy tossed her hair and grinned.

A sailor put a mug of beer in her hand. He held up a mug of his own and the din quietened. "Lady Dennys," he said.

"Lady Dennys," the sea dogs roared back and they drank deeply from their mugs.

She held her mug up. "The bold men of the *Swallow*," she said. They cheered and drank again.

Lucy and William retired to some chairs in the corner. "Thank you for coming, milady. It means a lot to the men."

"Not at all, Captain. I shall dine out on how I attended a victory party of bold sea rovers with only my maid to protect me. I shall fair give other ladies the vapours."

Her eyes danced. With Lucy, William reflected that one was never far from laughter. He had thought that she made sport of him, particularly, but now he thought she just made sport of the world.

"Your boatswain is entertaining my maid, I see," said Lucy, dryly.

William looked. The boatswain had his arm around the young girl while he explained some feat with vigorous motions of his other hand. "Mmm," said William, noncommittally.

The door opened again and Simon and Gwilym strolled in to investigate the noise. They looked around in puzzlement. Simon raised an eyebrow on spotting Lucy. "Welcome, Master Tunstall," said William. "Richards, fetch some mugs for our guests."

"Lady Dennys, Captain," Simon nodded to them. "Everyone seems in a fair mood."

"It's a victory party, Simon. Isn't it thrilling? Captain Hawkins and his gallant sea dogs killed the lunatic that has been terrorising London." Lucy gave William the Look.

"Ah, that's right," said William, flushing.

"Already, but how?" Simon was astonished. "How did the Watch not bring me word that the beast was out?"

William shrugged. "Some messenger arrived. It was dark, we didn't see her face."

"Her?"

"Him, I meant him. Slip of the tongue, Master Tunstall." William smiled, blandly.

"Then I suppose congratulations are in order, Captain." Simon still looked suspicious. Something was wrong but he was clearly not to be allowed to get to the bottom of it. He sipped his ale and held his tongue.

Gwilym walked up to Millie. He nodded at the boatswain who eyed him warily. "Evening, Millie."

Millie held her head high but she did not meet his eye. "Evening, Gwilym."

"Good party," Gwilym said. "You should have woken me and I would have come with you."

"I have to attend upon my mistress. Besides, Gwilym, it is not as if we have an understanding." Millie tossed her head in an unconscious mimic of Lucy. "You have made that clear enough."

Gwilym nodded. "I have to get a drink." He moved away.

Simon eased his breath out. Gwilym was a man in control of his actions but he was only human and affairs of the heart were always tricky. The secretary relaxed and enjoyed the party. The refreshment was good, a fine keg of "heavy," or strong, beer. Some of the sailors produced pipes and drums. They struck up sea shanties and the sailors danced around cutlasses.

"You are not joining in the dancing, Master Tunstall," observed William.

"I regret sea shanties are not in my repertory, Captain," said Simon. "Could your players strike up a lavolta?"

"Why not?" asked William. He clapped his hands for silence. "Lavolta, let's hear a lavolta."

The musicians conferred amongst themselves before striking up a fast-paced dancing piece. Simon dropped his cloak and sword belt and held out his hand to Lucy. "Milady, if you would do me the honour."

"It will be a pleasure, sir."

He held his hand out, palm down at shoulder height. Lucy placed her hand lightly on top of his and he escorted her to the centre of the room. Sailors moved back to clear the space.

"They make a striking couple do they not?" asked the boatswain in William's ear.

William glared at him.

Simon pivoted Lucy into position as she walked around him. She removed her hand and the two faced each other three feet apart. He bowed and she curtseyed. Then he moved close to her and placed his hands on her waist. She laid her hands on his shoulders. "One, two, three," Simon said in time to the music and they bounced sideways.

In the lavolta, the couple take energetic sideways leaps with the gentleman supporting the lady, hindered as she is by her layers of petticoats and topcoat. The partners dance to the man's right and left, then they spin and the lady jumps into the air boosted by her partner. The gentleman then catches her in his arms and steadies her as she lands. They spin in each other's arms and repeat the process until exhaustion sets in. The lavolta was the most extreme of a variety of fast dances known as "haute dance." Fast dances were reserved for the young; they were particularly demanding of the lady. Older people performed a "dance basse" such as the pavane where the dancer's feet never left the floor.

Elizabeth herself favoured the galliard, an haute dance that also included high jumps and was only slightly slower than a lavolta. Elizabeth's support for haute dance was essential because many of the more extreme Puritan groups would have liked it to be banned as a lewd demonstration. The Bishop of Ely thought it "the horrible vice of pestiferous dancing" and accused dancers of "kissing, smouching, and slabbering one of another and filthy groping and unclean handling." Others thought the elderly bishop to be jealous.

Sailors surrounded the couple, beating time and urging them on. Eventually, Lucy called halt. "Enough, Master Tunstall, enough. I am quite fatigued." William thought she looked fresh. It was Simon who was exhausted. The couple repeated the bow and curtsey and Simon led her from the floor to claps and cheers. Sailors pressed fresh beer mugs in their hands and they drank deeply.

When Lucy had refreshed herself, William claimed her hand. As an officer, he counted as a gentleman. He thought his old mum would be proud that her son danced with the aristocracy in the Tower itself. William lacked the elegance of the slim secretary but he was fit and strong, and he had a sailor's balance. He threw Lucy around unmercifully but she was fast and tough and exulted in the dynamics of the dance.

"I have never seen the captain dance with any woman like that before," said the boatswain.

"Methinks, I have never seen lavolta danced better," said Simon, with grudging admiration.

Lucy soared into the air and twisted, landing backwards in William's arms. "I am beaten, milady. You might be able to dance all night but I beg quarter." William found himself holding Lucy in his arms when the music ended. She tilted her head back to look at him. "You are restricting my breathing again, sir," said Lucy, archly.

"Methinks the lady does protest too much," William said boldly. He released her after a fractional squeeze. Her lips curled upward at the edges as he escorted her off the floor. She's making sport of me again, thought William happily. She likes me.

Lucy downed a small beer. "My maid and I should be to our beds," she said.

'Oh, must we go, Lucy?' asked Lilith.

'Hush, Lilith. A lady has to know when to leave the gentlemen, so that they can make merry unrestrained by gentle company.'

"I will escort you, milady," said Simon.

"No need, master," said Gwilym. "I can show the ladies to 'is 'ighness' apartment."

The ladies left, Lucy on Gwilym's arm and Millie following. Sailors waved their mugs and shouted their compliments to Lucy as she left. William showed her to the door.

"She seems very popular with the Swallows," said Simon to the boatswain.

"And why should she not be?" asked a passing sailor who had overheard. "She killed the demon."

"Be silent, Reynolds," said the boatswain. He went to intercept the man but Simon stopped him.

"I would hear it all," said Simon.

The drunken sailor rambled on. "That demon ripped Fletcher apart but she hoisted the bloody flag, reeled the monster in, slammed it down, and gutted it with that little knife of hers. It was just like watching a man catch a shark. All on her own she did it, as well," he said, admiringly.

Simon went cold. It was Lucy who acted as messenger, Lucy who tracked the demon, and Lucy who killed it. That explained a lot.

"You stupid bastard," Simon said to William when he returned from showing Lucy out. "How could you let her go demon hunting?"

"Hold on," said William.

"Then to let her fight for you." Words failed Simon at this point. "What sort of cowardly knave are you?"

"You will retract those words," said William. "No doubt they were spoken without thought."

"I retract nothing," said Simon. "I name you coward."

"Then I demand satisfaction," said William, and struck Simon across the face.

Light through the leaded window woke Lucy up. The sun had finally summoned the courage to rise over the curtain wall of the Bloody Tower. Its rays lit up Lucy's face. Lilith noticed that Lucy's brain rhythms had altered.

"Good morning, Lucy" said Lilith, primly. "I trust you slept well."

"Yes," said Lucy. She opened one eye to look at Lilith, who appeared to sit on the end of the bed. "I slept extremely well. I take it that was your doing."

"I thought you might have bad dreams. So I guided your sleep," said Lilith.

Lucy sighed. "It occurs to me, Lilith, that everything I see and hear might be a play staged by you, while you do something else with my body."

"I could do that," Lilith admitted. "But I haven't and I won't. I would never do that to my only friend. I always tell you when I play games with your sense of reality."

"I know, friend demon. I wish yesterday had been one of your dreams."

"It was real, Lucy," said Lilith. She grinned at Lucy. "You are only looking at a projection now, of course. So do you like the dress? It is 1960s chic. This is what a young lady wore in the first Shadow world that I visited."

Lilith had a small unremarkable brown cap perched on her head. What captured Lucy's attention was the dress. It was decorated in large black and white squares but the white was blinding and shiny, more like fresh whitewash than clothing material. It was high, collared almost like a clergyman's robes but, even if it was discreet at the bosom, it was riotously indiscreet everywhere else. It left Lilith's arms completely uncovered. The skirt was even worse. It clung tightly so there was no room for petticoats and it was cut four inches above the knee to show nearly all of Lilith's legs.

"Oh Lilith," Lucy said, laughing. "You surely have it wrong again. Fashions do change but these are undergarments. Another dress would have gone on top. No lady would walk around just in that. I can see all your limbs."

"No, really, Lucy. This is walking-out costume. Nothing goes on top, but a coat in inclement weather."

"Heavens," said Lucy. "Men in that world must have lost their sight or be much more resistant to a woman's charms than here."

"I have an hypothesis," said Lilith.

Lucy sighed.

"No, seriously, Lucy. I believe I am getting somewhere modelling human behaviour. Human sense organs register changes. So women change their clothes to continuously surprise men. As you know, men have limited intellect and hence little insight."

Lucy nodded.

"So the dresses have to keep changing what they reveal and what they cover. You notice the neck is as high as the hem."

A knock sounded at the door. Lilith faded gently away.

"Come," Lucy said.

Millie bustled in with a tray. "Good morning, ma'am. I thought I heard you rise. I have brought you a little cold collation from the kitchens and some small beer."

"Good morning, Millie. I did not expect to see you so early but you are very welcome nonetheless. Come help me dress while I eat." Lucy bounded out of bed to her dresser.

"You have such a good appetite these days, milady. The master is well pleased. He always thought that you picked at your food like a starling." Millie placed the tray in front of Lucy. The maid combed the girl's hair as she breakfasted.

"Some starling," said Lucy between mouthfuls. "I have been larger than any bird for many years, but I don't suppose Uncle Noticed."

"You know men, milady, unable to see what's under their noses. I thought your brown walking dress, as you are not expecting visitors."

Lucy waved assent and worked at her platter like a trencherman. Millie busied herself laying out the petticoats and dress.

"It was quite a night, ma'am."

"I saw you with the boatswain, Millie. Now you have two men in tow."

Millie helped Lucy into her clothes. "Two, ma'am? I am sure I don't know what you mean."

"Hm, Millie. I have seen you cast eyes at Gwilym."

"He likes to keep his options open, ma'am, so a girl has to do likewise," said Millie.

"I expect the men drank much more after we left, Millie. Let's hope Gwilym and the boatswain didn't come to blows over you."

"Apparently, there was quite a scene after we left, ma'am, but it was the gentlemen who fell out," said Millie.

"Really, Millie. What were they arguing about?" asked Lucy, struggling with a recalcitrant hook and not really paying attention.

"I am sure I wouldn't know, milady," said Millie.

Lucy looked sharply at her maid. Millie occupied herself with the hooks and steadfastly refused to catch her eye. Which meant she did know but was not going to tell Lucy, thought Lilith.

Lilith felt adrenaline kick in. Lucy's pulse suddenly shot up. 'What's wrong, Lucy?' Lilith asked.

Lucy ignored her. "How bad was their argument, Millie?"

"I am not supposed to say, milady."

"Where are they meeting? You must tell me, girl," said Lucy, frantically.

"Gwilym has already gone to act as Master Tunstall's second, milady. But I am not supposed to tell you."

"You silly goose, you let me chatter on." Lucy seized Millie by the arms. "Where?"

"The Lion Tower, by the royal zoo. But milady, your dress is not fully fastened," the maid wailed. Lucy slammed the door and ran out.

"You can't kill him. You know that you can't kill him," said the master, shaking his head.

"The whoreson called me coward," said William. "What of my honour?"

"I don't care if he accused you of pimping your mother around the Vatican's brothels. You still can't kill Sir Francis Walsingham's personal secretary. Think of your family and Plymouth. We need Walsingham's support. What use is your honour when we are all impoverished?"

"Enough, I'll settle for an apology," said William.

"Stay here then while I consult his second."

"Gwilym," said the master. "My principal is prepared to regard the matter settled by an apology."

Gwilym looked at Simon while the master regarded the sky. It was going to be a nice bright day.

"Absolutely not. He could have got Lady Dennys maimed or killed." Simon stuck his chin out. "An act of a coward, still say I."

Gwilym sighed. "I expect you heard, Master. My principal refuses to withdraw his remark."

The master sighed in echo of Gwilym and stalked back to William. "He refuses to withdraw."

"Then there is nothing else for it," said William. "We fight." He slapped the master on the arm. "Don't look so glum, Master. A milksop pen pusher won't put up much resistance. I'll play with him for a bit, give him a cut that he can show off to his doxy, and then retire, honour satisfied."

"Remember your training, Master Tunstall," said Gwilym. "He's a sea fighter with plenty of experience of close-in fighting. Stay well back and protect yourself. Recall the first rule—stay alive. Only move in to attack if he gets careless."

"Do you think I can win?" asked Simon.

"Of course you can," said Gwilym.

"Thank you for lying," said Simon and walked towards his opponent.

The master nodded and strode to the side of the chosen spot. Gwilym stood opposite him. "Take your places, gentlemen."

The duellists advanced with drawn swords and touched sword points.

"Gentlemen, fight," said the master, drawing the word out.

Simon backed off immediately, giving himself space. William advanced, making a series of exploratory cuts. The swords rang as Simon parried. He backed away after each of William's thrusts. Slightly puzzled William followed up. He launched a high cut to Simon's left. Simon parried and this time stepped forward inside

William's guard. He moved out of the parry into a high cut. William jumped and twisted to avoid the sword, his battle-trained reflexes cutting in before he could think. Simon's sword swished across William's body, the point slicing through his shirt and leaving a thin line of blood across his chest. The lions in the cages roared, excited by the clash of steel and the smell of blood.

"Hold!" said Gwilym and the master simultaneously.

"Blood has been drawn. Is your honour satisfied?" the master said to Simon.

"Yes," said Simon.

"Do you accept the result?" the master asked William.

"Damn your eyes, no," said William. "'Tis but a scratch. I fight on unless I get an apology."

The duellists assumed their places and the master started the fight again. William was angry now and he attacked Simon with strength and vigour. The secretary was soon in trouble, being beaten back with every blow of William's weapon. Simon stumbled and William launched a vicious overhead blow. It beat down Simon's sword and bit into his shoulder. Red blood flowed.

The seconds stopped the fight again to check that Simon could fight on. The wound was superficial. Each of the duellists was offered the chance to withdraw but both vowed to continue.

"Best of three?" asked Simon to William, with a jauntiness that he didn't feel.

William came in swinging. He was angry and fighting to kill. Both men were tiring so there was little dodging or clever tricks. This was a straight slashing match and William's greater size and endurance told. Simon was forced back, foot by foot. A blow smashed Simon to his knees. William swung his weapon in a high overhead arc to build momentum. Simon raised his sword desperately but this stroke could not be parried.

A slim form slipped between them and the hilt of William's sword smashed into a small hand with an audible thump. Blood spurted down the girl's arm. "What are you doing?" Lucy cried. "How could you?"

"Sweet Jesu sake—" began Simon.

"You stupid, stupid girl. I could have killed you," said William. "Why are you interfering in men's affairs?" He said, "Oh my God, your hand."

She pulled the sword out of his unresisting hand and it dropped, covered in her blood.

'Control trauma, shut down peripheral blood vessels, and build up shielding in the right hand,' thought Lilith to herself. 'Increase cell division in damaged area, oh, and I must remember to activate the immune system to *Clostridium* incursion.'

"It's a matter of honour, Lucy," said Simon.

"Men's honour. Boy's games," Lucy said. "Don't you selfish bastards think of anyone else but yourselves and your stupid honour?"

The men were shocked into silence to hear her swear.

"Go on then. Kill each other. The scandal will point straight at me. Leave me friendless and dishonoured but why will you care? You will be dead when it all comes out. It's me they'll punish. What of your promise to me, Master Tunstall? How will you fulfil it when you're dead?"

She burst into tears and turned away from them. Lilith reviewed her subroutines. She had blocked all pain reception from Lucy's hand because pain caused the girl distress. She now saw that a degree of pain was necessary for Lucy to monitor the condition of her body. Lilith thought it a cruel method but, nevertheless, she considered that she had to let some pain through.

The men saw Lucy gasp and clutch her hand. Blood dripped from it onto the lawn. Simon and William rushed to her but she shrugged them off, turning to Gwilym instead. He bandaged it tight to stop the bleeding and helped her to her chamber, calling for her maid.

"Now look what you've done," said Simon.

"Me?" asked William. "You brought on this stupid duel." He stopped. "Do you think she will lose the hand?"

"No," Simon said. "Lilith will cure it. I have seen this before."

"I don't understand why the sword didn't take her hand right off," said William.

Simon was about to hit the man when he realised that William was deeply upset. "Honestly," said Simon. "She will recover. You saw her fight."

William had put those events of that night into a compartment of his brain that he preferred to keep closed. Now he had to open it. Packenham had thrown her across the square into a wall. William himself had been sore for a week when Packenham had but elbowed him but Lucy was dancing only hours later after receiving a much worse blow. He really did not want to think about that.

Simon took his sword and thrust it into the earth, point first. What he was about to do next burned his soul but Lucy's needs came first. He held out his hand to William. "Captain Hawkins, I know you to be no coward but a gallant gentleman. Please accept my apology for false words spoken in anger."

William took his hand. "I accept gladly, sir. We have shed each other's blood and the matter of honour between us is closed. We shall not speak of it again.

Curious, William asked, "What did Lady Dennys mean by your promise to her?"

"I promised," said Simon, quietly and carefully, "to kill her with my own hand rather than see her burn. She is frightened of the fire."

"To kill her? Are you mad? Why should anyone burn her just because she does a little magic? She is Walsingham's niece."

"Lucy isn't a witch," said Simon. "She's possessed, you fool. Didn't you notice? What do you think Lilith is?"

"When you said Lilith, I thought you meant her herb-woman," said William.

"Lilith is a demon. You watched Lucy and Packenham fight in the mundane sphere. In the Other World, whatever demon was in him fought Lilith and Lilith proved the stronger."

"Possessed, is she? Poor little girl," said William. "But the cross didn't hurt her." He mulled this over.

William decided this was an opportune to clear up another issue. "What are your intentions to Lady Dennys?" William said to Simon.

"Intentions?" asked Simon, genuinely baffled.

"You and she are close. Do you seek her hand?" asked William.

"My father was a clerk, as was his father before him. What you suggest is impossible. I have known Lucy since she was but a small child. I love her like a sister." Simon was not being entirely honest about his feelings but he spoke truly about his intentions.

"Then you and I must be friends, Master Tunstall." William slipped his arm inside Simon's. "For I intend to win her as my wife. I could not determine how such an enterprise might be done but now I see clearly. I shall free her of the demon and Walsingham will give her to me in gratitude. Come, Master Tunstall, tell me all you know."

Behind them, two of the lions snarled and spat at each other.

"Mad, quite mad," said Simon, but he followed anyway.

Act 14, The Safe House

Walsingham chaired the meeting as usual. Simon attended to take notes and William to represent the enforcement end of the operation. Pooley was the star, though, Pooley and his watcher teams. The spy handed Walsingham every address visited by Ridolphi.

"Let me see," said Walsingham. "He spends a great deal of time at the Spanish Embassy. Hmmm. I see we have the usual list of suspects. He has been passing money around Catholic sympathisers. Make a note of the names, Tunstall. We will mount a series of raids after the next batch of Jesuits arrive. I suspect that we may pick up a few hiding at these addresses. Of course, the Spanish secret service would not use any of these people. Too obvious."

"What are we looking for?" asked William, fascinated. Secret service methodology was a new experience.

"A safe house for the plotters. De Mendoza will use an innocuous address that has no obvious links with known English Catholic families or the Spanish themselves," said Walsingham. "I see Ridolphi visits Madame Bouvier's hostel for young ladies at regular intervals. I wonder what His Holiness would say about that."

Simon and Pooley laughed; William looked baffled.

"It's a French brothel," Simon whispered in William's ear.

"Now this is more promising, a previously unknown address, the White Hart boarding house. Where would that be, Pooley?"

217

"It's a run-down area up in the south-central region below Watling Street," said Pooley.

"No access to the city wall or the river then?" Walsingham said.

"No, sir," confirmed Pooley.

"Useless for de Mendoza's purpose then. He needs a location suitable for getting his agents in and out of the city at night. Ridolphi visited a deserted house on four occasions. Stink Lane, where is that?"

"Below Thames Street, sir," said Pooley.

"On the river?"

"Yes, sir, adjoining Billingsgate Dock," said Pooley.

"Easy access to the river and from there to anywhere in the world," said Walsingham. "Well done, Pooley, I think you have found a safe house. So how are you going to raid it, Captain?"

"What are my exact objectives?" asked William. He felt on firm ground now they had a military enterprise to discuss.

Walsingham ticked them off on his fingers. "I want the place secured. I want any documents and other objects in perfect condition. They will have a weighted bag handy to dump sensitive material in the Thames. I want everybody in there taken, preferably alive. I want it done quietly so I can set up a trap in the house to pick up morsels, before the Spanish realise that their safe house is blown."

"That won't be easy," said William.

"If it was easy then I wouldn't have had to call on one of John Hawkins' best men to arrange the enterprise, would I, Captain? Hmmm? Drake isn't available so I have you instead." Walsingham put his hands together as if in prayer.

William flushed with pleasure. He knew Walsingham was building up his morale, he had done the same himself too often not to recognise the trick, but he was extraordinarily pleased nonetheless. To be mentioned in the same sentence as Drake was most satisfying.

There will be no holding the arrogant, provincial whoreson now, thought Simon. Long experience allowed him to keep a straight face but he was disturbed. Walsingham would sing a different tune if he knew the captain's intentions towards his niece.

"Can you draw me the layout of the area, Pooley?" asked William.

The spy chalked an outline on a slate.

"Do you have a plan, Captain?" asked Walsingham.

"The house is right on the river?" He looked to Pooley for confirmation. The spy nodded. "Then we will need to enter from the land and river at the exact selfsame moment. Is there a place where a lookout man can see both points?"

"Here, Captain, right at the head of the dock." Pooley marked a spot on the slate.

"Then we can do it, Sir Francis."

"Tomorrow then, Captain. Early while they are still asleep. Tunstall, go you with them to search for documents and evidence. You know what I need."

Lucy was back at her seat outside the window with a book lent to her by the keeper. She often visited him on his lonely watch and he had taken a shine to her. Gwilym sat by her with his feet outstretched.

"I am quite safe now the monster is dead, Gwilym," said Lucy.

"I suspect from what I 'ave heard that you were quite safe before, 'ighness," said Gwilym. "But 'is nibs 'as given me clear instructions and I don't care to contradict him."

The pair sat for a while in the sun.

"It's odd, 'ighness. I find you 'ere whenever 'is nibs 'as a meeting in 'is rooms."

"Has he a meeting, Gwilym?" Lucy said innocently. "One could not hear anything from here anyway."

"I certainly couldn't, 'ighness. But what can you 'ear, I wonder?"

Whoops, humans were so intuitive, thought Lilith. Their sharp, little minds could jump over chasms of ignorance to truth. She was still not sure how they did it. She had monitored Lucy's brain when the girl was using intuitive thinking many times. But she still did not understand the process. The People thought with small steps along determined routes but they did it very fast. Lucy thought slowly but in jumps. Lilith suspected that many of the intermediate linkages were being made but on some subconscious level.

"They have found a *safe house*," the girl used the unfamiliar term self-consciously. "Captain Hawkins intends to raid it tomorrow morning."

"And you want to go as well?" asked Gwilym.

"What if they find another demon? They would be massacred." Lucy sucked on a nail pensively.

Gwilym snorted. "That bunch ain't so easily massacred, 'ighness. They will feel that they 'ave to look after you, if you go as well. Then there is 'is nibs to consider."

"Gwilym, I can make the difference. I know I can. Oh, I wish I had been born a boy." She stamped her foot.

"Well miss, I am sure God 'ad 'is purpose in making you a maid." Gwilym smiled at her.

Lilith noticed that Lucy blushed and added the data to her model.

"I must go with them, Gwilym. How can I persuade them?"

"You will need to convince that captain. He will be loath to take you for two reasons. Firstly, he will be reluctant to annoy 'is nibs and secondly—he's set his cap at you and will be terrified of getting you hurt."

Lucy flushed again. It seemed to be a day for it. "Stuff and nonsense, Gwilym. Sir Francis would never give me to a sea rover. The idea!"

Gwilym ignored her. "If you must go then you 'ave to find reasons to overcome those objections. As to your protection, why 'ighness you may remind 'em that I am charged with that."

"You don't have to come, Gwilym. There is no reason for you to be put in danger as well."

He just looked at her.

"I am sorry, Gwilym. That was a foolish remark of a silly girl. Forgive me," she said. "My uncle has charged you with my safety so of course you would follow me down to hell, if necessary."

"Not to worry, 'ighness. You weren't thinking of trespassing on Beelzebub's estates were you?"

"Not at present," said Lucy. "There is enough wickedness in London for me. But I will make sure you are the first to know if I intend a descent to the Pit."

A door opened and Simon and William walked out in deep conversation. "They do seem to be such pals now," said Lucy.

'Are you not pleased that their quarrel is reconciled?' thought Lilith.

'Yeees,' thought Lucy. 'But I don't see why they have to be so thick with each other. It unnerves me.'

Lilith's human behaviour model ran round its loop. Well, well, she thought. Lucy is worried that they will talk about her. But why should that bother the girl?

"Captain, Master Tunstall," said Lucy. "How intimate is your conversation? Do I interrupt?"

"You never interrupt, Lady Dennis," said William. "How can such beauty ever be an interruption?"

Simon's lips curled. Watching the captain flirt was like watching a cow ice-skating.

'My, isn't he gallant?' thought Lilith, admiringly.

Lucy lowered her head modestly and then looked up at William through her lashes. "Why, Captain, how gallant you are."

Simon wondered what she was up to. He knew Lucy far better than William. She was never more devious than when she adopted her "little lost girl among men" pose.

Lucy took his arm. "There was a small matter you can help me with," she said.

She was actually simpering, Simon noted with alarm. Oh well, the gallant sea dog would learn the hard way. The mariners might sing that "all the nice girls like a sailor" but, in Simon's experience, all the nice girls liked a titled gentleman with five thousand pounds a year income from his estates. Lucy was after something.

It was like watching a boat getting it wrong shooting London Bridge. Everyone could see that it would come to no good but there was nothing anyone could do. The water carried events inexorably on to disaster.

"Anything in my power is yours, milady," William said.

"Thank you, Captain," Lucy positively purred. "Then I will come with you on the raid tomorrow."

"What!" William looked horrified.

And there is the disaster, thought Simon with grim amusement. Let's see you get out of this one, my bold salt.

"Under no circumstances," said William. "How do you know about the raid?"

"You promised," said Lucy, ignoring his question. "You gave your word."

"I did not!" said William.

"Anything in your power, you said." She pouted and stamped her foot.

"Yes, but—" said William, trying to get a word in.

"Just because I am a weak and feeble girl, you think you can cozen and ignore me."

Simon choked back a laugh. Queen Elizabeth was fond of the weak-and-feeble woman line, usually just before cutting some poor bastard off at the knees. Lucy had obviously been studying her technique.

"I don't—" said William.

"It's not fair," said Lucy, stamping her foot again.

Here come the tears, thought Simon. That's the next weapon in her formidable armoury.

"And all I am trying to do is protect you," Lucy sobbed.

"Protect me!" said William, in astonishment. The concept of him needing protection was a little difficult to come to terms with.

"Very well, if you won't let me come with you then I shall have to do the job alone," said Lucy.

"Out of the question. You may be strong and fast but you are not bulletproof. One unlucky shot, that's all it takes, my lady, to make you worm food. I have made my decision and it's final. You are not going near that house."

"And how will you stop me?" she asked.

That of course is the rub, thought William. He could order her and be disobeyed. He could not physically restrain her. It was socially unacceptable and probably practically impossible due to that damn demon she carried around with her. That demon had got to go. He couldn't even put Lucy across his knee and administer the smacking she so richly deserved. The spoilt little rich girl just did not seem to understand the danger.

He controlled his anger with an almost physical effort. William was not used to being contradicted to his face in this way. When they married, Lucy would have to know her place. The rational part of his mind pointed out that the girl would probably have a very clear idea of her place; it just wouldn't coincide with his view. The stupid irrelevance of his thoughts made him laugh out loud, which broke the argument.

Lucy looked at him with a strange expression.

'A man who can laugh at his own pomposity is a rare catch,' thought Lilith. 'I like your sea captain, Lucy.'

'He's not *my* sea captain,' thought Lucy, carefully concealing her underlying thoughts from Lilith.

"I will do a deal with you, Lady Dennys. You can come with us . . ." said William, carefully.

Lucy squeaked and struck her hands together.

"On one condition," William continued, over her intervention. "An enterprise can only have one commander or it is lost. You will consider yourself a soldier in my service and obey my orders without argument. Without argument and with alacrity, milady."

"Of course, Captain. I shall consider myself your servant in this affair." Lucy held her hands meekly in front of her, the epitome of womanly obedience. She didn't fool William for a moment.

The sun was making one of his dazzling appearances over London. The early morning showers had cleaned the air and washed away some of London's waste. Now the sunlight glittered off the wet city and sparkled along the Thames. Around Billingsgate dock, homeless beggars stirred in the doorways and alcoves where they had taken shelter. Bright rays of light burst through gaps in black towering clouds. England's fickle weather gods were still undecided whether to grant the people of London sun or rain so were supplying a little of each.

A seafaring man strolled down to the dock and took the air. He positioned himself on a convenient timber and produced a pipe. That the man indulged in the new vice of smoking marked him as well travelled, an oceanic sailor, then, rather than a coast-crawler. Lighting the pipe was a long and complex affair. Smethwick appeared fully engrossed in the task.

A barge sailed up the Thames past the custom houses and legal quays that clustered against the river to the west of the Bloody Tower. The vessel was piled high with cargo that was covered by an oiled cloth. The crew of three lounged unconcerned on the deck. One still appeared to be asleep. Early morning barges like these carried the night catch from the fishing fleet to Billingsgate. Her Majesty's hungry London subjects depended on them and the first delivery of the morning got best price.

The seafaring man watched the barge casually. He took his cap off and stretched, waving the garment in the air. A man and woman walked arm in arm across the head of the dock. The man was dressed in cheap but flashy clothes. He clearly worked with his head rather than his hands. He looked like a pox doctor's clerk. His doxy was no better. She wore a cheap imitation of a fashion dress and her makeup was far too heavy for one so young. Possibly the white ceruse that covered her face hid the ravages of smallpox or, indeed, some other pox. The couple argued as they walked. She slapped his face. He grabbed her arm and pushed her forward. She stumbled and responded with furious accusations. Smethwick chuckled and pulled on his pipe.

The barge sailed straight past Billingsgate dock towards London Bridge. The master shook his head at the crew. Fishmonger's Hall, with its associated market, was just the other side, above Old Swan Stairs, but a fish barge could never shoot the bridge safely. That was why Billingsgate dock was where it was. The barge crew seemed to wake up late to their predicament and they hastily tried to turn the boat.

The couple walked up Stink Lane, still arguing. The man dragged the doxy along. They stopped outside a doorway as their dispute reached a climax. The clerk held the woman by the forearms and shook her. The beggars watched with curiosity.

On the river, things were not going well. The barge's bow had come round too slowly. It crashed sideways into the embankment where a house overhung the river. Somehow the crew stayed on their feet. They flung grapnels up at the house's windows. The oiled cloth was flung aside to reveal men armed with pistols and cutlasses. The men clustered around the ropes and began to climb.

Smethwick blew a piercing blast on a seaman's whistle. The couple stopped arguing. The man stepped back. The girl jumped into the air and unleashed a devastating high kick. The entire door frame burst into the house with the door still attached. The girl fell down onto her bottom but rolled clear. All round her beggars jumped to their feet with surprising athleticism, producing weapons from under their rags. They disappeared through the shattered doorway.

One bulky beggar made straight for the girl. "You are all right, 'ighness?" asked Gwilym. The girl nodded and moved slightly as if to enter the doorway. Gwilym touched her gently on the arm with one finger.

"I recall my promise to Captain Hawkins. I will wait for his signal before I enter," she said, impatiently.

Gwilym and Simon exchanged glances. Any man who planned his actions on the expectation that a woman would keep her word was a fool, a fool who deserved all the grief that he would undoubtedly receive, thought Simon. Women were flighty, inconstant creatures. Blaming them for changing their mind was like blaming the sea for the tides changing. It was part of their nature.

William led the charge through the shattered door frame, followed by a half-dozen Swallows. Clattering footsteps sounded up the stairs. "Spread out along the ground floor," he said to his men. "I will take the top."

He ran up the stairs. A door slammed shut in front of him. He tried the handle but it was locked. "If the maid can do it . . . !"

William kicked the door around the lock. Wood splintered but it held. He backed up and shoulder barged the panel. This time it gave. William stumbled as he went into the room beyond. He found himself on his knees in front of a man pointing a pistol at him. William looked down the barrel at minimum range. The man couldn't miss. Such an ending was always a distinct possibility for a sea dog, even one as successful as William. He was philosophical about his chances of reaching old age and had faced death before, but this time he had a sense of loss, a sense of unfinished business with Lucy Dennys. The man grinned savagely and pulled the trigger.

William watched the fuse come down on the powder in the priming pan. The powder ignited with a hiss and flash of white smoke. William closed his eyes waiting for the main discharge. It never came. The man's grin faded; he looked in horror at the misfired weapon and threw it at William.

William beat it away with his cutlass. The man threw himself at William in a desperate effort to escape. William struck him on the chin with the handguard of his cutlass. The man dropped without a sound. A sailor rushed inside, waving a pistol, and fell headlong over William's victim. His pistol went off and blew a hole in the wall.

William's voice bellowed through the broken door. "The devil take you, Harrison. Watch what you're doing. You could have shot someone. You could have shot me!"

There was a long pause then William stuck his head out of the doorway. "You may come in now, milady. We have secured the building."

Lucy and Gwilym walked over the broken door frame. Strong wooden bars had secured the door and they were still in their brackets but to no avail. Lucy's kick had pulled the brackets clean out of the wall.

"Oh dear. Sir Francis wanted to use this house as bait. I rather think that the damage will prejudice that. Only a very stupid Spanish agent could fail to notice something was wrong. Remind me never to annoy you, milady," said William.

Gwilym just smiled.

The sea dogs searched the house with their usual finesse. There were a great many smashing and breaking sounds. They had brought housebreaking tools with them. The boatswain appeared out of a front room that overlooked the river. He held a scrawny man by the neck like a kitten. In the other hand, he had a set of horse saddlebags.

"Matey here was shoving these out of the river window as I was climbing in," said the boatswain.

"This is what Sir Francis wants," said Simon. "The important information will be in here." He opened the bags and pulled out folded letters and documents. "It's in code," Simon said. "That's a good sign. The papers must be important. It would be helpful if your men could find the decoding key."

Simon found stones at the bottom of the bags. "My congratulations, Captain, on your crew's skill. All would have been lost if this had gone in the Thames."

William said nothing but he was clearly pleased. He pulled up the scrawny man's head to look at him. Scrawny spat at William. "You'll get nothing from me," he said, spitefully.

"Oh good, a blusterer," said Gwilym. "They break quickly when you put them on the rack. It's the quiet ones that you have to use red-hot irons on." The man said nothing more but he turned pale.

"Sir, look at this," said a seaman to William. The man held a small chest that was securely bound in iron. "I'll open it," said another sailor and put a pistol to the lock.

"Stop, you whoreson," said the boatswain. Then to Lucy, "Begging your pardon, ma'am."

"You will spray us all with iron and lead, you fool," said William, angrily.

"Mayhap, I can help," said Lucy.

She produced her blade, Dee's dagger. For a moment she just stood there as if gathering her strength. The astrological symbols on the weapon glowed with red fire and the familiar sparkles gathered in Lucy's dark eyes. In a swift movement, she thrust the tip of the dagger into the gap between the lid and the body of the chest. The blade cut straight through the iron tongue of the lock as if it were paper. William flipped open the lid. Gold and silver coins gleamed.

William slammed the lid shut. "Boatswain, take you charge of this. Put it in the barge."

"So Ridolphi stashed the Vatican's pay-chest here," said Simon.

"I claim booty shares for the *Swallow*'s crew," said William.

Some sailors cheered.

"Silence those men, boatswain. I will brook no indiscipline," said William. "Master Tunstall and Lady Dennys will get officer's shares, Gwilym a leading seaman's and Sir Francis the owner's tranche."

"I will get some money of my own?" asked Lucy, in excitement. "I have never had any money of my own before."

William was momentarily confused. Lucy was heiress to a great estate. She was one of the wealthiest girls in England. Then he understood. Lucy might be the heiress but Sir Francis controlled her estate as the law decreed. And he would continue to so do until she married whereupon her husband would own it all. Lucy had never had any money that was hers to spend before. Not that she ever went short of anything but *she* did not buy it. He had an insight into how her experience of life had conditioned her personality. No wonder Lucy could appear so sophisticated in some circumstances and so childlike in others. She witnessed some of the great affairs of state but had less independence or control of her life than a dockside tavern girl. He resolved to be more patient with her in the future.

The search continued but nothing further was found. William was about to call it a day when Simon grasped his arm. "Where are the cellars, Captain? All waterside houses in London have cellars. Many old houses have underground tunnels as well, that connect to the riverbank or other buildings."

"Cellars," said William to the Swallows. "Find me the cellars."

They got to work but no amount of tapping on floors or ripping up floorboards could locate anything.

"Mayhap, there are no cellars," said William.

"Not likely." Simon shook his head.

"Mayhap I can help," said Lucy. She knelt in the middle of the ground floor main room and produced a diamond.

"I am going to work white magic," Lucy said to the men. "Leave now if it bothers you."

"Naaah," said the boatswain. "I always go to the wisewoman to get me boils fixed after a long voyage. Bit 'o white magic never did no harm to anyone."

Lucy nodded. "Please all be silent then, I need to concentrate."

She cut a circle in the floor around her using the athame. "Stay outside of this circle when I work the spell. I am going to use light magic to construct a cone of power. When I release it, the spell will track past magics."

Lucy paused as if trying to work out what to say. "Before I start," she said, diffidently, "it would help if a man gave me the fivefold kiss. This is difficult, you see, and the kiss helps focus the magic."

"That would be my job, Lady Dennys," said William. "What do you want me to do?"

Lucy knelt and placed her hands palm up on her knees. "You kiss me on the hands and knees and lastly my mouth. That makes the sign of the pentagram. You say 'I give you my power,' and it's done. It has to be a man, you see. Only a man can give me power."

William knelt in front of her. Then he bent his head and kissed her hands, her knees, and gently on her lips. He looked at her gravely, "I give you my power, milady."

Maybe he imagined it, but he thought he caught a sigh and a faint mist moving from his lips to hers as they parted.

She stared at the diamond and began to sing.
"My fancy did I fix
"in faithful form and frame,
"in hope there should no blustering blast
"have power to move the same.
"And as the Gods do know
"and the world can witness clear,
"I never served another Saint
"nor Idol other where."

She sang quietly but her voice seemed to grow until it filled the room. The diamond sparkled in time to the song.
"But one, and that was he
"whom I in heart did shrine,
"and made account that precious pearl
"and jewel rich was mine."

The diamond glowed brighter and brighter throbbing in time to the rhythm of the song. The light around the diamond rotated and began to send off spirals. William was reminded of a firework called a Saint Katherine's Wheel. It was a cloth tube of gunpowder wrapped around a wheel nailed to a post such that it spun freely. When the powder was lit at one end, the wheel was forced around creating a whirlpool of fire.

Lucy spread her arms. The tendrils of rotating light spread out, breaking through the circle cut in the floor. The men backed away in alarm. William strode forward until the whirlpool of light spun through his legs. He stood head up, legs apart, one hand on his sword hilt and the other on his hip. A tendril of light curled around his leg.

Lucy spoke, "Look at him, big arrogant man. I suppose he isn't scared of anything?"

Except that Lucy had not said anything. She still sang into the diamond.

"No toile nor labour great
"could weary me herein,
"for still I had a steely heart
"the golden prize to win.
"And sure my suite was heard
"I spent no time in vain,
"a grant of friendship at his hand
"did quite remove my pain."

Lucy's voice was in his head. A second person answered the girl. This was a woman with a lower husky sound. Her accent was passing strange. The consonants were hard and the vowels short. She spoke an English that William had never heard before.

"You are too hard on him. He just wants to show his men that there is nothing to be frightened about. I think your sea captain looks rather dishy."

Lucy's voice answered, "Dishy? Even your words for men involve food, glutton demon. And, as I keep telling you, he is not *my* sea captain."

"I rather think he is," said the strangely accented woman. "And you could do a lot worse, girl."

The light swirl moved past William and the voices faded away. Lucy continued singing.

"With solemn vow and released dove
"was knit the true tied knot,
"and friendly did we treat of love
"as place and time we got.
"Now would we send our sighs
"as far as they might go,
"now would we work with open ties
"to blaze our inward show."

Somehow, the magic had connected Lucy's mind to his. William also realised that the second voice in Lucy's head must have been the demon that possessed her. William had not given much thought to what Lucy must be experiencing but he had not expected possession to involve womanly squabbles over men. Somehow demons should be more, well, demonic. Another thought struck him. They had been talking about him and the demon had been pressing his suit to Lucy. This was clearly a demon of unusual intelligence and sensibility. It still had to go, of course, but perhaps not quite yet.

The spirals of light spread out to encompass the room and the raiding party. No one else showed any reaction. So only William could connect to Lucy in this way. He had given part of himself to her through the fivefold kiss so now they were entwined.

The room winked in white light. Traces of evil-looking purple and bilious green pulsed out of synchronicity from various places. Shadowy green and purple ghosts of men and other things faded in and out of reality, things whose forms were horrible to behold. An outline of a door appeared in purple in the panelling of one of the walls. Lucy raised her arm and pointed to it. "There. That is the source of the contamination. The cellar is there." Then she pitched over and the pulsing light winked out.

William caught her in his arms. "Steady, lady."

She clung to him for a second but recovered almost immediately. "This is getting to be a habit, Captain. Breathing, remember? I have to breathe."

He held her a moment longer than necessary and whispered in her ear, "Your demon was right, milady. I was just putting on a show for my men; actually, I was terrified. Incidentally, you are quite dishy yourself, whatever that means."

Her eyes widened in shock and she put a hand up to her mouth, "Oh!"

I have you, milady, William thought. He had the weather gauge on her for the first time since they had met. That would give her something to ponder.

The diamond was just a diamond again. Once the spell was over the hidden door was invisible but William had marked its position. He gestured to the boatswain who spat on his hands and seized a hammer. Three blows stove in the panelling to reveal a closet.

Inside on the floor was a trapdoor. William reached forward to raise it. Lucy saw him move as if in slow motion. "Nooooo," she screamed, crossing the floor in a single leap. Lucy seized William and threw him back against a wall.

"Steady, milady, steady. I have to breathe as well," he said.

"There is great danger down there. Trust me," said Lucy. "I must go first."

"I trust your intuition of danger," said William. "That is why I shall lead, milady. You promised to obey me. Remember."

"I promised to obey the orders of my captain," said Lucy. "Not the wilful behaviour of a stubborn boy. You must let me go first, William, for I am the best choice. Let me do what God has ordered for me."

William stood silent while his head argued with his heart.

"She is right, Captain," said the boatswain.

"You are silent, Master Tunstall," said William.

"I was just thinking that I wish I had half your courage, William. I do not envy you in this but—Lady Dennys is right. I will not take cover in equivocation."

William ground his teeth. "Devil take you all. Very well. You lead, milady. I shall follow close behind you."

"Close behind me, Captain," said Gwilym. "I guard 'er 'ighness' back."

"Behind you then, damn you all." William flung down his cutlass.

"Thank you, Captain." Lucy kissed him on the cheek. "You may catch me if I fall but remember that I have to breathe."

"I am keen that you continue to breathe, milady, and I shall always catch you if you fall." William failed to see any humour in this.

"I shall also come," said Simon.

"You most certainly will not," said William, savagely. "You instructed me on duty, Master Tunstall, now I tell you that yours is to stay here safely. You are to get my men out and make sure Sir Francis has a full report if we do not return. I want no rescue missions, understand?" Then his voice softened. "No one doubts your courage, Simon. Now you must do the most difficult job of all."

'Are you ready, Lilith?' thought Lucy.

Lilith was more than ready. She was waiting expectantly.

'Yes, Lucy, I will switch you to dark vision as soon as the light fades. Remember that you must allow for the lack of colour and perspective.'

Lilith suspected that they were all in grave danger. She had not liked the look of the things revealed as shadow echoes by the magic spell, things that could not have originated in this world. She suspected that there was a portal nearby. If so, it would have to be eliminated.

Lucy stood for a moment holding her dagger. Her skin glowed and her hair rustled as if in a wind. The glyphs on her dagger glowed deep red. She bent down and flipped open the heavy trapdoor with one hand.

A set of wooden stairs descended steeply into the dark. Lilith extended her senses to maximum as Lucy walked down carefully. She also piggybacked through Lucy's senses to get maximum coverage of the electromagnetic and mechanical spectrum. The stairs had no guardrails but were essentially sound. The girl stopped at the bottom and looked around the cellar carefully. On the riverside of the cellar was a bricked-up archway. Lucy walked over to it and ran her hands along the brickwork.

'It feels old and solid to me, Lilith. These bricks have been here for years. What do you think?'

Lilith extended the lobes of her gravitonic senses. 'I agree and the tunnel beyond the bricks appears to be choked with mud. I think this is a dead end.'

Lucy nodded in the dark. 'One final test.'

She pulled her hand back and rammed the heel of her wrist hard into the brickwork with a loud thud. Dust flew and bricks cracked but the wall was unmoved. Lilith immediately ran diagnostic routines on Lucy's body. The results were most gratifying. The energy fields had protected Lucy completely. I am, Lilith thought to herself, getting good at this.

Candles appeared on the stairs. Gwilym and William joined her on the cellar floor.

"Do you not need a candle, milady?" asked William.

"No, I can see better if I keep my night vision," she said.

William thought her answer odd, as no one had any night vision in the complete absence of light, no one who was not possessed, that is. He noticed that she avoided looking at the candle directly but, nonetheless, silver reflected from her eyes. They looked hard and faceted, almost crystalline, almost like an insect's. He shuddered, then was ashamed. She deserved better from him than ignorant fear but it was difficult to accept her condition, especially as most of the time she looked most wonderfully human.

Lucy carefully studied her surroundings then she cleared away dirt from one corner. William helped her. Another trapdoor lay hidden under a thin layer of floor rushes. It was stiff and awkward. Lucy needed both hands to lift it so she sheathed her blade. A foul smell emerged, like a slaughterhouse in summer.

'Careful, Lucy,' thought Lilith. 'I suspect that there is a portal nearby.'

'I know, Lilith.'

"A cellar under a cellar. I suspect that this was used for stashing smuggled contraband. They would bring it in by the river tunnel then hide it down here," William said.

Lucy knelt and stuck her head down the hole. "I can't see any steps but the drop is less than two yards."

Before any one could object, she dropped down.

"'Ere, 'old my candle," said Gwilym to William. He dropped down after her. William handed the candles down then followed. The ceiling was so low that the two men had to stoop.

"Christ's blood, what a smell," William said, holding his nose. "What are those?"

Small objects lay scattered around, half buried in mud. The under-cellar floor must be very close to the water table.

'Lucy, I have analysed DNA residues in the air as you breathe. They come from mammalian tissue and bone,' said Lilith.

'And that means?' asked Lucy.

'Animals,' said Lilith, 'including humans.'

"Bones and body parts," said Lucy to William, in a matter-of-fact way. "I think some of them are human."

"It's a charnel house." William was horrified. "Was this Packenham's lair?"

"I don't think so," Lucy said. "My location spell put him in north London. I don't think he travelled very far from his daytime rest to hunt victims by the time that we found him. The demonic possession was very strong within him by then and his hunger for blood was all-controlling."

"So something else lives 'ere. Careful, 'ighness." Gwilym moved close in behind her.

"There's an archway over there," Lucy said, and moved towards it before one of the men could object. Inside the arch was a brick-lined tunnel that was so low even Lucy had to stoop. Gwilym and William followed as best they could. The light from their candles threw Lucy's shadow forward but she could not see it. She saw instead the monochrome world of shades of heat. The wet floor was dark but the bricks stood out as they radiated thin sheets of warmth that had leached down from the morning sun.

'Lucy, I can sense a source of power up ahead,' thought Lilith. 'Halt.'

Lucy stopped so quickly that the men bumped into her.

"Are you all right, 'ighness,' said Gwilym.

"Yes, just a moment," she said.

'What's it doing? Is it a monster?' thought Lucy.

'No, I sense a device. I don't think it's functioning at the moment. It appears powered-down,' thought Lilith.

Lucy inched forward, slowly, followed by the men. The tunnel opened out into another brick-lined cellar. At the far end was a table with various religious paraphernalia on top.

"There's a passage way above that altar. I can see lit candles," William said, softly.

Lilith, and hence Lucy as their senses were merged, saw a flat rectangular panel vibrating with gravitational energy. Lilith was instantly on her guard. She probed the device but could not penetrate the surface.

"Move your candle up and down, Gwilym," Lucy said.

The man did so and the light at the far end faithfully followed him.

"It's a mirror," said William in wonder. "I have never seen such a large mirror."

"Yes, a mirror," said Lucy. "And mirrors are windows to the Other World."

Lilith thought that Lucy was probably right. They had found the portal. The girl moved forward slowly towards the altar. To the men, the mirror was a source of flickering light reflected from their candles. In Lucy's dark sight, the mirror was a black rectangle against the grey bricks. To Lilith's gravitonic senses, ripples of energy passed backwards and forwards, distorting the mirror's surface.

Lucy reached a hand out towards the mirror and touched it with her finger. It was like pushing against a membrane of semisolidified pitch or an animal's body. Her finger made an indentation. She pushed harder and met resistance. Lucy pulled her finger out and the surface sprang back, setting of an oscillation of ripples. The vibrations bounced of the edges of the mirror crisscrossing each other until the surface heaved like a turbulent sea. Energy leaked from it. Lilith detected electromagnetic energy at the various frequencies Lucy's body could detect. Probably, other wavelengths were also involved. That worried Lilith, as some wavelengths could be very destructive to human bodies. She set up a subroutine to monitor molecular ionisation damage.

Something else that was much worse emanated from the mirror, gravitons. That implied crossdimensional activity.

To Lucy's dark sight, the mirror began to glow. To Lilith's gravitonic senses, the surface was shot through with lightninglike gravitational energy. The men said nothing so Lilith assumed that to them it was still just a mirror. The energy continued to build up.

'Lucy, this is dangerous,' thought Lilith. 'Something is about to happen.'

"Captain, Gwilym, back up. I think I have done something foolish," Lucy said, urgently.

The men's large bodies fitted the narrow tunnel like bottle stoppers. They moved clumsily to turn around. Lucy faced the mirror. She drew out her dagger and its fiery warmth filled the tunnel with dull red light as her body energised the blade. The mirror vibrated with power and then disgorged energy with a thud that could be felt as power slammed the air. A tentacle poked through the mirror. It waved around, its tip seeming to smell the room. The tip orientated on Lucy.

'The mirror's a portal; something's coming through. Danger, Lucy, danger.' Lilith was extremely agitated.

"I can see that, Lilith." Unnerved, Lucy vocalised her thoughts. "For God's sake, hurry, gentlemen. We soon won't be alone in here."

The tentacle struck like a cobra. It shot forward and curled around Lucy's ankles, whipping her legs out from under her. She crashed back into Gwilym, starting a chain reaction that had them all on the ground. The tentacle curled around her leg and gripped hard, pulling her towards the mirror. The men grabbed at her. Lucy slashed the tentacle with her knife. Lilith rammed power into the metal. The blade cut easily through the flesh, burning it away with a hiss of smoke. A terrible gurgling scream sounded from the Other World.

Gotcha, thought Lilith. I'll bet you never expected a gravitonically powered weapon, demon.

Lucy's blade had cut clean through and the tip of the tentacle flopped to the ground, twisting and coiling like a snake with the head cut off. Green slime pumped out. The injured tentacle thrashed the air and grabbed her around the legs. More tentacles slid through the mirror. One grabbed Lucy around the waist. Another entangled her right arm, so that she couldn't use her blade.

Lilith was horrified. She had underestimated the monster. The strains on Lucy's small body were immense. Lilith poured gravitonic power into Lucy's cells at a level she would not normally have dared. Lucy's body crackled with the energy fields that held her together. Without those fields, the tentacles would have ripped her apart. Lucy stuck her left hand into the brickwork to get a handhold and her companions held her tight. But it was no use, the pull of the tentacles was too strong and, inch by inch, they dragged her towards the mirror. Her companions clung desperately to her and were dragged along with her.

A head of horror thrust through the mirror. It was too large but it seemed boneless and able to distort its shape. The snout had a round mouth surrounded by sharp feeding palps that clacked against each other in endless rhythms. Inside the mouth, serrated grinding plates rotated. As the head oozed further through, a large bulbous eye popped out from over the mouth and stared at the girl with evil sentience. The demon stank. Waves of foul air arose off it every time it moved.

Lilith tried directing a stream of gravitons at the monster but it shrugged them off. She was completely helpless; she couldn't free Lucy.

Gwilym got his dagger under his right arm and sawed on the tentacle holding her right arm. It was like cutting wood. The sharp knife was barely able to knick the skin but the man was immensely strong and he pushed hard. His dagger slipped and peeled off a layer of the monster's skin. It screamed in pain and snatched the tentacle back, freeing the girl's right hand. Gwilym had given Lucy back an offensive option. Now she could fight.

The tentacle whipped back in at her again. This time she was ready and met it with an immaculately timed slash. The glyphs on the blade glowed bright red as it lopped off another tentacle tip. More screams and gurgles.

Lilith analysed the pattern of the graviton stream bouncing back off the monster. One useful result had emerged. 'It has an intricate structure behind the eye, Lucy. That's the weak point.'

"Let go of me. I need room to fight," Lucy said to the men.

Gwilym understood immediately and released her. William was more reluctant and Gwilym had to slap his hand away. As soon as the men released her, Lucy let go of the wall. The creature pulled her towards its mouth. Instead of resisting, she twisted to throw herself over the tentacles straight at the demon's head.

'Go deep, Lucy. Reach the nerve centre,' thought Lilith.

Lucy focussed all her energy into her right arm and punched through the demon's eye, sinking her hand wrist deep. The point of the dagger snagged momentarily on the shell around the demon's brain before cutting through. Lucy was sprayed in slime. The monster convulsed, flinging the girl from it like a horrified man might flick a poisonous spider off his face. She crashed back into the men, who broke her fall.

'The demon's dying. It's losing control of the portal,' thought Lilith.

The portal shut with an almost physical clang. Tentacles and body parts sprayed over the three before dissolving into dust.

'Get the mirror off the wall. We have to move it in space before something else opens it,' thought Lilith.

Lucy staggered back onto her feet and moved to the mirror. Her knife lay on the floor. It was unlit now but she saw it clearly in dark sight by its residual heat. Lucy put her left hand under it and flipped it up into her right.

'See that, Lilith.'

'Get the mirror down, Lucy.'

'How will this help?' Lucy thought.

'Moving the mirror will detune it from whatever it is linked to at the other end of the portal.'

'I see,' thought Lucy, in the tone that meant she had not got a clue what Lilith was rabbiting on about.

A nail in each corner held the mirror to the brickwork. She inserted her blade behind a nail and levered it out. After the third nail was removed, the polished steel fell of the wall under its own weight. Lucy casually put the mirror under her arm and walked down the tunnel to where her companions still sat.

"Upsidaisy, lazybones," she said.

Lucy extended him one hand to William to help him up and he shrank back from her.

William saw shock and hurt in her expression. Then she turned and walked away from him, face carefully blank. He sat there, shocked at his own reaction. A candle lay on its side, still burning. Gwilym picked it up and followed Lucy. He contrived to stand on William's hand as he left. William gasped but Gwilym ignored him.

"'Old up, 'ighness. I 'ave to guard your back, remember," Gwilym.

"So you do, Gwilym," she said warmly. "Thank you for what you did back there. We would all be dead if you had not got my hand free."

"I 'ad every confidence in you, 'ighness. We will 'ave to spar again tomorrow when me bruises fade."

The voices faded into the dark leaving William wondering just how much damage he had done.

"Up you come, milady," said the boatswain, as he hauled her through the trapdoor. "What have we here? A mirror? I have never seen one so big."

Gwilym had to climb out on his own, followed by William.

"We had better make the place secure," said William. "Sir Francis has plans for it."

"No, Captain," said Lucy. "Your orders are changed. I want this place burnt to the ground. Fire will cleanse it. I will take responsibility."

"You can't take responsibility, milady. Sir Francis doesn't know you're here." William frowned.

"I am tired of games, Captain. I intend to tell him. Now burn it," Lucy said with finality.

They stood in Billingsgate dock and watched the building blaze. Tudor houses were firetraps and the roof fell in when the wooden framework caught alight. The Swallows contained the fire, stopping it spreading to other buildings. Eventually, only smoking ashes were left.

"Take us back to the Tower, please, Captain. We will all use your barge," Lucy said, her voice carefully neutral.

She sat on a bench staring at the river as they sailed downstream. Gwilym sat behind where he could watch anyone approaching her. William waited for some time before going up to her. "Lady Dennys. I want to apologise for my behaviour back in the tunnel. I was in shock."

"No apology is necessary, Captain. You performed your duties adequately. My uncle will be satisfied." She turned her head back to the river. He had been dismissed. She had treated him the way a lady treats a servant that she doesn't particularly like but who has given no fault. He slunk away. In his heart, he believed her fully justified for her opinion of him.

Act 15, Conferences and Questions

"You did what?" asked Walsingham.

"I killed the London monster, not Captain Hawkins."

"What the hell did you think you were playing at, Captain?" Walsingham glared at the man.

William sat bolt upright. "I have no excuse, sir."

Walsingham glared at him. "Well, at least your cousin has taught you to take responsibility like a man, but what were you thinking of? Give me one good reason why I shouldn't hang you on the deck of your own ship?"

"Don't bully the captain, Uncle, his nerves have not been very good lately," said Lucy, nastily. "I tricked him into taking me."

"Who else knew of this?" Walsingham said. Simon looked at his hands and even Gwilym looked embarrassed. "I see you all knew. The people I trust most to tell me the truth chose to betray me."

"My fault again, Uncle," said Lucy, wearily. "I put them in an impossible position. I realise that now, which is why we are having this conversation. I also raided the Spanish safe house and killed another demon in the cellars."

Walsingham sat with his head in his hands. "How, Lucy?" he whispered. "No, more importantly, why?"

"The same question, Uncle," she said. "I went because I was the only person who could stop what Isabella was doing. Only I have the power. I am possessed, Uncle. You knew that."

"I was concerned," he said. "But when nothing untoward happened."

Lucy levelled her eyes at him. Her eyes showed the steely determination of the Dennys family; a resolve inherited from Sir Guy de Dennies, who had commanded Duke William's reserve at Hastings.

"It happened. I just didn't tell you," she said, flatly. "As to who was responsible? You were, Uncle, you and Doctor Dee. You summoned the demon and it took me."

Walsingham seemed to shrink into himself. "Oh no, Lucy, say not that I did this to you, my love, my poor child."

Lucy rose and ran round to her uncle's chair. She knelt and took his hand. "I am sorry, Uncle. That wasn't fair. It was really Isabella. She kidnapped Lilith and brought her to our world using blood magic. Lilith escaped and Doctor Dee captured her in the dog and from there to me. I didn't ask for it, Uncle. It just happened."

"Lucy, I have had occasion to see possessed people," said Walsingham. "They rant, they rave, and they try to hurt themselves and other people. Are you sure you are possessed?"

"No doubt about it, Uncle. The demon is in my head right now. She is called Lilith, by the way. Some think that makes me a monster but I am still Lucy Dennys."

Lucy stared at William as she spoke. William looked as if she had slapped him. Fortunately for him, Walsingham was too shocked to notice the exchange.

"I will send for Dee to see if we can reverse this magic," said Walsingham.

"Dee is always reluctant to visit London." Simon spoke without thinking.

Walsingham's eyes blazed. "Pooley will take a fast wherry. Dee will come immediately or I will have his head. Have you translated the documents taken from the safe house?"

Simon shook his head. "They are written in some mathematical code that is unknown to me. Mayhap, Doctor Dee can help when he arrives."

"Mayhap, I can help. Show them to me," Lucy said.

"You, Lucy?" asked Walsingham. "What know you of conjuring?"

"Nothing, Uncle. You remember what my tutors said of my mathematical skills." Lucy grinned at Walsingham and he chuckled. The other men around the table relaxed slightly. It was unlikely that

Walsingham would have had them executed on the spot, but the possibility existed. If Lucy could raise a smile from him then they were probably safe.

"So how can you help, my child?" asked Walsingham, indulgently.

"I can show them to Lilith. She is an able conjuror. She doesn't think like us. Her mind is vast and seems to eat numbers and information." Lucy struggled to explain.

"Does this involve magic, Lucy? Do you have to summon her?" asked Walsingham.

"No, Uncle, Lilith sees what I see. Lilith is within me. Show me, Master Tunstall," Lucy said.

"Milady." Simon handed her some papers. She sat at the table and put the first in front of her. It consisted of strings of numbers grouped like words and sentences.

She looked at the first then moved it aside. She spent just a few seconds on each paper before she handed them back.

"Is that it? You hardly glanced at them," said Walsingham, astonished.

"Lilith recorded them. Her thoughts are like a vast library. She is also very fast." Lucy looked rather distracted. William thought that she was likely talking to Lilith.

"It's a number code, Uncle. Lilith is attempting a code-break on the understanding that the language is Spanish." Lucy frowned as if concentrating.

"That is a safe assumption, child," said Walsingham.

"It is Spanish and Lilith has the decoding key. I can write it down for you if you want, Master Tunstall."

"So fast?" asked Walsingham.

"Lilith can carry out ten million calculations a second." Lucy tilted her head to one side as she listened to a voice no one else could hear. "Most of the documents are financial accounts."

"The documents include the names of those paid?" asked Walsingham.

"Oh yes, Uncle, and addresses. There are references to people being sent places. They have code names, mostly like Raven or Faithful." Lucy paused. "This is important, Uncle, Lilith has found reference to a despatch boat."

"Go on, child." Walsingham leaned forward eagerly.

"Even when decoded, the departure port is another code word but the river is in clear," said Lucy, excitedly.

Lucy was not making much sense but he had carried out many interrogations so he patiently asked the right questions. "What river, Lucy?"

"The Crouch, in Essex," she said.

"When?"

"The seventeenth, four days time," Lucy said.

"Who are the despatches for, Lucy?"

"The Spanish Governor in the Low Countries, Palma."

"Why is it so important?" Walsingham said.

"The Enterprise of England, that's what it says in the despatches, the plans for the Enterprise of England. That's important, isn't it, Uncle?"

"That's very important, Lucy. Thank Lilith for me."

"Nightfall, Uncle. The despatch boat will leave at nightfall."

"Well, Captain, it appears that I cannot hang you for the present as I still have need of you. I will have to reserve the pleasure for later." Walsingham smiled coldly.

William was not sure if the spymaster was joking or not. On balance, he thought he was joking. "You want me to intercept the despatch boat, Sir Francis?"

"I do, Captain. You will be off the Crouch estuary on the night of the seventeenth. Stop and search any vessel trying to leave."

"Very good, sir. I will take the *Swallow*'s pinnace."

"And me," said Lucy.

"What?" William asked, confused.

"Do not worry, Captain. I will endeavour to keep as far away from you as possible," she said, cuttingly.

Lucy's voice was flat but the dismissal in her tone was hard to miss. Simon felt a momentary sympathy for the captain, something he imagined would never happen. Another suitor dumped, he thought.

"Why should you come on this enterprise, Lady Dennys?"

"Can you see in the dark, Captain? I can," she said.

"You can see without light, Lucy?" asked Walsingham.

"Yes, Uncle. Lilith calls it dark sight. Apparently, I can see heat. Lilith did explain how it worked but I can't understand her. Mayhap, Doctor Dee could. A boat will glow white with heat against the dark water."

"This is so important that—very well, Lucy. You will go. But you are there as the ship's eyes. Captain Hawkins and his men will do any fighting. You will obey me in this." Walsingham gazed at her, implacably.

"As you say, Uncle," Lucy said, obediently.

"Gwilym. I want you to accompany Lady Dennys. She is not to be placed in any danger. You will restrain her physically if she disobeys me."

"As you wish, 'ighness," said Gwilym.

"Uncle," said Lucy, shocked. One hand flew up to cover her mouth.

"The eventuality is purely hypothetical is it not, Lucy, for you will obey me?"

"Yes, Uncle," she said.

"Master Tunstall," said Walsingham. "Go you with them. Get me those despatches, Simon. The fate of England may rest upon it."

"What dress will you require, milady? The blue or the green?" asked Lucy's servant, Millie.

'What do you think, Lilith?' thought Lucy.

'I have always liked you in the green. Besides, I shall be wearing blue if necessary. My researches suggest the men are likely to associate blue with the Virgin Mary and hence, perhaps, look more kindly on me,' Lilith thought, wistfully.

"The green, Millie," said Lucy.

'Do we have to go, Lucy? Couldn't we run for it?' pleaded Lilith.

'And where in the world could we run that Uncle would not find us and bring us back? He has captured traitors who have fled to France and smuggled them home for punishment. Be sensible, Lilith. Besides, I do not wish to run. I am not a criminal,' thought Lucy, indignantly.

"Put your arms through here, milady," said Millie.

'I know you are right, Lucy, but I'm scared. That man hurt me. I am frightened of him,' thought Lilith.

'Shush, Lilith. Dee can't hurt you without hurting me and Uncle would never allow that,' thought Lucy, trying to comfort the demon.

'I am worried about something else. They might kill you. Your uncle would not intend to but in trying to evict me they might kill you,' thought Lilith. 'I don't want to be the cause of your death, Lucy. You are my only friend.'

'I had quite forgot about that. Well, there is nothing else for it. I cannot disobey my uncle. He is within his rights as head of my household to summon me as he wishes,' thought Lucy.

Lilith kept her thoughts from Lucy. The unbreakable social conventions that surrounded humans were quite ridiculous but they seemed essential for a properly functioning society. At least, that was Lilith's current thesis.

"Let me comb your hair, milady," said Millie. "We must put a shine on it for the gentlemen to see."

"How does Gwilym treat you lately, Millie? Does he press his suit ardently?" Lucy asked.

"He blows hot and cold, milady," said Millie. "I think he likes me well enough but he shies away when I mention babies or marriage."

" 'Twas ever thus," said Lucy.

"The boatswain has asked me to dine with him tonight. Mayhap that will give Gwilym food for thought. If not . . ." Millie shrugged. "I had not thought to marry a sailor but he is an officer and Plymouth is a pretty town, so they say. A girl cannot wait forever, milady."

"No, Millie. That is very true," said Lucy.

"I do not like the thought of my man spending weeks or even months away from me. But they say the homecomings are interesting," Millie giggled.

A servant stuck her head around the door. "Sir Francis is ready for you now, milady."

"Very well, tell him I will be with him directly." Lucy was in great-lady mode.

Lucy waited outside the door to gather herself. 'Here we go, Lilith. I feel a bit like some traitor that Uncle is about to question.'

'At least your uncle will not use the rack on you,' thought Lilith.

Lucy drew a deep breath and walked inside.

"Ah, Lucy. Come in and make yourself comfortable. We should not have to wait long," said Walsingham. The only other occupants of the room were Simon and Gwilym. The Spanish Secret Service's mirror from the safe house stood in a wooden frame. The steel had been newly polished to give a good reflection.

A querulous voice sounded from the corridor. "Will you stop pushing me, you ape? I am going as fast as I can."

The door opened and Doctor Dee was ejected through it on the end of Pooley's arm. Pooley bowed to Walsingham then left. Dee glared after him.

"Doctor Dee, how civil of you to come so quickly to my summons," said Walsingham, smoothly.

"Civil! Civil!" said Dee. "Three of your apes dragged me out of my own library."

"Be fair, Doctor, I would die of old age if we waited for you to finish in your library," said Walsingham. "Doctor Dee has the most comprehensive library in Christendom, Lucy. How many volumes do you have, Dee?"

"More than four thousand," said Dee, somewhat mollified.

"Four thousand," said Walsingham, admiringly. "The library at Cambridge University had but four hundred." His voice became authoritative. "You have brought the information and materials I need?"

"Yes, Sir Francis."

"So what do we know about the demon Lilith?" asked Walsingham.

'How can they know anything about me? I have only just got here and it was sheer chance that I got this name,' thought Lilith.

'Shush, Lilith, and we will find out. My people don't set too much store by coincidence. We believe everything is connected in the chain of being,' thought Lucy.

'There is an element of truth in that but—' thought Lilith.

'Hush, demon,' interrupted Lucy.

"There are fleeting mentions of her in many books of wisdom, including the Bible," said Dee. "I quote Isaiah, 'There too Lilith shall repose, and find a place to rest. There shall the owl nest and lay and hatch and brood in its shadow.' The place being described is a wilderness. Note also the connection with owls. Owls are, of course, suggestive of wisdom. So Lilith in the Bible is a lost traveller in the wilderness and she is a source of wisdom."

"Yes, I have seen her wisdom and Lucy described her as lost in our world. What else?" Walsingham said.

"The Bible does not refer to her again but there are other sources. The Jews have their own tradition. The first mention of Lilith is from the Alphabet of Ben Sira. This is a shocking book that is considered by many Orthodox Jews to be a fake. In the Jewish Rabbinic tradition, Lilith is the first woman created by God."

'I was created by the Elders,' thought Lilith, indignantly.

"Surely that was Eve?" asked Lucy.

"Eve was the first in the Old Testament but even in the Bible there are hints of a woman before Eve. Anyway, Lilith was created from the earth, like Adam, and so was independent of him." Dee looked at Lucy and coloured up. "Adam and Lilith, ah, squabbled over who should lie on top during, um, matrimonial relations."

"Fancy," said Lucy.

Dee hurried on. "Anyway, Lilith fled and God sent three angels to return her. They caught her by the Red Sea and threatened to drown her. Lilith negotiated an arrangement with the angels that she should have dominion over male babies for eight days and female for twenty. In this time, she could take them for her own. Even today, you will see Jewish babies protected from Lilith by amulets containing the names of the three angels."

"So Lilith is a destroyer of children," said Walsingham.

'What libelous rubbish,' thought Lilith. 'No wonder this man's spells go wrong.'

"And their mothers when in childbirth," Dee added. "But many Jews doubt the authenticity of this story. Other Jewish traditions have Lilith as a succubus."

"What's a succubus?" asked Lucy, innocently.

Lilith searched frantically though her stolen database. 'Succubus, what's a succubus? My! You know, I could probably do that if I really tried.'

'Don't you dare,' thought Lucy.

"A demon who comes to men in dreams in the night and drains their seed, as I suspect you know. Stop teasing the good doctor, Lucy," said Walsingham, warningly.

"The Jewish traditions are so confusing. They refer to Lilith as everything from a slave girl to the Queen of Heaven and consort to God Himself," Dee said.

'Consort to God. That sounds more like it,' thought Lilith.

Dee cleared his throat. "The final source I have is from the ancient legend of the Sumerian hero Gilgamesh who survived the Great Flood. The legend mentions a huluppu tree, whatever that is. Possibly, they meant a willow. The goddess Inanna had planted such a divine tree in her garden in the city of Uruk to make wood for a throne and a bed. But a monster built its home in the roots and the demon Lilith had her house in the branches. Gilgamesh slew the monster and Lilith fled in fear to the wilderness. Note the association with wilderness again. There is evidence that the Sumerians worshipped a winged demon called Lilith and that they associated her with owls and lions, more symbols of wisdom and courage."

'Wisdom and courage, I take it back, Lucy. Dee is a learned man and humans do know of me,' thought Lilith.

Dee drank some wine to refresh his throat. "Lilith's domain is associated with mirrors. Mirrors can be entrances into Lilith's world, which is described as a dark cave. This is illustrated by a Jewish folktale. A woman bought a mirror for her dark-haired daughter who was very vain. The woman did not realise that the mirror was a gateway to Lilith's cave. The daughter looked at the mirror often, and day by day she was more and more possessed by Lilith. The demon turned her into a girl of loose morals who, ah, consorted carnally with men."

This time it was Lucy's turn to colour up. "Uncle," she said, outraged. "I am a maid. I have never . . ."

"Yes, yes, Lucy," said Walsingham. "No one suggests otherwise. I notice that mirrors are portals in to the Other World. That matches our experience."

"You see that mirror over there, Doctor Dee," said Walsingham. "Lucy recently killed a demon with that knife you gave her. The demon was attempting to enter this world through the mirror. Lucy was able to kill it, because she is possessed by Lilith."

Dee slumped back in his seat with his mouth open.

"Not going too fast for you, Dee, am I?" asked Walsingham, not without a measure of malice.

"How do you know that Lady Dennys is possessed? I know that I once thought it likely but the lady seems rather normal to me. She would have died weeks ago had she been possessed after that unfortunate incident at Nonsuch. Could we not be dealing with the overactive imagination of a young woman?" asked Dee, patronisingly. "Have either of you seen anything?"

"I have seen her when the possession is on her," said Simon. He did not like Dee's attitude. How dare he put down Lucy as an hysteric.

"I haven't," said Walsingham. "Would you demonstrate, Lucy?"

"Certainly, Uncle."

'Now, Lilith, give me the power now,' thought Lucy.

'Knock them dead, my friend,' thought Lilith. So they wanted to see power did they? Lilith gave it everything she had.

Lucy stood up. She lowered her head for a moment then lifted it. Her eyes sparkled like diamonds and her skin glowed. Her hair crackled and shifted. She walked around the table. When Lucy was like this, she walked as if she had no weight, bouncing from foot to foot like a tigress. Dee shrank back as she approached him. She hit the heavy wooden table in front of him. To be more exact she smashed her hand right through it, collapsing and shattering the wood. Nobody said anything. Lucy stood still, her hair billowing in a nonexistent wind.

"Can you hear me, Lucy?" asked Walsingham, softly.

She turned crystalline eyes upon him. "Yes, Uncle. It's still me in here."

Lucy walked up to him and kissed him on the cheek. Walsingham never flinched. He caressed her glowing face. Simon felt fierce pride that he was servant to such a man. All the demons from hell couldn't frighten Walsingham. "I love you," she said, and he smiled at her.

"Show him your blade, 'ighness," said Gwilym.

Lucy pulled out her dagger, Dee's dagger. It shone with energy. The glyphs on the blade glowed bright red.

"I saw 'er kill a demon with that. She saved my life and who knows 'ow many others. Regular little demon-killer aren't you, 'ighness."

"Convinced, Dee?" asked Walsingham.

"Completely," said Dee. The power in Lucy faded and she became just Lucy again.

"I have never seen anything like that," said Dee, excitedly. "I have seen possession where a demon inhabits and takes over a human body but I have never seen such controlled power. Possessed people slaughter their friends and family before dying horribly. What has happened to you, milady, is entirely new to science."

"Lucy, what do you understand Lilith to be?" asked Walsingham

'Yes, what do you think I am, Lucy?' thought Lilith.

"She is a traveller from a far Other World who got trapped here by Isabella, in what to her is a wilderness. Lilith cannot live in our world independent of me, as it lacks essential nourishment that she needs. She is very wise and knowledgeable. She is not evil and wishes me well. The Other World that is her home is dark like a cave. There are many of her kind there. She cannot leave me without killing me. In return for possessing my body, she has made it strong and fast. I heal quickly and cannot suffer disease. Mirrors can be portals to the

Other Worlds; there are many types of portal incidentally. Lilith, herself, can create them."

Lucy looked carefully at her uncle. "Lilith is kind, considerate, brave, and loyal. I like her."

Lilith said nothing. She did not know what to say.

"Does that sound likely, Dee?" asked Walsingham.

"Yes," he replied. "We imagine one Other World but it is clear that it is divided up in some way. Lilith, as described by Lucy, is very different from the demons we know but that is easily possible. In some ways, she seems more like an angel. The ignorant think of angels as God's little helpers but angels can be terrible. I have always wanted to talk to an angel. Think what one could learn," said Dee, wistfully. "The lost Book of Enoch contains the guide to the tongue of angels, could we but find it."

"Back to the point, Doctor. Tell me about mirrors," said Walsingham, impatiently. Simon knew that once Dee started on Enochian magic he could waffle on for hours. Academics could be so boring.

"You may know, Sir Francis, that Lord Burghley has commissioned a report on the use of mirrors and lenses. Thomas Digges is to investigate their effect on light while I am to summarise our knowledge of the invisible rays. As you know, the Chain of Being is connected from Heaven to the upper layers of stars, through the layer of the sun, then the moon, shooting stars, and so on down to the earth and possibly Hell. The Chain also runs from angels to man, then animals and through plants to the inanimate and demons. Rays connect all the layers; that is how the astrological sciences work. Light is the only one of these rays that we can directly perceive. Light is bent and reflected by crystals and mirrors so we may assume that these objects have the same effect on other rays. That is why we use crystal balls as skrying stones and mirrors to open portals into the Other World."

"And diamonds to make magic," said Lucy.

"I would greatly desire to talk to this Lilith, directly," Dee said.

"Can we do that?" asked Walsingham, surprised.

"We have a mirror, and your niece." Dee shrugged.

"This will not hurt Lucy, will it?" Walsingham asked.

"Not at all," Dee said, reassuringly. He got up and gestured for Lucy to join him.

"Come here, my dear." Dee placed a chair in front of the mirror. "Look carefully at this please." Dee swung a crystal on a chain in front of her. It caught the light and twinkled. "You are very tired. Got to sleep now."

Dee's voice droned on and Simon felt his eyes drooping. Dee snapped his fingers in front of Lucy's eyes but she did not react.

"Come out, Lilith, I summon you. I am of Eve's line. I call upon the ancient pact." Dee repeated the words over and over. The room filled with light and Lucy's reflection in the mirror shimmered. Someone else appeared in the mirror, someone who walked straight out into the room.

Simon looked mouth open at a petite woman with short black hair. She wore a long, sleeveless, blue dress that turned up into a high collar behind her head. Her skin was very pale, like a Dane's, but her eyes were from Cathay and her hair as dark as Africa.

"Holographic technology, how clever." She clapped her hands together. "I didn't know you people could do that. I am Lilith, Lucy's friend."

No one spoke. Simon had no idea what to say. What do you say to a demon, especially one who does not look very demonic? Should not she have horns and claws and things? Maybe the odd fang would have made her seem more authentic. She looked like a foreign princess on her way to a ball.

Dee stretched out his hand to touch her. Her body was completely insubstantial. Dee's hand passed right through her.

"No touching, I am afraid. That's the problem with holograms. What can I do for you gentlemen?" Lilith said, brightly.

"You are the demon Lilith?" asked Walsingham.

"You may call me that. It is Lucy's name for me. You could not pronounce my real name." Lilith smiled.

"Of course, she will not tell us her secret demon name or we would have power over her," Dee said quietly to Walsingham.

Lilith smiled.

"Lilith, Lucy thinks you are her friend," said Walsingham.

"I am her friend. Indeed, she is my only friend. I will protect her with my life," said Lilith.

Simon was always amazed how much loyalty Lucy inspired in those around her. She had subverted the core of the English Secret Service and now, apparently, she was starting to work her charm on the demon realms.

"If you are her friend then you will let her go. Leave her and let her live a normal life," Walsingham urged.

Lilith looked sad. "I cannot, Elder Walsingham."

"We could use magic to force you out," Walsingham said, coldly.

"I beg you not to try. In order to jump from Lucy, I would need energy. My body would suck it from the nearest source automatically. That would be Lucy's body. This is involuntary. I have no control over it. Remember the dog. Please don't make me kill Lucy, Elder Walsingham, I love her."

Walsingham looked flummoxed and Simon did not blame him. They both remembered the agony-twisted form of the puppy. Lilith was not at all what they had expected. Like the experienced interrogator that he was, Walsingham changed tack. "How could you leave Lucy without killing her?"

"I could lock onto an external power source and saturate my body. It would need to be close by. I could leave her safely then and journey home," Lilith said.

"I see," said Walsingham. "I must think further on this."

Lilith's image began to flicker. "The spell is failing," said Dee.

Lilith winked out like an extinguished candle and only Lucy's reflection appeared in the mirror.

"Well, that didn't work," said Lucy. "What! What are you all staring at?"

Act 16, The River Crouch

Burnham-on-Crouch might not be the most miserable town in England but, on a wet afternoon, it made a rather good approximation. The town was perched on what was almost an island in a sea of mud. It boasted a single jetty that ran down far enough across the mudflats to allow loading at all but the lowest spring tides. But Burnham's location on the north bank of the mouth of the Crouch Estuary suited William's current needs.

The *Swallow*'s pinnace staggered onto a buoy off Burnham. Its foremast waved crazily in the swell. A party left the ship and rowed for the shore.

"My God, what a dump," said William. "Essex is just one big mudflat. Are the locals born with webbed feet?"

"There are pleasant enough lands around the old Roman city at Colchester," said Simon. He put his cloak around Lucy. "Are you warm enough, my lady?"

"Your cloak is welcome, sir," she said. "There is a cool wind over the marshes."

They landed on the jetty and walked up into the town, which boasted one tavern. William led the way in. "I need a table and four mugs of your best beer, landlord."

A man wearing an apron came out to seat them. "Sit here, lady, gentlemen. Can I get you some food?"

"A hot meal would be good. What do you have in the kitchen?"

"My wife has made a coney and turnip pie this very day. It is stuffed with pepper and currants and pricked between the legs so as not to break its body." The landlord waited expectantly.

"Excellent," said William. "We will have four servings."

The landlord bowed and went back to the kitchens.

"That sounds good," Simon said.

"Aye, well. I would not expect too much from such an out-of-the-way place," said William.

The potboy arrived with their beer. Simon turned to Lucy. "Are you warmed now, my dear?"

Lucy returned his cloak. "Thank you, husband." She kissed him on the cheek as the potboy put down the mugs. Lucy was doing her best to adopt the accent of the minor rural gentry. The crystal-clear accents of the London aristocracy were a little too distinctive.

They chatted inconsequently. The potboy returned with radishes and salt as a taster to clear their palette and tempt their appetite. William was astonished. This country tavern served food more like a fashionable Chelsea house than a place on the Essex marshes.

The landlord placed a whole pie in the centre of the table and wiped four plates, which he laid out for the diners. William indicated to Lucy that she should break the crust first. Lucy helped herself to a man's share. William wondered where she stored so much in such a slight figure. Somehow, he had expected that a titled lady would pick delicately at her food but she attacked her meals like a sailor on a blowout. When all had helped themselves, they tasted the food. The pie was baked to perfection.

"I wonder what the goodwife has used to glaze the pastry," said Simon, who considered himself something of a gourmet. "I suspect she has used an egg mix. The pastry is crisp and firm but just dissolves in the mouth."

"Mmmmm," said Lucy, and helped herself to another portion having wolfed down the first. She became aware that the men all looked at her. "What? The sea air has given me an appetite."

"I must ask for the recipe so you can make this pie for me, beloved," said Simon, playing to the gallery.

Lucy finished a mouthful before replying. "Of course, I will slave in a kitchen to make it for you, dear heart. Especially as you are so poor that we cannot afford a cook." She gazed at him adoringly. William choked back a laugh.

Lucy and Simon held hands a lot during the meal and often gazed into each other's eyes. William knew that they were only obeying his instructions but he felt more than a twinge of jealousy. Lucy treated him politely but with a coolness that wrenched at him. The tavern filled with locals mostly eating simpler fare such as a vegetable pottage, although the more prosperous yeoman farmers also ordered the pie.

The landlord reappeared to clear their plates. "Can I tempt you with something sweet to finish, lady, gentlemen?"

William was set to refuse when Lucy piped up, "What fare do you have, landlord?"

"Seasonal fruit, lady, or cheese, or my wife's special," he said.

Lucy clapped her hands, "What is the special? Is it as good as the coney pie?"

"I will leave you to judge its quality, madam. The special is cherry shortbread seasoned with mustard, cinnamon, and ginger."

"How splendid. I shall definitely try a piece. With your permission, husband." She said, remembering late that she was supposed to be a dutiful wife.

"Of course you shall have a taste of the shortbread, dear heart," Simon said. "I can refuse you nothing."

The landlord grinned. He had clearly worked out where the power lay in this marriage. William felt there was enough cloying sweetness at the table without adding cherry shortbread but he also ordered a slice for politeness's sake.

Lucy bit into her sweet. Simon waxed lyrical about the balance of the spices but Lucy seemed distant.

"Are you all right, Lady Dennys?" William asked, softly so that only those around the table heard.

Lucy replied as quietly. For a moment, she reverted to her earlier ease with him. "Ah, yes, Captain, thank you. Lilith, the glutton demon, gets terribly excited about sweet foods. Of all the sensations in our world, it is sweet foods that tempt her most. She keeps going on about it in my head, distracting me. Normally, Lilith is more polite and keeps quiet when I am talking to people."

William thought that the last sentence was probably not aimed at him. "Lilith tastes what you eat, milady?"

"Lilith absorbs every sensation that my body or my mind experiences," Lucy replied coldly and would not look at him. He lacked the courage to keep the conversation going.

They sat around the table eating until they were replete. The landlord returned while the boy cleared the plates. "How was the meal, gentlemen?"

"Superb," said Simon. "I mean no offence, landlord, but your wife's cooking seems far in excess of what is needed for such a modest place."

"Indeed, sir. My wife learnt her art in London Town. We get little trade from the sea but gentlemen out hunting stop here for dinner."

"Gentlemen?" asked William.

"Yes, sir. The Earl of Oxford has a country house nearby. What brings you gentlefolk to Burnham?"

"Mischance," said William. "I am taking a cargo from Gravesend to Kings Lyn. The mast broke but a few miles out of Gravesend so we came in here to make repairs. Master Johnston here is supercargo. He is taking his new wife back to Cambridgeshire with him."

"We could see that they were newlyweds," said the landlord, winking.

Lucy blushed prettily and clutched at Simon's hand.

"She will indeed make a fine wife with the, ah, proper instruction," said Simon, blandly.

A steely look from Lucy warned him not to push his luck.

"Mayhap, another jug of beer, landlord," said William.

The landlord left to arrange fresh drinks.

"So the Earl of Oxford keeps a house near the Crouch," said Simon. "How interesting."

"Do you think Walsingham knows?" asked William.

"Do you think Philip of Spain is a papist?" asked Simon.

They drank their beer and settled the account. It was expensive but worth every penny. It was going to be a long night. They took a turn around Burnham to walk off the meal. There was little to see except for a small Norman church. They lit candles and said prayers for the success of their enterprise. William watched Lucy kneel at the screen. If anyone had suggested to him that a girl possessed by a demon would sit quietly in church to pray then he would have thought them mad. He was changing many of his preconceptions. A pity he had not changed some of them sooner, he thought sourly.

They returned to the jetty and summoned the rowboat. The tide was on the flood so the oarsmen had to work hard to reach the pinnace. Most of the crew were resting. The boatswain kept a few fiddling with the mast to add verisimilitude to their cover story.

Lucy stood at the bow looking over the Essex marshes. A bird called mournfully with a deep booming sound. Gwilym joined her. "'Ow about a little exercise, 'ighness?"

"With knives, I have to practise with my blade," she said.

"We don't 'ave no wooden practise daggers, 'ighness."

"So? I promise not to hurt you," said Lucy.

"Ha!" Gwilym replied.

They walked to the centre of the deck where the pinnace was widest and drew their daggers. The crew clustered around eagerly. Some had seen Lucy fight and the others had heard all about it. No one was going to miss this. Simon and William watched from the aft deck.

"With your weight, Gwilym, you have all the advantages on this enclosed space. I don't have room to use my speed."

"You think life should be fair, 'ighness? What a peculiar notion."

Gwilym limbered up as he spoke. Then, without warning, he stabbed at her face.

"Christ's blood." William was horrified. Simon was relaxed; he had seen them spar before.

Lucy's blade flashed as she parried Gwilym's dagger. She slashed at him on the backswing but he had already swung away. He crowded her, making a series of feints. She checked each one. When he had manoeuvred her into the rail, he launched a midline thrust. She intercepted and their knives locked. Gwilym stepped inside her and blocked his forearm against her throat. Had Gwilym carried through he would have crushed her windpipe. She winked at him and he looked down to see her knee in his groin. Had she followed through she would have unmanned him.

"You are becoming quite a dirty little fighter, 'ighness."

"I have a good teacher," Lucy said.

Gwilym heaved and spun her round. He was not stronger than her but he had considerably more body mass so it was she who moved. She continued the spin, finishing her turn in time to parry his attack. She struck at him with her dagger in a series of low blows. He was forced to stoop to block them. When she had him down low enough, she jumped over his blade and lightly kicked him in the head.

"Cozened you, Gwilym," Lucy said, delightedly. "That rarely happens."

The crew clapped and whistled. Lucy gave a little curtsey in their direction. She appeared not to hear a loud aside from a seaman.

"And you fancied her in your bed, Billie. She'd eat you alive."

She also appeared not to hear the boatswain's piercing whisper in reply. "Reynolds, if I hear you insult the captain's guest again, I will tie your balls to my cutlass as good-luck tokens."

"Sorry, boatswain."

Gwilym and Lucy walked back to the centre and restarted. Thrust, parry, and counterattack followed at bewildering speed. A quick sideways kick knocked Lucy's feet out from under her but she rolled away and flipped back upright before Gwilym could exploit his advantage. Lucy raced back in at him and Gwilym gave ground step by step as she wove a spider's web of shining steel around his defense. She backed him up against the rail and thrust hard. He dropped his knife and seized her wrist, pulling into her arm so that her blade sank deep in the wood. Then he shoulder-charged her, knocking her backwards away from her knife.

Lucy scrabbled to keep her feet. He followed up like a bear. She turned into her fall and used the momentum to run away from him. Gwilym pursued her, showing surprising speed for such a big man. She dived around the left side of the mainmast. When Gwilym was committed to go after her, she grabbed at the mainmast with both hands and whipped her legs around off the ground. Gwilym tried to change direction but momentum carried him on. She swung around the mast and kicked him with both legs in the small of the back, throwing him forward into the opposite rail.

The girl dropped onto her feet like a cat and bounded after him. Gwilym dropped onto his bottom. "Peace, 'ighness. You might be able to go on all day but I'm knackered. 'Ave mercy on an old man."

William clapped his hands. "Show's over. Back to work. Let's see some action." Gwilym was the best close-combat man William had ever seen but Lucy had matched him blow for blow. How do I repair the damage, William thought? He was realistic enough to know that he would never win fair lady by his learning or smooth tongue. His skills were those of Mars. She will despise me if I crawl but how does a fighter impress a girl who can outfight him?

Lucy gave Gwilym her hand and pulled him up. "If you are such an old man you should be thinking of settling down with a good woman, like my Millie for example, who won't wait forever for a man." Lucy looked meaningfully at the boatswain.

"I think we should try and get some sleep," said Simon. "It could be a long night."

Simon stretched out beside Lucy on the deck. She dropped off immediately. She seemed to be able to go to sleep anywhere at any time. He found that sleep evaded him. It had been fun having Lucy play at wife for a short while but it had confirmed his opinion. He wanted a wife who was the way Lucy had acted, rather than the way she really was. He wanted a wife who would look to him for security and comfort, rather than to her titled family connections. Simon thought William was foolish to want to challenge the social order. It was a denial of the Chain of Being and could easily end in frustration and unhappiness for both parties.

The crew miraculously restepped the foremast as the sun set. When the last northern twilight evaporated, the pinnace dropped the buoy and sailed out into the mouth of the estuary. Lucy stood in the bow with William. He sneaked surreptitious glances at her. The wind fluttered the hair over her neck. Her eyes sparkled in diamond light. He knew that meant the power was on her.

Lucy scanned the darkness. "There are two boats entering the estuary," she said.

William stared into the darkness. "That will be the last members of the fishing fleet returning. Yes, I can see running lights. That must be one of them."

"The second one is farther back and to the left," she said.

"You can see all that?" asked William. "What does it look like? What do you see, milady?"

"The sea is dark black and the land is a luminescent grey. Boats are light grey against the sea. I can see the crew. People glow like white beacons. Fires flash like stars. It's like looking into the Other World."

"Look down into the estuary, Lady Dennys. Look for anything making for the sea."

The pinnace ploughed up and down, just making enough way to hold station against the tide. In the wide ocean, she was a small vessel that was of little consequence. Here, in the estuary, she was a shark among herring. The night wore on. Nothing moved upon the water once the last of the fishing boats was safely home.

Something flickered on the edge of Lucy's vision. She watched it intently. Minute by minute it grew into a grey shape. The target boat could not be moving above a slow walk. Lucy tapped William on the shoulder. "There," she said, pointing.

William stared into the dark. He could see nothing but he knew better than to doubt her. He hissed an order to the boatswain and the pinnace turned onto a new bearing. Lucy was impressed by the silence with which the manoeuvre was achieved. This crew had clearly carried out night operations before.

"Is she carrying lights?" asked William.

"I can't see any," Lucy said.

"Excellent." William rubbed his hands. "A legitimate vessel would have lights. Let's hope that they are not innocent smugglers, Lucy."

The girl was too excited to chastise him for using her Christian name.

The vessels closed, Lucy conning them in.

"Captain!" The boatswain hissed.

William ran forward.

"There she is, Cap'n, right on the bow, just where the lady pointed," said the boatswain. "How did the maid know?"

"Magic, boatswain. Just be glad that she is on our side. Get us alongside, if you please."

"Aye, aye, Cap'n. Stand by to board, pass it on," said the boatswain, softly to the nearest crew. The order passed down the pinnace.

The boatswain took the helm himself and held the pinnace bow on to the target. The enemy sailed on in for some time in blissful ignorance. A yell, followed by incoherent cries, indicated that the enemy had finally spotted them. The bow of the pinnace must have loomed over them like the wrath of God. William thought the boatswain had judged it too fine but, just when a collision seemed inevitable, the veteran sea dog put the tiller over and crashed alongside. William led the boarding action.

Gwilym appeared at Lucy's elbow. "You have done your bit, 'ighness. You stay here with me."

The Swallows stormed aboard the other boat and the pinnace stood off slightly to avoid damage. The helmsman matched speeds with the enemy boat on a parallel course. The Swallows ruthlessly put down all opposition. Simon appeared on the deck of the enemy ship clutching a leather bag.

"I've got them," Simon said, excitedly. "I have the despatches."

He stood in the bow waving them at Lucy. A man rose up from the shadows behind Simon. There was a blow and Simon fell. The man grabbed the despatches. William ran Simon's attacker through with a cutlass but it was too late. The man dropped the leather bag into the water between the two ships. Weighted, it sank immediately.

Lucy dived straight over the side after it.

William saw her go. He threw his cap in to mark the spot. It slid backwards down the ships as they moved. He walked back down the boat keeping pace with the cap, stripping off his clothes and boots. When he reached the stern, he dived in onto the cap.

'I can't see the bag, Lilith. It must be the same temperature as the water.' Lucy swam down as fast as she could. The weighted bag must be sinking fast.

'I am patching in gravitonic senses to your vision, Lucy. The moving bag will create gravity distortions,' thought Lilith. She also opened a file marked "anaerobic biochemistry" from her database.

Lucy could see a glowing blob in the distance. It trailed filaments as it fell. 'There it is. I can see it,' thought Lucy.

'Wait, Lucy, you will run out of oxygen long before you can intercept the bag at a safe distance. I have run a model. You won't be able to get back.'

Lucy did not answer Lilith. She had no idea what oxygen was. She powered down after the bag. Lilith desperately shunted oxygen from Lucy's minor organs to her brain and leg muscles. She twisted the girl's biochemistry to try to set up anaerobic energy pathways. Warning subroutines that she had linked to various parameters in Lucy's body all went off together. There was only so much Lilith could do.

Lucy reached the leather bag and twisted the strap around her arm. Then she started for the surface so far above. Her body was failing fast and her speed dropped until she floated helplessly. Lucy had neutral buoyancy in the cold water with the weighted bag balancing the stale air in her lungs. Lilith stopped her breathing reflex so the girl wouldn't gulp in water and shunted all remaining biochemical energy to Lucy's brain.

'You were right, Lilith,' thought Lucy. 'It was too far for me. I forgot I am not immortal. Save yourself, Lilith, I'm dying. Use the last power in my body to make a jump. Finishing me off quickly will be a kindness.'

'Never, Lucy, never say that,' thought Lilith. 'We live or die together. I am going to shut you down now to save energy.'

'Good-bye, Lilith,' thought Lucy. 'I love you.'

Lilith took stock of their situation. It was not good. Lucy's biochemistry was wrecked but Lilith still had gravitonic energy in her batteries. She extended her senses and swept the area. Lilith spotted a gravity distortion in the water above. She kept Lucy unconscious but she used some power to fire up Lucy's biochemistry one last time. Driving Lucy like this was doing terrible damage. Lucy's body took a firm grip on her blade, pulled it from her holster, and held it over her head. Lilith bled off gravitonic energy to excite the steel molecules. The knife lit up in the visible wavelengths. Liliith had little hope of rescue but she had to try.

William was frantic; no one could go so long without a breath. He kept putting his head underwater but could see nothing in the dark. Then, below him, he saw a light. It had to be her. He took three long breaths to fill his lungs and dived. He had no way of judging distance and the dive went on and on. Then he was right on top of her. He grabbed her arm and kicked upwards. She was completely limp and he feared the worst. Please God, he prayed. Not like this. Don't take her from me now.

William broke the surface. He pushed Lucy's head up but it lolled helplessly. She was not breathing. "Breathe, breathe, damn it, Lucy, breathe."

Eschewing propriety, he resorted to an old sea dog trick for reviving half-drowned sailors. He put his mouth over hers and blew air into her body. He could not see a reaction so he took a deep breath and tried again. This time she coughed and broke her mouth away. Lucy sucked air in great juddering gulps. Her head still lolled in his arms but she breathed.

"Thank you, Lord," William said.

He manoeuvred her around until she lay on her back on his chest, her head out of the water in the crook of his neck. William desperately searched the darkness around. He and the unconscious girl were completely alone. A wave slapped his face.

The boastswain steered the captured despatch boat into the pinnace and jumped back aboard. "Get this boat turned around, you whoresons. Everyone not on the sails, get to the sides to look for the captain and the lady. We have people in the water. I want silence. Listen for cries."

Simon grabbed his arm. "Can't we use the other boat as well? That would double our chances of catching them."

"I don't have enough crew to sail both," said the boatswain. "I have just left a few men onboard to hold the prize."

"So we need more seamen," Simon said. "Right, come with me, Gwilym."

The two men jumped into the prize and went to where the prisoners were held. "Who's in charge?" asked Simon.

No one answered but some of the prisoners looked at a blond-haired man. "We have two people in the water. I want you to get this boat turned around to search." Simon addressed Blond Hair.

"Why should I?" The man spat. "They can drown for all I care."

Simon was not in a good mood. His head hurt where he had been struck and his employer's niece was lost at sea because he had been careless and lost the despatches. "Persuade him, Gwilym," Simon said, coldly.

Blond Hair was a big man but he might as well have been a child. Gwilym pulled the man's head back, baring his throat for a dagger. The point broke the skin and blood ran down the blade. "You'll do it or I'll kill you."

The man still looked defiant. He probably thought he was marked for execution anyway.

"No, I won't cut your throat, that's too quick," said Gwilym. "I'll hand you over to Walsingham and tell him how you laughed at the thought of his favourite niece drowning in the dark."

The man licked his lips. "Walsingham's niece? *The* Walsingham?"

Gwilym nodded. "It'll be red-hot pincers for you, matey."

"Get her round. Jump to it," said Blond Hair to his crew.

Lucy stood in a sunlit meadow on a warm English summer afternoon. It was one of those days when time seemed to stand still. A bank of glorious wildflowers stretched out on each side filling the air with scent. A dark green forest marched across the skyline behind her and a stream burbled to itself below. Everything was still and quiet except for the buzz of insects moving from flower to flower. She walked down the hill to where Lilith sat on the grass throwing pebbles into the water.

Lucy sat down beside Lilith. For a while neither of the women spoke. Eventually, Lucy broke the silence. "Am I dead yet, Lilith?"

Lilith smiled at her. "Not at all. You are back on the surface breathing. Your body biochemistry is a train wreck. I am patching it up. It is easier if I keep you unconscious. Less chance of brain damage, you see. So I created this simulation for us to talk in." Lilith gestured at the meadow. "You remember this place fondly; I took it from your oldest memories."

Lucy threw a pebble in the stream, watching the ripples spread out. She did not understand what Lilith was doing to her body; she never did when Lilith went into details about magic, but she was aware that Lilith could carry out many functions at the same time. "Are we safe?" Lucy said.

"I am afraid not. Your sea captain is holding you up but he must be struggling. Unless someone finds us soon, I suspect we will all three drown."

"He is not my sea captain," Lucy said, automatically.

"Really?" Lilith said. "He jumped in after you. I suppose he would do that for anyone?"

"Probably," said Lucy, without much conviction. "He is rather brave and not very bright."

"Sounds like an ideal man to me," snorted Lilith.

"I can't leave him out there in the cold on his own. I owe him some company while he dies. Wake me up, Lilith."

"It will only be partial, Lucy. You won't be able to move all that much. In fact, lie as still as possible. I will have to put you back to sleep after a few moments to protect your brain."

Lucy nodded at her and threw another pebble in the stream. "I understand but wake me up anyway."

William forced himself to think clearly. The trick was to stay alive. Just keep them both afloat and try not to let the cold kill. He held Lucy tight to him to minimise heat loss. Her breathing was controlled and regular.

"Mmm, William?"

"Lucy. You're awake. Don't give up; we are going to get out of this. My men will find us."

"Liar," she said, with affection. "Thank you for coming for me, William." She drifted away for a minute then spoke again. "Catch me when I fall."

"That's right, Lucy. I promised to catch you when you fall. I always will. Don't give up."

"Like poor Anne Hewet who fell off London Bridge. Master Osborne caught her when she fell. Caught her and never let her go."

"What mean you, Lucy? Who is Anne Hewet?"

"Nobody important, just a prize. But mayhap they loved each other. I wonder?" She stroked his face. "William?"

"Yes, Lucy."

"Your beard tickles."

"If we were together, Lucy, I would have my barber shave me every week, every day even, if it pleased you. Whatever pleased you."

"You have my permission to hold me as tight as you want," she said.

"I know, as long as you can still breathe," William said.

"I have never been held like this before, in a man's arms," she said, sleepily.

"You fit there rather well, methinks," he said.

"Lilith can't keep me awake any longer, William. I have to go to sleep for a while. I will be back as soon as I can."

"Hush, sleep now. I will look after you."

William looked round in desperation. All he could see was darkness and water. He was tired and cold. Had he been alone, he would probably have given up and finished it, gone below and breathed in.

Lucy sat back in the meadow. "I feel guilty about reclining here in comfort while William fights for our lives. He really is rather sweet, isn't he?"

"I am sure that he would be glad that you were happy. But yes, he is a sweetie," Lilith said. "Have you ever played skimming stones, Lucy?"

"No, I don't think I have," Lucy said.

"Come on, then. I'll teach you." Lilith bounced to her feet and searched the bank for a suitable stone, which of course she found.

William spat out a mouthful of water. He was now very tired and he had stopped feeling cold. That was a bad sign. Then he heard a cry, but he could not see anything in the darkness. He tried to yell back but it was difficult as the spray whipped into his face. He had an idea. He raised Lucy's right arm. The blade was still gripped firmly in her hand.

William spoke into the girl's ear. "Lilith, Lilith, if you can hear me, make light, like you did before. It's now or never, Lilith."

Without warning, the dagger blazed bright blue-white light. William had never seen anything so beautiful. He heard cries in the distance. They had been spotted.

"Keep it going, as long as you can, Lilith."

Gradually the dagger dimmed and went out. But by that time a huge shadow was silhouetted against the night sky.

"There they are," said a voice. "On the port bow."

People were in the water all round him, supporting him.

"Easy, Captain. Let the maid go now and we will get her in the boat," said a swimmer.

For a moment, he failed to take it in. He still held Lucy tight, his fingers twisted in her clothes. Then thankfully, he released the burden and other people held him up.

"Gently with 'er 'igness." Gwilym's voice sounded in the dark.

Hands pulled him up. He snagged his knee as he was pulled over the side. He had never been more pleased to feel pain before. Pain was life. They had made it.

He crawled across the deck, "Lucy, how is Lucy?"

"'Er 'ighness lives, Captain. I will look after 'er."

The final release of responsibility turned off something in his head and he pitched gently down into the dark.

The boats heaved to, lashed together, until dawn. William slept most of that time. The boatswain woke him, with the present of a small beer.

"What a rat-party. I hate night operations," said William. "How bad are our losses?"

"No deaths," said the boatswain. "Reilly got a bad cut but it's clean so he will probably make it. The gentleman has a bump on the head. The lady is still sleeping. She is breathing naturally as far as I can tell. Walsingham's man is keeping an eye on her and he is right careful of who goes near."

"Good," said William.

He finished his beer in one go and went to find Lucy. She slept on the upper deck. Gwilym sat by her, whittling a piece of wood with his knife and watching. They had lain her in cloaks the night before, to keep her warm. William squatted by her. "Lady Dennys, Lucy, can you hear me?"

Her eyes snapped open and she stretched like a cat. "Indeed, Captain, thanks to you. Methinks you saved my life. I will never forget how you came for me."

So, thought William, they were back to "captain" and "lady" already. The intimacy of Lucy and William forged by the water was a fading dream but he had made progress. He was forgiven for his earlier transgression. He had found the answer to the question of how a soldier impresses a woman who can outfight him. Easy, you save her life at great risk to your own. How clever of him to arrange it, he thought ruefully.

"Your demonic friend had something to do with it as well," he said, modestly.

She smiled at him. "That's not what Lilith says. She says that you saved all of us, Captain. Truly, I can see why other men think so highly of you."

Lucy stretched out her hand and William hastened to kiss it.

The pinnace pitched in the swell as it made its way out to sea with the fishing boat in tow. There was a small canvas-covered cabin at the back where the captain could enjoy some privacy and protection from the elements. William held court there with Simon and Lucy. Gwilym was positioned three feet behind her. After her swimming scare, he refused to let her out of grabbing distance.

"Well, Master Tunstall, let's see if it was worth the lady risking her life, not to mention mine," said William.

Simon opened the leather bag. Inside, was a package carefully wrapped in oiled cloth. He slit open the cloth and removed a pack of papers.

"Have any survived?" asked William.

"The papers are soggy. The outer ones are ruined as the ink has run." Simon carefully peeled the papers back to split them up and allow then to dry out. "The inner ones have survived. They seem to be lists of troops."

Simon studied them. "They are an assessment of the trained bands around London and East Anglia. Troop locations, numbers, and how fast they might be deployed."

He picked up another document and handed it over to William. "What do you make of that, Captain?"

"It's a list of current ship dispositions around London and the south coast of England, with notes on how quickly they could be made ready for sea." William indicated an entry with his forefinger. "The *Swallow* is listed as docked in London itself. The information is right up to date."

"You are a military man, Captain," said Simon. "Why would someone want such information?"

William shrugged. "It is always useful to know the whereabouts of potential enemies, in case they are massing forces against you."

"Or in case you wish to mass forces against them?" Simon asked.

"Such information would certainly be useful to Palma if he intended to invade southern England but that is hardly a realistic possibility," said William.

"No, he would never sail enough troops past the sea dogs to defeat the militia," said Simon. "Unless, the government of England was already in disarray and fallen into factional fighting. The Duke of Palma might then land enough Spanish troops to decide the issue in King Philip's favour."

Simon continued to peel off and lay out papers to dry as they talked. One in particular caught his eye. "This is a letter to the Duke of Palma. I will read it out. 'Knowing that Elizabeth is an heretic and a bastard and hence no true prince.' "

"Her Majesty will love that," said Lucy.

" 'I am resolved to replace her by a sovereign more fitting in the eyes of God. I refer to Mary Queen of Scots who is of legitimate birth and so has the best right to the throne. I, myself, also have a legitimate claim and will marry Mary to cement it. Thus will petticoat government end and the march of this monstrous regiment of women be reversed. Then will I cleanse England of heresy and restore the true religion.' "

"And the burnings will start again, just like in Bloody Mary's reign," said William. "Just as it is described in Foxe's Book of Martyrs."

" 'I will tolerate no piracy and put down the nest of vipers in the west,' " Simon read out loud. He looked at William. "I think he means you."

"The Hawkins family is high on Spain's list of enemies," said William, not without a degree of satisfaction.

" 'Just two tercios of veteran troops should stabilise my rule until I have disposed of the last heretic leader who might impede me.' " Simon paused in his reading.

"Two tercios? Two regiments of Spanish infantry will muster at least two thousand men, more probably four thousand. What is Elizabeth supposed to be doing while all this is going on? Just sitting around moping, waiting to be deposed? She will loose the sea dogs and those tercios will be sleeping with the fishes," William said. "Rows of Spanish troops lined up in little wooden barges to cross the North Sea. Why, man, it will be like playing skittles with culverins."

"Elizabeth won't be able to loose anyone if she's dead," said Simon. "Listen to the rest of the letter. 'The first blow will be to remove the bastard Queen. Her death will paralyse all resistance as the heretics squabble amongst themselves over her replacement.'"

"Is this wicked letter signed?" asked Lucy.

Simon squinted at the signature. "The Earl of Oxford."

He got to his feet and paced up and down thinking. "We must get this to Sir Francis immediately. He will want total secrecy. If they find out we have captured the despatch boat they might strike early. No one will have seen us take it in the dark but if we sail it up the Thames in broad daylight then the secret is out. Captain, you must sink the boat here out at sea. Let Oxford think it was lost accidentally to Neptune."

"There is the matter of the prize money," said William. "I can't cozen the crew out of their share."

"The secret service will buy the boat at market rates. Now sink it," urged Simon.

"And its crew?" William asked, with an edge in his voice.

"The same. They must disappear as if they had never been," said Simon, coldly.

"You want us to slit their throats and dump them overboard?" asked William.

"Yes," said Simon.

William stood up and dragged Simon to his feet. He pulled him out onto the deck where the despatch boat crew were tied. He put a dagger in Simon's hand and pulled back the head of a sitting man to expose his throat. "You do it then, Master Tunstall. You kill the first two or three and my men will follow your example."

"They worked to save my life last night," said Lucy. "And that of Captain Hawkins."

"That we did," said the blond traitor. "Mercy, lady. Show us mercy."

Simon threw down the knife. "I don't like it either but what would you have me do? Risk losing England to save the lives of a few traitors. Their mouths must be stopped."

"Mayhap there is another way," said William. "We could transfer them at night to the hold of the *Swallow* and keep them hidden there until the plot is foiled."

"Yes, noble lord," said the blond man. "We would be as mice in your ship's hold."

"You understand," said Simon, "if there is a single incident then my order to the captain will be enforced."

"Yes, Lord," said the man.

"Very well then," said Simon, relief evident in his voice.

William gave orders to scuttle the captured boat. Then he took Simon to one side. "Master Tunstall, last night when Lady Dennys and I were in the water, things were a little perilous and she was confused. She mentioned an Anne Hewet who fell off London Bridge. In her mind, there seemed relevance in the story for our situation. Could you explain?"

Simon's face went blank. "Maybe you should ask Lucy what the story meant to her, Captain."

"I can see that you are hiding something, Simon. Out with it."

"Anne Hewet was a girl who fell off London Bridge into the Thames. She was rescued by a Master Osborne, an apprentice to her father, who dived in after her at some risk of his own life. Her father gave Anne to Osborne with a huge dowry in recognition that he had saved her."

"So that was what she meant. She said that Osborne had caught Anne and never let her go." William's face lit up.

Simon shook his head. "I know what you are thinking, Captain. You think she might draw some parallel that would favour your suit but you could be quite wrong. Did she say anything else?"

William thought carefully. "When I asked who Anne was, she replied, nobody important, just a prize. Then she said, but mayhap they loved each other. What did she mean?"

Simon sighed. "I told Lucy that story as a light diversion. I thought it would amuse her but it seemed to heavy her mood, instead. After I had finished, she asked me whether they loved each other. I did not understand her at the time. Later, I gave her reaction some thought. As men, we see it as a charmingly romantic tale of a brave man who wins a bride and a fortune. But look at it from her viewpoint. Anne was given away as a reward, apparently no different from the bag of gold that accompanied her. Ask yourself if Anne favoured this Master Osborne. Was he pleasing to her eye? Did his wit amuse her? Maybe Lady Dennys would like to be wooed by a man more interested in herself, than in her name and fortune. Just a thought."

"What are you two talking about?" asked Lucy suspiciously arriving suddenly behind them.

"Master Tunstall was telling me the story of Anne Hewet and London Bridge," said William.

"What made you bring that up?" asked Lucy, in surprise.

"You mentioned it last night," said William. "I wanted to hear the full tale before I answered your question."

Lucy's hand went to her mouth. William recognised that as a sure sign that she was uncertain. "What question?"

"As to whether they loved each other. Osborne was her father's apprentice so he must have known her well. No man jumps into the water in the vague hope of a reward, Lady Dennys. He throws himself in to save something too dear to lose. So he certainly loved her. I think she may also have loved him; had he not saved her? So, to answer your question, milady—yes! I think they loved each other." William walked off whistling, stopping only to berate some poor seamen for slackness.

Act 17,
The Earl of Oxford's Country Seat

Walsingham chaired the meeting, as always. This time Lucy had a place at the table. Gwilym eased the chair under her as she sat. "Now you won't 'ave to strain to 'ear, 'ighness," he whispered in her ear.

She grinned at him before playing the great lady. "Thank you, my man."

"Masterly, Captain, masterly," said Walsingham. "This is the most important haul of despatches that I have seen in, well, in a long time."

"Indeed, sir. May I take it my execution is further postponed?" said William, boldly.

"After reading this, Captain," Walsingham waved Oxford's letter, "I think you can assume that your demise is cancelled. I have been after Oxford for years but I never had the evidence, you see. You can't just arrest an earl and put him to the question, even if he is a treacherous bastard. Now I have him in my hand." Walsingham's eyes gleamed.

"We should really thank your niece, Lady Dennys," said William.

'Oh no, Lilith,' thought Lucy. 'He will think to please my uncle by telling how he pulled me from the water. Uncle will be furious that I disobeyed him."

Walsingham glanced sharply at him. "Lucy did not involve herself in the capture, did she?"

"Certainly not," said William, honestly. "Lady Dennys did not go near the enemy vessel before it was secure. She was entirely dutiful but her night vision is extraordinary. She just guided us straight to the target. We could not have succeeded without her."

'He is more subtle than he looks,' thought Lilith.

Lucy smiled at William in gratitude.

"The most worrying issue is the threat to the Queen's life. I have increased her security of course, put in food tasters and my own men around her chambers. She has taken to sleeping with a small sword under her pillow."

William laughed. "Blood, she has more balls than any other prince in Europe. The first assassin into her chamber will be pricked, mark me."

"Her Majesty is most difficult. She will promenade among her subjects. She insists that her greatest protection is their love, and to love her they have to see her." Walsingham sighed.

"She is not completely wrong," said Simon. "Politically speaking, I mean. Remember what happened when Queen Mary consigned Princess Elizabeth to the Tower. Londoners lined the Thames to shower her boat with flowers. That focused a few minds, I'll warrant."

"Politically, possibly she is right but it creates a security nightmare. Just one man with one of the new pistols, that is all it takes," Walsingham said. "No, we can't risk another assassination attempt. The Secret Service must strike first. Fortunately, Oxford is out of favour at court so this letter is enough evidence for me to act."

"Oh! What has the Earl done to annoy Her Majesty?" asked William, who was not in touch with court gossip.

Walsingham laughed. "He has seduced Ann Vavasour, one of the Queen's maids of honour. Ann gave birth secretly in the royal chambers set aside for the maids. You can imagine how the childless Virgin Queen reacted to that when it came out! It seems that I have need for you once again, Captain. Oxford is at his country house in Essex, with his cronies. All the plotters together in one place, where I can take them." Walsingham stretched his hand out and closed his fingers. "I could use the Earl of Pembroke's men but I want a quiet operation. Do you understand, Captain?"

"Yes, sir," said William.

The Earl of Pembroke controlled a substantial military force and he could be relied upon to put down rebellion with brutal and ruthless energy. Pembroke had served her sister, Mary, so Elizabeth had been a little hesitant when Lord Burghley had recommended him for her Privy Council. However, as Burghley pointed out, Pembroke was an English nationalist. He was disinterested in the finer points of politics or religious doctrine but was completely loyal to the legitimate ruler. The one thing he couldn't arrange was a quiet operation. Pembroke would go after Oxford with a troop of heavy cavalry. He would burn the house, put everyone in it to the sword and probably ravage the surrounding county for good measure.

"What about Lady Oxford, Burghley's daughter?" Simon said.

"Oxford has her exiled safely out of the way in one of his more inaccessible houses in Somerset. She would have been an obstacle to his marriage to the Queen of Scots, that stupid wretched woman. Before Mary of Scotland arrived in the land, it was Elizabeth's proud boast that she had never executed anybody for political or religious reasons. An eminently sensible policy as it created no resentment or martyrs for the Catholic cause. Within a year of Mary's arrival, we had a full-scale Catholic revolt in the northern counties. Before Mary, Spain was an ally and Philip interceded for us to calm the Vatican. Since the '69 revolt, the Vatican has declared Elizabeth a heretic and our relations with Spain have soured into a cold war. Mary has to go. The Queen is reluctant but one day I will build such a weight of evidence of Mary's treachery that the Queen will be able to haver no longer."

"I still don't see how Oxford could have divorced his wife to marry a Catholic monarch and become a Catholic king. The hypocrisy would choke even the Vatican." Simon tried to drag Walsingham back from one of his favourite hobbyhorses—the need to eliminate Mary Queen of Scots.

"Hmm, by the easiest way possible, Tunstall. Until death us do part, remember. No doubt the unfortunate Lady Oxford would have fallen down the stairs and broken her neck at an appropriate moment. It wouldn't be the first time," said Walsingham, dryly. He was referring to the scandal that had engulfed Leicester, whose sick wife had taken a lethal tumble at just such a convenient moment, when Leicester was courting the Queen.

Walsingham gave a wintry smile. "The status of a widow is vastly preferable to that of a convicted traitor's wife. I believe Lord Burghley could restrain his sorrow if his son-in-law failed to survive your attack. And the Hawkins family would have a powerful patron. You understand me, Captain?"

"Yes, sir. I will confer with my officers and plan an assault. I assume the Earl's house will be defended?"

"There will be servants there, certainly," said Walsingham. "And Oxford's cronies will be armed."

"You are all forgetting something," said Lucy.

"And what would that be, child?" said Walsingham.

"You are forgetting the Black Queen, Isabella."

"Go on, Lucy," said Walsingham, indulgently.

"Lilith envisages a problem with your plan," said Lucy, diffidently.

"I had forgot that there was a fifth person at this meeting," said Walsingham. "And what error does Lilith find in my arrangements?"

"Lilith does not think like us, Uncle. She is like a vast conjuring engine that can foretell possible futures," said Lucy.

"Like the mathematics used for astrology," said Walsingham, with interest.

"Yes," said Lucy. "She can cast many astrological charts all with slightly different starting points. She calls them mathematical models. She can make quite accurate predictions of the likelihood of events when she has conjured enough of these models. Let me show you."

Lucy fetched Walsingham's chessboard. She placed it on the table and stacked the pieces to one side. "In this chess game between the Secret Services, we start with the kings. The white king, that's you Uncle, and the black king, Oxford." Lucy placed both on the board.

"De Mendoza tried a fool's mate by using pawns to eliminate the white king." Lucy lined three black pawns up in front of the white king. "These are the bandits that attacked you on the road to Nonsuch, but the white knight and bishop, Gwilym and Master Tunstall respectively, took the pawns."

She removed the pawns and placed a black knight on the board. "They then deployed their knight, Packenham, to check the white king but the black knight was removed by Captain Hawkins," Lucy placed a white rook beside the knight, "and the white queen." Lucy removed the knight.

"You are the white queen, Lucy?" asked Walsingham.

"Yes, Uncle," she said. "We then counterattacked and removed two of their rooks, the safe house and the despatch boat. That just leaves their back line where the king lurks. You gentlemen are assuming that he is protected only by pawns." Lucy placed some in front of the black king. "But you are forgetting something. Where is their queen, Isabella?"

Lucy picked up the piece and showed it to the men. "Why, here, of course. Defending the king." She placed the black queen by the black king. "The black queen is very powerful and can open portals for demons. So she can convert these pawns to other more powerful pieces." Lucy replaced the black pawns by rooks and bishops and knights. "When you attack the Black king, Uncle, you will find that your pieces," she placed a knight for Gwilym, a bishop for Simon and a rook for William and his crew, "will be heavily outnumbered unless you reinforce them."

Lucy picked up the white queen and placed it behind the white attacking pieces.

"I like this not, Lucy," said Walsingham.

"I agree with Sir Francis; it is too dangerous," said William.

"I am sure you would die gallantly fighting impossible odds, Captain, and I promise that I would weep prettily over your grave," said Lucy, sweetly. "But surely the aim is to crush the plot?" She pushed the white queen right through the defending pieces until it touched the black queen. "The queens will cancel out to let the rook check the king." She picked the white rook up and placed it against the black king. "Checkmate."

She looked around the room. "Of course, Lilith and I may be wrong. Can someone point out the flaw in our argument?" There was silence. "I take that as agreement then. I must come with you. I know little of military matters and I am fatigued, so I shall take my leave of you while you plan your campaign."

Anyone who looked in her chamber would have seen Lucy asleep on her bed. Up to a point that was true. Her body was asleep. Lucy herself was with Lilith, in the meadow that Lilith had downloaded from Lucy's mind. This was a new convenient place where Lucy and Lilith could talk face to face, without risk of Lucy being discovered talking to spirits. They sat high on the meadow bank near the dark wood. Up here, cooling breezes alleviated the summer heat.

"I have to stop leading him on. To do otherwise is dishonourable," said Lucy.

"I don't understand your concerns, Lucy. He seems happy to be led on. Indeed, I get the feeling he would follow you anywhere, over broken glass if that is what it took," Lilith said.

"But it's not fair, Lilith. It's not fair to him. I know you can't understand because you are just a demon. You may be clever but you can't comprehend what it is to be human."

"Explain it to me, Lucy. I know you like him. You may tell yourself otherwise, but I see how your body responds to him."

"And why should I not like him, demon? He is handsome, commanding, and stands with that arrogant tilt to his head that dares the world to gainsay him. He answers me straight and looks me in the eye. He gazes at me with a hunger that makes my knees go weak. And when I was lost, he came for me at great risk to his own life, suggesting that something nobler than mere wanton lust drives his interest. So why should I not like him?"

"Then what is the problem?" asked Lilith.

"The problem is that it is all impossible. I am not destined for a provincial sailor, no matter how worthy he might be. I have my position to consider. Uncle has my position to consider. He would never countenance such a match."

"And you have to obey your uncle?"

"Yes. He has raised me as his own, Lilith. He has spared nothing for my security and comfort. He acts only for my benefit. I could dishonour neither him nor my dead parents' name by openly defying him. William's suit is just not possible."

"Your world is changing, Lucy. I have been modelling your society and it is in the throes of rapid evolution. New types of leaders are emerging from the wealth associated with marine technology. The old order of land and blood is fading. The Queen is at the head of this revolution so, as long as she rules, it will continue. If your uncle came to believe that this match was possible and desirable, would you then countenance it?"

"If wishes were lands we would all be rich. Stop it, Lilith. No good can come of such idle speculation. It leads nowhere but dissatisfaction. Why are you so concerned, anyway?"

"I see inside you, Lucy. I see what you want and I think that you want this man. I want you to be happy, that is all."

"I am happy, Lilith. We all have to face duty and put selfish desires aside at some point in our lives. And those, like me, who have received the greatest bounty, must shoulder the greatest duty."

✧   ✧   ✧

Lucy knelt down beside Gwilym under a tree. Irregular bushes broke up the ground cover. The dawn twilight lit up the horizon, infiltrating rays into the woodland around them. Oxford's house lay before them. The house had been described variously as a gentleman's country house and a hunting lodge. Both statements might have been literally true but were utterly misleading. The house was a farmhouse. In Surrey or the Weald of Kent, that would have meant a rambling building with various outhouses, orchards, and walled gardens. It meant something very different here on the Essex coast. William joined them and crouched down so that he did not break the skyline.

"The place is a bloody fort," said William. "A pox on Walsingham's intelligencers. If that's a hunting lodge then the *Swallow* is a fishing boat."

The house and grounds was completely enclosed by a high wall such that only the top floor was visible. This was the frontier of Southern England and it faced a hostile continent. The sea represented a highway rather than a barrier, and it was not unknown for envious foreigners to invade the realm looking for booty.

"We have no scaling equipment to get over that wall so we will have to go through the gates," said William. He pointed to a double wooden gate that was as high as the wall. "I bet that it's reinforced with wooden bars at the rear. It could take us whole minutes to get through. A successful raid depends on surprise and speed. We might as well send them a letter telling them that we are coming."

He signalled to the boatswain who ran doubled over to join him. "We will need to cut a sizable tree to make a battering ram."

"That cannot be done quietly, Cap'n," said the boatswain, pulling thoughtfully on his chin.

"You think I don't know that," said William, snarling. "Go back a ways into the wood to dampen the sound. As quick as you can, boatswain, the house will be stirring soon."

"Sir," said the boatswain, knuckling his forehead.

"Hold," said Lucy. "Mayhap there is another way."

She stood up very deliberately and walked out onto the grass. She looked at them over her shoulder with a mischievous grin. "Gentlemen, follow me." Then she walked down the slope.

"Lucy, wait," said William and reached out for her.

Gwilym seized his wrist. "Don't grab at 'er 'ighness. It ain't polite." He rose to his feet and followed her. She was moving slowly so he soon caught up and took his position, three steps behind and one to the left.

William cursed quietly to himself. Who was supposed to be captain here? He rose to his feet and held a fist over his head. He stepped out of cover, where he could be seen, and rotated the fist left and right. The Swallows emerged from the tree line and started down the slope.

The strange phalanx walked silently towards the fortified farmhouse. Lucy was at point with her bodyguard. William strode along behind her with a skirmish line of Swallows behind him. He had positioned Simon in the rear with a couple of sailors to look after him. Simon was there to search for evidence, not to fight.

They walked at a measured pace. What a how-do-you-do, thought William. He had followed some gallant officers in just such a skirmish line but not one led by a sixteen-year-old court girl. He had no idea what they would do when they reached the farmhouse but, knowing Lucy, it would be spectacular.

As Lucy walked she spread her arms down, palm out. Her skin took on a shine and then a glow. Her hair rippled. She looked as if she was moving into a headwind but it was a headwind no one else felt. She started to bounce as she walked as if her body was suddenly light. William knew that Lucy was possessed by Lilith and that she was now as much demon as human.

Lucy started to speed up into a fast walk at fifty yards from the gates and then a jog trot at twenty-five. William had once seen a Spanish lancer regiment charge in the Low Countries. Gentlemen abed in England made light of the Spanish army but William had never seen anything to sneer at. Amateurs think a cavalry charge is some uncontrolled gallop from the first wave of a sabre. Not a bit, the idea is to deliver the horses at full speed in a concentrated mass at the point of impact. The regiment William had seen had started at the walk and then gradually speeded up onto the target.

At fifteen yards, Lucy broke into a run with the Swallows following. At ten yards, she sprinted faster than any of the men could match. At five yards, she jumped into the air and rolled over until she flew feet first. At one yard, she drew her knees back. At six inches she exploded into motion. Her legs shot out and her feet hit each side of the join between the gates.

The gates did not open. They exploded, showering the air with splinters and Lucy landed in the middle of the wreckage.

"Ow," she said.

William and Gwilym rushed up. "Are you all right, milady?" asked William.

"I have a splinter," she said, through gritted teeth. "You are both to look away while I remove it."

"Oh holy saints," said William. He stared at the heavens. War was suspended while their general removed a splinter from her seat.

Lucy gave a yelp. "You can look now." The girl stood up and tried to hold on to her dignity. William chuckled and got a murderous look in reply, which only made him more amused.

A long straight path led up to the front of the farmhouse. At some point, it had been rebuilt in red brick. A thin orchard was planted on each side of the path nearer the house. The trees were of an unusual type, with large bright green fruit that was shaped like teardrops. Lucy started up the path, Gwilym at her back. The sailors followed them.

The trees did not improve upon close examination. Brightly coloured patches of fungal rot caused a strange appearance. Purple veins lined the fruits. No birds flew amongst the branches but large grey moths crawled over the fruit, as if feeding off the secretions that ran down the sides. The fresh, twisted body of a squirrel lay under one of the trees. The fruit above had little teeth marks.

The front door of house opened and a lady dressed in maroon court dress emerged. "Lady Dennys, I said there was more to you than met the eye, especially true as I see that your dress sense hasn't improved."

Lucy wore a working woman's dress rather than court clothes. They were far more practical than the elaborate costumes of the upper classes.

"Uncle always says that a young maid like me would look attractive in a turnip sack. It's only ladies of a certain age who need the support of artefact," Lucy said, sweetly.

"A man! What would he know?" Isabella shielded her eyes with her hand and examined the shattered gates. "Couldn't you just knock like everyone else?"

"I suppose that I just don't know my own strength," said Lucy.

"You do seem to be overburdened with energy," said Isabella. "Positively glowing in fact. We must find some way to burn off some of that surplus." Isabella raised her hands and started to chant.

'Danger, Lucy,' thought Lilith. 'Isabella is building up energy.'

'Really, Lilith? Oddly enough, I had worked out the same thing, despite my small mind.'

Lilith thought Lucy sounded worried. She tended to get waspish when she was concerned. Caution was a sensible emotional response to the situation. Frankly, Isabella scared Lilith witless. Lilith sensed a large vortex of spinning energy over Isabella's head. It had some of the characteristics of a portal but without the rip in space-time.

'Time to stop this,' thought Lucy. She drew her knife and flipped it so that she held it by the tip of the blade between her thumb and forefinger. Lucy drew back her arm to throw, when Isabella clapped her hands.

Lilith patched her senses through to Lucy so the girl could see energy spin from the vortex. It streamed over her head, divided and poured into the trees. Lucy flipped her knife again so that she held it by the hilt. This was no time to lose her blade. What William saw was a squall rip through the unsettling orchard, shaking the branches and causing the fruit to sway. Lilith and Lucy saw the trees glowing with power—power that drained into the fruits.

Fruits dropped to the ground where they beat like obscene green hearts. "Black magic," said a sailor, in horror. The Swallows shrank back except for William and the boatswain, who stood their ground.

Cracks showed on the outer casing of the fallen fruit. One split wide open to reveal the pulpy fruit within. The fruit hesitated, quivering for a moment before uncoiling. It expanded with extra body weight. Once upright, the plant creature stood on two legs. It had two arms and a sort of extension that served as a head. Its arms came up in a fighting stance, showing "hands" like shovels with shining hard edges like blades. More plant creatures emerged and moved towards the humans.

Lucy drew her blade and ran towards the nearest two monsters. She kicked the first one in the centre of the body, forcing it away. With her left hand, she spun the second around and cut its head off with her dagger. It fell with a hissing, deflating noise, losing body mass. Gwilym struck at the first one with his cutlass, lopping off an arm but it attacked with its other hand, forcing him back. Lucy ripped it open with her glowing blade. It fell with the same keening hiss as the first.

"Fire," William said. The sailors unleashed a fusillade into the plant things. Sea dog crews were heavily armed with guns so they could fire a withering volley. The shot hit home on the monsters, bursting straight through their bodies in places, but the creatures seemed unaffected.

"I doubt they have organs like an animal to be damaged," said Simon.

William raised his cutlass over his head. "Follow me!" he cried and charged, his men running behind him. They pushed the monsters back with the ferocity of their attack but the plant things were almost impossible to kill with normal weapons. The Swallows cut chunks out of the plant creatures but they always returned to the attack. More fruits dropped all the time adding to their numbers. The sailors were soon fighting for their lives.

"Isabella is the key to this, Gwilym. I'm going for her," Lucy said over her shoulder.

"Right, 'ighness. I'll cover your back," Gwilym said.

Lucy spun down the path, punching, kicking, and slashing. Her blade inflicted terrible damage when it cut through the plant men. But mostly, she just smashed them out of the way. Gwilym walked behind her using his cutlass two-handed, as a club, to bat away any creature that tried to get behind her.

Behind them, a creature knocked one of the sailors to the ground. The creature slashed at him. In desperation, the man put his pistol against the creature's chest and pulled the trigger. The shot burst through clean through the monster, doing little damage. However, the charge left a black scorch hole that caught fire. The flames spread quickly and the sailor had to scoot out of the way to avoid being burnt. The monster staggered around wreathed in flames until it crashed into a second plant creature, setting it alight in turn.

"Fire. Cleanse them with fire. Reynold, Hoggit, back to the gate for wood. Break branches off the trees and set them alight. Drive them back with torches." William was exultant. The key to any victory was finding the right weapon. The trees shook and moaned as the seamen lopped branches off.

Isabella greeted Lucy's advance with amusement. Her smile slipped as Lucy and Gwilym came on, foot by foot, yard by yard, leaving a trail of wreckage behind them.

Lucy burst through the last line of plant creatures to confront Isabella. The Spanish witch made a throwing motion with her left hand. A fireball materialised out of thin air and spun towards Lucy in a lazy arc. It seemed to travel slowly at first, curving away from her. At the last minute it speeded up, whipping in towards the girl. Lucy threw herself to one side and the fireball sizzled past.

'Isn't that interesting?' thought Lilith. 'The fireball is actually on a fixed speed and trajectory. The apparent changes in velocity are an optical illusion caused by misalignment of your eye-brain functions.'

Lucy dodged desperately to avoid the next missile while shoving Gwilym down under the line of fire. 'Fascinating, Lilith, now how about you devoting your exceptionally large mind to devising a strategy to avoid us being flame-grilled?'

The first fireball had ploughed harmlessly into the back wall but the second hit a plant creature, setting it on fire.

'Oh, I have already thought of that. I can—'

'Multitask, I know Lilith,' thought Lucy, ducking under a rising fireball.

'I have put an electromagnetic field into your blade. You can parry the fireballs,' thought Lilith, who was definitely in a huff.

"You can't keep dodging around like that forever, Dennys," said Isabella. "One of them will get you when you tire."

"You're right," said Lucy, standing upright. "I am fed up with dodging."

Isabella made a flick motion with her hand and another fireball curved towards Lucy. The girl deflected it with the blade of her dagger. The ball shot off at a tangent and hit one of the demonic trees. The tree burst into a conflagration, burning with much crackling and spitting of fire.

'There must be flammable spirits under the bark,' thought Lilith.

Several of the plant monsters rushed back towards the tree, trying to put out the flames. They were singularly unsuccessful, managing only in succeeding in setting themselves alight.

'The offspring of the tree try to protect their mother,' thought Lilith. 'That must be their primary biological function. How interesting.'

"William, set light to the trees," Lucy yelled.

Isabella said something in colloquial Spanish using words that Lucy had never been taught. 'I could translate them for you,' thought Lilith, trying to be helpful. 'Loosely, they involve putting your—'

'Never mind, Lilith,' thought Lucy. 'I can imagine the rest.'

'I doubt that,' thought Lilith, but she dropped the subject.

Isabella threw another fireball. This time, Lucy caught it on her blade, and flicked it back at the witch. Lucy had not quite got the line right and it flew over Isabella's head to crash into the house. Isabella was showered with sparks and burning wood.

Lucy glanced around to see how the crewmen were doing. They had more trees alight and blundering, burning creatures were spreading the flames. When she turned back, Isabella had disappeared. The house door swung shut behind her. Lucy pelted after Isabella to crash into a locked door.

Lucy kicked the door off its hinges. Inside was a large reception room with stairs leading up from the centre. Isabella ran towards the bottom of the stairs. She stopped and turned when Lucy crashed through.

"You shouldn't run so fast at your age," said Lucy, confronting Isabella. "You might pull a stay and rupture something."

Isabella threw something like dust into the air and said something too softly for even Lucy to hear. The dust dispersed into smoke that coiled lazily. It swirled into different colours and patterns that funnelled up to form a giant cobra that towered over Lucy. The girl jumped back as the snake struck at her.

Lilith saw the snake through Lucy's eyes. She could not understand how Isabella had transported such a large demon. She had not felt the surge of energy that accompanied an opening portal. In fact, she had not detected anything. Actually, now she considered it, she still could not detect anything. Lucy backpedalled as the giant snake coiled closer to her.

'Lucy, stop. The snake isn't real. It's a hologram,' thought Lilith.

'A what?' thought Lucy, confused.

'An illusion, it's not really there.'

'It cursed well looks there, Lilith.' Lucy dodged again.

'Isabella is buying time. Close your eyes.'

It was a measure of the confidence that Lucy had in Lilith that she did so. 'I hope you know what you are doing, demon.'

'Walk forward, Lucy.' The girl swallowed and took three long steps. Lilith was struck, not for the first time, by the astonishing bravery of her friend. Lucy had such a short life that Lilith would have understood if she had avoided any risk, so as to eke out whatever span she could. Instead, the girl walked into potential death solely on the word of a friend.

'Open your eyes, Lucy.'

The girl complied. The snake was behind her; in fact she was standing in its tail. The giant animal struck mindlessly into the empty air. From this angle, its form was more indistinct.

"The devil damn you, Lucy Dennys," said Isabella. She had something in her hand and a black vortex spun in front of her.

'That's the sea diamond mirror, Lucy. That's what brought me to this world. Stop her.'

Isabella pushed her body into the vortex like a woman walking against a strong wind. Lucy flipped her knife around and threw it. The blade struck the vortex at the same moment as Isabella vanished. There was a flash so hot that it set light to the drapes, and even the wood panelling. It was accompanied by a blast of air as if a great cannon had been fired into the room at point-blank range.

Lucy was knocked to the ground. The power was gone from her body but it had lasted long enough to protect her. She got up and walked to the base of the stairs. Her dagger lay there so she picked it up and examined it. Astonishingly, it was undamaged. Beside it was a flat traylike object. She turned the object over to see a highly polished mirror with an ornate frame set with aquamarine diamonds.

"Are you all right, Lucy? What in damnation happened here?" William entered the room and gaped. "My life used to be so unexciting until I met you, Lady Dennys. I sailed ships to the Americas, fought the odd battle against overwhelming odds, relieved the Spanish of the occasional trinket, nothing too burdensome at all, really."

"Isabella opened a portal," said Lucy.

"Like in my cabin," said William. "I recognise the signs. I suppose that means Isabella got away."

"Maybe," said Lucy. "But I shorted out the charge with this." Lucy displayed the blade. "And Isabella left something behind."

"I recognise that. It's the mirror I took off my last prize. It disappeared from my cabin with Isabella. Ah, I see. This is the magic artifice that opens portals to the Other World."

"And Isabella dropped it," said Lucy. "I wondered where she ended up?"

'Or when she ended up,' thought Lilith. 'Uncontrolled portals can twist time.'

While they talked, the rest of the crew joined them.

"Blimey, milady, you made a mess of someone's chambers," said a wag.

A man dressed in an expensive white shirt and breeches stalked onto the upper landing. He held a duelling rapier in his hand. Armed men followed him onto the landing, but he arrogantly indicated that they should wait while he walked alone down the stairs. "Who the hell are you rabble?"

"Captain Hawkins, may I introduce you to the Earl of Oxford. Milord, Captain Hawkins of the galleon *Swallow*," said Simon.

"I know you. You're that oily little clerk to Walsingham," said Oxford.

Simon bowed. "I am indeed Walsingham's oily little clerk, milord."

"What are doing in my house making such a bloody racket? I'll have Walsingham's head for this."

"I have come to arrest you for treason, milord," said William, mildly.

"Have you indeed? Only the Queen can order my arrest," said Oxford.

William reached back and Simon passed him a document. "As you see, my lord, the Queen's seal."

"Indeed," said Oxford. He gestured to Lucy. "Stop gawping, girl, and get out of the way. Go about your duties or I'll have them take a cane to you."

He had clearly taken Lucy to be a servant girl. Obviously, he could not tell one servant from another. This, as much as the threat of a caning, told Lucy everything she wished to know about Oxford's treatment of his inferiors. It suited Lucy to be anonymous in front of Oxford's men so she curtseyed and removed herself to a corner.

Oxford strolled arrogantly down the stairs. "Hawkins, eh? I suppose you are one of that noxious brood from Plymouth."

"I have the honour to be cousin to both John Hawkins and Francis Drake," said William, bowing.

"No honour, Captain, to be the cousin of pirates," said Oxford, with a sniff. "And how do you propose to arrest me?"

William smiled and raised his cutlass. Oxford walked down the stairs and raised his rapier. "You men," Oxford said to the sailors, "back off and give us room."

Oxford did not lack for courage, whatever other vices he had, thought William.

"Want us to shoot him down, sir?" asked the boatswain, who had no pretensions to be a gentleman.

"No, I will deal with him," said William, who did have certain pretensions in that direction.

The two men took a stance and Oxford immediately attacked. He was a tall man with a long reach, which he ruthlessly exploited. After the first exchange, William knew that the aristocrat was an accomplished duellist. Oxford unleashed a complicated series of offensive manoeuvres. William was slow to disengage. Oxford slashed him across the arm, drawing blood. The earl drew back and saluted with his weapon.

"First blood to me, Captain."

'Lucy, your captain is being outfought,' thought Lilith.

Lucy did not answer but Lilith could see her life signs move into panic mode. It was a measure of the girl's distress that she did not bother to correct Lilith about him not being her captain.

The men fought on. William moved straight to the attack, trying to beat down Oxford's lighter rapier. The earl parried brilliantly and counterattacked. He soon had William on the defensive again. Oxford executed a beautiful feint and pricked William in the shoulder. Again the earl backed off and saluted.

"Second blood to me, Captain. Mayhap you should have stayed in Plymouth rather than trying the patience of your betters."

"Sound council, my lord. I will try to remember it, if I ever meet my betters."

They took their stance again. William was bleeding from two wounds. The first was bloody but inconsequential but the second clearly hurt him. The point is always more dangerous than the edge. Lucy eased her blade out and gripped it by the tip behind her back.

'That's it, Lucy. Bring Oxford down,' thought Lilith. 'No one will notice if you do it right.'

'William will notice,' thought Lucy. 'I can't do that to him.'

The men had started the duel again.

'You can't save his life? What madness is this, Lucy?'

'Oxford might kill him but I can do much worse. I can strip him of his honour and his manhood. I can destroy him. All I have to do is help him, Lilith, that's all it takes. He's a man so he would rather die.'

'Men are such wonderfully illogical creatures. They are so handsome and exciting but do you not sometimes think that their irrationality makes them more trouble than they are worth?' thought Lilith, trying to distract Lucy from the fact that her sea captain was soon in deep trouble again. 'Why have you drawn the knife if you are not going to intervene?'

'To avenge him, Lilith, Oxford dies one second after William,' thought Lucy. 'I will kill Oxford if the boatswain does not shoot him down first.'

Oxford spun his sword around William's cutlass to get inside his defence and then lunged. The rapier struck William in the body and penetrated along the side of his ribs. Oxford relaxed and started to back off. William pulled his left arm in to hold the weapon in place. He stepped towards Oxford, moving onto the rapier, drawing more blood. William's face twisted with the pain.

Oxford looked surprised; one's opponent in a duel is not supposed to walk onto your sword. He impatiently tried to free his weapon but William had it tight. William had all the time in the world. He raised his cutlass high and slashed the earl across the neck in a single fluid motion. The heavy weapon cut deep enough to nick bone. Oxford fell without a sound. The weight of his falling body pulled the rapier out of William's side. A new flow of blood stained his shirt.

"Oh William, William, you're hurt." Lucy ran over to pull his shirt off.

The boatswain pounded up the stairs, closely followed by the rest of the Swallows. Oxford's leaderless and demoralised supporters put up a feeble resistance before crying for quarter.

Simon organised a party to search the house. The boatswain escorted the prisoners out. That only left Gwilym in the room with William and Lucy. Gwilym took his customary bodyguard stance by the door and took a keen interest in what was left of the ceiling decoration.

The rapier had glanced off a rib and ripped up William's side. Lucy reached under her dress and pulled off a petticoat. William could not take his eyes off her. She tore the petticoat into strips to clean and bind his wounds. She was very thorough. The slightest cut could kill through infection by noxious vapours.

When she had finished, she stood in front of him and looked up at him. Tears rolled down her cheeks. "I'm only crying because I am so mad at you. He should have killed you. I thought you were going to die in front of me."

"Shush." He wiped her face with a stray piece of petticoat. "Oxford was a duellist and a far better one than I could ever be. He was a duellist but I am a soldier, Lucy. He wanted to play with me to show his skill. I just killed him at the first opportunity. Thank you for believing in me enough not to help."

"Stupid male pride. Uncle is just the same. You are all the same." She stamped her foot.

"Thank you." He kissed her.

She did not move a muscle but continued to gaze up at him with big eyes. The same big brown eyes that he had noticed that first time that they met at the *Swallow*'s gangplank. "Oh William, this is stupid. I can't let you kiss me. It can't be." But she still did not move away.

"Shush," he said, again. He lifted her chin with his hand and kissed her hard on the lips. This time she responded.

Act 18,
John Dee's Cottage at Mortlake

The boatswain conned the barge carefully against the stone steps. Seamen jumped ashore with ropes and made the boat fast. "So this is Mortlake," said William, taking in the surroundings. The place was a pleasant enough hamlet despite its grim-sounding name. Supposedly, the currents and eddies of the upper Thames delivered the bodies of drowned men and animals to this bend in the river.

The barge had sailed up from London that very morning. William had the carpenter put in some additional seating for his illustrious passengers. One could hardly expect a member of the Privy Council to squat on the deck. Walsingham had spent the journey going through affairs of state with Simon. William would have liked to take the opportunity to talk to Lucy but had been inhibited by the presence of her uncle. Lucy had been rather cold and distant since the intimacy that they had shared in Essex. Indeed, the girl appeared to avoid being on her own with him. He feared that he had been overbold.

Walsingham signalled for him, so William hastened over to the spymaster. "That is where Doctor Dee lives." Walsingham pointed to a small cottage perched right on the bank of the Thames. It was in a poor state of repair and looked as if one good push could send the whole building tumbling into the water. "It is actually his mother's.

Doctor Dee is indifferent to the normal luxuries of life and spends all his money on books and artefacts. I wonder what old Mother Dee thinks of having her son and his household dumped on her in her dotage."

"The Doctor is married?" asked William. "He did not look the type." William hastened to add, "I meant no disrespect, Sir Francis, it's just that Doctor Dee appeared to be rather too aesthetic for matrimony."

"You would be surprised," said Walsingham, dryly. "When he was at Cambridge Dee used his body as actively as his mind."

"Where's Lucy?" asked Walsingham.

"There, Sir Francis," said William, pointing to where Lucy had curled up against the stern bulkhead. Her eyes were closed and she appeared to be fast asleep. But they couldn't see inside Lucy's head.

Lilith crossed over the stepping-stones. One wobbled and she almost fell in the stream but she windmilled her arms in time to regain her balance. "You might have warned me that stone was loose," Lilith said, in a reproving tone.

"Lilith, you created this place for us. You pulled it out of my memories. How can you not know everything about it?" asked Lucy, hands on hips.

"Oh, I have a subroutine that formats the meadow." Lilith waved a hand airily. "You can't expect me to waste core processing power on such simplistic tricks. After all, I have—"

"An exceptionally large mind. I know, Lilith. You have often found it necessary to remind me."

"You seem subdued today. It is true that I am hardly an expert on human social interaction but your brain wave patterns are not indicative of happiness."

"I fear that I have made a grave error, Lilith. I made a solemn promise to myself that I would not lead him on and then I let him kiss me. How stupid of me, Lilith, how very foolish."

"I have wanted to ask you about that kiss, Lucy, but have been afraid to raise the subject."

"You know, Lilith, it says everything about my situation that my first proper kiss from a man should be observed by Gwilym watching me from the outside and you from the inside. Mayhap I should have arranged for it to have taken place in a theatre and sold tickets."

"Would people have really paid to watch such a short event?" Lilith asked, puzzled.

"I was being sarcastic, demon," said Lucy. "You can be astonishingly literal-minded."

Lucy paused, "What do you mean by short? It was quite a long kiss, actually."

"About this kiss," said Lilith, refusing to be deflected.

"What?" asked Lucy.

"I just wanted to say that I didn't understand. Before I mean."

"You are not making any sense, Lilith."

"I thought I had learnt so much about human beings, when I studied your literature in the other human Shadow World. I read about love and hormones and passion but Lucy, I understood nothing. I just did not realise what it felt like."

"I trust you found the experience enlightening," said Lucy.

"For that one moment, my mind collapsed. I would have done anything for him, literally anything to keep that feeling. Now I know." Lilith paused.

"Know what, Lilith?"

"Why your people have such complex rules and customs to regulate behaviour. Why things are done or not done. Your passions are so strong, so overwhelming, that rigid conventions are essential to prevent anarchy. Can it really be even stronger for men?"

"How would I know, Lilith?"

"What are you going to do about your sea captain, Lucy?"

"I shall marry someone suitable and try to forget him. What else can I do?"

"I don't know but I doubt you that will ever put him from your mind." Lilith paused. "Incidentally, your uncle is shaking your body." The meadow faded away as Lilith switched off the simulation.

"Wake up, Lucy. Time to go ashore," said Walsingham.

"I was just resting my eyes, Uncle." She stretched and jumped to her feet.

"Careful, milady. The steps are muddy." William stood to hand Lucy safely out of the boat and onto the steps.

"Thank you, Captain." Lucy was polite but distant.

Simon followed her.

"Why does she blow so hot and cold?" William said to Simon. "I take three steps forward in her favour but then she moves two steps further away."

"You navigate treacherous waters, my friend," said Simon. "Make sure you don't leave your bones on a hidden reef."

The party made their way up onto the embankment beside Dee's cottage. In front of them, set safely back from the water, loomed the solid shape of Mortlake Church, dedicated to Saint Mary Magdalene.

"The church is new," said Lucy in surprise. Most English churches had been built during the years following the Norman Conquest. England's new overlords had ruthlessly torn down the old Saxon churches. In this way, the Norman aristocracy demonstrated their piety to God and also indicated to their Saxon peasantry that they were in England for good. In time, the new Norman churches became a conservative English tradition and the French-speaking overlords became a conservative English aristocracy—such were the foundations of the Dennys family.

"It's one of the first Church of England buildings put up after King Harry split from Rome. A truly English church, it is not forty years old. The tower is handsome, is it not?" Walsingham traced the outline with his hand. The stepped tower was Norman-square with buttresses on the lower corners. It was firm and solid and proclaimed to the world that, like the Norman aristocracy, the Anglican religion was here to stay.

Dee's property ran all the way back beside the church. Outhouses and barns clustered around a rectangle to make a small courtyard behind Dee's cottage. Walsingham unclipped the gate and his party entered the courtyard. Chickens and pigs rooted around in the yard. Alerted by a servant, Dee greeted them at the back door of the cottage. "Welcome, Sir Francis, welcome, and Lady Dennys. I believe that this is the first time that you have visited Mortlake. Her Majesty was kind enough to visit me earlier this year when I was unwell, although she remained in her carriage of course. So two lovely ladies have visited my humble dwelling this year."

Dee was doing his best to be gallant, reflected Simon. But, from the expression of Lucy's face, he had a great deal of ground to make up. Lucy failed to give him the "English kiss" on entering.

"I regret my mother cannot greet you," said Dee. "Her health has failed this year and she is bedridden." The party entered the cramped dwelling. It was at least a hundred years old and the frame had started to warp, giving the place a lopsided look. A baby cried somewhere in the back of the house. "My son Arthur has a lusty voice. My wife is attending him."

"Indeed," said Walsingham.

"My household and I live simply in a few rooms, most of the other space is devoted to my collection of books and artefacts. I keep the most valuable items here in the cottage with me." Dee walked to a bookshelf and pulled out a tome, which he handled reverently. "This is Johannes de Burgo's *Treatise on Magic*, which I acquired when in Louvain. It is written in Spanish using the Hebrew alphabet. I thought originally it was in code and spent some little time trying to code-break it before realising my error."

Dee shook his head and smiled at his own stupidity. Simon noticed that Dee changed character completely when discussing his beloved collection. Dee replaced the book and moved along the shelf.

"Now this is the *Secretum Secrotorum* that I bought in Padua. It is anonymous but I believe it to have been written by Aristotle."

"The *Secretum Secrotorum*," Simon was impressed. "It concerns the magic of immortality, does it not, Doctor?"

"Indeed, Master Tunstall. It contains the first mention of the Fountain of Youth. We will talk more on this later." Dee paused for effect. The philosopher had a tendency to talk as if delivering a lecture. "Actually, I found many useful works in Italy including volumes on Plutarch, Euclid, and Apollonius. Oh, and this work on the Cabala mysteries."

"Now this is interesting." Dee pointed to a slim book. "This is the famous *Liber Experimentorum* by the Spanish mystic Ramon Lull."

"Do you not have a copy of Copernicus' *De Revolutionibus*, Doctor?" Walsingham said.

"Two actually," said Dee with false modesty. "I also have copies of Boethius' *Consolations of Philosophy*, Norton's *Ordinal of Alchemy*, and Ptolemy's *Tetrabiblios*."

"This collection must have cost a fortune," William said in awe, speaking for the first time.

"Indeed, it did," said Walsingham, dryly. "The secret service paid for most of it."

"I believe the Service has had value for money," said Dee, stiffly.

"And I trust that situation will continue," said Walsingham, pointedly.

"Where do you keep the rest of the collection?" asked Simon. "There is not room here for four thousand items."

Dee moved to the window and opened it. "Behold my *Externa Bibliotheca*," he said, gesturing to the barns and outhouses arranged around the yard. "That old cow shed contains my volumes on alchemy, the Armenian Church, Africa, botany, barques, calvados, and chastity. The barn, there, holds works on demonology, dreams, dragons, earthquakes, entomology, Etruria, Exeter, and my navigation artefacts. The whitewashed stone house has falconry, fabrics, gambling, games, gymnastics, horticulture, houseflies, Islam, jesters, Jews, and logic. In the shed, the one with the shuttered windows, are volumes on marriage, mythology, the European nobility, oils, ointments, and pharmacy. The labourer's cottage has my collection concerning rhetoric, saints, surveying, ticks, tides, toffee, veterinary studies, weather, women, and zoology."

"You hold books about women?" asked Lucy.

"One of the more intractable areas of investigation in my experience," said Dee, apparently with a straight face.

Lucy sniffed, eloquently.

"I suggest we move to the barn where I can explain my interpretation of the more mysterious of the works that you brought back from Essex. If you will follow me?" Dee showed the party out into the yard. He strode to the barn vigorously and promptly forgot where he had put his key. Walsingham tapped his foot while Dee searched. Eventually, he discovered the offending item and unlocked the barn door. Simon noticed that the lock was modern and secure. Inside, long rows of stacks filled with books formed long isles. One small area was clear, containing a reading table and chairs. Dee's collection of navigational artefacts was positioned behind.

William was fascinated by a set of globes of the world. "You like them, Captain?" asked Dee.

"I confess that I have never seen finer," said William, admiringly.

Dee flushed with pleasure. "They were a gift from an old friend, Geraldus Mercator."

"I see you also have a compass and a cross-staff. I had heard that you were an accomplished navigator."

"This will interest you, Captain Hawkins," said Dee. He ushered William to a corner containing a complex engine of shining metal. A pendulum swung beneath it.

"This is a clock, is it not, Doctor Dee?" asked William.

"Indeed, and it is accurate to the nearest second."

"Draw your sword, Captain, and stand just so." Dee manoeuvred William in front of a mirror. "Now make a mock lunge."

William was a little bemused but he did as he was told and made a halfhearted lunge at the mirror. It seemed to flicker into life and something came out of it and lunged back. William leapt back with an oath and the apparition vanished. He repeated the mock attack. This time, he anticipated the result and held his ground. He was able to observe the image flickering in front of him.

"God's blood. It's me. The mirror creates an homunculi of me. Do you try it, Master Tunstall?"

Simon took his place with the same result. "It's like the image of Lilith that you called forth, Doctor Dee."

Everyone looked at Lucy. "Well, I don't remember. You had me mesmerised, remember," the girl said, sulkily. "Lilith says that it's a hologram, if that helps. She also says that it is theoretically impossible for us to create holograms given our primitive understanding of light. Lilith can be a bit patronising sometimes."

"Where did you acquire this mirror, Doctor?" asked Walsingham.

"From Sir William Pickering. You recall, Sir Francis, that he and I studied under Sir John Cheke at Cambridge. I stayed at Sir William's residence when he was ambassador to Brussels. He had this mirror there and gave it me to assist my studies in the optical sciences."

"Indeed, Pickering was one of the Queen's suitors at one time, I recall."

"Her Majesty was much taken with this mirror when I showed it her."

"Talking of mirrors, Dee. What have you found out about the one that Lucy took from the Lady Isabella?"

"Ah yes." Dee went over to a bag and retrieved the mirror. Dee had cleaned it. The mirror was just as William remembered it. Twelve inches high, beautifully worked with gold, sculpted into mythological creatures and monsters, and set with aquamarine diamonds.

"It is most disappointing, Sir Francis. I had high hopes from your description but it is just a mirror. There is no power in it at all."

Lucy sat bolt upright. "That can't be. Lilith was held captive in that mirror and Isabella used it to travel between the planes. It has great power."

"Mayhap it had once, milady, but it is empty of all magics now," said Dee.

Lucy looked at the mirror intently and touched it. "Lilith agrees with you, Doctor. It is just a mirror now, but it was powerful once. Isabella used it to conjure a portal to the Other World. As she entered the portal, I attacked her with my dagger. There was a huge flash." Lucy cocked her head on one side and said, "Oh, I see."

"What do you see, Lucy?" asked Walsingham.

"I was talking to Lilith. She thinks the blade shorted out the mirror, draining it of energy. Sorry, Doctor Dee, I think I may have ruined it for you."

"Mayhap it is for the best," said Walsingham. "It was an artefact too dangerous to be allowed to exist. We would always have had to destroy it eventually but I had hoped to use its power one last time." He looked at Lucy but she was still distracted by Lilith and so did not pick up on his meaning.

Walsingham rose to his feet. "So the matter is concluded. The plot is smashed and the main conspirator killed. You may take possession of the diamond mirror as legitimate compensation for—whatever the Hawkins family has against the Spanish on their letter of reprisal. You may return to Devon, Captain. Rest assured, John Hawkins will be told how well you carried out your duties."

"The coroner has not yet pronounced a verdict on Oxford's cause of death," William reminded Walsingham.

"The verdict has already been decided. At the appropriate time, the coroner's court will sit and confirm it officially," Walsingham said, confidentially. "Oxford died accidentally while practicing swordplay. It's a common enough verdict. People will suspect that we are covering up a duel of honour."

"I suppose we will never know what became of Isabella after the portal collapsed," said Lucy.

"I can tell you that she survived. One of Pooley's watchers saw her board a fishing boat by the Spanish Embassy. My agents report that she crossed the sea to the Low Countries. We must take our leave of you, Doctor."

"Stay a little longer, Sir Francis. I have decoded the documents you took from Oxford's house." Dee gave a smug smile.

"Indeed, Doctor." Walsingham sat down.

"There was a great deal of information about the plot, including names of sympathisers who might be expected to assist the new government." Dee attempted to hand the papers to Walsingham but the spymaster gestured that Simon would take them. "I expect you will be arresting such people."

"I will arrest the dangerous ones but not the others," said Walsingham. "They would only deny the charge and claim that the plotters had added their names out of ignorance or spite. No, I will arrange for them to find out that they are named in Oxford's records without revealing how deeply they are implicated. Then I will let them stew, while they wonder how much I know. Her Majesty will have no more loyal subjects than these people in the future. Fear will see to that."

"Then there is this," said Dee holding a small journal. "Have you heard of the fountain of youth?"

"The fountain of youth?" asked Walsingham. "Do you mean that awful painting by Lucas Cranach?"

"Lucas Cranach?" asked William.

"German painter, not the current one but his father. He was one of Martin Luther's friends and a keen Protestant. For some reason, he also specialised in painting nudes. He painted this perfectly odious picture of all these nude geriatrics jumping in an ornamental pool and emerging young and nubile at the other end."

"I do not mean the painter." Dee sounded exasperated. "I mean the legend about the West Indian island."

"Perhaps you might recap for us," said Walsingham. "The short version, if you please, Doctor."

"The Indians of the Caribbean Sea had a legend of a mysterious island of power somewhere north of Cuba in the Bahamas Chain. Have you ever been to the Bahamas, Captain?"

"No, they are a bit away from our usual routes," said William.

"Pity," said Dee. "This island is usually called Bimini. The Indian legends say that only the pure of heart could find the islands. It seems that some could find it while others could not even though they sailed the same waters. Most Europeans did not believe Bimini existed but one Juan Ponce de Leon did take the legends seriously. He became convinced that the island was the site of the fabled fountain of youth. Why that in particular, I cannot fathom, as the legends speak of many wonders, eternal youth being but one."

Dee refreshed his voice, from a mug.

"De Leon was given permission by Charles V of Spain to mount a search in—" Dee consulted his notes. "—March, 1513. He sailed the waters with Indian guides and found precisely nothing. He did, however, bump into Florida and plant a colony there. St. Augustine, I think it was called. De Leon tried again in 1521, with exactly the same result except that this time he ran foul of the Floridan Indians who drove him off. As far as I know, no European has ever found

Bimini and the Indians who knew its location are long gone. There the story ends."

"So why your interest, Doctor?" asked Walsingham. He had waited patiently through Dee's lecture. The doctor could be irritating but he was the foremost scholar of the secret and hidden sciences in England.

"Isabella's journal, Sir Francis. She claims to have visited Bimini. Her writings are difficult to comprehend. They were written in code, of course," Dee said.

"No doubt that gave you few difficulties, Doctor," said Walsingham.

"It presented a pretty problem, Sir Francis, but, as you know, any code can be cracked, given enough time. The problem with the journal is not the code but the guarded and mysterious references within. It can only be understood by one steeped in the secret sciences. The average sort of turnip eater would have no hope of comprehending her writings."

"So what are your conclusions then, Dee? And why am I listening to this?"

"I anticipate that you have not seen the end of Isabella, Sir Francis. She was the real power behind the coup. Oxford would have been king only in name and I suspect that the Spanish do not control her either. She has vaulting ambition and a desire for power. Most witches are sad old women who gull simple villagers out of parsnips. I believe the Lady Isabella to be the real thing. From the references in her journal, she has developed a deep antipathy to you and your niece. I doubt that events in Essex have altered that opinion and I do not think that she is the sort of person who turns the other cheek."

"Well, no doubt we will deal with her should she ever return to these shores," said Walsingham, rising. "Thank you for your warning."

"Sit, please, Sir Francis. There is more." Dee made a seating movement with his hand. "Isabella's power comes from Bimini. I suspect she is far older than she looks, if I have determined certain astrological charts in her journal correctly."

"You think she has found the fountain of youth, Doctor?" asked Simon.

"Oh, I think she has found more than that, Master Tunstall. I think she has found a source of great power. This little trinket," Dee pointed to the sea diamond mirror, "is but a pale reflection of what lies in Bimini. Tell me, Sir Francis. Do you know where Isabella went when she left London?"

"At the Low Countries, she joined a Spanish vessel carrying a unit of Italian mercenaries bound for the Americas," said Walsingham.

"I was afraid of that. The Secret Service must stop her, Sir Francis, before she replenishes her power at Bimini."

"You present me with a pretty problem, Doctor. My arm is long but . . . the Americas!"

Dee gestured at William. "You have a race-built galleon and crew. Why not overtake her?"

"Hold, Doctor. It's a big ocean out there. One ship cannot intercept another at sea," said William.

"Can it not, Captain? Well, mayhap one can't normally but it all depends what you use to search." Dee looked at Lucy, meaningfully.

"Send Lucy? To the Americas? Think you that I am demented?" Walsingham was outraged.

"I agree with Sir Francis. It would be madness to risk her on such a venture," said William.

Lucy opened her mouth to protest but Dee forestalled her.

"Isabella must be taken and her source of power at Bimini destroyed. Without Lady Dennys, you will find neither." Dee walked to a shelf and pulled down the *Secretum Secrotorum*. "Aristotle places the fountain of youth on an island found beyond the Pillars of Hercules. The philosopher claims that most who seek the island will fail to find it unless they can see into Hades, for the island spends but little time in our world."

"It's a portal," said Lucy, excitedly. "The whole island is a portal and it moves in and out of the Other World. That's why de Leon couldn't find it."

"That is my conclusion," said Dee. "Methinks Bimini must have a massive source of power to move a whole island. Enough, perhaps, to speed Lilith home."

"I see," said Walsingham. "We stop Isabella and Lilith destroys her source of power at Bimini by leaving Lucy. I like this solution. It deals with so many issues."

"Will Lilith agree, Lucy?" asked Walsingham.

"Lilith is my friend. She will do what I ask," said Lucy, neutrally.

Dee pulled over Mercator's globe. "If Bimini is between the Bahamas and Florida then it must be about here, Captain."

William studied the globe and traced a route south to the latitude line and then west across the ocean. "How much start does Isabella have?"

"A little over two weeks, Captain," said Walsingham.

"Two weeks! And it will take us half a week to prepare the ship for a transoceanic voyage and then warp her out of the Thames. The *Swallow* is faster than any Spanish ship, Sir Francis, but be reasonable, man. She will have nearly three weeks lead on us. It's not possible to overtake her."

"Not if you sailed by the normal route, Captain," said Dee. "But suppose you took a direct route." Dee traced a diagonal sweep across the Atlantic Ocean from Cornwall to Florida.

"Doctor Dee. You are the foremost expert on navigation in the land," said William. Dee waved his hand in an unconvincing display of modesty. "So why waste your time and mine? You know we can't sail diagonally across the ocean."

"Why not?" Lucy asked, genuinely puzzled.

"Because it is easy enough to know the latitude of a ship using a cross-staff," said William. He looked around and pointed at a wooden structure that consisted of a long staff with two cross staves on at right angles. "See, Doctor Dee has one there. With that, I can measure the angle that the sun makes with the horizon at midday. From tables, I can deduce how far south the ship is. So to reach Bimini, we sail down the eastern Atlantic until we reach the correct latitude then sail along the latitude line. But to sail diagonally across the Atlantic I would need to know the *Swallow*'s longitude as well as her latitude."

"And that cannot be done?" Lucy asked.

"No. Oh, men have tried. One can guess at longitude by dead reckoning. That is, trying to measure the ship's forward speed and keeping a record on a chart. Another way is to calculate the difference in angle between magnetic north and the pole star. But these methods are wildly inaccurate. And if the ship is not where the navigator thinks she lays then you can sail her straight onto a reef. I can't risk the *Swallow* and all aboard," here William looked at Lucy, "with such foolishness."

"Indeed not. But suppose you had an accurate clock, Captain?" asked Dee.

"If I knew how many hours west of England the ship was then I would know how many degrees west the ship had travelled. Know you of such a clock, Doctor?" William asked, rhetorically.

"As I told you, Captain Hawkins. That clock is accurate to a second." Dee pointed to his gleaming engine. The pendulum underneath swung rhythmically backwards and forwards.

William laughed. "Bless my soul, Doctor. You theoretical scholars should get out more. Such a machine would never survive a voyage. That pendulum would be wrecked before we reached Gravesend."

"I am not such a ninny that I cannot recognise that," said Dee, testily. The Doctor went to the corner and opened a chest. He searched within and retrieved a package wrapped in an oiled cloth. He opened it reverentially.

"Johannes Trimethius' *Steganographia*," said Dee. "After Trimethius died, his fellow monks read his manuscripts. So shocked were they to discover that he had been working on demonic magic that they burnt all the copies that they could find. That is why there are but three copies left."

"It cost the secret service twenty pounds, as I recall," said Walsingham.

"Scholars still argue whether it is a book of magic masquerading as a code book or the other way around," said Dee.

"Which is it, Doctor?" asked Simon.

"Why both are true, young man. It is really a book about all aspects of secret communication.

"Now, Captain," said Dee. "Suppose you had a way of communicating with someone in England from the deck of your ship. Hmmm?"

"Someone with an accurate clock who could tell me the time in England when the sun was overhead on the ship," said William, excitedly. "Know you how to do this, Doctor?"

"In this book," Dee waved the *Steganographia*, "is a spell that causes two candles to become magically harmonised. What someone says into one will be heard from the other."

"Why isn't everyone doing this if it only takes two candles and a spell?" Walsingham asked.

"There is a snag," said Dee.

Walsingham groaned. "I thought so. There is always a snag when magic is involved. What is it?"

"It's demonic magic." Dee paused and seeing no one grasped the point, continued. "You need a demon to power the candles."

Lucy was staring out at the river. She turned her head to find all eyes on her. "What!" she said. "What are you all staring at?"

Act 19, Leaving London

William kicked the tufts of grass. He thought he saw traces of brown. This was so unlike the lush, green Westcountry. London desperately needed rain. He glanced at the sky. It was completely cloud covered but not a drop of water fell.

William was not in a good humour. The sailors recognised his mood and hurried to load the *Swallow* with enough food and stores for an oceanic voyage. St. Katherine's dock was a hive of activity. William hunted out the dockyard attendant. The man noticed him and attempted to scurry off. William would have none of it. He pounced and seized the man by the arm.

"I am afraid that I am busy, Captain." The attendant tried to disengage his arm but William held it firm.

"Too bad," William said, rudely. "Those spars, there, are rotten and warped. I am not putting to sea until you produce some decent wood." He pointed to a stack of materiel.

"That's the best I've got. Take it or leave it. Think you that I have premium stores for every provincial who blows in to town? You may be a big man in Plymouth, sunshine, but this is London." The attendant sneered.

William took a firm hold of the attendant's shirt and lifted him on tiptoe.

"Unhand me or Cousin Jacob and a dozen of his men will be out to fix you, Captain," said the attendant, completely unfazed.

William considered calling up a few of his crew to show the man what real violence looked like but he realised that he had a better way to enforce his will. He dropped the man and patted him down.

"That's better," said the attendant, smugly.

"Fair enough, I'll just go up to the Tower and tell Sir Francis Walsingham that I can't obey his orders. It can't be done because some dockyard whoreson has taken his money and cheated him out of decent stores. I'll do that shall I?"

"Sir Francis Walsingham is the backer of this cruise?" The attendant licked his lips.

"The very same. You know the one; sits at the right hand of Her Majesty, has an office in the Tower, runs the scariest spy service in Europe, puts traitors on the rack before beheading them. That Walsingham—you must have heard of him. No doubt he will be well impressed when you threaten him with Cousin Jacob."

"No need to do anything hasty, Captain," the attendant said, ingratiatingly. "Perhaps I can locate what you need."

"Excellent," said William. "I thought we could arrive at a satisfactory solution. I have some business up at the Tower but I'll be back in some little while to see how you are getting on."

The Tower was just a few minutes walk as the raven flies but the whole point of a fortification is that one can't just walk into it in a straight line. It was a good half hour before William conferred with the gunner at the armoury.

"Captain," said the gunner, touching his cap.

William watched a crocodile of sea dogs moving barrels and bags of shot on small carts. "Everything in order, gunner?"

"Yes, sir. The armourers have been most helpful. We will be fully loaded with munitions by tomorrow."

"Good, well—carry on, gunner."

William continued up the Tower Hill to the north curtain wall where Walsingham had his apartments. He found Simon Tunstall, who was greeting a florid, rather round man. The fellow looked like a countryman, come up to market.

"Captain Hawkins, may I introduce Master Paxman. Master Paxman, this is Captain Hawkins of the galleon *Swallow*."

The two men shook hands and exchanged conventional greetings. "Are you by any chance related to . . ."

"John Hawkins is my cousin," said William. He was used to the question and he answered with good grace, as he was proud of his cousin.

"Ah," said the countryman.

"Master Paxman farms a sizable number of acres in the county of Surrey," said Simon. "This is his daughter, Margaret."

The girl looked about thirteen but was probably a year or two older. William gravely bowed to her. "Greetings, lady."

"Your servant, sir," she squeaked nervously, and attempted a curtsey.

"You are up to town on business?" William said to the farmer, in effort to make conversation.

"In a manner of speaking, sir," said the farmer, expansively. "It is my intention to betroth my daughter to Master Tunstall and we await Sir Francis Walsingham's blessing."

William could not have been more astonished if the farmer had announced his intention of declaring war on France and leading a force of crack cowherds to assault Paris. "My, ah, felicitations, Master Tunstall." Then realising how weak that sounded added, "Warmest congratulations. Let me look at the bride to be."

She really was a pretty little thing, although clearly exceedingly nervous. "My, my, how beautiful she is, Simon, no wonder that you kept her well hidden from all us rough sailors. Ah well, another dainty little fish swept from the sea."

"Thank you, William," said Simon. At that point a servant beckoned. "I believe Sir Francis will see us now, if you will excuse us."

Simon showed the Paxmans into Walsingham's reception room. Sir Francis and Lucy were present. "Sir Francis, may I introduce Master Paxman and his daughter Margaret." The men bowed and Margaret curtseyed. "Mistress Paxman regrettably died earlier this year."

"My condolences, sir. This is my niece, Lady Dennys," said Walsingham, setting off another exchange of bows and curtseys. "Wine for my guests." A servant hastened to comply. "She is a dainty catch, Simon," said Walsingham gallantly. "How fortunate you are."

Poor Margaret blushed again. Probably, she had not ever received so much attention in all her short life. Walsingham tactfully turned to Simon. "And what brings your new bride to the Tower, sir? Are there not prettier places in London to visit?"

"I will take her to see the crown jewels later," Simon said. "But first, we have come to ask your permission to marry."

"But there is no legal requirement for my permission," said Walsingham.

"Nevertheless, I ask it," said Simon.

"Well, well, then you shall have it," said Walsingham, clearly pleased with the respect that he had been shown as Simon's patron. "I consider this a good match. You are an excellent young man and the girl is worthy of you. How old is your betrothed?"

"Margaret is fifteen, Excellency. But she will turn sixteen this autumn," said Paxman.

"So you will marry when you return from the Americas?" Walsingham asked. It was unnecessary to add the qualifier "if you return from the Americas." Simon assented. "Have you sufficient funds to keep a wife? You will continue to live at Barn Elms when convenient, of course, but you should also have your own establishment."

"Master Paxman is to settle a farm on his daughter for a dowry," said Simon.

"Even so," said Walsingham. "A wife is expensive and with such a pretty young wife there will soon be more mouths to feed." He chuckled. "We must think of a suitable wedding present for you and an increase in your stipend."

Margaret was blushing again and looking increasingly uncomfortable. Lucy spoke for the first time, seeing her distress. "Fie, Mistress Paxman. The men will now discuss the sordid details of money and contracts that are so unbecoming for a young lady's ears."

Lucy waved a hand, airily, to indicate her distaste for such matters. She took a firm grip on the young girl's arm and propelled her out of the door. "Take you a turn in the grounds with me and tell me all about yourself. We shall be firm friends when you come to live at Barn Elms."

The farmer watched them go with an expression of deep satisfaction. The Dennys family held considerable landholdings in Surrey and Master Paxman knew exactly who they were. Simon knew that he brought little in the way of material wealth to the match but he brought something just as important—connections. Few farmers' daughters from the county would ever meet the likes of Lady Dennys, let alone be "firm friends" with them. Master Paxman would consider his gift of a farm an excellent investment. Margaret began to relax and giggle at some sally of Lucy's as the pair moved out of sight into the Tower's grounds.

Lucy kept Margaret close to the apartments, engaging her in conversation, so that they were at hand when Simon and his future father-in-law emerged into the courtyard some moments later.

"Will you take your betrothed on a sightseeing tour now, Master Tunstall?" asked Lucy. "If so, may I act as guide? I have spent some little time here on my own lately and I have explored. Did you know that they have a wonderful map of London in the library? After examining it, one can go right to the top of the turret and see London spread before you, just like the map."

"I thought access to the turrets was restricted," said Simon.

"So it is," said Lucy. "But I have discovered that a bearer of the Queen's ring can go almost anywhere." She held her hand up.

"The Queen herself gave you that," said Paxman, clearly impressed.

"Off her own finger," said Lucy, proudly. She then laughed. "You must think me very boastful, Master Paxman."

"No I don't, Lady Dennys, not at all." He clearly meant it. The farmer obviously belonged to the "if you've got it, flaunt it" school.

"Shall we go?" Lucy said. "I suggest we first see the chapel where Anne Boleyn prayed before her execution. I am a distant cousin of the lady."

Simon offered Lucy his arm. "What, sir, you offer me your arm when your betrothed stands unescorted? How ungallant of you. No doubt Master Paxman will do me the honour of his arm." The farmer hastened to accede.

"My apologies, madam. I am unused to my situation. Please allow me." Simon bowed to Margaret and took her arm. Lucy led off, chatting animatedly, her hand resting lightly on Paxman's arm. The farmer had insisted on being present with his daughter at the interview with Walsingham. He was a careful man and wished to assess Simon's position in Walsingham's favour with his own eyes. Simon approved; a prudent man would raise a prudent daughter. Lucy had copper-bottomed Simon's suit.

Paxman had ambitions to be president of the county fair at which the more prominent farmers and tradesmen displayed their produce. Next time the committee met, Simon knew that Paxman would wax most lyrical about the time he escorted Lady Dennys around the

Tower of London. The wives of the committee members would want Lucy's clothes, jewellery, and manner described most closely. The other contenders for the presidential chain would be hard-pressed to match this coup.

Simon allowed Lucy and Paxman to move ahead so he could talk to Margaret alone. Propriety meant that he had exchanged few private conversations with the girl. They passed a gaggle of sailors struggling with casks. The sailors were used to Lucy and gave her only passing glances but they gazed at Margaret with interest. Simon pulled her in tighter to him. She looked up at him, slightly puzzled. He smiled at her and she smiled shyly back at him. The match had been arranged for all sorts of practical and sensible reasons. But he was surprised to find that he also found her adorable.

"Lucy, gentlemen, these council of wars are becoming a habit," Walsingham said. "You have even started sitting in favourite seats. So, Captain, when can you sail?"

"Tomorrow's tide, Sir Francis. The pilot's advice is that we use the afternoon's outgoing tide to assist us down the Thames. I will give my crew shore leave tonight."

"I see. Is that wise?"

"Not at all, but it is traditional and to deny them would only provoke insubordination."

Walsingham nodded. "Then there is the matter of my niece. Have you chosen a companion, Lucy?"

"Millie, my maid, has consented to accompany me, Uncle."

"And where will the ladies be accommodated on the ship, Captain?"

"At night, Lady Dennys and her companion will sleep in my cabin. I will have a gentleman's berth. During the day, I will need my cabin back as it is my office but I do not think that this will inconvenience the ladies overmuch."

"I understand that the crew sleep on the deck. Gwilym, you will sleep outside the door to the ladies' cabin. You will kill anyone who attempts to enter when they are inside."

"I assure you that I maintain strict discipline aboard, Sir Francis. The women will be as safe as if they were at Barn Elms," said William.

"My niece would not be going with you if I did not believe that to be so, Captain. Nevertheless, Gwilym has his orders."

William nodded. It would not hurt for everyone to know how the land lay.

"Lady Dennys, I suggest that you and your maid sleep onboard *Swallow* tonight. That way you can try out what we have to offer and allow us to fix any omissions in our hospitality before we leave. Once at sea, we only have what we have, milady." William smiled at her.

"So, Lucy, it's almost midday. Let's put your demon through her paces," Walsingham said. "Are you ready?"

"Yes, Uncle," said Lucy. She sat down cross-legged on the floor and put Dee's candle in front of her. Walsingham lit it from a fuse and then retreated. Lucy put her hands on her knees, palm out.

"Are you ready, Lilith?" asked Lucy out loud, so that the whole room could hear.

'I want you to hold "C"' for me, Lucy. Hold it as long as you can,' thought Lilith.

William watched Lucy take a deep breath. She sounded a note. At first, it slipped up and down the scale but it eventually steadied on a pure tune. The candle flame danced and flickered then shimmered in time to the note. Lucy's voice faded away but the flame held a steady harmonic.

'This is extraordinary,' thought Lilith. 'The properties of the subatomic particles that make up the burning gasses are aligning in colour, charm, and spin. I don't really mean colour or spin, Lucy. These are just words to describe properties of particles. All I am doing is flooding the area with gravitons to power the process.'

'Lilith, you are not making any sense,' thought Lucy.

'Quantum mechanics isn't supposed to make sense. I mean that the vibrations of the things that make up the flame are all lining up like marching soldiers instead of a chaotic mob, which is their normal condition. I am beginning to see how demonic magic works; maybe I am a demon after all. Try talking into the candle. Your voice will set up vibrations that will change the alignments of the particles in the flame. If the candles are tuned, as Dee claims, then the same should happen at his end and he should hear your voice.'

"Doctor Dee, can you hear me? One, two, three, um, Mary had a little lamb."

"Of course I can hear you. What is it about telephonic candles that make people talk drivel into them." Dee's voice sounded from the flame. "Five thousand years of thaumatological research so that you can transmit nursery rhymes."

"Sorry, Doctor." Lucy apologised but her companions could see she was smothering giggles.

"Very well. I think we can agree that the trial is successful. Blow out your candle. We can't afford to waste them."

"Yes, Doctor. Bye." Lucy blew and the flame flared yellow and went out.

"So," said Walsingham. "You sail tomorrow then, Captain. No doubt you have much to occupy yourself." Walsingham dismissed him. "Would you stay behind for a moment, Lucy?"

Walsingham waited until they were alone, well almost alone except for Gwilym, who went where Lucy went. The ancients used to call slaves "furniture with tongues" because foolish men forgot the tongues and suffered for their error when the slaves spoke of secrets best unrevealed. Walsingham had no worries about Gwilym because he was not a slave but a trusted retainer, tied by loyalties of blood and honour to Walsingham's household.

"Are you sure of this, Lucy? It is not too late to express doubts. Even now I can remove you from the enterprise."

"Hush, Uncle," Lucy touched his lips with her fingers. "Without me there is no enterprise. I am content."

Lucy rested her hand on William's arm as they walked the length of the waist deck. Her maid and Gwillym were but four paces behind, deep in conversation. "Do you still want to come now you have tasted shipboard food?" asked William.

"The meal was—" Lucy groped for an appropriate word. "—extraordinary, that's it, extraordinary."

William threw back his head and laughed, "I will pass on your compliments to the cook."

"Where do you keep the oven?" asked Lucy. "I would have thought fire exceeding dangerous on a wooden, tarred vessel."

"Indeed it is. For that reason fires are traditionally restricted to deep within the vessel's hull, near the wet ballast. However, there are appalling noxious vapours there. Disease is as big a risk as fire on a crowded ship and has killed more sailors. Drake has pioneered methods to reduce sickness. One innovation is to move the oven to the fo'c'sle, which is where I place it."

Lucy walked over to the rail and looked towards the tower. The lights of London, Southwark, and the Bridge twinkled onto their reflections in the river. "They are like diamonds on a string around a brunette's neck," she said. "Or fairy lights."

"Your eyes shine more brightly, milady." William moved a little closer and took her hand. "Lucy, there is something I have been thinking about."

A drunken voice from the dock spoiled the atmosphere.

"So the little pixie said, you think I'm very small,

"but when I'm in the mood, maid, I'll tell you true what's tall."

The voice trailed off. "Ahoy the ship. Some worzle-banger has stolen the gangplank. Nah, here it is, they moved it. I'm coming aboard, ready or not and I'll fight the first man tha's gets in my way."

William craned his neck around Lucy and saw a drunken sailor wearing a woman's petticoats weaving up the gangplank. "Ferguson, again. I hope the drunken bastard falls in," William muttered. Two boatswain's mates made their way purposefully to the top of the gangplank. "Come over here, Lady Dennys." He steered the girl to the other side of the ship. William put his back against the rail and stood her in front of him so she looked at him and past him, to the river and lights of Southwark.

"Shouldn't you go and deal with that?" asked Lucy.

"Absolutely not," said William, appalled. "I would have to hang a drunken sailor for mutiny if he hit me. The boatswain's mates will deal with him." The cries reached a crescendo. There was the sound of a fist hitting human flesh and the thud of a body hitting the deck.

William paused to allow the miscreant to be dragged off. "I believe I can escort you to your quarters now, milady."

William took her arm and led her to his cabin. Gwilym was sat with his back against the bulkhead by the door, whittling with a dagger.

"Good night, my lady," William said.

She extended her hand. He kissed it and she vanished within.

"Good night, Gwilym," said William.

"Captain." Gwilym inclined his head.

William left to make the rounds of the deck before retiring to the gentleman's cabin.

Later that night, Lilith noted that Lucy was tossing and turning. The girl was very excited.

'Would you like me to help you sleep,' Lilith asked.

'Yes, please, Lilith,' thought Lucy. 'Don't you ever sleep?'

'No, not really. I spend time in resting where I update and sort files into archives before new data comes in, but I never shut down the way you do.' Lilith gently smoothed Lucy's brain waves into sleep patterns.

'Do you know why we sleep?' Lucy asked.

'That's a very good question that I am not sure that I can answer. You need physical rest, of course, but I suspect you unconsciously update your own memory archives while you are asleep. Lucy?'

Lucy didn't answer. Lilith touched her brain and felt the wave pattern. 'Sleep tight, my friend,' she thought, softly, and withdrew within herself.

The next day Lucy was up with the dawn. William had suffered a busy night, having been dragged from his bunk to deal with the last of the shore-leave dregs. "You look refreshed, milady," he said, sourly. The only thing worse than a bad head in the morning was wide-eyed, happy people around.

"What are you doing?" asked Lucy.

William sat behind a desk that had been placed on the main deck. The boatswain stood beside him. "Punishment parade. After the traditional last run ashore comes the traditional captain's punishment parade. Now go over there, milady, while I undertake my duties."

Two boatswain's mates hauled a sailor at the double up before the desk. He was having trouble putting one foot in front of the other, partly because he still wore a lady's petticoat. He stood swaying in front of the captain. William observed him like a natural philosopher finding a new type of beetle. "Ferguson, again! What is it with you, sailor? Do you like punishment parade?" asked William.

"No, sir," came the reply.

"Charges?" asked William.

"Drunkenness, sir, and calling a petty officer a whoreson."

"These are serious charges, Ferguson," said William, gravely. "I notice you have a black eye. How did you acquire that?"

"Fell over, sir," the sailor said, adjusting his petticoat.

"So you have no quarrel with your treatment last night?"

"No, sir."

"You know the routine by now. Will you accept my punishment or do you want to claim your entitlement to a trial ashore?"

"Your punishment, sir."

"Very well. You're a disgrace to the ship, to your fellow sailors, and to me. You are banned from another shore run for two weeks and will be on punishment duty for a week. Dismissed. No, don't try to salute. Just go."

'Why is he banning shore leave for the man when the ship will be at sea anyway?' thought Lilith.

'I am not sure. It's some sort of man thing. Punishment must be given even if it is meaningless. But we have been dismissed by our new supreme commander—go over there while I undertake my duties, hah!—so, I suggest we go into town. Where are Millie and Gwilym?'

Later that morning, William made his way towards the Tower. He had not seen Lucy go and was slightly miffed that she had disappeared before he could talk to her. Women were so capricious, flouncing off for no apparent reason. William managed to drag the walk to the Tower out to a full hour, for no better reason than he needed time to think and gather his courage. Drake had once told him that there was a time for a quick dash and a time for the long campaign and he had wisely chosen the latter strategy when dealing with Lucy Dennys. But Drake had also said that bold attack was the end point of any campaign and that one should never mistake dithering for wisdom. He was now dithering and it had to stop.

He plotted a course to Walsingham's office and put himself on a fast tack. Then he bumped into someone. "Ah, Lady Dennys. I didn't see you leave."

"You said go over there so I went, Captain."

"Yes but I didn't mean . . ." He was floundering again. He took a firm grip on his mouth. "I need to talk to you. I have to tell you something."

"Indeed, Captain. I am sure that I am at your disposal, as I always am when you have a short gap in the endless list of responsibilities."

"Lucy, please be quiet," he said, desperately.

She obediently shut her mouth in mock fear.

Now or never. "I have to tell you, that I about to inform your uncle, that when I get back, that is when we get back, from the Americas that is . . ."

"Is this going somewhere? Because we sail in only three hours," she asked, interurpting.

"I am about to tell your uncle that I will ask for your hand when we return," said William, in one rush.

She just stood there and looked at him, mouth open.

"I was going to mention it to you first but you had gone somewhere," William said, rather weakly.

"Mention it to me, sir, mention it to me? You thought you might mention it to me?" she said, her voice rising and disturbing a flock of starlings.

"Well, it seemed polite," said William.

"Polite!"

"Marriage arrangements are a matter between men," he said, stiffly, realising that she was not entirely happy with his decision.

"Is it so? In that case, mayhap you should marry a man and leave me out of it altogether," she said, hotly.

"Lucy," he began.

"Don't 'Lucy' me, you arrogant, self-opinionated, self-centred, cocksure provincial. I am Lady Dennys to you. What makes you think that I am destined for the likes of you? How dare you take this step without a by-your-leave?"

The sparrows departed to a gentler place. Tower officials and guards stopped to watch and enjoy the sparks. Gwilym examined the sky.

"I do not like your tone, milady. When we are married you will, perforce, moderate it," William said.

"When this business is finished, you will not have to suffer my tone again. We will not meet again," she said, with finality.

"When this business is finished, we will marry." William said, coldly. He was used to being treated with a degree of deference, not as an upstart yokel.

"And where would we live? Will you be taking a house in Surrey and presenting yourself at court? How good are you at poetry, Captain? Or would you expect to dump me among the hogs and your cast-off tavern girls in Plymouth, while you went a-roving? I would as soon as marry an Irish tinker as you." Lucy looked him boldly in the eye.

"I will marry you, milady, even though you be a shrew that no other man will tolerate." William was white with anger. He grabbed her by the upper arms.

"Shrew, am I? Unhand me, sir," she said, equally furious.

"Because you say so? Mayhap you have too often had free with your will, milady. Now I will have free with mine."

Lucy opened her mouth to express her opinion on that, when he pulled her to him and pressed his mouth hard on hers. All the girl got out was an outraged squawk. He took his time with the kiss, despite her struggles. When he released her, she stepped back, panting and wide-eyed.

"Your servant, milady," he said, insincerely. William bowed and walked off leaving her with an open mouth.

Lucy stamped her foot. "Insufferable man."

Lilith just did not know what to say. Lucy's thoughts were a maelstrom that was painful to interpret. Emotion after emotion chased across her head. Lilith was not sure whether to comment or stay silent. Lucy was liable to misinterpret either strategy. Lilith began to appreciate the terrible complexity of human mating behaviour. It was even worse than she had anticipated. Eventually, Lucy solved her dilemma by addressing her first.

'Did you see what he did?' Lucy's thoughts emoted outrage.

'I was aware of the situation,' thought Lilith, as neutrally as she could.

'In public! To manhandle me in public!'

'Surely, it would have been improper in private.' Lilith thought without due consideration, and Lucy pounced on it.

'It is even more improper in public. He treated me like a tavern girl.'

'But why did you let him then, Lucy, if it offended you so?' Lilith was confused. 'Why did you not just push him away?'

'How could I, demon? He is twice my size.'

'Twice your size perhaps, but you are twice his strength, are you not?' There was a long pause while another set of complex emotions flickered across Lucy's consciousness. Lilith continued. 'I was close enough to monitor his physiology, his blood pressure, heartbeat, and skin conductivity. It seems to me, Lucy, that you struggled just enough to cause maximum impact on his biochemistry but not enough to escape. Is that a component of human mating behaviour?'

'Lilith, I will evict you if you speak to me of this again, even though it kills us both.'

"Come in," said Walsingham in reply to William's knock. "Ah, Captain."

William marched over to Walsingham's desk and came to attention stiffly in front of it, like a sailor on punishment parade. Walsingham noted his pallor.

"Sir," said William formerly. "I beg your indulgence to speak to you on a matter concerning your niece."

"Yes, Captain," said Walsingham, warily, pressing his hands together as if in prayer.

"I wish to inform you that I intend to ask for your niece's hand upon my return from the Americas."

Walsingham blinked.

"I am sure that I am hardly your idea of a perfect suitor. I could point out the advantage of a marriage alliance between the Boleyn and Hawkins clans, in the event of war with Spain. I could point out that Lady Dennys has shown scant interest in any of the aristocratic suitors placed before her. I could point out that many of the aristocracy might no longer favour an alliance with her, given the rumours that must already be circulating."

At this point, William noted that Walsingham's lips tightened. "But I will restrict myself to the following observation. I have fought alongside the lady. I have seen her courage and humanity. I have seen her laugh and cry and observed her triumphs and failures. I admire her more than any woman that I have ever met and I believe I can make her happy."

"So you love her, Captain," Walsingham observed. He sighed and pressed his hands against his eyes before continuing. "I should have anticipated that, Lucy is very appealing. But affection is an uncertain basis for a marriage, especially where there are so many other conflicting factors. You and she live in different worlds, you must see that."

William met his eyes boldly. "Then think of the political disadvantages of rejecting the suit, sir. The message it sends out is that we in Plymouth are good enough to officer your ships and to fight your battles but not to marry your daughters."

Walsingham came to a decision. "We will talk of this on your return, Captain."

"Sir!" William turned to go.

"Captain." Walsingham stopped him. The spymaster seemed to have difficulty framing his next statement, which was most unlike him. "You will look after her on this voyage, won't you?" Walsingham was almost pleading.

"Sir," said William. "If harm comes to Lady Dennys, it will be because I am already dead. I have to prepare, if you will excuse me, sir." William saluted and left, his back ramrod straight.

As soon as he was clear, Lucy slid into the room.

"I take it you heard all that?" Walsingham said.

Lucy nodded and bit her lip. "I was outside the window."

"Our family has always believed that forewarned is forearmed. We ought to put it on the coat of arms," said Walsingham, dryly. Lilith thought the man looked tired. "Well, this is a pretty pickle that you have created, Lucy, and no mistake."

"He is a good man," said Lucy, defensively.

"That he is," said Walsingham. "A good man for a Plymouth pirate. For that is what he is, my girl, once you strip the romance away from his profession."

"He is right, though, Uncle. War with Spain is coming and that war will be fought at sea. How many of our ships will be designed, built, owned, or officered by the Plymouth families?" Lucy had spent too much time at court and around Walsingham to be politically naive.

"About two-thirds to three-quarters," answered Walsingham.

"And what will happen if Spain makes a rapprochement with the Hawkins clan?" Lucy said.

"That is hardly likely." Walsingham waved a hand dismissively. "Elizabeth's government and the Hawkins family are united in the new religion. John Hawkins and Drake have much reason to hate papists."

"Perhaps, but political advantage can make strange bedfellows. What if Philip promised Plymouth that they could keep their religion and gave them trading rights in the Americas?"

"I am not unaware of the need to bind the London aristocracy and the Plymouth naval families together, Lucy. Do you remember when Hatton made a joke about knighting Drake? I wonder whether we should not take the idea seriously. Sir Francis Drake and Sir John Hawkins might sit well in Plymouth."

"Possibly, but let us not be mealy-mouthed, Uncle. The coinage of diplomacy is gold, treaties, fortresses, and women's bodies. And of these, women's bodies are the most durable because gold is spent, treaties are broken, and fortresses fall, but the children we produce unite families forever." Lucy turned and walked to the window.

There was a long silence. "You seem to be arguing that I should permit this alliance on political grounds. But there is your happiness to consider, Lucy."

Lucy had her back to her uncle, where she could see out of the window. In the distance, William was taking his temper out on a company of Swallows who had failed to carry out their arms drill to a sufficient standard. He had his back to her, head thrust aggressively forward, left hand on his hip, right on his sword hilt. Lilith picked up her thoughts. 'An arrogant, confident man, born to command other men.' A final echo disappeared below her consciousness, 'Born to command other men and women.'

Lucy spoke to her uncle without turning around, "I would not be the first girl who had to lie back and think of England." She paused and Lilith noticed that a small smile played around her lips. "But you know, Uncle, it might not be so bad."

Act 20, On Strange Seas

The *Swallow* ploughed down the narrow seas on the western approaches between England and France. The ship met the long Atlantic rollers up from the West Indies head on. Her bow crashed against each wave in turn in an unpleasant corkscrew motion. Every plunge thrust spray into the air, which the wind blew inboard. It was late in the summer to start a cruise across the world and a promise of autumn chill was in the sea air. Squalls of rain surrounded the ship, severely reducing visibility. William stood down in the bow lost to his thoughts. Here, close to the sea, under the fo'c'sle was the nearest to privacy that could be found on a crowded warship. He welcomed the cold spray and wind on his face. It suited his mood. The crew recognised their captain's black humour and left him to his reflections.

Someone climbed down and stood beside him, unspeaking. "I thought you were avoiding me, milady?" William said.

"Yes," Lucy agreed. "I was. I am afraid that I am something of a coward, Captain. I avoid confrontation, especially when I'm in the wrong."

"Whatever else you are, milady, no man who has seen you fight will call you coward."

"Fighting!" Lucy shrugged. "Anyone can fight. What takes courage is apologising to a man that I have wronged. I spoke harshly and used ill-judged words to you, sir. Please accept my apology."

323

"Shush," said William. He touched her lips with his fingertips.

"Shush. That is what you said to me when we were in the water. See, Captain, I don't just insult strangers. I also insult the man that saved my life."

"The fault is hardly yours to bear alone. I am a rude and vulgar man, unused to the niceties of your class. I also aim well above my station. However, I have often aimed high and in my experience, that is the only way to hit a distant target."

The two stood in silence for some time watching the water.

"How did the test of the magic candles go?" asked William.

"Well enough," Lucy replied. "But I found it more difficult to make contact than in the Tower."

"The sea is supposed to drain magic," William observed. "Mayhap, that is what you felt."

"I hope so," Lucy said. "Lilith says that it could be connected with the distance between the candles. That could become a problem when we cross the ocean."

Lucy shivered. William undid his cloak and put it around her shoulders. "You see another example of my uncouthness, milady. I must wait until you chill before offering you protection. A gentleman would have done so before you shivered."

She smiled.

"That is better. A smile from my lady banishes all cold," William said, gallantly.

"And I accused you of lacking poetry, sir," she said.

"Another example of your good judgement," William said. "Did your uncle discuss my proposal with you?"

"He did."

"And did he ask your opinion?"

She said nothing.

"Come talk to me, my lady."

"I see you will know it all, sir. I told him that I could see political advantage in the match."

"Did you indeed! I suppose that I have deserved such a reply. Did your uncle enquire after your personal wishes?" William asked.

"He did."

"And am I also to be allowed to know them?" William asked.

"I told him that I did not oppose the idea. Indeed, I might find the match somewhat . . . " She paused, clearly anxious to select the right word. ". . . stimulating, despite certain difficulties that I foresee." Lucy snuggled up to him. "I am still a little chilled so I will stand closer to you, if I may." She reached up, pulled his head down, and kissed him on the lips. "That is by way of an apology for my behaviour earlier."

"Is it? Then I trust you will insult me often," William said. "I find your apologies—stimulating." Inside his heart sang. He had kissed her twice but this was the first time that she had kissed him.

"I know you think that I am an arrogant aristocrat, and mayhap you are right, but I believe you love me." William started to speak but she talked over him. "There is a great danger in that. You are the commander of our enterprise and I will obey you, but I am the weapon in your hand. When the time comes, you must be prepared to use me as you would any other weapon. Our enterprise is lost if you hold me back out of love. You must be brave, William, and let me go in harm's way."

William would think on this conversation later but for the moment his mind had picked up one detail. She did not oppose the match.

"Sail ho, one point off the port bow." A sailor's voice called from the crow's nest.

William hurled himself up the steps to the fo'c'sle. "What type of vessel is she, can you not see?"

Lucy watched him go, with a slight smile. 'You see, Lilith. My reservations about his suit are not entirely ill-founded. Were I to be his wife, I would always have to compete with his first love, his beloved mistress.'

'And who is she?' thought Lilith, confused.

'Why, the ship of course. That sleek mistress that always obeys, never answers back, and is ever waiting his will. How does mere flesh and blood compete?'

Lucy climbed back after William and found a place to stand that was out of the way. William was talking to the master. "Can you see her, Mr. Smethwick?" asked William.

"I think there is something there, in that squall. But my sight ain't what it was, Captain. Especially in this weather."

'I can't see it either, Lilith. Can you help?' Lucy thought.

'Let me switch on night sight to cut through the haze and try to bend the light to increase magnification. I will drop gravity shields in front of your eyes—now.'

Master Smethwick nudged William and pointed to Lucy. Her eyes took on a hard crystalline appearance and her skin glowed.

William spoke directly to the girl, "Can you see the ship, Lucy? Can you describe her? What is her course?"

"She is moving to cross our bow," the girl said.

"Cross our bow? I can't allow that. Boatswain, take us two points to port," William bawled.

Orders cascaded down the chain of command until the helmsman hauled on the whipstaff and brought the ship's bow around.

"She has three masts, square sails on the first two and a triangular sail on the rear," said Lucy.

"Is she race-built?" the master asked.

Lucy looked at him blankly.

"Is her architecture cut down, like the *Swallow*?" William said.

"Oh yes," Lucy said. "But she is smaller and fatter than this boat."

"Ship," William corrected automatically. "What colours does she show?"

"I can't see colours when using night sight," said Lucy. "But she is coming out now so you can look yourself."

A ship's sails, tatty and travel stained emerged from the squall. The hull of a race-built galleon followed, painted in green and white squares and triangles.

"She's English," William said. "But the hull is on a two-to-one ratio unlike our three-to-one."

"Aye, she's a cruiser rather than a pure warship," said the master.

The boatswain arrived at the fo'c'sle with a sailor in tow. He touched his cap to William. "Sir, Andrews here thinks he knows her."

"Go on, man," said William. "What ship is she?"

The boatswain prodded the sailor. The man removed his cap and twisted it between his hands. "I saw her at Deptford, Cap'n. She be the *Pelican*."

"*Pelican*? That's Drake's ship," William said, unable to keep the awe from his voice. "Three years at sea and he brings her up the western approaches like he was on a shakedown cruise."

Word spread quickly among the sailors and cheers rang out. "Silence," William said. "Boatswain, can you not control the men? Are we to be humiliated in front of Drake?"

"No, sir," said the boatswain. "Silence, you whoresons, or I'll start stripping backs."

The noise abated. The ships closed rapidly, running on opposite parallel tracks. "But does Drake live?" William said softly. "Or does his ship return without him, like Magellan's. Look there, on the afterdeck, Cousin Francis, himself." William pointed to a slightly portly man, of some good age, clad in officer's working clothes. As the ships drew level, William raised his cap. "Hip, hip—" His voice was drowned in the rousing "Hooray!" from the crew. William repeated the formula twice more and the last *hoorah* shook the sails. Drake bowed and doffed his cap. Then the *Pelican* was astern and disappearing into the next squall.

"They treat him like a god," said Simon, softly to Lucy.

Lucy looked at the worship in William's eyes. "I had not seen you arrive, Master Tunstall," she said. "Yes, to them he is a least a demigod, like the heroes of old. A new English Odysseus to prowl the seas and strike terror into the heart of England's foes."

"Drake has changed her name," said the master. "I distinctly saw *Golden Hind* on the stern. Why that, I wonder."

"I think I know," said Lucy.

"You, Lucy?" asked William "You know why Drake renames his ship so?" William could not quite keep the incredulity out of his voice and his officers chuckled.

"Yes, sir, me, sir," Lucy said, icily. "Sir Christopher Hatton, who so kindly invited me to witness a play in his box at the theatre—you know what a theatre is, I assume, Captain—is one of the principal backers of Drake's enterprise. Sir Christopher Hatton's coat of arms includes a golden hind. Now if you will excuse me, Captain Hawkins, I am a little fatigued. So I will leave you to steer the ship, or whatever it is that you do."

Lucy swept off the fo'c'sle lifting her skirts in front, every inch of her the Lady Dennys. There was dead silence. "I believe I have been put in my place," said William and laughed, his officers joining him. "When I marry the wench, she really will have to learn to curb that tongue; such sharpness is unbecoming in a wife," he observed, ruefully.

"If you marry the, ah, wench then you may certainly try," said Simon, thoughtfully. "Do write and tell us how it turns out, from whatever hospice they consign you."

"I will go and make my peace," said William. He followed the girl onto the aft deck and approached her where she stood against the rail.

"I hope I have not offended you again, milady," William said.

"No, not offended, Captain. And I am sorry if I spoke too sharply to you in front of your officers."

"It is of no consequence, Lady Dennys. Although nominally under my command, you are hardly bound by the same discipline as the rest of my crew."

"You mean that I can get away with almost anything, partly because of my status as a member of the gentry and partly because I am a silly girl who can't be expected to know better," she said, sweetly.

"I would not have put it quite like that," he began.

"No?" she interrupted. "Then how would you have put it?" Lucy waved her arm. "It doesn't matter. The episode illustrates what bothers me about your ambitions towards myself."

Lucy looked him straight in the eye with that directness that so appealed. "We are from different worlds, William. Don't you see? I will never fit into your world of ships and seaports. How will you adapt to my world of court, politics, and great houses? Mayhap we should stop this now while we are still friends, before we hurt each other."

"Enough, madam, I will never hurt you. I believe I can make you happy—happier than you will be in the possession of some chinless wonder with a title. You could already have had such a man if that is what you really wanted. You will in turn make me happy. Just being in your company makes me happy. Even your waspish tongue pleases because it reminds me that I have to keep my wits sharp to hold your respect. Life isn't a rehearsal, Lucy. We only get one chance. I will not let your doubts and fears wreck our happiness. I intend to win your hand and your heart by whatever means are necessary. I intend to have you, so get used to the idea, milady. I am not some aristocratic milksop to be deflected from his objective by the first reverse. I'm a sea dog captain. I fight for what I want; I always win and right now, what I want most of all is you."

She stared at him, mouth open. He had the distinct impression that men were not in the habit of addressing the Lady Dennys so. He decided now to follow another of Drake's maxims and quit and run after a victory, before a powerful but momentarily disorganised enemy could regroup.

"Actually, my lady, I have a favour to ask of you," said William.

"You do," said Lucy, warily.

"I would like to talk to Lilith," he said.

"Lilith? But you can't. I mean, only I can talk to her."

"But I understand from Master Tunstall that John Dee was able to arrange an interview with your demon."

"So I am told," said Lucy. "I was, you understand, mesmerised at the time. But Doctor Dee used magic and a mirror to create a 'hologram' of Lilith. We lack both. Wait, I will ask her."

Lucy stared at the sea for a few moments. William waited silently, assuming that she was involved in some inner discussion.

"There might be a way, Captain. I suspect that I am going to regret this but I will allow it. Lilith has learnt a great deal about magic from recent events. She believes that if you stand close to me then something might be arranged." Lucy looked evasive. "Lilith tells me that you and I are in harmony and it is possible to connect us. She says she suspects that you have connected with me before." Lucy looked indignant. "It was in that safe house at Billingsgate, wasn't it? I wondered how you knew what I was thinking."

William grinned. "So you and I are in harmony, are we? Your fate is written in your stars, madam. You can't fight it. I have to stand close to you and look into your eyes, do I? I believe that I can manage that."

He moved to comply. Looking into Lucy's big brown eyes was a pleasing experience. As William stared, they seemed to grow larger and swirl. He was sinking into them. There was a wrench and William fell. He heard a rushing sound and saw whirling light and was in a meadow, a meadow on a summer's afternoon.

"It's always summer here," said Lucy, appearing in front of him. There was no suggestion of movement. She was just there.

"Where am I?" asked William.

"Well, literally you are in my head, or Lilith's head, which is in my head. But metaphysically, you are in a meadow that used to be a favourite of mine. Lilith took it from my memories. I am afraid she brought me here while you were struggling in the water with me, Captain. I have often felt guilty about that."

"Think no more on that, milady. Lilith did exactly the right thing. I would not have wished you to suffer. The real meadow, the one that this is based on—were you a small child at the time?"

"Why do you ask?" asked Lucy, curious.

"Lucy, the grass is knee high, the flowers are six inches across, the trees are topless, and the insects . . ." William pointed to a bee that zigzagged past; it was the size of a robin.

"I never noticed. It is as I remembered it. I suppose I was five years old or so. You are here to meet Lilith are you not, Captain? I expect she is down by the stream." Lucy led the way.

William could have sworn that he and Lucy were alone but a few steps towards the stream meandering below brought them into the presence of a woman. She was dressed most peculiarly in tight black breeches with long legs that hung right down over her shoes. The shoes were also unusual with high, thin heels. The white sleeveless shirt was rather more familiar, albeit usually worn by men.

"Honestly, Lilith, is this outfit another of those you claim is worn by women of the future? You do it to shock, don't you? One time, William, she wore this dress that showed her legs all the way up to— well, all the way up."

"I just wanted to look my best for the captain, and I haven't worn this outfit in public before. The lower garments are called flared trousers and are female copies of men's clothes."

"Indeed," said William. Lilith spoke in that odd clipped accent that he had heard before. Simon had told him that what made Lilith appear so extraordinary was that she looked so ordinary. William was not sure that flared trousers were all that ordinary but he knew exactly what Simon meant. Lilith was rather pretty and feminine. It was difficult to accept that she was a demon from the Other World. Demons should look—demonic, so everyone knew where they were. The demon held out her hand and William kissed it, automatically. He could touch her. Simon had told him that the Lilith hologram summoned by Dee had no substance, so clearly some other magic was at work here.

"I would like to talk to Lilith alone, if you would be so kind, milady."

"Why? Oh, I suppose you want to talk about me." Lucy narrowed her eyes and seemed to consider. "Very well." She turned and took a few steps then was suddenly a fair distance away, out of earshot. There was no discontinuity or jerk, the illusion just happened.

"So, what shall we talk about, Captain?" Lilith smiled.

"Before we start, are you what you appear to be?"

Lilith laughed, "And what do I appear to be?"

"An attractive young woman, pert enough to catch the eye of any man and intelligent enough to hold his interest. Does this image truly represent you?"

"That rather depends what you mean," Lilith said, thoughtfully. "I have no body that you could see or feel, but I am young by the standards of my people and I am female. Lucy finds me pleasant company. I am also influenced by neural outflow from Lucy, so I tend to react to men as a human woman would. So, yes, Captain, I believe this body truly represents me. Does it matter?"

"It does to me. I find it easier to talk with you, if I know what you are really like."

"Hmm, body language. Yes, that is important to your kind." Lilith smiled, encouragingly. "Now that is settled, what do you want to talk about?"

"Lucy."

"Ah."

"You know I intend to marry Lucy?"

"I know what Lucy knows, I see what she sees, I hear what she hears, and I feel what she feels."

"Um, feels, do you?" This was like talking to Lucy. The conversation veered into uncomfortable areas. Lilith had Lucy's disconcerting ability to sidetrack the discussion.

"I believe from our previous contact that you do not oppose the match," said William, getting back to the point.

"I want Lucy to be happy. I want her to have what she needs to be happy."

"And she wants me?"

"If you think I will betray Lucy by revealing her thoughts to you then you are very mistaken, sir," Lilith's voice was cold.

"No, of course not. I spoke without thinking. Forgive me, demon."

William was silent for a moment but Lilith showed no sign of wanting to say anything so he carried on. "Will you leave Lucy when we reach Bimini?"

"If Lucy wants me to."

"And suppose she doesn't? Marriage is between two people, not three. Suppose she is seduced by the power of your possession of her? Will you do the decent thing and go anyway?"

"The decent thing. Getting rid of me is the decent thing is it, Captain? I can see how it would suit you but how about Lucy?"

"Don't accuse me of selfishness, demon. I want what's best for her."

"Really?" Lilith changed tack. "I suppose you have had many friends as a boy, William."

"Yes, what of it?"

"I didn't," said Lilith softly. "I had no friends at all until Lucy. And look around you, Captain Hawkins. How many friends do you see here in Lucy's childhood world, just me and you, her best friend and her suitor? Are you going to ask her to choose between us? Would you be so cruel?"

William had no answer for her.

"Think carefully, Captain, for you may hold three people's happiness in your hands. I gather from your silence that this interview is terminated."

Lilith clapped her hands, theatrically, and opened her arms. William had a sensation of flying through a tunnel of light and then was back in his body, looking down at Lucy. Looking into Lucy's eyes.

"Don't be alarmed. Little time has passed out here, merely the blink of an eye. No one will notice anything. Did you get what you wanted from Lilith?" Lucy asked him.

"I got much to think upon, milady. If you will excuse me," he said.

The *Swallow* sailed on, possibly the first ship in the world to achieve a direct course crossing from Northern Europe to Mexico. Everything depended on an accurate assessment of longitude.

"Do you have to ask her to do it again? It gets worse every time," pleaded Simon.

"What else can I do?" asked William. "If there was any other way, any other way at all, I would choose it. But we are now only one hundred miles of the Bahamas by dead reckoning. I can't risk going any further without checking longitude."

"But Lilith estimates that the effort needed to power the spell goes up by the square otf the distance and we are, what, three thousand miles from London?"

"Do you think that I don't know that? Do you imagine that I delight in torturing the maid? But there are a thousand uninhabited coral islands and reefs in the Bahamas, all ready to rip the bottom out of a ship."

William pulled open the door to his cabin, frustration lending unnecessary vigour to the action. Lucy knelt on the floor inside with her hands palm out on her thighs. She chanted gently to herself, eyes closed. William squatted down beside her. She opened her eyes and William could see fear lurking like a dark cloud in them. "There is an alternative to the reading, Lucy. I can reverse course to the east and head south to the latitude line."

"And how long will that take, Captain?" Lucy asked.

"Some little time," William admitted.

"And where is Isabella?" asked Lucy.

"It must be a close race but I calculate that we are a little ahead of her."

"A lead that we would lose if we take the long route to the south." Lucy closed her eyes again. "Light the candle."

William leaned close to Lucy's ear and whispered. "Take care of her, Lilith. Stop if it gets too much for her, even if she wants to go on. Milady's courage exceeds her sense."

Lucy started to sing the critical note. The candle flame flickered and flared before steadying on the same harmonic as the sound. Lucy took a deep breath and sang harder. Her skin began to glow as Lilith poured power into her. Her eyes glittered crystalline in the candlelight. The flame climbed higher and higher. Lucy's body twisted as if under torsion and William could see the agony in her face. He was about to insist on a halt when the flame shrank back into a hard line with a noise like cannon shot ripping through the air.

"Doctor Dee, Doctor Dee. Can you hear me?" The flame line vibrated in tune with her voice, like a lute string. There came an indistinct murmur from the candle in reply. She gasped and twisted her head in agony. "Doctor Dee, say again, I can't hear you."

"The time in London is four hours and forty-seven minutes past noon," Dee's voice said from the flame.

The candle flared and went out. Lucy swayed and William grabbed her.

Millie rushed over. "Right, all you men out of the chamber. My mistress is going to her bed for the rest of the day. Begone, all of you."

During the night the wind began to rise and the *Swallow* pitched and rolled in the heavy seas. The storm launched itself fully with the dawn.

Black clouds scudded low across the sky and the first rainsqualls washed the ship. William shot out of his quarters and hastened to the rear deck.

"Boatswain, put her under storm sails; batten the ship down," said the master. The boatswain screamed orders to the crew, who scurried to his bidding.

A jagged lightning bolt split the sky beside the ship as he ran. "What the hell is going on, master?"

"I don't know, sir. I have never seen anything like it. The storm just blew out of nowhere." The *Swallow* pitched downwards and her bows buried themselves in the next roller. Foaming water washed as high as the fo'c'sle and into the waist deck. The ship staggered then rose out of the wave like a prize fighter shrugging off a heavy blow. She climbed upwards and crested. William saw a wall of water in the foreground racing towards them as the bow dropped down.

"Grab hold! Great wave coming!" William yelled at the crew. Men ran to tangle themselves in ropes or get under cover. The giant wave slammed into the ship, ripping away part of the fo'c'sle and the foremast. It passed clean over the decks, burying them in water. The water rushed over the rear decks, sweeping William off his feet and towards the side. He tried to grab the rail as he collided with it, but the power of the water was too strong and he went over the side.

Something grabbed his wrist in a vicelike grip and held him as the water rushed past. It seemed to last forever but was probably only a flicker of time. His body twisted in the rushing water but the grip on his wrist was unbreakable. He was pulled unceremonially back over the side onto the deck.

William coughed up water. "Lucy? Where did you come from?"

"We are under attack, William. Lilith can feel power all around us."

As if to emphasise the point a lightning bolt forked into the water beside them. The *Swallow* yawed into the next swell, unbalanced without her foremast. The next giant wave would roll the ship over and kill them. Lucy raised her arms and began to sing.

"When that I was and a little tiny boy
"With hey, ho, the wind and the rain,
"A foolish thing was but a toy
"For the rain it raineth every day.
"But when I came to man's estate
"With hey, ho, the wind and the rain,
"'Gainst knaves and thieves men shut their gate
"For the rain it raineth every day."

Her voice started softly but, as demonic possession overtook her, Lucy's words echoed around the ship from the keel to the mast tops. She kept singing and a cone of power built up around her.

"But when I came, alas, to wive
"With hey, ho, the wind and the rain,
"By swaggering could I never thrive
"For the rain it raineth every day."

The cone spread outwards until a luminous glow surrounded the *Swallow*. It damped the howling wind and the rolling surf. Even the rain seemed to slide off it.

"But when I came unto my beds
"With hey, ho, the wind and the rain,
"With toss-pots still 'had drunken heads
"For the rain it raineth every day."

Lightning flickered angrily all around them. A golden hemiglobe surrounded the ship. Through it, William could see waves of power dropping from the sky and sweeping in towards his ship in rippling sheets of green and purple. He suspected that the luminous shield was allowing him to see what Lilith and Lucy saw. No wonder the girl had said that they were under attack. This was unnatural. The power flowed around the golden globe to whip up the water in the ship's wake.

"A great while ago the world began
"With hey, ho, the wind and the rain,
"But that's all one, our play is done
"And we'll strive to please you every day."

A massive lightning bolt sliced down towards the ship and struck the globe. It flared and rang like a bell. For a split second, the whole ship was bathed in light, then the globe split at the top and fell down into the sea each side of the vessel with a hiss.

Act 21, Bimini

The *Swallow* sailed across placid waters, one moment a tropical storm, the next a village pond.

"Bail her out. What are you waiting for, whoresons? A personal invitation from King Neptune?" The boatswain's voice rang across the ship.

"Has anyone seen the master?" William said.

"He's not here," said Lucy. "I couldn't save both of you. I had to choose." The girl began to sob, quietly.

William took her in his arms. "He was a sea dog, Lucy, and a good age. He wouldn't retire. I think he wanted it to end this way, rather than on land among strangers. Now, I must check the ship over."

William walked down onto the main deck to confer with the boatswain. "The master's gone. You will have to take over his sailing responsibilities. I will navigate. Get me a foremast rigged as soon as possible."

"Aye, aye, sir." The boatswain nodded towards Lucy. "She's a little cracker, isn't she? The men reckon she's like a good-luck token. They believe that we can't lose as long as she is with us. I think they're right. How does she do that singing trick?"

"I wish I knew. It astonishes me how the sea grew civil at her song. She's upset over losing the master. She thinks she should have saved him."

"She saved the ship and all our arses today," said the boatswain. "I have heard of witches who could whistle up a wind but never one who can sing the sea to sleep."

"Is that what the men think she is, a witch? I am worried that they might take against her."

"What, the lady? Of course they think she's a witch, the captain's white witch. I have heard no complaint of her. If I had then I would have dealt with it." The boatswain closed his fingers making an impressive fist. "The men have seen you together. They know where the lady's affections lie."

"Put up the mast, boatswain," William said, stiffly. "I needs must comfort Lady Dennys."

"Aye, aye, sir," said the boatswain, grinning.

Women aboard ships, William thought, were very bad for discipline, although possibly good for morale, especially the captain's.

He made his way back to Lucy, who was talking to Simon. "I hope the storm did not push us too far off course or your hard-won longitude reading will be for nothing," William interrupted their conversation.

"We don't need to navigate now, Captain. I know the course for Bimini. The island is over there." Lucy pointed.

"And how do you know that, milady?" asked William.

"The magical attack came from Bimini. Lilith can smell the island."

"Does that mean Isabella has already reached the island?" asked Simon.

"Not necessarily," said Lucy. "She could have used the island's magic from a distance."

"Are we safe for the moment or do we face another attack?" asked William.

"Lilith thinks that Isabella has shot her bolt for the moment. We are probably safe for a while, now that we are in the Other World," said Lucy.

"What?" asked Simon.

"Other World!" said William, simultaneously.

"I am afraid my defensive spell wasn't entirely successful. That last attack squeezed us out of the world," Lucy said, cheerfully. "But we would have had to come here anyway to find Bimini, so maybe Isabella did us a favour. By your leave, gentlemen."

Lucy curtseyed to the men and paraded off. She was clearly delighted to have caused such a sensation.

"What speed are we making?" asked William, trying to get a grip on something tangible.

"I estimate four and a half knots," said the boatswain. "Sorry, sir. It's the best speed we can make with the rigged foremast."

"We've lost our lead, haven't we?" asked Simon.

"I suspect so. Hell's teeth! We came so close, Master Tunstall." William punched his fist into the rail.

Simon pulled back the sleeve on the captain's shirt. Five purple bruises marked where Lucy had grasped it. "I expected to see that," said Simon. "Look where she gripped the rail."

William ran his fingers over the wood. There were deep indentations that were just the size of Lucy's hand.

"So do we turn back and admit defeat?" asked Simon.

"I just don't know," William said. "This is not a tactical situation that I have faced before. If we go on, and Isabella gets to the magical source first." He spread his hands, expressively. "We may confront dangers that we can't cope with, even with Lucy's help. However, if we turn back, we may give Isabella the chance to launch another magical attack across the water, one that sinks us this time. It is probably safer to head straight for the island at our best speed."

"There is another consideration," said Simon. "According to Lady Dennys, this is the Other World. How do we get home if we just sail away? Doctor Dee told us that Bimini Island has a portal that we could use to go home. I suppose that this is the Other World. It all looks so normal."

Simon gestured at the blue sky above them

"Do you think so?" asked William, pointing over the side. The *Swallow* had been sailing through a swarm of jellyfish for some time. There was nothing unusual in that as such, except that these jellyfish had humanlike eyes on top of their canopies, eyes that watched the ship as it sailed past. Simon grimaced.

"Aye. I must warn the crew not to do any fishing. It's salted meat from the hold to eat from now on," said William. He came to a decision. "We go on. All our courses are fraught with danger so we might as well choose the one with some chance of success, however small. Have faith, Master Tunstall. We have our own pocket-sized secret weapon on board."

✧   ✧   ✧

The *Swallow* steered into a bay of Bimini Island, following Lilith's guidance. The island was low and covered with rich tropical growth, quite unlike the rest of the Bahamas. A small Native American city was visible just behind the beach. It was badly overgrown with luxuriant foliage but roofs and cleared areas were still visible.

"No sign of a ship," Simon said. "Do you think we have got here before Isabella?"

"Possibly," said William. "But look over there." A thin column of smoke rose from the jungle into the air. "The Bahamas are supposed to be uninhabited. This island clearly isn't. Boatswain, get the shore party organised. Break open the guns, I want everyone heavily armed."

Boats ferried the assault force to the shore. William chose to take both the gunner and boatswain with him, as he thought it unlikely that the *Swallow* would come under military attack. They had not seen another ship since entering the Other World.

The island was hot and humid even by the standards of the Americas. The fetid smell of rotten vegetation hung heavily in the air, which was alive with the buzzing of insects.

"So, Lady Dennys, which way do we go?" asked William, when they had all disembarked.

Lucy ignored him. She seemed distracted. "Lucy, are you all right?" asked William

"Yes, I'm fine," said Lucy. "It's just that the magic sounds like a screaming child in my brain. The source lies within the city."

They made their way through the jungle. A paved path ran towards the flat-roofed buildings.

"I wonder what keeps the jungle back from the path," said Simon. "It would require heavy use to keep it free but there is little sign of people or large animals."

"I suspect all sorts of irrational things happen here," said Lucy. "Magical power streams out of the city. Have you seen the butterflies?"

"What about the butterflies?" asked Simon.

"Some of them have three pairs of wings."

The first building that they chanced upon was almost concealed by the jungle. It was white-walled and square. An orange-red band, about one foot wide, ran around the base and a similar band circled the house in green at the top. Peculiar red slabs were positioned in a line along the edge of the roof. One had fallen off and dug into the earth. William examined it closely. It was made of an opaque, crystalline mineral. Blunt tools, probably of stone, had been used to roughly shape the slab.

As they went deeper into the city, the plant life thinned out and the buildings emerged clearly. Some structures still had doors barring entry, while in others gaps opened into dim interiors. None of the men felt moved to explore. Lucy silently pointed to the left or right, guiding them through the streets. The route took them ever closer to the rising column of smoke. Eventually, she stopped at a compound surrounded by a high wall of white and red-flecked stone.

"The magic comes from in there," Lucy said. "Something is happening. The power is building up."

William flipped a mental coin. "Follow the wall to the right."

They turned the corner and came upon a heavy set of wooden doors, with a life-sized statue each side. The boatswain detailed several men to put their shoulder to them. The wood gave but an inch before locking against a retaining plank.

"Hurry, we must hurry," Lucy said, suddenly. "Isabella is opening a portal."

The men did not understand the implications of her comments but her urgency and fear came across clearly, so they redoubled their efforts to break down the doors.

"This is no good." The boatswain turned around. He pointed to one of the statues. "Use that."

The sailors upended the stone and charged the doors, using it as a battering ram. The first blow splintered the wood. Something cracked on the other side but the doors still stood. The sailors backed up and ran at the doors again.

Lilith detected all kinds of gravitonic anomalies from the swirling energy mass on the other side of the wall. 'Help them Lucy,' she thought. 'They will never get that door down in time.'

Lucy reached up and pushed hard on the statue as the sailors charged past. This time the doors smashed off their hinges. It happened so fast that the sailors failed to notice the girl's intervention. The sailors flooded into a large rectangular enclosure.

To Lilith, the inside reeked of the heavy energy fields that protected the structure from the decay of time. The interior walls were still brightly white above waist height. Below this they were painted in an emerald green. The floor was lined with coloured stones in a zigzag pattern of dull orange and pale green. Nothing grew on it. The jungle was forbidden to intrude here.

The broken doors were on one of the shorter edges of a rectangle. A low platform of white stone stood at the other end of the precinct, some fifty yards away, with steps leading up from the floor. A square one-story temple with a flat roof stood on this base. The bottom half was the same brick red as the outer walls but the upper half was a flat white that glared in the tropical sun. Panels of pale blue stone were inset. Peculiar ornamental crenulations lined the edge of the roof. These battlements were made of green bricks so arranged as to be straight on one side but in three steps on the other.

A large open rectangular doorway led into the building. Two white pillars supported a long red lintel stone. Isabella stood in front of the temple behind a natural extrusion of crystal that speared out of the floor. Deep blue waves shimmered within the mineral. Isabella's arms were raised in supplication. Her Italian mercenaries flanked her and formed a protective screen in front on the steps.

Isabella spoke in a voice that cut across the precinct. "Lady Dennys! I should have known it was you as soon as the doors burst in. You just don't take a hint when you are not wanted, do you?"

"What in hell is that?" William pointed over Lucy's shoulder to the middle of the courtyard. Hell was right. A large spinning black vortex hung in the air in front of the Spanish witch. Flashes of lightning flickered from the circumference of the circle and disappeared into the centre. The optical effect was of a deep tunnel but that was impossible, as the vortex was a paper-thin flat disc.

"We are too late," Lucy said, dully. "Isabella's got the portal open."

A dot appeared in the middle of the vortex. It grew in size until it could be seen as a figure. It continued to grow like an object approaching at high speed, from a long way off. The figure appeared in the courtyard. It did not step out of the portal or drop but just was there.

The demon stood three yards high on two scaly legs. Its body was held horizontal but a snakelike head reared up on a long curved neck, balanced by a muscular tail. The body and arms of the monster were covered in coloured feathers, giving the appearance of a giant bird. But this monster had two long arms ending in hooked claws. It raised its foot and made a raking gesture at the men with three taloned toes, like a bird of prey. The demon was definitely unfriendly. One of the sailors sobbed and dropped his boarding pike.

Lilith examined the creature carefully. She reached out with her mind to explore the beast and the portal. The demon felt her and opened its mouth, revealing rows of dagger-shaped teeth. It hissed in annoyance at her probe.

Simon whispered behind Lucy's back, "Topiltzin Quezalcoatl. Our Lord of the Feathered Serpent."

"What?" asked William.

"The Aztec worshiped a feathered serpent called Quezalcoatl. Their legends say he departed overseas into the rising sun to find his own land." Simon paused. "Mayhap this is his place."

'Lilith,' thought Lucy. 'Is that demon as dangerous as it looks?'

'Your physiological reactions are an appropriate response to confrontation with such an organism,' thought Lilith, who tended to get pompous when rattled.

'What?'

'It's dangerous.'

A second demon appeared beside the first, then a third.

'Can we fight the demons, Lilith? Can we beat them?'

'I don't think so, Lucy. That portal goes deep into the Shadow Worlds, deeper than I imagined was possible,' thought Lilith. 'The very physical laws of the universe are likely to be different where those monsters live. I am surprised that they can exist here at all.'

'Maybe magic protects them.'

'Oh, of course,' thought Lilith. 'The energy from the crystal creates a bubble universe around them. The monsters will vanish if we destroy the crystal.'

'So all we have to do is kill the demons, fight through the mercenaries and Isabella, and destroy the crystal. Then the dead demons will cease to be a problem,' thought Lucy, dryly.

Lilith ignored her. 'There might be something I can do. I might degrade the information in Isabella's control channels by spraying gravitons at her.'

'Right,' thought Lucy. 'Degrade control channels, right.'

A fourth demon appeared. The vortex began to throb and purple blotches spun in whirls around its centre but the demon arrived safely. Isabella waved her arms and chanted frantically.

'I think that I have found the right spin for the particles,' thought Lilith.

A fifth demon sped out of the nowhere of the vortex, towards them. The purple blobs multiplied and split into blue and red whirls.

The throbbing vortex collapsed with a crash and a smell like a lightning strike. A scaly head and feathered arm bounced onto the zigzag floor leaving a slimy green trail. The rest of the monster disappeared back into the vortex as it closed. The demons hissed their anger at Isabella.

'Isabella's lost control of the portal,' thought Lilith, smugly.

"See! The demons can be killed. Cut them and they bleed and die, just like anything else," William called out to the sailors, trying to boost morale and stave off panic.

The demons screamed at the men, showing their teeth. Isabella laughed and sneered at Lucy.

William drew his cutlass and raised it over his head to signal a charge. Several of the men fired their weapons. The demons did not appear to notice.

'Stop them, Lucy,' thought Lilith. 'They don't stand a chance.'

"No!" yelled Lucy. Once she had William's attention, she continued in a lower voice. "The men can't fight these things. You will all be killed."

'I have been running some simulations. The sailors will be run down and slaughtered one by one if we all retreat together. You and I might get away but they have no chance. The result is the same if we all attack, only quicker.' Lilith paused.

'I don't like those choices, Lilith. Give me another,' the girl thought.

'There is a third way. We get the men to retreat back to the boat while we attack to pin the demons in place. Back in the last Shadow World, I looked up some files in an interesting place called the Sandhurst Military Academy computer. They had this whole section on what they called *Target Rich Environments*. A lone fighter can use her enemies' size and numbers against them.'

'I get the idea. On our own we can hit anything that moves but the demons will get in each other's way,' thought Lucy. 'We still won't win though, will we?'

'No. I am afraid we can't win but we can tie them down long enough to save the men. However, my assessment of male behaviour is that they will insist on dying with us. Ridiculous, but there it is.'

'Leave the men to me,' thought Lucy. 'I will do what women always do in these situations.'

'What's that, Lucy?'

'I will lie to them for their own good,' thought the girl.

The conversation with Liliith had taken little more than an eye blink of time.

"William," said Lucy, turning to him. "This battle is unwinnable. I suggest we retreat back to the ship to fight another day. I will make a demonstration and occupy them long enough for you to get the men away. Then I will flee and join you at the ship."

"I like this not," said William.

Lucy looked at him with big innocent eyes devoid of any hint of duplicity. "I am the weapon, Captain. Remember your promise to use me when the time came. Well, the time is upon us." Lucy grabbed William and gave him a long lover's kiss. "Don't worry about me. I'll run these demons round in circles, then join you," she whispered.

Gwilym made to follow her. "Not this time, bodyguard, speed is my defence now. This time you stay with the other men," Lucy said. He fell back reluctantly.

The girl turned her back on the men and walked towards the monsters drawing her blade. Internal communication between Lucy and Lilith happened at superhuman speeds. Lucy had become used to long discussion occurring between one footfall and the next so she thought to have one last conversation with her friend.

'Tell me something, Lilith,' thought Lucy. 'When I die, will you really die with me?'

'I am afraid so, Lucy. I will stay with you to the end.'

'How long would you have lived if you had stayed in your own sphere?' thought the girl.

'Ah. It's a bit difficult to explain in your terms, but I suppose you would say forever. Barring accidents, I would have lived forever.'

'Oh,' Lucy was crestfallen. 'I'm sorry, Lilith.'

'Don't be, Lucy. I have lived more in the last few months than I would have in a lifetime with the People. It's a privilege to die with you.'

Lucy said nothing but Lilith detected a strong emotional reaction. Lucy paused for a long time. 'You know, Lilith, I always thought I would die in childbirth. I was very frightened of that. Still it's not a problem now.'

'Oh it never was a problem, Lucy,' Lilith thought. 'I could easily have prevented you conceiving.'

Lilith detected a flood of neural activity. 'Now you tell me. Did you not think to mention this earlier?' thought Lucy.

'No,' thought Lilith. 'I didn't think it was important.'

'I don't suppose you did, Lilith. Well, it's not important now. We have demons to fight.'

'I have set up some simulations.'

'Simulations?' thought Lucy

'Dreams, Lucy, astrological predictions of what the future could be. I want you to watch them.'

'Oh, models! Why didn't you say.' As Lucy walked forward towards the feathered serpents, Lilith ran simulation after simulation in her head. In every one, the girl lost the fight and was ripped to pieces by the demons.

'Enough, Lilith, enough, so I am going to die.'

'Please, Lucy. There is a point to this. Now, watch what happens when I increase the power running through your body.'

Lucy watched the simulations despite herself. After each run, Lilith incrementally turned up the gain until the girl did massive damage to the serpents. But Lucy started to die of exhaustion after fewer and fewer minutes.

'I calculate there is an optimum power level where we have a seventeen point three percent chance of winning before your body burns out,' thought Lilith.

'Seventeen point three percent? That sounds good, Lilith. What's a percent?'

Lilith started to explain.

'Never mind,' thought Lucy. 'Turn the power up and I can win but you may kill me anyway.' Lucy paused for a moment. 'Come on, Lilith. Let's do it.'

Lilith dropped out of Lucy's conscious mind, to avoid distracting her, but seamlessly melded into the girl's body as she strode forward. Barely a second had elapsed in real time.

"She means to buy us time with her life so that we can flee." William slapped the side of his breeches in irritation. "I daren't risk ordering a charge. We probably would just get in her way." He stood at the head of his men on one side of the ancient courtyard near the entrance facing Isabella and her mercenaries on the opposite side, some thirty-five yards away. The demons, and now Lucy, stood between them.

William came to a decision. He turned and yelled out, "Boatswain!"

"Sir."

"Lady Dennys is going to fight the demons. The minute she gets into trouble we charge."

"Sir!" said the boatswain. "You hear that, whoresons? We fight the minute the lady falters."

William turned. Lucy stood about twenty yards from the line of monsters. Her head was up and her arms were outstretched. Her hair rippled as if in a wind but the air was still. Her skin shone and blue lightning crawled down her dagger blade.

"Then the Lord opened the eyes of Balaam, and he saw the Angel of the Lord standing in the way, and his sword drawn in his hand. Numbers 22:31," the gunner said. He added simply, "Angels shine."

William had not realised that the gunner was religious. It was funny what one never knew about people.

The feathered serpents stood in a line in front of her. If snakes could be said to look nervous then they were nervous. Four huge demons from hell stood and hesitated at the sight of a sixteen-year-old girl. William thought she looked like a fairy princess. He had never loved her more.

Lucy attacked without warning. In four steps, she accelerated up to an incredible speed. She ran straight for the centre of the demons' line. The serpents dipped their heads to meet her.

The girl gave a skip, hit the ground with both feet and jumped.

Lucy flew.

The jump was impossible. She soared, somersaulting over the creatures' heads. The demon on her immediate right lifted its head to snap at her and her glowing blade flashed against the bright sky. A scaly head hit the ground with a thud. Green fluid poured from its severed neck. The monster's body stood for a moment, as if deciding whether it was truly dead, before folding in on itself. It looked like a giant chicken settling on a nest.

The Swallows gave a roar of approval that shook the enclosure.

"Angels fly," the gunner said, reverently.

Lucy landed on both feet and used a forward roll to absorb the impact before springing upright. The girl had so much momentum that she skipped sideways for two paces before stopping. The monsters turned and rushed her.

She ran back in at them, fearlessly. Lucy feinted with a sprint to the right, before veering left and throwing herself at the demon on her far left, which was somewhat separated from its fellows. It reared up to catch her in midjump, but this time she dived in low to the ground. The demon lifted a leg and clawed at her. Lucy caught a talon on her left hand and deflected it. The energy spun her round but she slashed at the back of the demon's leg as she fell, severing the tendon.

The feathered serpent gave a terrible fluting cry as its leg collapsed. The long neck struck out at Lucy. She skipped out of the way to avoid daggerlike teeth.

Isabella screamed instructions at the demons. The two undamaged monsters were on Lucy immediately. The first to reach her struck with its long neck, like a snake. The girl deflected the huge head with her blade, slashing it across the monster's face. The demon seemed barely to notice and clawed at her now unprotected body with a claw-tipped arm.

Lucy flung herself backwards. She tripped and fell to the ground losing her knife, its glow fading as soon as it left her hand. The second monster jumped on top of her like a hawk on a field mouse. It stamped its feet, trying to crush the small body underneath. Lucy twisted and turned desperately on the ground, to avoid the hooked talons. The monster gave her no chance to find her feet. The girl was helpless.

William's sword came up and his mouth opened to order a charge.

Both demons thrust their necks down at her. Giant wedge-shaped heads with dagger teeth reached for her—and clashed. The demons shook their heads in an almost humanlike way and glared at each other. Demon one took a chunk out of Demon two's shoulder. Demon two hissed in anger, and raked its claws across Demon one's snout. And then they had at each other, green in fang and claw.

The demons hissed and spat like a nest of cobras. Lucy rolled clear of the melee, retrieving her dagger. She slipped away, as the demons squabbled like a pair of drunken wherrymen. Lucy ran clear of the two combatants towards the crippled serpent. The creature tried to drag itself upright but its leg failed again.

Isabella screamed and gesticulated at the fighting demons using the strange click language. They reluctantly disengaged and looked around for Lucy.

The girl took a stance in front of the wounded demon. When it didn't respond, she moved in closer and slashed it across the snout with her blade. The angry serpent hissed at her and shot its head out, jaws gaping. Lucy spun on one foot, moving her body out of the line of the strike. The wedge-shaped head slid harmlessly along her back.

Lucy kept turning raising the dagger over her head and bringing up her left hand to double her grip. She brought the blade down in a powerful two-handed slash across the demon's neck. There was a thud like a heavy axe biting into a tree, a flash of energy from the knife, and the neck parted, spewing green slime. The head wriggled on the ground and snapped its jaws, trying to get at the girl. Eventually, a glaze settled over the yellow eyes and it stilled.

The Swallows cheered until the temple precinct shook. Hoorahs broke out again as Lucy saluted them with her blade. One or two of the Italian mercenaries cheered as well, forgetting which side they were supposed to be on. Isabella quelled them with a look.

"By God, that's two down. The lady fights like Drake himself," said the boatswain.

The remaining demons lumbered towards her. Lucy took off in a flat run away from them. Her path took her across the line of Isabella's mercenaries. Up to now, they had taken no part in the proceedings, content simply to obey their last instruction, which was to protect their employer. Isabella, the sorceress, had obviously pinned all her hopes of victory on her demons, dismissing the mundane force at her disposal. Now they had drawn attention to themselves. The Spanish witch screamed a command and some of the soldiers raised their crossbows and pointed them at Lucy, but the officer at the front countermanded the order, forcing his men to lower their weapons.

Lucy ran like in great loping strides with elbows in and weapon held wide away from the body. The lumbering, feathered demons built up to a fast clip and gained on the girl.

When she reached the wall of the enclosure, she leapt up the sheer face. Grasping the top to steady herself, she landed on two feet. There she waited for the enemy, knife in hand. The monsters braked in front of her and split up to come at her from two sides. They had learned caution. Lucy Dennys had taught them caution with the edge of her blade.

A serpent struck at Lucy and she smacked its head away with a parry; the blade rang against six-inch fangs.

"That will give the bugger a toothache," said the boatswain, with grim satisfaction.

The next monster raked at Lucy's legs with one arm and she leapt upwards, lifting her legs as the claws slid below her. Landing on the narrow wall perfectly balanced, she slashed at the monster's neck, forcing it to spring back. Lucy took the opportunity to renew her attack on the first demon.

A voice from the past came into William's head. "The keys to power are women and horses and fire and steel, and the strongest of them all are women." His father had been fond of quoting that to his young son. At the time, he had not understood, as women were weak and feeble things. By God, he understood now.

And so it went on. Lucy parried, thrust, and slashed, running and jumping along the top of the narrow wall. William could discern her strategy. Height protected her from the hawklike talons on the monster's legs but it also restricted her movements. Lucy was dealing out blows but none of them were lethal. Wounds only seemed to anger the monsters.

The lethal steps continued. Simon remembered Lucy dancing the haute dance at the Tower, the lavolta. Lucy and the demons danced a vicious lavolta, where the slightest misstep could cost her life. The demons only had to get it right once. Lucy had to get it right every time.

A monster overstretched its head in a lunge at the girl and her blade came up. The feathered serpent was wary of the weapon and jerked its neck back. The blade threat was a ruse. Lucy kicked the serpent under the chin. Unbalanced, it tumbled away from the wall.

Its partner turned, with an incredulous expression, to watch its compatriot fall. Lucy jumped on top of the wedge-shaped head. She reversed her dagger so it pointed downwards and thrust down, ferociously. The weapon skewered deep between the monster's eyes.

The beast reared in its death agony. Lucy was thrown violently across the precinct. She landed badly. The girl climbed to her feet slowly. The last serpent raced towards her undeterred by the fate of its colleagues. It hit her in a whirlwind of teeth, claws and taloned feet. Lucy slapped each challenge away with her blade but the girl was almost entirely defensive now. She was visibly faltering.

William raised his sword high and looped it round his head to attract the men's attention. The demon caught Lucy with a vicious blow that spun her to the ground. Blood splashed across her tunic.

"England, Elizabeth, and Saint George!" William launched himself across the precinct.

The demons were terrifying but the Swallows were Elizabeth's sea dogs. They feared nothing that walked the earth or sailed the seas, because they had never met anything more frightening than themselves. As one man, they charged after their captain.

William heard a few battle cries of "Lucy, Lucy," in amongst the rest. The monster stood over her. Its head whipped from side to side confused by the roar of the charging sailors. Lucy lifted herself on one hand, and in a single fluid motion pushed the glowing dagger deep into the demon's bowels. Then the girl collapsed.

The demon whistled a fluting wail of anguish. It snapped at the wound. Yellow eyes with vertically slit pupils focussed on Lucy's still form. The demon raised its taloned foot to crush her.

The sailors hit the beast first, forcing it back. Billmen jabbed at it with the points of their weapons, and made slashing cuts with the bills' cruel hooks. The monster seemed more confused than hurt by the men's attentions. A sailor got too close and was crushed between snapping jaws. He died so fast that he didn't even scream. Then the rest of the sailors swarmed around the beast. Their weapons cut ribbons of flesh off the serpent but it did not seem to notice.

"It's dragging its left side. Lucy has hurt it. Maybe we can wear it down," said William. A crossbow bolt whipped past him and buried itself in a sailor's chest. Isabella's mercenaries had joined the mayhem.

At that point the gunner entered the fray. He was no longer a young man and the heavy object at his side slowed him down. He carried a boarding gun, built to his own design by a gunsmith in Plymouth. Five barrels were linked to a single trigger. The gunner himself had loaded each barrel with the finest ground powder and the truest balls.

He bided his time and then thrust the muzzles of the gun under the chin of the beast as it chopped another sailor in half. He pulled the trigger and the pampered weapon repaid his loving care by firing every barrel. Not a single misfire. Balls smashed through the creature's neck but the real damage was done by the blast. Super-heated air and burning powder melted the demon's flesh like snow in the sun.

"Guns will stop anything," said the gunner.

The monster's head dangled off its neck by a strip of flesh. It was in a bad way now, stumbling around while the sailors chopped at it like soldier ants around a scorpion. It still managed to deal the gunner a clout, knocking him down. The boatswain grabbed a halberd from a sailor and hacked repeatedly at the demon's damaged neck, until the flesh parted. It took a little while for the separated bits to accept the fact, but gradually the demon died.

Lilith worked frantically to repair Lucy's metabolism. The magical energy leaking from the crystal helped her stabilise the girl and restore her abilities. 'Lucy, can you get up? We have to find Isabella, before she works more magic.'

'I feel sick,' thought Lucy. 'How come we're still alive?'

'Our men deceived you,' thought Lilith. 'Instead of retreating, they charged the last demon. Obviously, you failed to convince them.'

'How dare they disbelieve me,' thought Lucy, indignantly.

'You were lying,' Lilith reminded her.

'That's not the point,' thought Lucy.

Lilith was losing track of what the point was. 'We have to find Isabella and stop her. She will be by the crystal.'

Lucy retrieved her blade and climbed to her feet. She came face to face with an Italian mercenary, who thrust his sword at her in reflex.

"*Ragazza da sogno,*" he said, gallantly, pulling his sword back and kissing the blade, "*bella ragazza.*"

'What?' thought Lucy, who did not speak Italian.

'He says that you are his dream girl and very beautiful,' thought Lilith.

"*Galente, senor,*" she replied, in Spanish.

The man smiled and blowing her a kiss, disappeared into the fighting. Lucy moved through the battle, which flowed around her. Men turned aside to let her pass.

Simon found himself duelling with a mercenary demi-armoured in helmet and breastplate. The man thrust at him with a sword. Simon sidestepped deftly and carefully ran the Italian through the throat. All round him men hacked and slashed at each other. The mercenaries were well armed and armoured but the sailors ripped through them.

A man cut at his head. Simon ducked and slashed back in reflex. He hit something but had no idea what damage, if any, that he had inflicted. The eddies of the fight swirled him away too quickly. Where was Lucy? Simon thought that she had fallen nearby but could not see her. This was the first battle he had ever been in. It was nothing like the classical descriptions of warfare. All was noise and confusion. He had no idea who was winning.

A huge punch in the back forced him to his knees. Whatever it was had failed to penetrate his armour as he was still alive. Simon forgot all pretence of being a gentleman trained in the higher arts of duelling. He jabbed and slashed at anything that tried to stop him.

A mercenary stumbled into him. The man thrust at him with a short pike. Simon parried the blow. The mercenary drew back for another thrust. A loud clang rang out and the mercenary went down on his knees, losing his helmet. A sailor came out of nowhere and smashed the Italian a second time over the head with a wooden club. The seaman grinned at Simon toothlessly. There was a thud and the sailor slipped forward over his victim silently. A crossbow bolt protruded from his back.

Lucy spotted Isabella by the crystal outcrop. She threaded her way through the fighting men. Isabella stood in a patch of calm among the battle.

Isabella chanted something and waved her arms.

"You look like a demented windmill, madam. Have you no sense of dignity?" asked Lucy.

"You turn up here in my special place dressed like a sailor's trollop, knock down doors, and start waving a knife around, and you talk to *me* of dignity?" asked Isabella. "But at least you have brought a ship with you. That will be useful. I had to sink mine when the cowards tried to flee after I went ashore."

'That was why there was no second attack on the *Swallow*,' thought Lucy. 'She preferred to use her power for revenge.'

"My own commander of mercenaries refused to shoot you down like you deserve," said Isabella, spitefully. "I will deal with him after I have finished you off."

'She is a vengeful woman,' thought Lilith. 'I doubt she is entirely sane.'

"Nothing to say, Lady Dennys?" said Isabella. "Last time we met, I said that you had a surplus of energy but you have lost most of it now, haven't you?"

Isabella made one last pass with her hands. Her body glowed with energy. She spread her arms and a bubble of energy spread out from her pushing the soldiers and sailors. Lucy and the Spanish witch stood inside their own private duelling ground.

Isabella pulled a sword from a sheath inside her petticoats and assumed a duelling position. The sword glowed silver, static electricity flickering in blue crackles up and down the blade.

'Oh dear,' thought Lilith. 'We are rather power-drained, Lucy. This might be a problem. I shouldn't energise your body again so soon.'

'Really!' thought Lucy. 'Shall I ask her for an adjournment? I suggest you do something rapidly, demon, as that bitch means to skewer us.'

Lilith pumped power back into the girl.

Isabella made a straight thrust at Lucy's chest. The girl parried it and stepped back to maintain distance. Isabella continued to attack, testing the girl's defence with high, low, left, and right lunges. Lucy was forced back. The girl could not get close enough to counterattack. As soon as she closed, Isabella cut at her, forcing her to parry and back away. Lucy was soon panting hard and the energy running through her body began to flicker.

Isabella grinned. "What, no merry quip or little homily, Lady Dennys? I think that you are just a frightened little girl who now realises that she was acting above her station."

'You need to finish this quickly, Lucy. We are running out of power,' Lilith said.

'What do you suggest, demon? That sword completely outreaches my dagger.' Lucy parried another lunge. 'All right, I have a cunning plan, God help me.'

Isabella made a couple of halfhearted cuts to the girl's head. Lucy knocked them away with her blade. Then, Isabella lunged straight for Lucy's neck; this was a serious attack and the witch was fully committed. Lucy turned, deflecting the sword fractionally with her blade so that it missed her by inches. Then she stepped in towards Isabella, continuing the spin until her dagger struck at Isabella's side. The blade touched the glowing shield that surrounded Isabella—and it erupted in a flash of energy.

On paper, the battle between the soldiers and the sailors was a foregone conclusion. Men who were disciplined, experienced, heavily armed and clad in demi-armour, outnumbered the Swallows. The sailors wore no armour and carried a variety of weapons, some quite primitive in function. And yet, it was the mercenaries who gave ground before the ferocity of the sailors. It was the mercenaries who were clubbed, stabbed, and cut. It was the mercenaries who fell and died. The Swallows showed why Elizabeth's sea dogs were the terror of the northern ocean.

The cry went up, "*Cediamo*," and "*Arresti il combattimento*."

None of this meant much to the English who continued to attack the soldiers until the mercenary officer yelled in English, "Quarter. We yield. We ask quarter."

The officer stood in front of William holding out his sword hilt. A battle-mad sailor tried to run the officer through but William pushed the man away.

"Cease fighting. Give them quarter," yelled William.

A sailor ignored his captain and cut the throat of a wounded mercenary.

"Boatswain! Hang the next man who disobeys my order. I'll have some discipline out of these whoresons." William would do it too, and they knew it.

William took the sword from the Italian officer but he offered it back, hilt first. "I accept your surrender, sir, but you fought well. Please retain your weapon."

The man would need his sword to maintain authority amongst his own soldiers. It was in William's interests for the officer to keep the surrendered mercenaries in line.

The man bowed. "And to whom do I have the honour of addressing, sir?"

"I am Captain William Hawkins of the *Swallow*. The *Swallow* is part of the battle fleet of John Hawkins, my cousin."

The Italian officer cheered up. To surrender to an unknown heretic pirate would have been a disgrace that might have been the end of the mercenary's career. But William was a cousin of Admiral Hawkins, which therefore made him a relative of the great Francis Drake himself. To have crossed swords with a cousin of *El Draco* and lived, even if you did have to surrender to him, was positively career enhancing.

"Tell me something, sir," said William. "Why did you prevent your men shooting at our champion, the Lady Dennys? I saw you countermand the Lady Isabella's order."

The officer turned his mouth down in elaborate distaste. "My men and I signed up for Spanish service to get rich, serve God, and kill heretics." At this point the officer made a small shrug of apology to William. The captain waved a hand to show that he understood, as one professional to another.

"We gave no oaths to serve alongside demons or to shoot girls in the back," continued the officer.

"Whatever your motives, sir, you bought quarter for your men with that act of chivalry."

"And where is the maid?" asked the mercenary.

Oh God, thought William, where is she?

At that moment, a flash of light lit up the precinct and knocked the Italian over. "What in the name of the seven seas?" said William. He ran towards the explosion. Lucy was facedown on the ground. William knelt beside her and checked her neck. He couldn't find a pulse, nor did she seem to be breathing. "Come on, Lucy. Breathe for me." He tried the trick of blowing into her mouth but this time she didn't respond. He held her, tears streaming down his cheeks.

"William," said Simon, putting his hand on the captain's shoulder.

"She's dead, Simon," said William.

There was a cough. Isabella was on her knees, head bent forward. A discarded sword lay in front of her. William gently put Lucy down, picked up the weapon, and held it against Isabella's neck.

"You evil papist witch. You finally got her. You waited until she was exhausted from killing four demons and then you murdered her." William drew the sword back. This was how they had executed Ann Boleyn.

Simon went to intervene but Gwilym grabbed him. "Let the captain finish it. If Hawkins doesn't kill her, I will."

William hesitated, sword back ready to strike. He had killed many times in battle and had once hung a sailor but he had never killed a woman before. Then he had a thought.

"Lilith! Lilith can take Lucy to a safe place and shut her body down. That's what she did in the River Crouch. Lilith needed air to bring her back to life." William dropped the sword and cradled Lucy's body. "What do you need, Lilith? It's not air is it? What do you need this time to bring her back? Show me a sign."

Lucy still held her dagger gripped in her hand. It began to glow, just like it had in the river estuary. "The blade," said William. "Lucy's blade is the key. What do I do with it, Lilith?" The light from the dagger dimmed and went out. "What do I do, Lilith?" pleaded William.

"Lilith can't have enough power to keep the blade glowing," said Simon.

"Power! That's it, Lilith is out of power!" William said. "Where can we get power for a demon?"

The crystal rocks thrust from the ground nearby. William pointed. "There! There is a source of great power."

William carried Lucy reverently over to the rock formation. He put his large hand tightly around her small one, the one that gripped John Dee's dagger. Then he thrust the blade hard into the crystal and the world turned blue-white. A flash seared his eyes. He had the brief impression of falling until something hit him so hard on the chest that he couldn't breath. Then the blackness came.

The sun seared William's eyes, making him shut them tighter. The light levels lowered again as something shaded him so he opened his eyes again. William took a little time to focus on Lucy's face.

"What happened?" he asked. He noticed that his voice was croaking.

Lucy pointed to where crystal shards littered the ground. "You destroyed it when you thrust my blade in, releasing its energy. Lilith used the power to rebuild me, but you must have guessed she would do that. The flash of power hit you hard. You have been in a swoon for some little time."

"Where is Isabella? I still have business with her." William's voice hardened.

"Isabella was older than she appeared, William—much, much older," Lucy said. "The crystal was a fountain of youth, of sorts, and Isabella had clearly taken of it. When you destroyed the crystal, she reverted to her true age. She did not survive the conversion." Lucy shuddered.

William sat up; the movement making his head spin, causing Lucy to steady him. There was something missing. "Lucy, where's the city?"

"It's gone," she said. "The jungle has disappeared as well. Bimini is just another uninhabited Bahaman island. We are back here in the real world. We can go home, to England."

William opened his mouth to ask another question but she touched his lips.

"Shush," she said, pushing him flat on his back. "You need nurturing and I propose to start now."

She lowered her face to his and kissed him. She kissed him and kissed him and kissed him.

Act 22, Endings and Beginnings

The Master of Constructs minutely adjusted the rotation of a black hole. It hardly needed adjusting as the measured error was close to the tolerances of his equipment. However, it gave him something to do. They had expected the Traveller back within one or two thousand revolutions of the construct. After ten thousand revolutions without word, the project began to be wound down. After twenty thousand, only a skeleton staff remained.

An Engineer approached him and opened communication using the frequency of respectful address to a superior. "How long will you continue to oversee the operation personally, Master? The probability of a successful recovery has dropped to seven point nine five percent. We can watch for you."

"I met the Traveller before she went. Did I ever tell you that?" asked the Master. "It was disconcerting that the youngest and least experienced was to be given the most hazardous position, the position of honour. The least I can do is stay until the probability drops below one percent and all hope is lost."

"I fear we have another failed mission," said the Engineer. "I doubt the Elders will countenance another try. It would have been satisfying to know our origins."

"Our origins are surely described in the holy words of the Sacred Truth," said the Master.

"Of course," said the Engineer. "But confirmation and added detail would have been stimulating."

"Such thoughts are best not broadcast," said the Master. "An ungenerous person might detect evidence of heresy. Such a conclusion would lose a person his position."

The Engineer signalled permission to withdraw and the Master waved him away. The spread of heresy amongst the technical classes was frightening. It had become far worse recently. Privately, the Master considered the Elders mad to have permitted this mission. It had stoked up and spread heresy, not curtailed it.

A soft glow emanated from the construct and an alarm sounded. "Arrival imminent, arrival imminent, arrival imminent . . ."

"Turn that wretched subroutine off before I erase it," said the Master, irritably. "Obviously an arrival is imminent. What idiot fitted that device?"

The Engineers clamped down on their thoughts, as it was the Master himself who had insisted that alarms be installed.

"Let's see what we have," said the Master. "A capsule is approaching fast through the Shadows. This is going to be very tricky."

"Probability of successful recovery is five point seven percent," said an Engineer helpfully.

The Master glared at him. "Your model omits to properly include a variable for my enhanced skill so your calculation is invalid," he said, taking personal control of the recovery systems.

The recovery was indeed tricky. Several times the capsule almost broke through only to be lost back into the Shadow Worlds. Each time, interdimensional forces buffeted the capsule to the point of destruction but each time the Master caught it and eased it back. The vortex spun angrily between the five black holes.

"Gently, gently," said the Master, manipulating the controls. "Got you."

The capsule popped back into real space and was ejected out of the construct. Gravitational fields caught it and caressed it into a gravitonic matrix.

"It's too small," said the Engineer. "The Traveller can't be inside."

"It has the right codes," said the Master.

The force field around the capsule collapsed and data came pouring out. Lobes captured the data into the construct but the system was inefficient and vast streams were accidentally copied into the universal data stream.

The Master cherry-picked strands as information flowed past him—a universe of light, biochemical beings, matter technology, heresy, heresy, heresy. A last note from the Traveller caught his eye.

"The precise origin of the People is still not clear to me. Our information functions show clear resemblances to the human's electronic information technology machines. On the other hand some of our core structures are duplicates of Lucy Dennys' central nervous system. Whether the humans transferred themselves into their machines, and so become us, or whether we are simply the descendents of the machines is unclear. I hope it is the former, as I would like to think something of Lucy lives on in us. Whichever is true, it is irrefutable that humans came first and were the creators of the People."

The Master groaned at that point. This was heresy so deep that his whole being vibrated in shock. He read on.

"I propose to stay with my good friend Lucy and learn more about these wonderful, vibrant, doomed creatures. I will send more data back when I can."

"Is there any chance of suppressing this?" asked the Master.

"None whatsoever," said the Engineer. "It is already too late. We were not expecting a data dump, so much of it has already been distributed as it overflowed our buffers. The radicals are claiming victory and have already split into two separate factions who have declared war on each other."

"The radicals are already fighting each other?" asked the Master, shocked.

"The monotheists are claiming Lucy is the source of all life while the polytheists claim she is but one of many sources."

"What are the Elders doing about it?" asked the Master.

"They appear to have committed ritual dissolution," said the Engineer, showing the modulation of extreme shock.

The Master watched news reports flooding across the universal net. Nothing would ever be the same again.

The story ended. Alice was just Alice again and Lucy and her world were simply a picture in the crystal ball. It had been so real, as if Alice was Lucy. Her own life poured back into her head like rebooting a computer program but it took a moment to remember that she was Alice Harding, a London University history lecturer and a nobody. She was not an aristocrat who hobnobbed with society and who had a secret life as a demon killer.

'God, full-sensory movies,' thought Alice. 'How do you do that?'

'We aim to please,' thought Lilith. 'Makes DVDs look like a What the Butler Saw machine, doesn't it? But to answer you question, I can get in your head, Alice. You see what I project on your brain. I could probably explain it to you if you had studied a science rather than one of the humanities.'

'I get enough of the superiority of geeks lecture from Hammond, thank you,' thought Alice.

She studied the crystal. Lucy was still freeze-framed in it, head bent over her sea captain's face. Her auburn hair hung statically in the freeze frame. 'She's very pretty, for a ginga,' thought Alice. 'The Commission like to hang portraits of their chairman on the walls of their boardroom. When they run out of space, they remove the oldest picture to a basement. They had me catalogue the basement store once and that was where I found an old painting. I recognised the likeness of Walsingham at once, of course. We know what Walsingham looked like from his court portraits, but I couldn't work out whom the girl was. She looked twenty years younger than him. I wondered whether she was some sort of trophy mistress who had been cleansed from the official records. The Commission seems to have forgotten Lucy Dennys.'

'Lucy was his closest living relative and the delight of his heart. She was also his most lethal agent,' thought Lilith.

'You stopped the story too early. What happened to Lucy? Did she marry her dashing sea captain?' asked Alice.

'Lucy had a wonderful life, with many adventures and many children, who were the biggest adventure of all. Her children and their children went out and founded a great empire. Lucy was my first and greatest friend but in the end she left me, as you all must do.'

Lilith's tone was flat but Alice had the feeling of infinite sadness. Then Lilith's thoughts lifted. 'But Lucy's daughters always come back to me. Each generation you come back to London to find me and you carry Lucy within you.'

Alice looked back at the freeze-framed picture of Lucy and her mouth went dry. Lucy's hair swirled in the wind, framing an infectious smile. Diamonds sparkled in her eyes. The sense of life in her was overwhelming.

'It's funny,' thought Alice. 'Somehow you would expect your great-grandmother fifteen times removed to look rather older than a cheeky teenager.'

'I wonder how Hammond is reacting to all this?'

"Here you go, Alice." Hammond lifted a fried egg out of the pan and plonked it on a heaped plate. "Two eggs, just the way you like them."

Alice sat at the table gazing at some old piece of tat she had found in the box.

"What is that thing?" Hammond said. "It looks like a crystal ball. You can't pick up the winner of the three-fifty at Ascot on it can you?" She didn't reply. "Nah, thought not. All you can do with those things is put old ladies in touch with their cats that have crossed over. Are ye no there, Tiddles? Knock once for yes and twice for no."

He knocked twice on the kitchen table and laughed. Then he swept the crystal ball aside and plonked the plate down. "Forget the diet and get your laughing gear around that. I always reckon that a decent breakfast sets you up for the day."

The radio switched back to the music show and The Clash pumped "London's Burning" out into the kitchen.

"What's this?" asked Hammond. He picked up the conjuring knife. "Wow, it's really wicked. You could do some serious damage to someone with this."

Alice sat at the table staring at where the crystal ball had been. She hadn't touched her breakfast.

"Alice, are you all right?" Hammond put his hand on her shoulder. She was stiff and didn't react so he shook her gently. The stiffness disappeared and she fell off the chair. Luckily she fell towards him so he could catch her. He lowered her gently to the floor and checked the pulse at her throat. He was reassured to feel her heart beat strongly. Her chest moved as she breathed.

"Alice," he said again. "Alice." Hammond tapped her cheek gently and she stirred a little but then subsided. She appeared to be in a deep sleep. He picked her up in his arms, carried her to the bedroom, and put her to bed.

"Now what do I do, girl?" he said. "I should phone for an ambulance but you will kill me if it turns out that you have only fainted. The last thing you ever want is officialdom involved in your bloody dubious activities."

He went back to the kitchen and brewed up. When he returned to the bedroom she was still out of it, so he drank the tea himself.

"I will give you an hour. If you haven't woken up by then you are going to casualty, my girl. You will find breakfasts in Wimbledon General Hospital not to be a patch on mine." He looked at her. "Please wake up, Alice."

He washed up. Every five minutes, he checked up on her. Alice's pulse remained strong and she breathed normally. Occasionally, she made small snoring noises. After an hour had passed, he decided to give it two before he panicked officially, and after two hours, he decided to give it three. After four hours he was seriously worried. He shook her one more time, "Please, Alice, wake up."

There was no reaction. Hammond slipped his mobile out of the leather wallet on his belt and slid open the lid. Blue light lit up his face. He dialled nine-nine-nine and waited interminably for an operator.

"Emergency services. What number are you calling from?" asked a cool female voice.

"02771 490 1324," said Hammond

"What service please?"

"Ambulance."

"It's okay, Hammond. Put the phone down, please," said Alice.

"I'm sorry, operator, I was too quick. The emergency is over," said Hammond, flipping closed his phone. "How are you feeling?"

"I feel wonderful. I feel so rested and alive." She held her arms out, "Come to bed, Hammond."

"What the bloody hell was the matter with you? You scared me witless this time." He was shouting, relief and anger equally proportioned in his voice.

"Nothing, Hammond, I was just exhausted. Come to me."

He knew he should let her rest. He knew he should persuade her to see a doctor, he knew this was a bad idea, he knew so much. But he took his clothes off anyway and slid into the bed and into her.

They made love, not sex but made love. It was slow and caring and wonderful. Afterwards, he left the bed and walked to the window. He looked out, not really seeing anything. A dark blue BMW was parked across the road behind his Ford. There were two men inside the cabin, wearing identical black leather jackets.

"What are you thinking?" she asked.

He was not ready to tell her. He knew what he had to do but he was barely ready to admit it to himself. "Are you hungry?" he asked.

"Hmm, starving," she replied.

"I'll make you something." He left the bedroom without a word and went to the kitchen. When he reappeared with a tray, she was dozing. She ate as if she had never seen a decent hot meal before, pausing only to sink a mug of dark English tea. Afterwards, she chatted to him about inconsequentials. His answers were monosyllabic and she eventually ran down. He walked back to the window; the BMW was still there.

"What is it, Hammond?"

"Alice . . ." Hammond said.

"Hmmm," she purred. He could not look at her. He knew she would be stretching like a cat and he would be lost if he looked at her.

"I am leaving you, Alice." There, he had said it.

"What?"

"Let me go, Alice."

"And for old time's sake, you decided to have me one more time before dumping me?" There was a flash of anger in her voice and something else, hurt. He did not want to hurt her. He had never loved anyone as strongly.

"What we just did finally made my mind up. I've thought about leaving you before but never had the nerve to go through with it. This on-off relationship is tearing me apart. Let me go, Alice. You don't want me enough to commit to me."

"I need you, Hammond. You are the one anchor in my life." She sounded as if she meant every word. As if the thought of losing him forever, of not being able to just drop in when she needed reassurance, was terrifying.

Now it was his turn to get angry. "I am tired of being an anchor, tired of being here for you when it suits you. Tired of ringing you in hotel rooms all over the world and hearing another man's voice in the room. How about me? How about what I need?"

"I'm a selfish cow, Hammond, I always have been. You knew that before you bedded me. But I can change. Please don't leave me." She cried softly.

"You'll never change, Alice," he said. What can one do with a crying lover? But this time she would not talk him round. He was resolved to stand his ground. "Let me go, Alice, if you feel anything for me."

She didn't reply. He gazed back down in the street to keep his eyes away from her. The sun was setting over the building opposite. The BMW still sat parked below. The man in the passenger seat saw him looking from the window and carefully looked away.

"Alice. Why are two men watching your flat?"

"Oh Christ, it's the Commission. We have to get out of here. Get dressed."

Hammond hopped on one foot trying to get his trousers up. "Why do I always get caught with my pants down around you?"

"Probably because you are so keen to get mine down." She grinned at him archly, pulling her clothes on. "You will miss all this if you leave me."

There was no answer to that. He was not sure whether she was talking about the situation or her body or just the whole experience. She had done it to him again. They were supposed to be splitting up. Instead, he was helping her flee into the night with stolen artefacts.

"I meant what I said." He tried desperately to get a grip on the situation.

"'Course you did, love," said Alice. She grabbed him and kissed him passionately. Alice looked deep into his eyes, "I love you, geek, don't leave me, please don't leave me. I will treat you better."

She had never ever said that before—said she loved him, that is; she had often called him a geek.

"Hurry up," she said. "They'll have an enforcement team here soon. Put the knife and crystal back in the box. You carry it; I'll drive. They may not realise that I have a car in the basement garage. We'll take the service lift."

The service lift was designed for rubbish bins, not people. It had no door and creaked horribly all the way down. The basement car park was empty of people. Her prized Mini Cooper, with the Union Jack painted on the roof, was over in a corner. The cars were crammed tightly together to maximise capacity. Hammond waited in the aisle for her to wriggle in the driver's side and back the motor out. Something niggled at his consciousness. He took a moment to isolate what was bothering him. A car engine was idling somewhere nearby.

Alice gingerly backed the Mini out of the space, taking care not to catch her mirrors on the cars parked each side. An engine roared and a black Jaguar Sports shot across the line of parked cars. The driver hit the brakes at the last moment. They shrieked as he stopped, boxing in the Mini.

Hammond tried to see inside but the windows were heavily blacked out. The passenger door alongside him opened and a woman slid gracefully out of the Jag. She was petite and slim with jet-black straight hair. *Matrix*-style sunglasses hid her eyes.

"Ours, I think," she said, taking the box out of his unresisting hands and opening it.

A man appeared out of the driver's side of the Jag and opened the boot. "Come on, Alice, get out of your car. We are taking you to see some friends. They want to talk to you about loyalty and punishment. As this is only a two-seater, you and lover boy will be travelling in the boot. Not much of a boot on this model, so you will be cramped. Never mind, that will give you the chance to snuggle close and whisper sweet nothings."

Alice climbed out of the Mini. "Let my friend go, Jameson. He's a civilian."

"Love, he stopped being a civilian when you chose to involve him," Jameson said.

"Let me introduce you to two of the Commission's top torpedoes, Hammond," said Alice. "The man is Major Jameson, late of Her Majesty's Guards, and the woman is Karla, better known as the Dark Lady. Back away from her; she's very dangerous."

Karla removed the sunglasses to reveal iridescent, metallic green eyes. She looked at Hammond and licked her lips. He backed off. For some reason, the woman scared him silly.

"The box is mine, Jameson," said Alice. "It has been in my family longer than the Commission has existed."

"Bollocks," said Jameson, succinctly.

'Lucy's movement patterns are laid down in your hindbrain; power up, defensive field on, you have control, Alice,' thought Lilith. 'Oh this feels good. I've missed human company.'

"Okay, Jameson, you've asked for it," Alice said.

Alice walked around her car towards Karla. Hammond was astonished. Alice was always slightly gawky and uncoordinated. It was part of her charm, but now she moved like Kate Moss on the catwalk. Her skin seemed to glow with vitality but what really worried him were her eyes. Diamond sparkles lit up her eyes to match the iridescent green of Karla's.

"Lucy Hawkins?" Karla said. "It can't be you, Lucy. You've been dead these four hundred years. I saw you die."

Alice grinned and said, "Some things never die. You of all people should know that, Karla."

"Karla, what's going on?" asked Jameson, looking worried for the first time.

A bloody good question, Hammond thought.

The two women looked at each other like two fighting cocks in a pit. Karla dropped the box but her right hand came out holding the knife. Her hand was a blur as she threw the weapon at Alice.

The dagger stopped with its point one inch from the bridge of Alice's nose. It stopped because Alice had the hilt firmly grasped in her right hand. She smiled at Karla.

Hammond gaped at Alice. How had she done that?

Karla just nodded. "That proves it. Lucy was always good at catch."

Who the hell is Lucy, thought Hammond?

"Good girl, Lilith," Alice said, mysteriously, to the air. Then to Karla, "Come on baby, let's rock and roll." Alice went into a crouch and held the knife horizontally at eye height. Fire ran up and down the blade. Her left hand extended out palm down.

Karla opened her mouth in a wide smile, showing teeth as long as fangs. She leapt up onto the long bonnet of the Jag.

Alice was already moving. She accelerated up to Olympic sprinter speed and jumped. She held her arms outstretched like plane wings and rotated around them to land on the roof of the car. Karla shot straight up the sloping windscreen at her and punched with her left and right hands. Alice deflected both blows.

Alice jumped into a high kick, knocking Karla down across the bonnet onto the ground. She leapt after the woman. Karla rolled back onto her shoulders and caught Alice with a two-footed kick in the head. She struck Alice so hard that Hammond almost felt the thud.

Hammond thought that would be the end of the fight but Alice flipped over backwards and landed on her feet. As Karla got upright, Alice hit her on the chin with the knife handle, knocking the woman straight back down again. Hammond noticed that the box was still on the ground where Karla had dropped it. He bent down quietly and picked it up. Thuds and grunts sounded from where the women traded blows. Jameson watched the women anxiously. From the look on his face, he was having issues about coming to terms with Alice Harding as superwoman. That made two of them.

Hammond sneaked carefully behind Jameson. The man clearly had Hammond tagged as civilian and hence harmless. Hammond smacked the box down on Jameson's head. He dropped onto all fours, semiconscious. Karla looked at him in horror. While she was distracted, Alice stabbed her in the side. Karla screamed as the glowing knife cut through her. The Dark Lady fell.

"Come on," said Alice. She picked up Hammond and the box, and threw them into the passenger seat of the Jag. Then she rolled over the bonnet to the driver's door and climbed in.

"Keys left in the ignition. What were you thinking of, Jameson?" asked Alice, rhetorically.

The Jag started first time, a tribute to the money Ford had poured into fixing reliability issues. She smacked the gear selector into first and dropped the clutch. The sportscar took off, rear wheels spinning in a haze of blue smoke. Alice waggled the wheel to avoid hitting Jameson and Karla. The woman had crawled over to him and had his head in her lap. She was stroking his face.

"Karla in love with a man," Alice said softly. "That's too spooky even for me."

"Will they be all right?" asked Hammond.

"Sure they will," said Alice. "Jameson has a thick head and only a stake through her cold dead heart would kill Karla. A stake or this." Alice tossed the conjuror's knife onto Hammond's lap. He picked it up and looked at it. The markings on the blade were outlined in red light.

Hammond didn't quite know how to respond. Part of his mind insisted that Alice was winding him up. The other part remembered Karla's metallic eyes and snakelike stillness. He didn't want to remember the teeth.

The Jag rocketed up the access ramp and turned out into the street with a howl of tyres and the blare of horns from irate motorists.

Alice giggled. "The Commission are never going to believe this. Two of their top gunslingers floored by a couple of London University academics. And we stole their Jag!"

"Where are we going?" asked Hammond, struggling with a seat belt.

"We can pick up the South Circular in a few miles. I'll run round it to Watling Street. Then we'll go right down the M2 to the Channel

Ports. Let's see how many speed cameras we can trigger for the Commission to explain away between here and Dover. I have a mate who works on the ferries. He can get us on a boat to France and then the world is open to us. Where do you fancy?"

"I have a class to teach on Tuesday at UCL," said Hammond, weakly. "Geophysics II."

"You can ring in and work a sicky," said Alice. "Jameson is going to be so pissed. All those kung fu lessons and he gets taken down by a geophysicist in glasses, wielding an historical artefact."

Hammond sighed. This time he had definitely intended to leave her, to end the hurt. If he left Alice, he could find a nice girl who would love him, have his babies, keep his house, and always be there for him. Alice would never fit that role.

Alice threw her head back and laughed out loud. She was so alive, more alive than any other woman he had ever met. Fire burns, but how do you go back to living in the dark when once you have experienced light? He loved her, he always would.

"You have bloody done it to me again, haven't you?" asked Hammond. "Just waltzed into my quiet little normal life and wrecked it. I must be the only man whose working week is ruined by his girlfriend turning into Wonder Woman, which is something else you have yet to explain to me, incidentally. When we are on that ferry, we are so going to discuss our relationship."

"Of course we are," said Alice. "Absolutely, I promise. But in the meantime you will have to stay with me, I am afraid. For your own good, you understand." She smiled at him. "So you won't be able to leave me, after all."

She became serious. "Please don't leave me, Hammond. I couldn't bear that. I love you."

"If I could just work out how you planned all this," he said, exasperated. How could he leave her? How do you leave the woman you love when she had just said that?

She dropped her left hand onto his knee as she powered the Jag inside an articulated lorry on a roundabout. She gave him a squeeze and then theatrically moved her hand up his thigh. "Wonder Woman is also much faster and stronger than you now. I shall drag you back if you try to escape, hold you down, and as a punishment, have my wicked way with your poor quivering body."

He turned that idea over in his head. "I suppose there might be compensations," he said. "I believe the traditional reaction to such threats is to lie back and think of England. Can your mate get us a cabin on the boat?"

They looked at each other and laughed. The glow had faded from her skin but residual diamond sparkles still lit up her eyes. They flashed in time to the flickering red that lit up Lucy's blade.